The
AUTOBIOGRAPHY
of MY BODY

The
AUTOBIOGRAPHY
of MY BODY

DAVID GUY

A DUTTON BOOK

DUTTON
Published by the Penguin Group
Penguin Books USA Inc., 375 Hudson Street,
New York, New York 10014, U.S.A.
Penguin Books Ltd, 27 Wrights Lane,
London W8 5TZ, England
Penguin Books Australia Ltd, Ringwood,
Victoria, Australia
Penguin Books Canada Ltd, 2801 John Street,
Markham, Ontario, Canada L3R 1B4
Penguin Books (N.Z.) Ltd, 182-190 Wairau Road,
Auckland 10, New Zealand

Penguin Books Ltd, Registered Offices:
Harmondsworth, Middlesex, England

First published by Dutton, an imprint of New American Library, a division of
Penguin Books USA Inc.
Distributed in Canada by McClelland & Stewart Inc.

First Printing, February, 1991
10 9 8 7 6 5 4 3 2 1

REGISTERED TRADEMARK—MARCA REGISTRADA

Library of Congress Cataloging-in-Publication Data

Guy, David.
  The autobiography of my body / David Guy.
    p. cm.
    I. Title.
PS3557.U89A94 1991
813'.54—dc20   90-13920
                                                                                    CIP

Printed in the United States of America
Set in Century Schoolbook
Designed by Leonard Telesca

PUBLISHER'S NOTE
This is a work of fiction. Names, characters, places, and incidents either are the
products of the author's imagination or are used fictitiously, and any resemblance to
actual persons, living or dead, events, or locales is entirely coincidental.

To the Men:
Bill
and Bill and Rusty
and Don and Dick
and Bob and Bob and John and Andy
and Guy and Chris and Charley
and Sy and Victor and Joe and Mike and Lex
and Dick and Richard and Bob
and Levi and Mark and Tom and Ray
and Robert and George . . .

Acknowledgments

I would like to thank Joe Marion and Jim Dykes for their expert professional opinion concerning various technical aspects of this novel, Joe in particular for his numerous readings and his almost infinite capacity to find mistakes in what I had done. Both of these men were helpful in discussing my early ideas for the book, as were Laurel Goldman, Michael Brondoli, and Kristin Paulig. For their helpful suggestions concerning later drafts, I would like to thank Sherry Huber, Ginger Barber, Alma Blount, Gary Luke, and Arnold Dolin. And for their kind patience with my strange moods while I was writing the book, I would like to thank Alma, my son, Bill, and my cat, Satchel.

If a fool would persist in his folly, he would become wise.

—William Blake,
The Marriage of Heaven and Hell

PART I

ONE

This city has changed, and not for the better. It seems to have changed every time I come back. I will admit as much as anyone that the skyline has improved, with new buildings that might not be masterpieces but are at least visually interesting, bright and new. It is also true that the air is much improved since the steel mills closed down; you can more or less breathe now, and you don't run into those strange sulfurous smells, though you also don't see the incredible evening colors, oranges and pinks and sometimes almost purples, that you used to see around the mills. That was something people never mentioned in those days. Pollution could be beautiful.

So I am heartened every time I return to Pittsburgh. It seems to have taken the shaggy character of an old city and added the flash of a new one. But then I step out into the streets, and they seem to have been cleared out by the construction; they don't have the crowded, busy, ants-at-a-picnic feeling that I love about city streets. The buildings look interesting even when you get down beside them, but when you walk inside you find just a bare lobby, stone and marble and a few plants in pots. An alcove or two of elevators. A guy is standing there in a uniform wearing a walkie-talkie that puts him in touch with God knows what, and he tells you that you are welcome in the lobby—you can walk around and look at the marble and plants (though not, I'm sure, if you're a vagrant trying to get in out of the cold)—but you can't go upstairs unless you have some business. It would be a little obvious, at that point, to drift over to the directory to see what businesses there are. Who wants to go upstairs anyway, if your only chance for a view is to get into somebody's office? So the buildings look good on the skyline, they even look good when you get down beside them, but they're not for the people in the city. They're for the people who work in them. This is America's most livable city, but there's nobody in the streets when you go out there. Maybe that's what they mean by livable.

I'm thinking of an old building called the Jenkins Arcade that they recently imploded and carried away as a pile of rubble, leaving a hole in the ground. (I'm sure they'll fill it with something. Men are always filling holes with things.) It wasn't what you would call charming, God knows, long high forbidding hallways, brick floors, heavy wooden doors with frosted glass, stuffy steam heat that could produce a fainting spell in the heartiest constitution. It was the kind of place where you figured dentists worked with pliers. DR. FRANK-ENSTEIN, you expected to see in block letters on one of the windows. But downstairs, on the first floor, where the surface was white marble, the lobby was surrounded by brightly lit shops, a candy store, a luggage store, a tobacco shop. Everybody was there, businessmen in dark suits, hurrying off for a Pittsburgh businessman's luncheon (Polish sausage and a draft beer); secretaries—they weren't businesswomen yet—getting in some shopping on their lunch hour, clicking along on high heels, with bright dresses, great legs; a small army of women shoppers, middle-aged and older, wearing threadbare overcoats, their doughy faces flushed with exertion, seven or eight shopping bags somehow suspended from their hands; second- and third-shift mill workers, wearing a couple days' growth of beard, a kind of grime in their skin that never washed out; gangs of kids. After a trip to the dentist you could wander in the crowd, stop in the coffee shop for a milkshake. Ease the pain a little. There's no such place in these new buildings. There's no place where people just go. They've taken away the city and replaced it with a corporate headquarters. They've removed the human element.

I want my city back.

It was a bitter cold day when I returned, temperature in the teens and a hard wind blowing, a light dusting of snow around, so there were fewer people out even than usual. This trip, for the first time ever, I was staying downtown, at a hotel up near the top of the triangle. I thought it best this time not to stay at home, though it's no home I ever knew. The Senator and the Duchess, after all these years of living in that huge house, finally moved to an apartment, in a building my sister calls the Hall of Fame, because so many of the city's former notables live there. I'm talking about people you thought were dead, and you weren't all that wrong. It's a fabulous apartment, huge as apartments go—you could park a truck in the kitchen—but any apartment is small when you're a guest, especially when you have to buzz for the elevator every time you want to leave. That place can feel a little tight even under the best circumstances.

This time I thought it would be tight in other ways as well.

I set out on a walk almost as soon as I got to the hotel, because there's nothing more depressing to me than a hotel room when you're alone, unless it's a hotel lobby. (I think that's why whores have always done such a bang-up business in hotels. Men aren't horny up in those rooms. They're lonely.) I was headed not exactly for the Point, but in that general direction, looking for a street with a little life in it, when I stumbled across Mellon Square. The first place Sara and I ever kissed. I hadn't remembered that until I saw the place. I'd have been hard-pressed the day before even to name the first place we kissed.

It had been an August night, but a windy one, the first chill of autumn in the air. The wind was gusting so hard that a misty spray blew on us now and then from the fountains. We hardly knew each other at that point, and there were other people around, taking in the evening, and it wasn't even quite dark yet, but when we walked out into Mellon Square it seemed so pretty and romantic, with the lights shining through the fountains, that we started to kiss. It wasn't that the kisses were great, but that we fell into them, came together and started kissing; she wanted to kiss me and I wanted to kiss her. I was twenty years old, and that was the first time I had ever felt that. A woman who simply wanted to kiss me. Kisses that just happened.

So twenty years later, stumbling across that spot, I started to cry. In my body crying was held in for years; there are eighteen or nineteen years of it coiled like a beast waiting to spring, so it never comes out gently, tears pouring from my eyes. I always sob, and groan, with a huge heaving at my chest. It came on me so hard that I had to lean against the building. What the hell, there was hardly anyone on the streets anyway. What people were there wouldn't have stopped for something like that. It was too scary.

I think I could have come across any other moment from my past and it would have been okay, or come across that moment at a different time. It wasn't that I wished things were different. In a moment of clarity I can look back and see that it all happened with a great clanking inevitability. But I was standing at a cusp of my life, a huge accumulation of rounded-off experience behind me, a gaping emptiness ahead of me. I felt full and whole and utterly lost all at once. I felt lost, but not afraid. I had been in the dark wood for so long that I had grown comfortable there. Then I stumbled across that moment from the past that had seemed to hold such promise, when I thought that a feeling of togetherness meant everything was going to be all right.

That night twenty years before had been a turning point in my life, though I would hardly have guessed it at the time. I thought I was doing one thing when really I was doing another. I thought I was impressing a woman by taking her to an elegant restaurant; then she ordered pork chops, for God's sake, and coconut cake with ice cream for dessert. She showed me how the girls had taught her to float the cream on her coffee at boarding school. We stumbled out into Mellon Square and into all that kissing, which tasted of her coffee and of the mild onions from her salad, tastes I rather liked. I thought I was impressing a woman, or seducing her (*that* would have been a first), when really I was forming a friendship and falling in love. (Such is the strange turn of my libido. I fall in love with friends.) Twenty years old, and that was the first time I had ever felt a woman wanted to kiss me. Was it any wonder I chose to stay with her, even if the kisses weren't perfect? Twenty years later, I thought of all the happiness that followed that moment, and the pain, happiness and pain that both seemed a part of that moment, and I started to cry.

Not a soul so much as looked at me. You call this a city? Where are the old ladies with the shopping bags, their coats smelling of mothballs? Where was the grizzled old wino who would happen along and offer me his bottle? Where the hell were the nuns?

I recovered after a while, wiped away the tears and blew my nose. (I'll be fine, really. Just a slight nervous breakdown.) I think I'd needed to cry. There is a certain tension in coming home, a sadness. It wells up from your stomach and into your chest, like an ache, or a scream. You have to get rid of it, because if you don't—and I've done this one—it flows into your muscles and comes out as anger (men characteristically do that), or you swallow it back and it becomes anxiety and depression (women). I felt better after I cried. My whole body felt more relaxed. Maybe they should have a room for that at the airport. A place with padded walls where you can stop to cry, or scream, whatever, if it's home you've arrived at. Throw yourself against the wall a few times. I bet it would cut traffic fatalities in half.

There is a street of vice that runs through the heart of the city. I always head there when I return, if only to touch base with a part of myself. That was the only place in the city where I felt entirely relaxed, where I didn't have to live up to something. It was also a place that gave me a wicked thrill, from the time I was a boy. Just the fact that I knew it was there, a streetcar ride away. We're talking about a boy who lived in a very scrubbed-up home, who fled that not only to get his hands dirty, but also because there was something that he wasn't getting. I remember, for instance, the simple— essentially erotic—thrill of taking a streetcar to the seamy side of the city, buying cigarettes from a machine (I always bought Luckies; I figured I might as well die in real agony), and walking around the streets to smoke them. Tobacco was the very scent of wickedness, and the pain of sucking that smoke into my lungs disguised another pain (probably a cousin to the pain I had just relieved by leaning against a building and crying). I don't smoke cigarettes now, but I can bring back that thrill by picking up a fresh pack and inhaling them. It practically gives me a hard-on.

I didn't have to go all the way downtown to smoke in my earliest days, but eventually I did—along that street of burlesque houses, novelty shops, what they called art theaters in those days. Anyone who saw me would have said I looked horribly out of place. I thought I had found my true home. In one way vice was terribly tame in those days; in another it had an excitement it will never have again. A glimpse of bare tits gave you a thrill that nothing could nowadays. The anticipation of seeing a little pussy (maybe they'll finally show it this time; maybe they'll make a mistake and show it) lent the whole enterprise an incredible air of suspense.

I used to wander those streets, glancing into the novelty shops—the doors were open in warm weather—my heart thumping as I saw the tough downtown kids. They had dark skin and wore dark clothes, had hair that glistened; they pinched a cigarette between their thumb and first finger. Their eyes flashed when they saw me. Fresh meat. They almost started to laugh. (You have to picture a soft kid, baby-faced, thirty pounds overweight at the age of fourteen, sporting a crewcut that belonged on a six-year-old. An essentially kind, gentle boy, who would all his life be taken—correctly—for a soft touch. He is smoking a cigarette and glaring, trying to look tough. This baby-faced glare only makes him look more innocent.) The one adult wore a grimy apron that held change, a short dark cigar in the side of his mouth. Only once did I ever go in, walked up to one of the machines that said 25¢ beside the silhouette of a female figure. I looked at the machine and looked at the guy with the cigar. He looked at me. I took out a quarter and looked at the guy. He didn't say anything. I stepped to the machine with the quarter, found the slot. He still didn't say anything. I deposited the quarter, peered into the viewer, saw a bare-breasted woman—huge tits—smiling back at me. "You ain't eighteen, kid," the guy with the cigar said, stepping up to me. "Get the hell out."

It was the same essential impulse that took me back to that street in subsequent years, the same feeling of ease. (No need to hold yourself up. You've touched bottom.) I was the same good little boy who wanted to get his hands dirty. We are all, at any age, every age we've ever been. The ante had been upped, of course. The boy who at fourteen would have given his left nut (as we used to say) for a glimpse of pussy could now—at the age of thirty, say—see all he wanted, page after page of women holding it open. (When in Virginia, Visit the Luray Caverns.) And if he put that same quarter into a machine, he would see that bare-breasted woman not just smiling, but opening her mouth to get it around something, opening wider, wider . . .

The ante was also upped in other ways. On the second floor of those buildings (maybe this had been true in the old days too) were dark quiet rooms bathed in black light, with heavy scarlet shag carpets. Women sat on the couches in skimpy bathing suits, and the guy at the desk spoke a kind of code (French, English, Greek) that left things essentially vague, but we were definitely beyond the realm of mere looking. The first time I was up there, probably somewhere around that thirtieth year, I gave him fifty dollars, about midway on the price scale. I wasn't at all sure what I had paid for.

This is the same baby-faced fat kid smoking cigarettes and trying to look tough, only now he is an adult in a business suit, trim and handsome, still essentially boyish. It is the same little guy wearing an apron and smoking a cigar, only now he is a tall thick blocky Italian, scar tissue around his eyes, an essentially romantic expression on his face of weariness at the pain of being human.

He nodded toward the couch. "Take your pick of our lovely ladies," he said.

I chose a tall woman, extremely thin, who seemed to have the friendliest face. Daphne, was her name. I realize that I was in a horrible den of iniquity, that people are expecting a den-of-iniquity story, but I was also in Pittsburgh, where a certain awkward but genuinely friendly warmth pervades every transaction, even, I have no doubt, a Mafia hit ("How ya been?" before they machine-gun the poor bastard to ribbons). Daphne actually took my hand as we walked back, said, when we arrived at a room with a huge waterbed, "You get comfortable, sweetie. I'll be right back," then took me straight to the sink when she did get back, washing me carefully and looking me over. She was pulling, looking for a discharge. "How's this little fellow today?" she said.

"You mean big fellow."

"That's what I meant. Big fellow."

"Fine."

"Stepping out for a little exercise."

"He hopes."

"He came to the right place."

It wasn't a moment before we were on the waterbed, me on my back, her down between my legs, holding the friend she had just been introduced to. She was all skin and bones. You could have played her ribcage like a xylophone. She had large brown nipples, a small swell of tits beneath them.

"What you paid for was half-and-half," she said. She must have known how confusing that international smorgasbord had been. "But you only get to come once. We also do other things, which cost more. That stuff he said. You can pay me back here."

There is sometimes in sexual encounters—as in other encounters—what I think of as a human moment, when we let down the barriers, allow our spirits to touch. It doesn't always happen by any means. It doesn't have to do with other feelings. It doesn't have to do with love. It might happen in the most casual, sordid encounter. It was about to happen in that encounter. I was going to say something that would ease her mind. I would tell her exactly what I was looking for, which is always a question in such situations. I would save her what could have been considerable physical exertion.

"I just want to get blown," I said.

She smiled, and gave me the thumbs-up sign. Never had it seemed more appropriate.

"Except that I'd like to hold you first," I said.

"What?"

It was risky, what I had just asked for. I could have gotten along fine if I'd never brought it up. But now that I had, if I didn't get it, the whole thing would be ruined.

"I'd like to hold you a minute. I'd like you to come up and hold me."

"Oh. Sure."

"I don't pay extra for that?"

"No, sweetie. Free of charge."

Oh Christ, the human body. Hair against my face. Its scent in my nostrils. We wrapped our arms around each other, entwined our legs. She smelled of sweat. It smelled good. I squeezed her hard and she squeezed me back. I was getting a slight scent of milk.

"You have a baby," I said.

"Sleeping in the back. No titty-sucking for you."

"You can suck for both of us."

She laughed. I didn't want her to suck yet. I didn't want to let her go.

"Your heart's pounding like a son of a bitch," she said.

"I love this."

"Your dick got hard."

"I think he likes you."

"I like him too. You're a good guy. I'm going to treat you right."

Jesus, if she only knew. She already had. She could skip the blow job.

She did treat me right, as it turned out. She worked with a kind of agonizing slowness that was intense beyond belief. I groaned, and shuddered. "Scream your head off, sweetie," she said. "We're soundproof in here." When I had finished, she moved up on my body with an impish look in her eye and deposited the contents of her mouth in my navel. It overflowed.

"Either you got to come less," she said, "or we got to drill you a bigger belly button."

I wonder how many times she used that joke.

There are people, of course, who can't understand why a nice man like me would ever have wanted to visit a woman like that. They figure there must be something wrong with me. There are others—and this is probably a larger group, more likely to belong to the social class I grew up in—who understand that I might want to do such a thing, but find it unbelievable, and unforgivable, that I would talk about it. These are sophisticated people, who know that there are all kinds of bizarre behavior in the world. But they believe that certain things are just not *said*.

I understand how they feel. Those are my people, after all. But I believe that, whether we acknowledge it or not, there is—beneath the level of language and thought—another life, a deeper life, that we all lead. I think of it as the life of the body. For a few months in my fortieth year—initiated, it seemed, by that fit of crying, a last moment of sadness for what had gone before—I went through an experience that threw a light on that other life, focused it and made it clearer. It was as if those few months were a prism; I could look into them and see my whole life reflected.

I believe in talking about the life of the body, because if we don't acknowledge it, if we don't make it a part of us, it poisons our lives. It makes us enemies to ourselves, strangers to ourselves. And it will make itself known; it will erupt into our lives in some messy way, like an old bulldog we had years ago who in a fit of senility staggered over and took a dump on the Duchess's snow-white living room carpet. The poor old boy needed our attention. He got it.

Women like Daphne are behind me now, years in the past, not because of this new virus that has shown up (although for that reason I hope it's in the past for her too; I hope she lives out in Penn Hills with three kids and spends her evenings testing the depth of her husband's belly button), but because that doesn't do it for me anymore. My thirteen-year-old prick that jumped up and danced at the wink of an eye, my nineteen-year-old prick for a passionate kiss, my thirty-year-old prick for the clutch of bare flesh . . . Those things still turn me on. But they are no longer what I want. I can literally say that my cock doesn't want them. What I do want is much more vague. I dream of a situation where the defenses are down, the barriers are down. The woman says who she is and I say who I am and we're both just interested, attentive, not wishing things were otherwise, because we've heard it all before, and because we know everybody's crazy some way, and because we know that the only real problem is wishing things were different. That's where the trouble comes from. Our defenses are down, and our hearts touch. As we lie there—I'm afraid I picture an older couple, mid-fiftyish perhaps, while in the present I'm just turning forty—we are smiling, content. And lying between us—soft, but heavy, and also, somehow, content—is my cock.

My Mother's Embrace

My mother was a stylish dresser. Since I grew up with that fact, since things were always that way around my house, I didn't know that her devotion to clothes was out of the ordinary. I thought all women were like that (and that my sister, with her perpetual wardrobe of sweatshirts and blue jeans, was in that regard not quite a woman). My mother had four closets full of dresses, I mean jammed solid with dresses—you could hardly get your hand in to take one out. Every one of those closets was cluttered with shoes, all these weird little pairs of women's shoes arranged neatly on the floor. She also had, in one of her rooms—the woman had several rooms—a dresser with three drawers full of pocketbooks, because you had to have the pocketbook that went with the shoes that looked nice with the dress that was appropriate for the occasion. . . .

I can't imagine the amount of time it took to purchase and maintain such a wardrobe. She was always giving away dresses to a secondhand boutique the society women had, so she had to replace those, and it always took her hours—at least any time I was around—to make up her mind about buying so much as a handkerchief. In my mind to this day, the most boring thing in the world is to go shopping with a woman. As soon as we step into the store, I am overwhelmed with a wish to lie down in the corner and go to sleep. At this point in my life I will go shopping with a woman if she holds a gun to my head. That's the only way.

I used to love it when my parents got dressed to go out for the evening. God knows it happened often enough, three or four times a week. It was a frequent pleasure in my life. We lived in the huge house that my mother had grown up in. It was more than we needed for the five children we eventually were, much less in those early years with just Helen and me, but that was another thing I never questioned. We lived in a mansion.

The children's dinner was early, out in the kitchen with Doris—hamburger, I swear to God we had some form of hamburger five or six nights week—and after dinner I would play in the huge south room, but in a place where I could see the long sweeping staircase. Their grand exit, I suppose you would call it, though really it was like a grand entrance, coming down those stairs. They arrived separately, since they had separate rooms. The Senator usually came down first, then went off to read the paper and have a quick drink. Whether he was down or not, the Duchess made an entrance that was worthy of a state dinner. Was it for me, sitting down in that corner of the south room? Was it for the walls? Was it in preparation for an entrance at the place where she was going? I never knew.

I used to like the way the Senator looked too, jaunty and relaxed, practically dancing down the stairs. In my mind that is still (perhaps because I seldom look that way) the way a man should look. He would be wearing a blue suit; I don't remember him ever wearing anything but a blue suit, with a white shirt and black shoes. The only thing with any flash was his tie, which had maybe a few red stripes. He was a big man, but a graceful one. It wouldn't have occurred to you to call him fat. He looked the way men were supposed to look in those days. (A man did not have a salad for lunch in those days, except maybe on the side. He had a thick soup with a small steak and a baked potato, or red snapper with fried potatoes, all this after two or three drinks, and I swear to God if he had a piece of pie with his coffee nobody so much as blinked.) He would have shaved again in the evening, and spruced up, put on some after-shave. He would be smoking a cigarette. "Hello, Charlie," he would say, picking me up to throw me around a little, or stooping down to wrestle. "How's it going, Chas?" He was always in a good mood when he was going out with the Duchess.

I sat waiting for her. First I would hear in the upstairs hallway that peculiar sound, silk against silk, whatever, that women used to make when they walked. Undergarments. She always stopped at the top of the stairs to check in her pocketbook for something. She always had whatever it was. Standing in profile to me, she would turn her head in my direction, quizzically, as if someone up on the second floor had called her. Then regally, as if a thousand eyes were on her—with her head always up; she didn't so much as glance at the steps—she made her way down. She walked slowly, and gracefully. There was a slight air of procession to her steps, though they also seemed perfectly natural.

I don't remember any of her outfits specifically (I'm sure that if I could describe one at this point it would sound fairly ridiculous), but I do remember their effect on me. For one thing—and I don't see how this could be, but it is the impression I have—I never saw the same dress twice. If I did, the times were too far apart for me to remember. The first thing I thought every time I saw her was, This is a new dress. There was always something slightly surprising about it. Either the color was an interesting shade, or there was an unusual pattern to it, or the style was new. The dress was surprising, but never stunning, or daring; it was always in impeccable taste. How does she do it? her women friends must have thought. She always finds exactly that dress. Always surprising. Never daring. Always in perfect taste.

She was a tall slender woman, with chestnut brown hair, ice blue eyes. Her hair hung just to her shoulders. Her face was thin, her features perfect. I was thrilled to see her. After her regal descent, her descent for a thousand eyes, she would walk down the front hall and notice me sitting there. (Had she really known all along that one pair of eyes, anyway, was riveted on her?) She would smile at me, in an intimate way, just the two of us. It was as if you knew a great ballplayer, Mickey Mantle or somebody, and after he had hit a home run and trotted around the bases, maybe touched his cap to the crowd, he noticed, just before he got to the dugout, that you were sitting beside it, and he smiled at you, and winked.

The Senator would happen along at that point. He was a physical man, couldn't seem to walk by without touching you, though if you were a boy he was as likely to goose you or punch you in the arm as anything. Get you in a headlock and give you a Dutch rub. You were always on your guard with the Senator around. He would make some physical gesture toward the Duchess, to embrace her, or give her a kiss, but she would never let him. "Don't muss me, Bruce," she'd say. "Don't muss me."

That's right, I would think. Keep your filthy hands off her, you crude bastard. She's too beautiful to touch.

But I have often wondered about that. Didn't it bother the Senator, never getting to touch his wife? Didn't it embarrass him at least, right there in front of his son? It never seemed to. It seemed to be just what he expected. (Did he ever come home from one of those parties—where she had looked absolutely radiant all evening, comported herself perfectly—and throw the Duchess down on the heavily carpeted stairway, rip her dress off and take her, right there where she had made her decorous descents?) They seemed to be a perfect couple, the Senator and the Duchess. They were a model of what men and women were supposed to be in those days. That big boisterous good-looking guy who was always trying to get his hands on you, but who always seemed slightly embarrassed or ashamed about it. That slender, delicate, beautiful woman, who was always trying to keep herself for the occasion she was attending, and who always told him to take his hands away.

The Duchess had a certain way with her babies. Fastidious, is a word that comes to mind. She didn't actually take care of them that much. She had three people to help around the house, and most of what Doris did was child care. But the moments when the Duchess did care for her babies loom large in my memory. Changing the baby, for instance. She never did that where she was, as some people do, but always went up to the baby's room, with mats and plastic and buckets and all kinds of paraphernalia around. I can see her to this day, doing everything out at arm's length, holding her breath, wincing, practically averting her eyes. God knows it is hard for anyone to clean up shit with dignity, and I'm sure I've looked plenty uncomfortable doing it in my time. But the Duchess had a particular problem.

Feeding the baby was bad enough. I think of how much women went through back in the fifties to feed a baby, when it could have been so easy. It seems typical of that bizarre decade. There was the whole thing of sterilizing the bottles, which was a tremendous production. You started by disassembling them and scrubbing the parts with special brushes. There was a huge metal pot with a rack inside it where you boiled them in water, the whole contraption rattling away on top of the stove. All this was before you even mentioned the word milk, though the word that you actually mentioned was formula. You mixed that in the kitchen, out of a powder, then poured it into the bottles and heated it (not too hot! I can still see the Duchess shaking a drop out of the nipple onto her wrist, to test the temperature). Once all that was done, the baby, who must have been starving half to death at this point, could eat.

Except that even then the Duchess wasn't ready. She had to prepare for any eventuality, spread diapers around everywhere a baby might toss his cookies. She was as particular about her slipcovers and her carpets as she was about her clothes. She also had to drape several diapers on herself (this is a woman who was never dressed in rags; her housedresses were as nice as most people's evening clothes). With roughly the same care with which you see those guys handle radioactive particles, all dressed up in special suits, she would pick the baby up, hold him at arm's length—he might erupt from any of several orifices—then rest him on her arm and place in his mouth the most sterilized nipple in all the world. After a moderate period of feeding came the most perilous moment: burping the baby. She would put the bottle down, sit the baby up, then slowly, at arm's length—he seemed so heavy—hoist him into the air (Look out, fellas! This thing could blow any time!) and, very gingerly, place him on her shoulder to wait for the little sound—*Bap!*—that signaled the All Clear. Jesus was I relieved when that went off.

I don't think the Duchess enacted this procedure all that

often. Only when Doris had a day off or something. But I feel as if I was there on every occasion, as if I saw her a million times, looking pained, annoyed, finding her baby a heavy burden as she handled him out at arm's length. I used to feel sorry for her, that she was working so hard. I wished I could do something for her.

A couple of years ago I visited Helen and some of her lesbian friends in Maine, where they go for a month every summer. Ordinarily it would have been out of the question for a man to so much as stop in and say hello, much less stay for a week ("Has one of you dykes started to pee standing up?" somebody would yell from the bathroom, as she slammed the toilet seat down in disgust), but Helen told them she would vouch for me, and that if she had a chance to see me for a week in the summer she was going to do it. No one loves me more than Helen, and there is a fierceness to her that is hard to deny. I think that if one of those women had made a critical remark about me Helen would have ripped her tits off. On the fifth night, when we were sitting around on newspapers eating lobster, one of them said—and this was a hell of an admission for this particular woman—that she thought I'd be all right if I weren't a man. Didn't I want to do something about that? She'd heard there was an operation. I told her I would stay the way I was just to prove that a man could be all right, to stand as an example to her. And that, anyway, whether I had an operation or not, I was still the best pussy-eater in the house. This remark brought hoots of soprano derision from these women. They were rolling around on the floor, holding their heads, throwing lobster shells at me. But it was true. There wasn't a woman there who was a more devoted student of cunt than I was.

I like lesbians. I like their attitude. I loved staying in that house. I think it was the only place I've ever really felt at home.

One of those women was so recent an addition to the lesbian ranks that she had a baby only a few months old. Her former boyfriend had had some kind of problem with parental responsibilities. He'd had the same problem in an earlier relationship. The baby was born and he started to hyperventilate or something. Had to lie down in a corner in the fetal position. She'd half expected it to happen, though that didn't make things any easier when it did. She was so disgusted she became a lesbian.

Never have I seen a woman more devoted to a baby. Not only did she take him everywhere she went, but she always had him pressed against her body. She was a large soft woman, with mammoth tits, so he was always riding around on a mountain of warm flesh. Sometimes she would lie on her back and let him crawl around on her. He must have thought he'd died and gone to heaven. If he got hungry she'd just lift up her T-shirt and let him suck. (She didn't have to sterilize her tits. She didn't have to heat her milk. It wasn't called formula.) She wasn't in the least bit embarrassed about that. Nobody around but us lesbians, after all.

Anyway, at some point, after seeing her handle the baby that way for days, and feeling—to tell the truth—more than a little envious of the little bastard, I finally said something. "God. I don't think I ever got that kind of affection when I was a child." And Helen, standing beside me in a T-shirt and jeans, looking as little like the Duchess as anyone possibly could, said, "That's right. Our mother would have held us out there with a pair of tongs if she could have."

I was stunned. I had made that remark in a casual way, off the top of my head. I hadn't expected to have it confirmed so resoundingly. It was something I had felt only vaguely, in my bones. I hadn't quite admitted it in my head. I could see in that moment all that that simple fact had meant to Helen's life, and to mine. It had had vast ramifications. I stood there and stared at it.

A few years ago my marriage ended abruptly. Came home one night and the woman was gone, as the song says. It seemed totally out of the blue, though anyone who hadn't had his head firmly planted up his ass would have seen it coming miles away. Six years before, at a time when I had been deeply depressed and hadn't been there for her, Sara had fallen in love with another man. I knew she had started an affair—she had been perfectly honest about it—but I figured it would blow over. Within a few months I figured it had blown over. How could anyone be more desirable than I was? In time I came out of my depression and wanted to resume my marriage, in fact to be more intimate than ever, only to find that her feelings for me had died, and those for the other guy had deepened. The old sad story. The woman pick up and gone, as the song says. I can't say as I blame her. She'd had to live with a zombie for a while there, and she couldn't take it. She shouldn't have been asked to. On the other hand, I don't blame me either. I'd had to be a zombie for a while there. Otherwise I would have died. Or become a normal human being. I'm not sure which is worse.

Anyway, it was a crazy time. I've always been what is known as a problem sleeper, but at that point I put on an exhibition that should assure me a place in the Insomnia Hall of Fame (after I've died, which is the only way a person like me is ever sure of getting some sleep). For three straight nights I didn't sleep at all. Not one wink. After that there were two months when I got only three or four hours a night. I would wake up at some bizarre time—3:45 is a good example—and spend the rest of the night staring into the blackness. Which seemed to bear a strong resemblance to the rest of my life.

A part of the weird and inexhaustible energy that was keeping me awake had to do with the fact that I wasn't being touched. Sara and I hadn't been having much sex in the last months of our marriage (all right, we hadn't been having any), but we had still been touching. We spent ten or fifteen minutes, for instance, hugging in bed every morning before we got up. We had an unspoken agreement to ignore the hard-on I got. In a way it was all so nice because we did ignore it. Those hugs were like a faint allusion to our past passion, as if we were eulogizing it, but they weren't sad. They were friendly. Sensuous and luxuriant. They were lovely.

The loss of that feeling after Sara left, the sheer absence of a physical being in my life, was driving me a little crazy. I was having withdrawal symptoms. My body needed a fix.

All kinds of weird things were running through my mind at that point, especially at night. Most of it made no sense at all. It was as if someone had turned on a tape recorder and was playing it full blast, at some advanced speed. When it did slow down, when the noise died down a little, images appeared to me. One was a scene from my childhood that had often passed through my mind through the years and that must have been one of my earliest memories. It was a kind of tableau. I was a boy of five or six, standing beside my mother as she sat at her dressing table doing her nails. At first that was all I saw in it. I just knew that that image kept coming back to me.

I should mention in connection with all this something that is probably already apparent, that my family was not physically demonstrative. The Senator was a fairly physical guy, though there was always that embarrassed air about his affection. He had to turn it into a wrestling match. But the Duchess had some definite physical limitations. I could see them clearly in how we were with each other as adults. We only saw each other about once a year, but you would never have known that from our greeting. It would be stretching the definition to call what we did a hug. Our bodies did not come together, though they might brush each other, or bump. Our hands touched neutral places. The shoulder. The upper arm. She would offer her cheek for a kiss, and make a half-hearted attempt to kiss me, though all she usually got was air. The whole thing was something of a formality. It was as if—to use an old sports term—we were walking through it, and would do the real embrace later. But the real embrace never happened.

I wouldn't have said at that point that there was anything wrong with all that. It was the way I had been raised. If I saw people behaving in another way (as a teenager, for instance, I had an Italian friend who used to be showered with kisses at the slightest provocation by his mother, his aunts, his grandmothers), I thought *they* were strange. I hadn't yet had my realization about the way I'd been handled as a baby. I'd spent much of my adult life running after women's bodies like one of the Marx brothers, but I didn't see anything wrong with that. All men—as the expression goes—do that.

Anyway, in the midst of that crazy time, when that image kept returning to me, I decided to look at it for a while, to try to remember what surrounded it, to see what it was about. It must mean something if it kept coming back. I spent several nights staring at it. I don't know if what I came up with is factually accurate—I think there's a good chance it is—but psychologically it's dead on the mark. As a lifelong storyteller, who knows that the story is not really in the facts, I can say with some confidence that this is What Happened:

I had come home from school and was alone with the Duchess. It was a moment I had often dreamed of. It seems a simple enough wish, for a boy to be alone with his mother, but in a house where I had an older sister, where my father might pop in any time, where there were three servants, and where—most notably—my mother had an extensive social calendar, it didn't often happen. In fact, this unusual circumstance—that the house, or at least the second floor, was empty except for the two of us—may be the detail that made this moment memorable, because the feelings that attached to it must have come up countless times. The Duchess was sitting at her dressing table, filing her nails. Her face was immaculately made up. Her soft brown hair hung just to the shoulders of a blue silk robe she was wearing.

I was coming to her with a problem, something that had come up at school. The Duchess wasn't overly fond of problems—I imagine that's why I went through my youth keeping them to myself, being a model child—but it was a part of my dream to go to her with a problem, something I was scared of or worried about. I'm sure that, as my parents always did, she brushed the problem aside. "You're not afraid of *that. You're* not worried about *that."* It was a way they had of trying to diminish the problem, so it wouldn't bother me. Actually, they were failing to take seriously something that was very real to me. They were eliminating a difficulty for themselves, avoiding the need to deal with it.

"No," I said. "I guess not."

And thereby betrayed my truest self.

My body, as I stood there, took on a strange feeling. It was an overwhelming restlessness. I didn't know what to do with myself. I wanted to jump out of my skin. I wanted to roll around on the floor and scream.

Probably the problem I had come to the Duchess with had no solution. I had come for something else. My mother said whatever words she said. She gave me a little kiss. She probably patted my back. I was supposed to take that and go back into my room. Back into my life. And everything would be all right.

But thirty years later, sleepless in a dark house, my wife finally gone, I saw—and it was a stunning revelation—what I had wanted. It might be more accurate to say that I admitted what I had wanted. I finally let myself want it. I wanted my mother to hold me. To turn to me from that dressing table and open her arms to me, take and hold my whole body—my chest, my stomach, my legs, my face—against hers. As I saw her do that (it was such a *relief* to see it, finally to admit it) we fell back on the bed, my body wrapped in hers. As I saw them lying there, that six-year-old boy—my early precious self—and his beautiful mother (whom he watched with such rapt attention as she came down the stairs) I recognized that embrace. It was the embrace I always sought from women, anytime we went to bed. It was the thing I had to have to feel all right. It was the absence of that embrace that I was feeling now (in the way that, at a moment of crisis in our lives, we often go back to earlier moments). It was that strange feeling in my body that I had felt when I was six that was surging through me now, keeping me from sleep.

For the first time in my life, I had remembered wanting to hug my mother.

And for just a moment, with the kind of certainty that we feel only in our bodies, I knew: *that* was what I had wanted, all those times I thought I wanted a woman.

TWO

Two cities appear in my dreams. I have named them for what they are like and for the feelings they evoke, since neither one has recognizable landmarks. The city I think of as New York is enormous, virtually limitless, and moves at a terrific pace, traffic whizzing by, though the sidewalks are not overly crowded. The landscape of buildings is tall and majestic, and very regular, like a fortress. I have an appointment in those New York dreams, but it is never important, and I have plenty of time to get there. I always walk, and the point of the dreams seems to be the trip I am taking. The rush of the great city around me, my leisurely pace as I enjoy it.

The city I think of as Pittsburgh, on the other hand, is close and convoluted, slightly claustrophobic. In that city I am looking for something, usually a woman, though not some particular woman. The street of vice in that city—strippers and dirty movies and magazines—is always just around the corner and is open to the air, but dark, like a parking garage. Everyone wanders through. I hurry along streets lined with skyscrapers, trudge up hills, duck into buildings, looking for a place where I can find a woman. Often it is in an office building: beside the dentist's office, the jeweler's, whatever, is the place where you get a woman in this city. Sometimes I find the building, sometimes the room, sometimes I see the woman, but the encounter I'm looking for—whatever it is—doesn't take place. My Pittsburgh dreams have an unfinished quality to them. They begin in frustration and end in confusion.

I find these dreams vaguely embarrassing. To spend my nights walking through large open-air adult bookstores. Office buildings with whorehouses in them. I have told the dreams to Helen. She makes a living listening to dreams, as a therapist. Her practice is limited to women. The Dyke Shrink, as her friends call her.

When she talks about dreams, Helen doesn't quite sound like herself. She doesn't hesitate, or mumble, or shrug. She doesn't speak crudely. She speaks sentences that fall with a thud.

"The New York city is the city of your career," she says. "You have things to do there, but you are relaxed and content. You know who you are. The Pittsburgh city is the landscape of home. There you are still searching. What you're looking for is acceptance, which is what those places, whorehouses and adult bookstores, mean to you. A place where you can be who you think you really are. Which is actually just a part of who you are."

"Don't editorialize," I said.

"Probably the dream comes up because of some way you've failed to accept yourself during the day. Nothing to do with sex, necessarily. So you have this dream. Anyway. You're not going to find this acceptance in a whorehouse. You're not going to get it from a woman. You're not going to get it from anyone else. You've got to give it to yourself. Find that place inside you and walk in there to stay. You've got to be your own whore."

She should write a book. *How To Be Your Own Best Whore.*

"Why is it in an office building?" I said.

"That has something to do with your work. Your career. Or maybe the career you didn't do."

There are whores up in those buildings.

"You speak with such authority," I said.

"I'm just taking a stab at it." She took a sip from her beer, slightly embarrassed. We were sitting in her living room. I don't think she really knew where those interpretations came from. She started talking, and they rumbled up. "Ignore me if you want."

"It always sounds just right," I said. "That's what drives me nuts."

She smiled, shrugged.

"*You're* my favorite whore," I said.

"I'll be your whore anytime. How do you want it, big boy?"

My dream landscape is accurate to Pittsburgh. It is an oddly convoluted city. The downtown area is a triangle, famously formed by two rivers coming together to form a third, and the streets are also on that triangular plan, so that in places they come together at funny angles. Up at the top of the city, where my hotel was, the streets looked fairly normal, but down near the Point they can be weird, very short, and slightly claustrophobic where the buildings are tall. That was the part of the city I was in now. I mention these things because the one major coincidence in my story is about to take place, and I want to suggest that it was at least in a likely location, and that it made sense for me to be there. I was down in those small out-of-the-way streets because I was looking for the city as it used to be. For the people who used to be there. I was looking for a touch of humanity.

The store I was standing in front of was called Womanbooks. It had caught my eye because I am drawn to any bookstore, and because I was surprised—and delighted—to find a new one downtown, and because it had a bright and attractive window display, though before I noticed the name of the store I was puzzled by the odd mix of books. There were classic titles by Edith Wharton and Jane Austen and Willa Cather, followed by modern masters like Anne Tyler and Alice Munro. The latest hardback by Marge Piercy was displayed front and center, flanked by a number of her paperbacks. There was a row of pop psychology—*How to Get the Love You Want* and *Women Who Love Too Much*—that segued into a clutch of books on sexual technique and dysfunction, followed by some books on women's sexual fantasies. There were books of leftist political theory and some small-press lesbian novels. At the bottom of the display was a whole row of the Virago series. After puzzling over this display for a few minutes I noticed the store's name in the window, followed by a motto: Celebrating the Diversity in Women's Reading.

I should say so.

Beside the window, and perpendicular to it, was a counter, and sitting behind the counter was a woman. She turned to look at me. The face that within a few weeks I would think of as the most beautiful in all the world was gazing out at me, and I must say that, as I look back on it, it seems pleasing, but rather ordinary. (Much of the beauty in that face came from its animation. The life she breathed into it.) She wore large spectacles with thin black frames that had slipped partway down her nose. She wasn't bothering to push them back up. She had luxuriant red hair that hung straight to her shoulders, not quite a fiery red, actually a kind of burnished color, but all the prettier for that. Her mouth was slightly too large, her lips too thick; it was almost an ugly mouth, but somehow—as she bit the corner of a lip, pressed her lips together—it drew your attention. It seemed hungry. There was an ample sprinkling of reddish freckles all over her face, but even they, against her pale skin, were attractive. Without them she wouldn't have had enough color.

She was wearing a gray turtleneck with a white, loose-fitting cotton dress on top of it. Her posture was extremely expressive. I would call it Female Resigned. Her legs were spread. Her shoulders slumped. Her belly stuck out. This was a posture that the Duchess—to pick another female wildly at random—would never have assumed in her life. It said: I know I Look Good so I don't have to look good. Nobody's telling me to suck in my belly or close my legs. There is—as this posture might suggest (and as a more traditional female posture would deny)—a cunt under this skirt. Feel free to get interested, but the rest of the package goes with it. Including the brain. And the heart.

The face that gazed out at me was blunt and inquisitive. Curious, but not terribly so. She would check me out, if I wanted to stand there, but she wouldn't go to the trouble of pushing her glasses up on her nose.

The odd thing about this face—and the coincidental thing

about the moment—was that I had seen it before. It had been different then. The face had been rounder and fuller. The body had also been fuller, not fat, but a little on the soft side. Broad at the hips. The hair hadn't been luxuriant, or even especially noticeable. It had been what Helen called dyke hair, one of those little Gertrude Stein caps. I hadn't been sure if it belonged to a dyke or not. I believe that ambiguity had been intentional. This woman liked to keep you guessing. She also liked to move around in both communities. Anyway, the face was different, and the body was different, and as I stared in the window I kept superimposing the old person on the new one, back and forth, back and forth, trying to see if it fit. I couldn't decide. I was still trying to make up my mind when I opened the door and stepped in.

"We're moving to Shadyside in a few months," she said. "This is just a place to get started." She was answering the inquisitive expression on my face, which she took to say, What's a classy store like this doing on this godforsaken street? "You can come in," she said. "Men are allowed. If they behave."

"Andrea?" I said.

"Yes."

"It's Charles Bradford."

She stared at me. "Charles. God. Without the beard. It takes a minute."

She stepped out from behind the counter to hug me. We hadn't actually been close in the old days, I doubt if we had ever hugged, but it was a gesture among a certain segment of my generation. We're comfortable with our bodies, it said. We're okay with them. We're cool.

"It's been a while," she said.

"What. Ten years."

"At least."

"And you're still here."

"Others may come and go."

"You work here."

"Hey. I own it."

"You've gone respectable on us."

"Don't let it fool you. I'm still the same person underneath."

It was in the mid-seventies that I had known Andrea, back

when Sara and I, in a moment of insanity, had tried living in Pittsburgh. I had started writing for a local underground newspaper, partly because I thought that would connect me with the people I wanted to know and partly because the paper was looking for writers and was glad to have me. It was a dinky little publication, mostly just distributed around the universities, but it commanded great respect among the Left. You'd have thought it was the *Village Voice*. I was still trying to figure out what I wanted to do, using this paper that anyone could write for to help me find out. (But I wrote some great pieces for them. I have never let a publication's pay scale determine how hard I worked.) It gave me something of an identity. It also gave me a reason not to throw myself more wholeheartedly into the political struggle. I was Press.

Andrea—also a reporter for the paper—wasn't like that. She was a much different-looking person in those days, of medium height and slightly dumpy, with that short rust-colored hair that was often disheveled and little rimless glasses that seemed always to have slid partway down her nose. She never wore anything but blue jeans and sweatshirts, and her nails were bitten to the quick; she was a chainsmoker of Camels and a prodigious coffee drinker. But she didn't for one minute try to maintain the objectivity of the press. When she went to cover some kind of demonstration—and she was always requesting such assignments—she would join right in, and if she got carried off by the police, biting and kicking and shouting obscenities, all the better. She was happy to file her story from a jail cell. She had no feeling that what happened to her should be divorced from the rest of the story. What happened to her *was* the story, far more interesting—as far as she was concerned—than the whole background of the demonstration.

She was also not like me in that she didn't care in the least about the writing of the piece. I would spend hours on my stories, going through draft after draft, while she would throw down any old thing and let the editors fix it up. She didn't care if they rewrote her pieces entirely, as long as they gave her the byline. She wasn't working for that paper because she wanted to be a writer or even a journalist. She was just looking for a way to be at the center of the political action.

The rumor was—and this kind of rumor was widespread in

those days—that she was at the center of the action in other ways as well. If you were up all night with her getting out an issue, and you wanted to take a break about two in the morning to fool around, she didn't—as we would say nowadays—have any problem with that. She would find a spare office somewhere, or just a closet if she had to. She would no doubt have offered a philosophical explanation for her actions. We were supposed to fuck each other in those days. It showed our solidarity. She wanted to give herself to the movement in any way she could. She wanted to give her body to it.

Andrea was an extremely impressive and articulate person as long as she was giving you the party line on something. She could give you the pro-choice position, for instance, at the drop of a hat, and expertly parry any counterargument you came up with. It wasn't that she had thought it all out, but that she had heard all the arguments. She had an insatiable appetite for political discourse. It made her pants wet. She could have written, or at least spoken, the whole issue of *The Nation* every week (if you left out the poetry and book reviews). All you had to do was give her the topics. It wasn't my impression that she read all that much. She got it all by word of mouth. She went to bed with those self-involved political types and let them talk.

She also knew every bit of gossip on the Left. Who was screwing whom. How they were liking it. What they were into. I suppose a lot of people will tell you those things if you just ask. She was especially delighted to report on someone's gender preference. If she didn't know it by rumor she claimed to know it by instinct. "She *is* a lesbian," she would say. "I'm just not sure she knows it yet."

She had a strong tendency to divide the world up into us and them, and was willing to allow a single fact to make the difference. "He isn't sure about capital punishment" or "He thinks we need some nuclear deterrent" meant, as far as she was concerned, He is a total asshole. She was also very capable of concealing such an opinion, showing one face to a person while speaking of him very differently to others. In that regard she was political in the worst sense. You could actually figure out more from the little details of how she acted toward you—if you could see past the inevitable flirtation—than by what she said to you.

I had never been sure how she felt about me. On the one hand I worked for that newspaper, which raised me practically to the status of a god. On the other hand I wasn't willing to dash off to a protest at the slightest provocation. In the midst of a driving rainstorm or whatever. I always wanted to make a judgment as to whether or not a protest would do any good, something she never gave a moment's thought. I was married, and didn't noticeably fool around, which doubtless made me a wimp in her eyes. She would have liked to sneak me off to a spare office late some night and see what kind of man I was. Furthermore, Sara had taken my name, which Andrea considered the most cowardly and traitorous thing a woman could do. That probably cast a shadow on our whole relationship.

Now, ten years later, a change had obviously taken place, though I didn't know how profound it was. The closely cropped dyke hair of the old days had grown out bright and red and beautiful. The face had thinned, showing her features better. So had her body. (The ass that she had waved in the face of the Left in the old days had been quite a hefty item.) The stylish clothes were a big change from the old days, when she had seemed to want to look bad, as if to show what she was going through. Mostly, though, the change was in her face. Her tough-woman exterior seemed subdued. There was a tenderness, a vulnerability, in her eyes. The girl in her, which she had always suppressed, seemed to be showing through. It was as if someone had slapped her in the face, hard, and said, "All right. Cut the shit. Show us who you really are." And she was still trying to decide.

"So." I gestured around the store. "When did all this happen?"

"A couple of years ago. Me and another woman. A university professor who didn't get tenure. At first she was going to fight, then she just said fuck it. The whole system's corrupt anyway. She'd rather work for herself."

"How's it going?"

"Surprisingly well. There seems to be a real market for this kind of store. Women will even come to this totally shitty location. Not that we have books that other places don't. But you can browse more freely here. Some guy isn't going to be eyeing you. And you don't have to worry about buying *Lesbian Sex* or whatever. Nobody's going to look at you funny at the cash register. But we do want to move to Shadyside. Closer to where our clientele lives. That's where we wanted to be all along, except that the rents are so high. We weren't sure we could do that volume of business. But it looks like we can."

Andrea was good at selling herself. Presenting an idea. She already had me convinced.

"I didn't know you were a book person," I said.

"You didn't picture me curled up in front of the fire every night. With my Jane Austen or something."

"Not exactly." *The Story of O* was more like it.

"I don't know. I've been into this and that. Never especially books. If you'd told me ten years ago that I'd own a bookstore someday I'd have laughed my ass off. But I got it into my head that I wanted to own a business. And the woman I opened it up with knows books inside and out. She's been an avid reader since she was a kid. For me it's more of a gathering place, where women can talk to each other, and feel free, and maybe work on politics."

The place looked great to me, bright and well-lighted, with floor-to-ceiling shelves along two walls and several movable display cases out in the middle of the floor. There was a couch at the back, and an automatic coffee maker beside it on a table, and a little alcove of magazines and literary journals.

"I see your articles," she said. "You're doing great."

"Thanks."

"Do you make a living at that?"

"Only part of one. I also have some money from my Uncle Egbert."

That was my way of referring to money I had from my family, on my mother's side. One of those elaborate trusts devised by aging capitalists. I'm sure they never thought they'd be supporting a journalist on the Left. It wasn't all that much money, but it meant the difference between working as a free-lancer and having a job at some publication. I was deeply grateful to Uncle Egbert.

Andrea let this odd reference pass.

"Are you and Sara still together?" she said.

"No. Not for a couple of years."

"I'm sorry."

There was a genuine sympathy in her eyes. A look of real sorrow. She had soft green eyes, very expressive.

Was there something else going on behind those eyes, as she heard my words?

"What about you?" I said.

"I married Arthur Grossman."

Perfect. If she was actually going to get married, if she was going to surrender to a bourgeois institution to that extent, it would be Arthur Grossman she would do it with. He had been a kind of father figure—perhaps it would be more accurate to say an older-brother figure—to the New Left in Pittsburgh. He was a political science professor, and as soon as he had gotten tenure in the late sixties he had started to raise hell, leading protests, giving speeches, writing inflammatory letters and articles. He could be found around campus at all hours, in bars and coffeehouses, expounding his ideas. There were periods when he hardly taught in his classes, just chatted with his students about what was happening in the news, which he said was more to the point than their textbooks. He was the only person in the city who knew the party line better than Andrea, who might have been able to footnote it for her. They were a perfect match. He was a feather in her cap, as she was in his.

"You still together?" I said.

"Nope. He left four months ago. Took my kid."

That was the fact that gave everything meaning. Her look of resignation as I stared in the window. Her blankness of affect as we talked. The pain in her eyes as I had spoken of breaking up with Sara. The way her face had trembled slightly when I asked about her situation. Her eyes had gone beyond softening now, were dissolving altogether. Her face was collapsing.

"Decided he'd rather stick his dick in some other woman."

This statement had its startling aspect. It wasn't that it was crude. Andrea had always had without a doubt the crudest vocabulary of any woman I had ever met, and that was saying something in my generation. You'd have to go back to a mill worker or a thirteen-year-old boy to match it. It wasn't that it was bitter. Andrea had always had a depth of bitterness in her that seemed to have nothing to do with her present situation, that seemed to have its roots in her distant past. She was simply too angry all the time for it to be something in the present. But when I was in the store there were three women browsing, and now two of them had come to the counter. One looked unshockable—she was buying one of the Anne Rice vampire novels—but the other, who was standing at the register with a book by Rosamunde Pilcher, looked positively matronly. She didn't seem the kind of person you would express such feelings to, especially not in that language. Andrea's words were also startling because, though I had known her in the past and we had traveled in the same crowd, we hadn't been intimate. We certainly hadn't confided in each other. It wouldn't have occurred to me to say such a thing to her, though I could have said something similar.

But Andrea didn't hesitate for a moment. Now she was weeping bitterly, tears pouring from her eyes. She spoke through her sobs. This transformation had taken place in a matter of seconds.

"Decides he wants to stick his dick in someone else. His dick gets hard for someone else. So he *leaves* me. *Takes* my *kid.*"

"I'm sorry." It seemed a feeble response, but I couldn't think of anything else.

"Not as sorry as I am." She let out a sob that sounded like a groan. "That stupid prick."

"We're all sorry, dear," the matronly woman said.

"The slimy son of a bitch."

The matron took a small package of Kleenex from her purse and offered it. Andrea snatched out a tissue without so much as noticing where it had come from. Of all the things I came to admire about Andrea, the one I admired most was her astounding ability to burst into tears. A few weeks later, when she was crying about some trivial matter (she *always* cried the day before her period started), when I held her against me and felt the sobs in her soft little belly, fluttering against my rock-hard belly, I thought, That's where the pain is for all of us. In that vulnerable spot. And that's why it's hard for me to let it out. I've held it in so long it's locked tight.

If I could have cried like that I'd have been the most emotionally healthy person on earth.

"That's all men are interested in, is their dicks." Andrea was actually addressing these words to the matronly woman. "Where he's going to stick his dick is all a man ever thinks about."

"I know." The woman shook her head.

"He decides he wants to stick it somewhere else. So he *leaves.*"

She still seemed to find this fact startling, four months later.

"It's terrible," the woman said.

"Takes my only kid."

This would seem a good time to mention—though I need to emphasize that it would be months before I put the facts together and came to this realization—that the things Andrea was saying were not true. Her husband had not wanted to leave her, he had simply wanted to have an affair, something she had done several times during their marriage. He had told her what he wanted (she hadn't always been so forthcoming in the same situation) and she had thrown him out. She had more or less forced him to move in with the other woman. And he hadn't taken her son. They shared custody. She actually saw the boy a little more than he did.

It was also true that, the whole time she was saying these things, weeping profusely, she was putting the woman's book in a bag and ringing it up, taking her MasterCard and filling out the slip.

"I lost my kid because of what he wants to do with his dick."

"It's shameful," the matronly woman said.

"Men try to figure out what to do with their fucking dicks and they fuck up the whole fucking world."

"*That's* the fucking truth," the third woman said.

"Andrea," I said. "Maybe I'll come back later."

I don't have a problem with women's tears. That is, I do, but I have learned to handle it. I have learned to stay with a woman while she is crying and not want to bolt, or quiet her down. I also don't have a problem with women's anger against men, though I had the distinct feeling that I was about to get hit over the head with a MasterCard machine. But I didn't think I was doing any good by being there. I couldn't think of anything to say. I couldn't think of any way to comfort her. She looked as if she might sit there and cry for the rest of the afternoon. (*I* had brought this on?) There was also a certain, I don't know, surreal aspect to this whole scene that was driving me crazy.

"You don't have to come back." It seemed to have slipped her mind that I was there. "You can just leave."

"I *want* to come back," I said.

The matronly woman turned to me. "I think it would be best." For me to leave, she meant.

"You don't want to come back," Andrea said. "I might get hysterical."

"That would be okay."

"I might embarrass you."

"I won't be embarrassed."

She turned back to the counter, took a long deep breath, and, in that instant, stopped sobbing. "I might be busy."

"I'll come at closing time."

"There could still be customers here."

"I'll wait."

"I might still have work to do."

"That would be all right."

She turned a look on me that seemed positively hostile. "You'll help me with my work?"

"If you want. Or I could leave and come back when you finish."

"That doesn't sound like much fun."

"I wouldn't mind."

"So come then. Come any time you want."

"I'll come at closing time."

"It's a free country. I can't stop you."

"If you feel like it and have some time, we'll talk."

"If you feel like it too. Don't come on my account."

That conversation could have gone on all day. Anything I said, she had an answer for. I figured I just had to walk away. I nodded to the other women, headed for the door. "I'll be back at six," I said.

"If you *want* to," she said.

I opened the door and was hit by a gust of arctic air. As I stepped into the gray afternoon, the door shutting behind me, Andrea yelled out one last thing.

"You might be coming back to a crazy woman."

I should have listened.

Movie Kisses

A void opens in the psyche and the demons enter. You don't know why you aren't being hugged (it is your body that feels the absence of hugs; your mind doesn't know what the hell's going on), so you invent explanations. You decide that you are not huggable. Not lovable. You might assume that you are inherently unlovable—always an attractive theory for the morose psyche—or, more likely, that you have done something wrong that is preventing you from being hugged. You search through your life for the offending act. Countless possibilities present themselves. You believe that if you improve your behavior you might be hugged. You will make up (by being *so* nice) for your inherent unlovability, or you will atone (by being *such* a good boy) for the thing you have done wrong. So you tiptoe around, figuring out what The Woman wants, never saying what you want, never making waves.

This strategy definitely falls into the "Hope Springs Eternal in the Human Breast" category. Don't you ever notice that, no matter how nice you are, how much you tiptoe around, you never get the hug you want? (You'd have a better chance running up to your mother and taking it. Throwing her down on the stairway where she makes her decorous descents . . .) How long do you continue this behavior? Ten years? Twelve? Thirty? Forty?

In the meantime, you must find compensations. It is impossible to live when you are getting so little of what you want. If you can't have what you really need, you take what you can have. These compensations cannot be out in the open. They would betray your image as a nice boy. So you take them furtively. They become a part of your secret life.

The most readily available compensation is in your imagination.

In the movies of my youth, the woman had—like my mother—shoulder-length straight hair that curled up at her shoulders. She had a luscious creamy complexion, large soft lips—always dark with lipstick—and moist limpid eyes. In every movie, it was a key moment when she and the man first kissed. There was an awkward pause in what they were saying, their sentences trailing off (you *knew* what was coming) as she looked up at him with her doelike eyes. The screen might mist over slightly. He moved toward her, perhaps taking her waist in his hands, and she leaned almost imperceptibly toward him, closing her eyes. Their mouths gently met. Her arms encircled his big strong shoulders. Their lips melted together, but did not open. Their heads might move passionately from side to side.

Many boys my age—five, six, seven—acted as if they hated such scenes, retching and gagging, but though I pretended with them (thereby betraying my truest self), I loved those kisses. I looked forward to them in every movie. My heart filled with longing as I watched.

I began at an age before memory a fantasy life that has continued ever since. At any spare moment—always, for instance, when I lie down in bed at night—my mind turns to fantasy, and it is a constant background to whatever I'm doing. In my childhood, when I knew nothing about sex, all my fantasies were of kissing. They were strange little vignettes. I imagined that I was in the presence of an older woman, one of the movie starlets, say, from the screen. For some reason she had decided to be nice to me. It wasn't that I attracted her (I was only seven years old!), but something else. She saw my loneliness. She took pity on me. Sometimes I invented a reason. ("Charles, you've just won that raffle you entered a few

weeks ago. The first prize is five thousand kisses from me.")
She would walk to a chair and sit me in her lap and kiss me
and kiss me, with the passionate lengthy kisses that I thrilled
to on the screen. Her lips were large and soft and warm. Her
hair was silky. Her arms encircled me and did not let go.

It was a vision of the eternal loving female, of unconditional love that has no end. Was it strange to be having such
fantasies at that age, to be virtually obsessed by them? Would
a psychiatrist regard such an obsession as abnormal? ("This
child will go on to become a raving pervert.") I have no idea.
I'm not interested in normal behavior. I'm interested in the
child I was, father to the man I am. That child was obsessed
with kissing. He thought about it night and day.

There are details of those fantasies that must not be overlooked. The woman and I were not equals. She was fifteen years
older, much taller and more mature, astonishingly beautiful.
She did not kiss me because she wanted to (that would be absurd!), but because she knew I wanted to. I had done nothing to
earn those kisses. They had come out of nowhere.

Isn't this rather obviously the fantasy of a boy who wanted to
kiss his mother? Who wanted from his mother an unconditional
physical affection, a warmth and enveloping that had nothing to
do with who he was or what he deserved? Haven't all of us wanted
such love? (And, failing to find it, projected it elsewhere? To mention only the most obvious example, we have projected it onto
the image of an unconditionally loving God. How quaint! To at-
tribute human feeling to the Creator of all there is.)

That fantasy—oh! those fifties movies—was the basis for a
sexual wish that I was to have for the rest of my life.

There was a girl whom I kissed regularly at the age of six or
seven. Her name was Rachel. (My thing for Jewish women goes
way back.) She was the sister of my best friend, Alan. It was in
many ways a classic situation. He knew that I kissed his sister
(he himself kissed her, or so she told me), but we didn't speak
about it, and I didn't do it in his presence. I waited for days when
he wasn't home, or times when the three of us were playing and
he had run off somewhere. I wanted to keep those kisses a secret.

This was sexual reality, not sexual fantasy. The differences
are vast. She might have said no, for instance, and broken my
heart (she never did, God bless her). She was not bigger or more

sophisticated than I, she was not beautiful, she did not wear lipstick and have long silky hair. She was a funny-looking little Jewish girl with cheekbones as big as plums and brown hair in pigtails. She smelled of garlic (preparing me for the dark sophisticated Jewesses of my later years), and when we kissed, clutched together like wrestlers in a desperate clinch, I felt her teeth pressed against my mouth, which was vaguely disturbing. I felt that a kiss should be all mouth, soft, warm, and smooth. The way it seemed on the screen.

But there is something to be said for reality. The heart-pounding excitement of asking Rachel if she would kiss me, and seeing the smile come over her face. The real flesh, her big thick Jewish lips, moistened quickly by her tongue. Her hot hands clutching the back of my neck, a little too hard perhaps, but you had to like her enthusiasm. Her breath on my skin as she breathed through her nose (otherwise the poor girl would have suffocated). The thrill we got from those moments, and the happiness. The secret we shared.

Rachel and I did other things, took our pants down and let each other look, played doctor—all the classic moves—but those things seemed strange and frightening. It was with kisses that we loved each other, and it is the kisses that have remained a vivid memory. Alan and I stopped being best friends when I was eight, and I didn't kiss another girl for years. I missed it terribly.

I also vividly remember—speaking of reality—seeing my parents kiss, which is the one way I ever saw them come close to being sexual. I remember in particular a ritualistic kiss that they often exchanged when the Senator came home from work. I watched it dozens of times. It must have held a strong attraction for me. (It must have expressed what I wanted to do.) He would have gone to the closet to hang up his hat and coat. She would come out to meet him. He would put his hands on the small of her back; hers would rest on his shoulders. He would look down at her, but she would lower her eyes until she was not quite looking at him. She wore a slightly embarrassed expression. They kissed once, twice, modest little kisses. Their lips were pursed and round. The Senator might lift her into the air a little. The Duchess would redden and give an embarrassed laugh, lower her head even more. Their mouths did not melt together. Their lips didn't open at all. Their kisses were more chaste than those on the screen.

I have in later years become obsessed with those kisses, spent hours seeing them again, examining them for meaning. (This fact undoubtedly says far more about me than it does about my parents.) Why did they kiss in that embarrassed, chaste way? Did they not want their children to see a more passionate kiss? (Why did they *do* it, if it made them so uncomfortable? Did they do it for us, to show us what a kiss—or a loving relationship—should be?) Or was that the only way they kissed? The possibility seems absurd, but there was something about the way the Duchess kissed—something in her embarrassment—that suggested that might be all she did. There didn't seem to be any give in her. That was the way she was.

At the time I saw those kisses—the memory seems to be from when I was five or six—I didn't know there was another kind of kissing. I had never heard of French kissing, and didn't until I was eleven or twelve. There was no suggestion of it around my house, and it wasn't—as it is today—shown in close-ups on television and movie screens. It seemed an exotic art, and I was thrilled to hear about it, but not surprised. I had known there must be something more to kissing. I was sure I would like it. I couldn't wait to try it.

I didn't kiss a girl that way until I was seventeen. That doesn't sound like a long wait in retrospect, but it was an eternity to go through. I was overweight and shy in my youth—my wishes stuck in my throat—so I didn't go out much. I tended to go out with girls I had a crush on, so I was afraid to kiss them. Afraid I'd ruin everything. (There was nothing to ruin.) But when I was seventeen I had a date with a younger girl, also overweight, not especially pretty, with whom I didn't care what happened, and when we got back to her house we sat in her car and kissed fiercely and avidly for half an hour, our mouths open as wide as we could get them, our tongues battling for supremacy, our lips sucking at each other and making all kinds of weird noises. We didn't know each other, and had no idea if we liked each other, didn't know what the hell we were doing, but we both had the same terrible hunger. It was a fabulous evening, and has remained in my memory when far more sophisticated and romantic evenings have disappeared. My balls ached for two days.

I have often wondered what that extraordinary craving was. It seems obvious to say that it was a hunger for my mother's breast (that rubber nipple just didn't get it), but it also seems too fierce for that. Not everybody who didn't get breastfed can be walking around feeling that way. It is a hunger that continues. I don't feel I've made love unless I've kissed until my lips are bruised and lifeless, my tongue limp. I am eternally grateful to that girl I went out with when I was seventeen, who showed me what kisses could be, demonstrated an oral craving as vast as mine.

It is for that reason that, years later, kissing Sara in Mellon Square, I should have noticed that—though she was passionate, and genuinely wanted to kiss *me*—Sara did not kiss my way, that her idea of a kiss was lightly, tenderly, to open our mouths and touch just the tips of our tongues. At first I thought she was just proceeding slowly, but in time I realized that was really the way she liked to kiss. Nothing wrong with that. But it made our kisses a paradigm of our whole relationship, me always wanting more, her always holding back, drawing away. Soon the holding back became habitual; it preceded any actual encounter. So the hunger increased. . . .

Or was that the situation I actually wanted? Was my real wish to duplicate the relationship I had seen between the Senator and the Duchess, or the one I'd had with the Duchess, because that pattern was easy and familiar, and told me what I believed to be true about myself? And because, of course, I could then have my compensations. I could have my secrets. Which I had grown to love almost as much as the things they were compensating for.

Sometimes I have felt—and I know this doesn't make any logical sense; it makes some other, deeper, kind of sense— that all my yearning, all my oral craving, was just a wish to break down those decorous scenes of kissing I had seen when I was young, to reenact them and make them different. The embarrassment on the face of the Duchess when she could not—at the thought of a kiss—look into her husband's eyes; her closed pursed mouth, which had no give to it, which seemed to disapprove; my big boisterous father, cowed into embarrassment over wishes he had every right to. No! I want to shout, as I look back on that scene. That isn't passion! That isn't love! I want their mouths to open and their tongues to intertwine; I want him to carry her to the bedroom and work his mouth down into her bodice, suck her nipples until she is breathless and aching; I want him to throw her onto the bed and sink to his knees, hike up her skirt and tear off her underpants, take her thighs onto his shoulders and show her a kind of kissing that is deeper yet.

Because I wasn't kidding Helen's lesbian friends—that is one sexual act I am devoted to (is it any wonder, given my history?); it is another one that sounded strange when I heard about it but that I knew I would like, I knew I was born to do. Back in those days when I had never even seen a cunt, when cunts were just a rumor, just a myth, like the unseen God, to think not only of seeing one but putting my head right there. My mouth. My tongue. The first time I did it I loved it, and I soon became, with the help of some brilliant teachers ("A little slower, darling. A little higher. Oh!") a black belt, if not a Zen master. The short springy hair, with that ripe odor clinging to it, the most enticing of all human odors; the soft moist texture of the flesh, the most beautifully textured flesh on a human body (with the possible exception of the penis); the tiny little bump that, when licked, produces such an extraordinary reaction; the deep mysterious cavern into which you can thrust your tongue and find an even stronger, brinier taste; the moisture that pours into your mouth and rolls down your chin as you lick and suck and (very gently!) bite; all the reactions you see in the thighs and belly and up into the breasts, moans and shudders and screams and convulsions. This is my Ode to Pussy-Eating! My ultimate sexual act, after which even fucking often seems—pardon the expression—anticlimactic. Though I go ahead and do it anyway. What the hell.

My number's in the book.

There is a certain irony to all this. The little boy who was such a woman-pleaser, who tiptoed around trying to be *so* good, has, by violating every principle of that early training (you put your mouth *where?*) become the greatest woman pleaser of all. I spent all those years being a good boy, hoping I would get hugged. Now I am a bad boy. You should see the hugs I get.

THREE

I have only seen the Duchess cry once in my life. That seems a strange—perhaps an incredible—statement, but I'm sure it is true. I remember the moment so well—a moment not otherwise memorable—that I'm sure I would remember any others.

It was an afternoon when my friend Alan was having a birthday party. I was seven years old. I loved Alan (God knows I loved his sister), but I didn't especially love his birthday parties. For one thing, I was the only Gentile there, perhaps the only non-family member. This kid had cousins coming out his ass. They were all very close, and as soon as they got to his house they started laughing and screaming and running around, Alan with them, in a way that I didn't like. They paid no attention to me. They were probably excluding me on purpose, as kids will do at that age (when we're older we do it in more subtle ways). He always had an elaborate party, taking us to lunch at the Pittsburgh Playhouse and then to a children's matinee. I found the food too fancy there, and the atmosphere oppressive. I also didn't like the plays (give me a good TV show anytime). Mostly, though,

I felt like an outsider with those kids. I couldn't stand being cut off from my friend like that. I hated to see him behave in what I considered to be a stupid and inconsiderate way (though I'm sure the two of us had been just as bad many times). So, though I had accepted the invitation when it came ("Of *course* you want to go to Alan's party. You'll have a *won*derful time"), I suddenly realized, on the day of the party, that I was face-to-face with four hours of agony, but that there was a way to avoid it. I went to my mother's room and told her I didn't want to go.

I can easily imagine the conversation that ensued, though I don't remember it. The Duchess would have told me what a delightful place the Playhouse was, how delicious the food was in the dining room, how much I'd enjoy the play. I'd have told her I'd much rather have a hot dog and watch TV. She'd have told me how much fun I'd have with all those children. I'd have told her I hated those children. (I would be gaining confidence here, starting to realize the extent to which I'd been had in this situation.) She would tell me—and from her standpoint this would be the ultimate weapon—how much it would mean to Alan if I'd come to his birthday party, how disappointed he'd be if I didn't. I knew that was bullshit. He wouldn't so much as notice if I wasn't there. He was surrounded by family at his birthday party, that was what it was about, and I didn't really belong there. I could even imagine the fun we'd have the next day, when I'd take his present to him and we'd open it, just the two of us.

The Duchess wasn't a mean mother (pardon the expression), and she didn't want to make me do something I didn't want to. I'm sure that her reaction in this situation was complicated, that it had to do with the fact that her child was doing something that she believed to be terribly wrong, that she was frustrated because she couldn't make me see the light, that she was afraid of offending Alan's mother (especially, perhaps, because they were Jewish). The fact remains that this was a once-in-a-lifetime moment. I have been with her at far more emotional and important moments and never seen a tear. But when she stood from the dressing table on this day, to call Alan's mother and tell her I wasn't coming, I could see tears in her eyes. I could see that she was crying.

I knew that I had just done something terrible. The worst thing I had ever done in my life.

From the perspective I have now, the Duchess's reaction seems perfectly appropriate. She virtually lived for social obligations, for knowing what the world expected her to do and doing it. If you ever wanted to know what your social obligation was, if you ever needed that clarified, you just had to go to the Duchess. She always knew. On the other hand, I don't think she had any idea what she wanted. If you had asked her that—No, no, I don't want to know if you *should* go to that party, I want to know if you *want* to go—I don't think she would have known what you were talking about. That distinction didn't exist for her.

I would have done anything to stop her from crying. I would have gone to the party. I would have gone to a dozen parties. By that time the Duchess wouldn't have let me. She could see that I didn't want to. I was feeling that combination of enormous delight (I got out of it!) and overwhelming guilt (You shouldn't have done that!) that most of us feel when we have done a socially unacceptable thing. I think that one of the ways the world divides up is in the proportions in which we feel those things. For me, the guilt has always outweighed the delight. And in this case, the fear of having hurt my mother (If my mother doesn't love me, who will?) was stronger than anything else about the experience.

When things were all over with Andrea, when I finally sat down and told Helen the whole story, the first thing she said was, "You should have told me she cried the first day you saw her."

I didn't know what to do with myself that afternoon, after I left the store. I had been at loose ends earlier in the day, but that was nothing compared to the way I felt now. I hadn't eaten lunch, I was trying to let a small snack they had served on the plane be lunch, but I suddenly realized I was ravenously hungry. The stress of the moment had touched some hungry place. I could also see that, since I was going back to the store at 6:00 (I had checked the hours on the door as I went out), and wouldn't be heading for Helen's until after that, I might be eating rather late. So I walked up to the old Hotel William Penn (from a room of which a despondent young journalist named John O'Hara once almost jumped, thereby nearly robbing the world of some of my favorite writing), sat in their grand if somewhat faded dining room, and had a club sandwich and a bottle of beer. There were nine or ten well-dressed black men scattered around at other tables, and I began to think that maybe the city had changed, that the business community had opened up in a whole new way. But later that evening I drove past the Civic Arena and saw the marquee, and realized I'd had a late lunch that afternoon with the Harlem Globetrotters.

By the time I got back to Womanbooks the day looked much worse. I didn't think it would snow—it seemed too cold for that—but the sky was a dark gray, the wind even more bitter than before. People were heading home from work, so there was a lot of traffic, but there still weren't many people on the sidewalk. You had to be nuts to be out there. It was like night on Andrea's street, and the streetlights had come on. As I looked in the window I saw that none of the possibilities she had mentioned had come about. She was standing in the store alone, waiting for me.

Andrea told me later—some weeks later—that she had thought I was coming back to the store to fuck her. I had heard her story, seen her vulnerability, assumed she was ripe for the plucking, and come back to pluck her. Since I had nothing better to do that afternoon.

I was astounded when she told me that. I would never have taken advantage of a person's pain that way. For perhaps the only time in my life, I was seeing a woman with absolutely no thought of having sex with her. Then or any other time. I just wanted to speak to her without those other people around.

"You thought *I* would do that?" I said to her when she told me.

"I didn't know you then."

"Would *you* have done it?"

"I was in pretty bad shape. I'd have done almost anything for some affection. I was going to wait and see how it went. How you came on. But I was sure that was why you were coming."

"Wouldn't you have thought I was a total asshole if I did something like that?"

"Sure. But doesn't it sound just like a man?"

Not that she had any problems with men.

And why, one might have asked, would she have even considered having sex with a total asshole?

When I opened the door and stepped inside, she said, "Lock it."

"What?"

"It's past closing. I was waiting for you to get here. The keys are in it. Lock it."

I turned around. The keys were, indeed, in the door. I locked it.

Andrea was standing behind the counter, unpacking a box of paperbacks. She looked up at me over her glasses.

It seems extremely important at this point to describe how she looked, and I can see it clearly in my mind's eye, but I need to be careful how I say it. Andrea was a woman, she was every bit a woman, the word girl would never have come to mind in her presence, but sometimes, in a particular kind of emotional situation, I felt I could see the girl in her. She was at one of those vulnerable moments in her life when she was closely in touch with past moments, she could revert to them easily. When I came in the door and saw her—solemn, pale, staring at me with wide sad eyes—she looked like a little girl who had done something wrong and was about to be punished. She looked like a girl who had been hurt before and was afraid of being hurt again. She looked as if she might fight back this time.

I stepped up to the counter and spoke. "Andrea. I'm sorry that stuff came up the way it did. With those people around. It was so awkward. I didn't know what to say."

"Okay." She nodded.

"I just wanted to tell you how bad I feel for you, and that I've been through the same thing, though it's different for everybody, and that if there's anything I can do for you, anything at all, I'd like to do it."

She didn't quite say anything. She nodded her head solemnly and mouthed the words "thank you," though I didn't hear anything. Then she took her eyes away from me, looked at the counter, put her hands on the box she was unpacking, and started to cry again. Huge tears fell from her eyes. She started to sob.

I stepped behind the counter to hold her. She didn't embrace me strongly—as if she didn't have the strength—but she positively fell against me. I was supporting practically her whole weight. She didn't make much noise when she cried, but her body shuddered. She sobbed and sobbed.

"Maybe you could, just, hang around for a while," she said. "Spend some time."

"Sure."

"I get so lonely."

It ached in my heart to feel her cry like that. This woman I didn't even know. I wished I could take her whole weight on me. Absorb her pain. I had never felt anyone give herself to crying like that. Her whole body sobbed.

At the same time, in the interest of honesty, I need to say that there most definitely was something sexual to it. I may have come to the store without a sexual thought in my head, but no sooner had I gotten there than a woman had thrown herself into my arms and started sobbing against me, a feeling not all that much different from the throes of passion. I was smelling her hair, smelling her body. (Andrea had the best natural smell of any woman I had ever met. That was a strong part of what attracted me to her. The scent of her armpits was a faint echo—in this case a prefiguring—of her cunt, and her cunt was ambrosia. I think I could stand to see her at this point, perhaps to talk to her, but if I took her in my arms and smelled her body I think it would break my heart.) I don't mean that I started to think about sex, or wanted to fuck her. But something was happening.

As suddenly as she had started crying, she leaned back, pulled away from me, snatched a handkerchief from a shoulder bag sitting on a chair, and stopped. She heaved a huge sigh, dried her eyes. "I don't know why I'm crying," she said. "I'm better off without the son of a bitch. My life is *so* much better." She held up the handkerchief. "I wear out three or four of these a day."

"It's good for you."

"You think?"

"Crying's great for you. It releases tension."

"I've got to be one of the most relaxed people in the world, then."

She put her handkerchief back, moved the shoulder bag to the floor, and started unpacking the box again.

"I mean," she said. "For instance. If I were married right now, if this whole thing hadn't happened, here's what I'd be looking at. I'd have to close the shop, get my kid, go to the market to buy something for dinner. Not knowing if my husband—Jesus, I even hate the fucking word—was going to be home for dinner or not. I'd buy enough for him, just in case. Then I'd go home and fix the food, wondering if he was going to be there. When it was ready I'd wonder if we should go on without him. I'd sit there getting hungry, trying to decide. Then we *would* go on, and the food would be cold. We'd sit there eating alone. I'd finish dinner and put the kid to bed, getting his bath, doing that whole thing myself, then Farty Artie would come home and tell me he'd already eaten, which wasted half of what I'd bought. I'd give it to the dog or something. It also meant I had to clean up, since it didn't make sense for him to clean up after something he hadn't eaten. I would have done everything at that point. It was all perfectly logical. I'd walked into it with my eyes wide open. He'd told me he was undependable in the evenings, that he often wouldn't be home. But what the fuck was *I* getting out of all that, I'd like somebody to tell me? What was in it for me?"

Excellent question.

"Now I can just go home and fix something for myself. Scramble some eggs or something. Eat quietly. Stare at the walls all night."

She lowered her eyes again and the tears poured out, her body starting to sob. I moved toward her, but she held up her hand, held me away.

"I'm not going to do that again," she said. "It's too easy. Don't humor me."

I didn't see anything easy about it.

She heaved a big sigh and looked up at me. "Why don't we get out of here?" she said.

"Out of here?"

"I've got some errands to run. A dress to take to the cleaners. All within a few blocks. You could walk with me. It'd cheer me up."

"Okay."

I wasn't sure how long I wanted to stay. I had dinner plans with my sister, though there was still plenty of time before I had to be there. But I had come to let Andrea talk, and she didn't seem talked out. She still seemed to be teetering on the brink of despair. And the odd thing was that—even on this grim subject—I enjoyed her conversation. She had such a bristly, angry, obscene way of talking about things, a crazy verbal energy. She actually made it all kind of funny.

She stepped to a little room at the back to get her coat, and the dress she was taking to the cleaners. She had to walk around and turn off some lights, turn off the heat, set the burglar alarm and lock the door. "Jesus, what a wind," she said, as we stepped out into the evening. The wind was icy down there near the Point, as it whipped up from the rivers. She took my arm as we walked along the sidewalk, past some shops. She held it tight.

"So what was Arthur doing that whole time?" I said. "When he wasn't coming home."

"Working, was the blanket term. That meant talking. This is a man who could run his mouth all day. He ran his mouth for a living. With students, he said, though it could have been anybody. He'd sit in a bar talking politics, and I swear to God if he wore out the students he'd take on a bum off the streets. He'd take on the bartender. In some dirty seedy bar."

"Drinking too much."

"No. He'd be sitting there with a draft beer, one sip taken out of it. Waiting for some poor unsuspecting slob to sit down beside him. The only reason he ate dinner at those places was that somebody else wanted to. That was the excuse he needed to talk to the person."

It was funny—though this is always the way—how the thing that made her furious was probably also the thing that attracted her in the first place. The fact that he had such a passion for his subject. Couldn't stop talking about it. I can imagine that it was in one of those seedy bars that they first came together, meeting for lunch, say, then talking right into dinner. He leaned forward in his chair, elbows on his knees, a fire in his eye, while she was slumped back in her chair (in the position Female Resigned), taking it all in, her cheeks flushed with excitement. Finally she would take him to her apartment—knowing her as I do now, I'm sure this is how it would be—and, throwing him on his back, fuck his brains out, doing all the work herself. They would talk politics far into the night, her cunt dripping.

Finally he had found someone who wanted to listen as much as he wanted to talk. Who could take whatever he could dish out. She had found someone who could fill her up. She had wanted to believe it was just for her. She hadn't realized it was for anybody who stumbled along.

We had stopped at a store just a couple of blocks down from Womanbooks—and around the corner—called the Leather Report. "I do the books for these people," Andrea said. "Brings in a little extra money. This is another woman-owned business. Couple of lesbians. A pretty tough pair. I just need to pick up some things." The store had closed at 5:00, so she took out some keys to let us in, locked the doors behind us. She turned on some lights. "I'll just be a minute," she said, walking toward a counter on the left. "Have a look around." The store's space was roughly the size of Andrea's, but it had two display windows, and seemed a lot more open. There was a glass case of smaller items up front, change purses and key rings and gloves. There was a rack of long coats up there too, and a small display of boots. But most of the merchandise was on racks at the back, jackets and pants and skirts, all black leather and hung in rows, shining under the lights. It gave off that strong smell of new leather.

Andrea had taken a couple of checkbooks from a drawer under the counter, glanced through them for a second, and put them in her shoulder bag. "The thing about old Artie," she said, "was that when he finally got home, I *wanted* to talk. About our kid. Our so-called relationship. Or just about how he really was. Not what so-and-so said about Central America. But how he was doing. What his life was like. He didn't know what I was talking about. He didn't have a clue."

Now we were getting into a slightly more familiar area of female complaint about men.

"And sex. Jesus. It didn't exist."

Extremely familiar.

"Do you know how much we were fucking at the end there?"

"I don't know. Twice a day?"

"I'd say once a month. On the outside. If it was a good month. You know, the moon was right or something. Once a fucking month. Even then it wasn't especially good. I mean, you'd think a normal man. I don't mean he wasn't normal. But you'd think most men would be going out of their heads by that time. They'd really give you a bang. Bite you or something. You're ready for it after a month, right? But it was this very quiet thing. Kind of polite. Why am I telling you this?"

"Beats me."

"I'll tell you one thing. If he could fuck like he can talk, I'd have been one happy woman."

The mood swings in this conversation had been nothing short of spectacular. It wasn't just that she could stop and start on a dime. It was the incredible range she covered. We had already moved through fear, sorrow, resignation, anger, and despair. Now we were in some kind of whimsical hilarity. No telling where we were headed. Wasn't it about time to cry again?

"For instance. I went out with this guy a few weeks ago. My one date since I separated. I mean, I like to get laid as much as anybody"—a vast understatement, in my opinion—"but most men, at this point in my life, I just can't stand the conversation long enough. I'd rather watch television and have a late date with my vibrator. That's a hell of a commentary, isn't it? Television's better than conversation. It's a hell of a statement about men." It was a hell of a statement about the person who stated it. "Anyway. We went out to dinner. I mean eventually we did. But we were going out to dinner, at this lavish place he invited me to. So I wore this fancy dress I have. It's the dress I'm taking to the cleaners. Would you like to see it?"

"Sure."

"Would you like to see me in it?"

We had moved beyond the realm of mood change here into confusion, perhaps incoherence. I didn't know what the hell was going on. I didn't—as the expression goes—know whether to shit or wind my watch.

"I don't know," I said. "Sure."

"Do you like to see women in clothes?"

"In or out. Either way."

She smiled. "Do you like to see women model clothes?"

"I don't know."

"Jesus. Why can't men express a simple opinion nowadays?"

"I'm sure I would like it. I've just never seen one."

"You've never seen a woman model clothes?"

"I've never even had one bring it up."

"Listen. I *love* to model clothes."

"I'm very happy for you."

"Let me put this dress on for you."

"Be my guest."

She took off her coat, grabbed the dress, and disappeared into a dressing room at the back. One thing I find interesting about women is that, though they might spend hours dressing, though you can wait forever while they do what they call dressing, the amount of time it takes them actually to take one garment off and put another on is minuscule. She popped out of the dressing room in about thirty seconds, looked at herself in the mirror, fooled with her hair, and turned to me.

"Now. What does this dress say to you?"

It looked to me to be mostly cotton. I'm not too clear on fabrics, but it was thin, whatever it was. It was black, a pullover, simple but somehow also elegant. What this dress did above all else was cling. You saw everything that was beneath it. There was even a slight indentation at Andrea's navel. Her nipples were announced with a fanfare of trumpets.

I believe the Duchess would have worn a slip with that dress.

Andrea's mood had changed again. She was smiling, no trace of tears anywhere. She was smiling as if in anticipation of a joke.

"Charles," she said, as I hesitated. "What does this dress say to you?"

"It says Fuck Me."

"Exactly."

"It has Fuck Me written all over it in tiny letters."

"I know. This guy who came over. My big date. I gave him a drink. I sat him on the couch. I could actually see him get interested. Staring at my body. He had ants in his pants. I went over and sat beside him. I said, 'Are you sure you want to go to dinner right now? Are you sure that's what you want to do?' It turned out it wasn't. He had to call the restaurant and tell them something had come up. He couldn't honor his reservation. Well. Something had come up all right.

"Anyway. Five months before. When I was still with Arthur. It was our anniversary. We went out to dinner. I wore this dress. Nothing underneath. I mean no underpants, even. I mentioned this fact to him. He didn't seem to react. Spent the whole evening talking about the Middle East. Hardly noticed his food. Then we went home, and *nothing happened.*"

Her smile widened. She had just said the punch line.

"Can you believe it? *Nothing happened.* He didn't have the common courtesy to fuck me on our anniversary. When I had worn this dress. He didn't even cop a cheap feel."

"You're better off without him."

"Isn't it the truth? I'm about the same without him. My biggest expense is still batteries for my vibrator."

That vibrator did keep coming up.

I look back on this conversation and am stunned at all I didn't see. It was tremendously exciting, and I can see why I was excited. I don't blame myself for being excited. But I can't believe all that I missed. It was about two inches from my nose.

"So," she said. "Are you into leather?"

"I don't know."

"You don't *know* if you're into leather?"

"I've never had the money."

"Come and take a feel."

This woman had a way of putting things.

We walked to the long racks at the back, where the jackets, pants, and skirts were hanging. We stood there and felt them. I crushed a jacket to my face and smelled it.

"This is fabulous," I said.

"Isn't it?"

"It's like skin."

"It's the next best thing to skin. But we've got one more test. Wait here."

She grabbed something off the rack and disappeared into

the dressing room. The effect when she came out was even more striking than before. She wore the pale gray cotton turtleneck she'd had on earlier. Without a dress on over it, you noticed that it was clingy too, and rather thin. Beneath it she wore a pair of bright black leather pants. They gave off that leathery sound as she walked. She still had a broad smile on her face.

"Now Charles," she said. "Don't be afraid."

"I won't." It turned out I liked women modeling clothes.

"You have to use your imagination."

"I have an excellent imagination."

"You're my husband."

My imagination did have *some* limits.

"We're going to embrace, Charles. Will you be embarrassed?"

"I'll try to bear up under it."

"Remember. You're my husband."

"I remember."

She came into my arms. I smelled her hair again. Her body. She melted against me. The blouse was soft under my hands.

"Now Charles," she said. "You're my husband."

"I remember."

"Where do your hands want to go?"

"Well . . ."

"Be a man, Charles. Put your hands where they want to go."

I did. The leather was cool and soft. The place on her body was also soft.

"Now do with your hands what they want to do. What they absolutely positively have to do."

I crushed her ass like a ripe fruit. She yelped and jumped against me. I felt a gasp of hot breath at my ear. Her ass was soft, like the leather. She stepped back and pushed me away.

"You pass," she said. "Jesus." She swallowed hard, took a deep breath. "You go right to the head of the class."

"Thanks."

"I'm going to check for bruises in the morning."

"I'm sorry. I got carried away."

"That's what you're supposed to do. That's what leather is all about. In the last two years with Arthur I wore a leather skirt four times. Every time I embraced him repeatedly. He was my husband. He never touched the leather."

"God."

"I finally put his hands there. It still didn't do anything. He didn't squeeze me." She shook her head. "I think he spent too long in graduate school."

That, in my experience, usually had the opposite effect.

"So," she said. "Do you see anything you like?"

You better believe I did.

"How do you mean?" I said.

"Some of these leather items are for men, too."

"Oh?"

"They have some male customers. They're not crazy about it, but they do. These leather types are a world unto themselves. Motorcycles. Tattoos. I'm talking women here. Now and then some bull dyke comes in and asks if they have any specialty items."

"What's the answer to that?"

"The answer is yes. Wait here a minute."

In a way, I suppose, this was all getting weirder and weirder. It was hardly the kind of evening I'd expected. But I was glad I had come to see Andrea. I'd gotten to say what I wanted to. She seemed much cheered up. I could see that I might want to see her some more while I was in town.

She returned only as far as the dressing room, which didn't have a door but a curtain, hanging from a curtain rod. She was holding something behind her back. "Come here," she said. "I'll show you what these leather types are into."

I walked to where she was standing. She positioned me halfway into the dressing room.

"Hold your arms up," she said. "Close your eyes."

I did. She slipped something onto one of my wrists, then, after a moment, onto the other. I looked up. It was a pair of leather cuffs, suspended from the curtain rod.

"That's a specialty item," she said.

I looked at her. She was inches away, smiling.

"This is what they're into," I said.

"What we're into," she said. "Me and my leather buddies."

Now she tells me.

"What do you do now?" I said.

She reached up to my shirt, located my nipple, and squeezed. A little too hard. I bit my lip, shifted uneasily from one foot to another.

"Anything I want," she said.

Into the Dark Room
with the Woman

The thought of my grade-school teachers as objects of erotic attraction—a natural place to turn, once I had exhausted other options—would be funny if it weren't so tragic. The wire-framed spectacles. Steel gray hair drawn back in a bun. The tarnished dentures. Massive arms with loose flesh hanging from the underside. The flower-patterned dresses. Those heavy black shoes with the short thick heels. The body odor. Even a boy as desperate as I would have been hard-pressed to find a mother substitute among those women. I might as well have looked among the linebackers of the N.F.L.

There were a few rays of hope. The math and gym teacher was a short fiery woman by the name of Mrs. Longiotti. She was not pretty—thin-faced, with a pronounced overbite—but she had bright black hair, an olive complexion, and the quick graceful movements of a miniature athlete. The energy surging through her body made the whole classroom rumble. There was also an English teacher, Miss Kirkland—a thin, pale redhead with a pasty complexion, a pained look on her face—who was at least young. She had the energy of her anger. A body you might like to make contact with.

There was no body contact for a boy like me. Always cheerful—my face fixed in a broad smile—deeply studious, perfectly obedient (he is *so good*). Even at school, among those substitute mothers, I did not get the embrace I wanted. Mrs. Longiotti did not keep me after school and, in appreciation of the model student I was, give me long warm hugs, passionate Italian kisses.

Another kind of student did get touched. Grabbed and shaken. Thrown over the teacher's knee. Mrs. Longiotti wielded rulers and yardsticks like a martial-arts expert, and Miss Kirkland once spanked a boy so angrily—I was sitting only a few feet away—that spit flew from her mouth. Once, in a cold fury at four boys who had been fooling around, she took them one by one into the cloakroom. The rest of us were dead silent, but the walls were thick in those old schools, and the doors were heavy. We didn't hear a thing. Each boy emerged after a few minutes shamefaced and weeping, holding his fists to his eyes. What had happened in that dark room with that woman? What had she said? What had she done? The boys didn't tell.

All I knew was that, frightened as I was, I wanted to go into that room with that woman.

There was the obvious attraction—for somebody who was always doing what he should—of being bad, being adventurous, doing what *I* wanted for once, and then, oddly, being rewarded for it. At least getting some physical contact. The bad boys had a much closer relationship to the teacher than I. It was violent and mercurial, but it was close. The physical contact of punishment would have absorbed that strange energy in my body. Spanking was oddly passionate, oddly like (though I didn't know this at the time) lovemaking. The woman would grab and clutch me. Throw me across her knee. Her skirt would be soft. It would make that rubbing sound against her nylons. Her thighs would be warm. My prick would rub against them. She would smack my bare skin in rhythm. My body would jerk and thrust. I would shout with every smack. The reality of a punishment might have been terribly painful, deeply humiliating—I'll never know—but the fantasy of it was enchanting.

Punishment would have fulfilled me also in another way. I knew in some deep place that I must have done something wrong; otherwise I would be getting the hugs I needed. A good spanking might wipe the slate clean. I would be forgiven. I wouldn't be bad anymore. I could be embraced. I could be loved.

In time I worked through various fantasies and imagined the perfect scene. I had been kept late after school. All the other children were gone. I had, technically speaking, done something wrong, though actually I was quite innocent. (I had been late to school because I rescued a helpless infant from a burning house. Something like that.) There was a deep sadness in my teacher's eyes. She loved me, but she had to do this thing. Though we were already alone in the classroom, she took me into the cloakroom, where nobody could possibly know what we were doing. She took down my pants and underpants, drew me across her lap. The punishment was fierce, loud smacks and screams, but afterward there were tears in her eyes as well as mine, and she held me a long time, comforting me. "I'm sorry, Charles. Oh. I'm so sorry." There was a tremendous closeness between us. It was a moment we would always remember. I could feel that she loved me.

There was something in all of us when we were young that understood the excitement I felt. We were scared to death at the thought of being punished but also terribly excited by it; we talked constantly about the punishments at school as by far the most interesting things that happened there. We played school and acted them out. I had a friend who was a bad kid and had been spanked at school (already I was into rough trade), and he was not at all surprised when I questioned him and wanted to pretend about it. We took our pants down and spanked each other in my father's car. It was tremendously exciting (I can still see that moment, and feel my ambivalence, my wish not to hurt him—I was a gentle boy— and my simultaneous wish to hit him hard and hear him scream, see the imprint of my hand on his flesh), and I knew it was a kind of taboo play; I wouldn't have told an adult about it. But it didn't seem weird. It wasn't any weirder than a lot of things we did.

Such fantasies would come and go in my youth. They might be quiescent for months or years—I had plenty of other things to fantasize about—then flare up again. By the time I was a teenager they did seem distinctly weird, and I felt weird for having them. Not long after I learned about sex, I read in a sex manual—in a chapter on perversions—about a boy who had gotten excited when he was caned by his governess and who continued that sexual predilection into later life. The description of that punishment—"Now you're going to get a whipping. And every night for eight nights you'll get the same"—inflamed me like nothing else I had ever read. I masturbated to it so many times that I memorized it. I haunted bookstores and libraries, looking for other descriptions of beatings; I spent hours of my youth fruitlessly leafing through books. I wrote my own scenes and masturbated to them. I longed to see spankings in real life, though I rarely did, and though I was put off by real anger or brutality. There had to be an air of complicity for me to enjoy that fantasy, a willing victim, like that boy with his governess. Spanking was far from being my only sexual fantasy when I was young, but it was a major one. It took me to a level of excitement that nothing else did.

FOUR

There is a new bus way in Pittsburgh, one of those urban innovations that is striking just because it is so simple and obvious. They had a railway line that was sitting around and rotting, so instead of going to all the expense of trying to revive the trains for transportation—a chancy proposition at best—they paved the line over and made it an expressway for buses. No other vehicles at all. Now those frustrated ulcer-ridden bastards who have spent their whole lives fighting city traffic (they should really make this route a reward for years of service) can pull onto the expressway and let 'er rip, roaring along as fast as their buses will go. The surface is smooth, the stops well spaced. It only serves a part of the city, but it is fairly convenient to my parents' place, very convenient to my sister's. As we rocketed along the expressway that evening, the landscape dark except for some lights from houses on the hills, the passengers' weary and numb faces reflected on the insides of the windows, I was glad to be on the bus, sheltered from the wind and the blare of the city.

That had been an awkward moment for me back at the

Leather Report with Andrea. It was a joke, of course, and had not really gone beyond that. But it was obvious that what she had said, and what she had done, had pressed a few buttons of mine, and that the same things were pressing some buttons of hers. We had wandered into a place of sexual excitement—at least I was wandering—and there was something in the embarrassment and closeness of the moment that made sex very attractive. I think that sex often happens because people can't stand a certain closeness; they look into each other's eyes until they can't take it, then bury their faces in each other's shoulders, or passionately kiss, to hide their shame. I was feeling at least the beginning of that kind of excitement with Andrea. The easiest thing, once we had uncovered that vulnerability, would have been to make a pass at her. But that would have stifled whatever intimacy had started—sex is an old familiar routine, which we can walk through unconsciously—and I was at a place in my life, a strange new place, where I valued the intimacy more than the sex, even if intimacy meant embarrassment. So I didn't lean down and kiss her, as she twisted my nipple, and we faced the awkwardness of dance partners who have missed a step and lost the beat: Now what?

"One of these days we're going to get together, my friends and me," Andrea said, as she removed the cuffs, "and turn you on to this."

"Sounds scary."

"It is. Especially once you've met my friends."

All that proved to be just talk. Andrea didn't have such friends.

She walked away from me, taking the cuffs with her. She was suddenly subdued. I felt a hardening in her.

She had taken what happened as a rejection.

"So," she said, as she put the cuffs away and turned to me. It was as if I had become a different person. "What brings you to town?"

I took a deep breath, slowly let it out. The conversation was about to change levels.

"My father had a heart attack," I said.

"God." She paled. "You should have said something. I stand here talking about my little problems."

"Your problems aren't little."

"Was it serious?"

"Apparently not. This was several weeks ago. They said right away it wasn't life threatening. My mother told me not to come then. There were so many people around. She thought it would be better when he got home. I'm not at all sure I'm the person my father should be seeing when he's recovering from a heart attack."

"Really?"

"We're okay if we stay on certain subjects. We just never do. Everything's fine for a while. Then it all collapses."

We could see it coming from miles away, the conflict that always got us. It was as if we were at a railroad crossing, and from far away we heard the whistle, and saw the smoke. And we just stood there. Was the truth that we were somehow paralyzed, that we couldn't move? No. The truth was that we wanted the train to hit us.

"I won't speak to my father," Andrea said. "Haven't for years. I won't see him."

"How come?"

"He hurt me when I was young. I've never forgiven him. I never will."

That was one solution. We love our parents and hate them, and in that conflict there is great pain. It's tempting to choose one side and eliminate the ambiguity forever. But you lose something when you do that. A part of you dies. No matter which side you choose.

"I'll tell you about it sometime," she said.

There was none of the ambivalence about this moment that there had been about the other one. She cried about her husband even while she was calling him a bastard. About her father there was only cold hard anger.

"I'd like to see you again," I said.

I had come to comfort her, not wanting anything else to creep in. But I had done that now.

"Are you going to be around?" she said.

"I might. My sister wants me to stay awhile. She thinks my father is going through some larger crisis that this heart attack is only part of. She wants me to stay with her. My parents want me to stay with them. I just want to get the lay of the land. I'm staying at the William Penn for a day or two.

That's one thing about being a free-lancer. I can relocate with no trouble."

"Are you seeing your father tonight?"

"I'm seeing my sister. I'll see him in the morning."

"Well." Andrea had brightened. "I'm at work at least part of every day. You can call me or come by." She was writing numbers on a pad, tore the sheet off and gave it to me. "These are work and home."

"I'll definitely call. Whatever I decide."

I hadn't realized it yet, but Andrea would be a factor in the equation.

She saw me to the door. We hugged. She had such a strong embrace, which was also soft and tender.

"Thanks for coming back," she said. "It was sweet of you."

"I wanted to. I was glad to."

"It meant a lot."

As she pulled away from our embrace, she looked into my eyes, as if wondering, really, what was behind them. She didn't seem to come to a conclusion. But she leaned forward and, lightly, kissed me on the mouth.

My sister was a woman whose life seemed too good to be true until you realized all she had done to bring it about. She had bought a house in Shadyside when it was a funky little racially mixed neighborhood. Now the house was all fixed up and the neighborhood was one of the poshest in the city. Her office was an easy walk from the house, in a brand-new office building. Also within walking distance were the gym where she worked out and the tennis courts where she played. She lived almost entirely in a world of women. They were her friends, lovers, political allies, clients. You didn't know where one thing left off and another began.

Helen had been a girl who the girls thought was beautiful and who the boys didn't even notice. She had exactly the same features as the Duchess; in one way the two of them were dead ringers and in another they didn't look a bit alike. Helen didn't do that flirty, vulnerable, little-girl thing with her eyes, which was about 60 percent of why the Duchess was so attractive. Her gaze was magnetic to men. Helen just frankly stared, interested in what was there. That put men off in a way. It frightened them. They felt they were being examined. They were. No more, of course, than they were examining her.

Behind all this, no doubt, was the fact that Helen realized at an early age that she couldn't compete with the Duchess on this level, that she was up against one of the all-time greats at being demure and attractive, everybody's little girl. She dropped out of the race altogether, wore blue jeans and sweatshirts, skipped the makeup. When she did dress up, as a girl, she didn't look right. The clothes seemed to belong on somebody else.

She was a serious person, not in the sense of not being funny, but in the sense of not being frivolous. She smiled and laughed when she felt like it, not in order to make herself attractive. She was an excellent student, a superb athlete, a leader in the class—her friends just *couldn't* understand why she didn't have more dates—but the major activity of her first twenty years was music. The Senator, for some reason, had made this his pet project, starting her on piano lessons when she was four and closely monitoring her progress. It wasn't that he especially cared for music. He just seemed to think this was a suitable thing for his little girl to do. She continued lessons throughout her youth and gave a recital every year. She was technically adept, but—though I never said this to her—I always felt there was something missing. She could play the most difficult pieces without a mistake, but in another way the whole thing sounded like a mistake. I eventually decided that the missing ingredient was a real love of music. Those performances weren't hers. The whole fact of being a musician wasn't hers.

She was the most understanding of sisters all through my youth, and I adored her. I had my own kind of lonely and rejected adolescence, and she spent hours with me, advising me, encouraging me, sympathizing with my problems. She got me dates and told me what to do on them (that didn't mean I could do it). She had friends over who talked endlessly about boys and romance, and she sometimes let me sit in. She didn't talk much about the few dates she had. Once, however, some prissy fucked-up bastard at school who had had a date with Helen told me in the hallway that she was a good kid but had left his finger a little smelly, and by the time they pulled me off him I had broken his nose and blackened one of his eyes. I got suspended for three days. Helen did talk to me that time. "I wanted to try some things with him," she said. "Not because I liked him. I just wanted to try them. But it wasn't good. It wasn't fun. He was really just embarrassed. I felt like a piece of meat."

She proceeded to tell me how a girl should be touched, how it would feel good. Now if I could just find a girl to let me try it.

She could have gone to college anywhere, done almost anything, but she chose to go to Oberlin and study music. It wasn't that she wanted to. It was more the way a woman becomes a nun because she believes she has a vocation. I had a vague bad feeling about the whole thing, which I was too young to put into words. It seemed to me that she was cutting herself off from so much to go off and do something she didn't really enjoy.

For all you could tell from the outside, she did fine. She had a solid career as an undergraduate, went on to graduate school. She kept giving recitals, playing more and more complex pieces, and I traveled to attend them. I kept waiting to hear that flair appear in her playing that would make all the difference, that would turn what she was doing into music. Finally one year she gave a recital at which she came out, sat at the piano, and didn't play. She sat with her shoulders up, hands in her lap, and stared at the keys as if she were about to begin, but she never did. At first the audience thought she was concentrating, preparing herself, and they waited politely, but after a while they started to move around in their chairs, then to talk. A wave of uneasiness swept over the room. People coughed, fidgeted; a couple of them laughed. Finally Helen turned and gazed at the audience for a moment—that frank curious stare with which she had greeted so many men—and walked away. And in so doing, walked away from her whole music career. She was twenty-four years old.

What she didn't tell me until years later—at the time she said she "just couldn't" play—was that she'd been having an affair with her professor, a man thirty years older than she. He was an extremely difficult teacher, would berate and mock her all through their sessions, then afterward, when her nervous system had turned into limp spaghetti, would fuck her, as if that made everything better. Her personal life had gotten all tangled up with her vocation. She didn't know if her professor liked her or just liked her ass; she didn't know if he thought she had talent or just wanted to fuck her. In an obvious way, of course, this situation just acted out the feelings from another relationship and raised questions that had existed in Helen's life since she was four years old. Why was she doing all this? Who was she doing it for? In time she decided that she couldn't have done music for herself at that point if she wanted to. There was too much pressure from the outside. She couldn't unravel the tangle.

This kind of crisis, in which you stop doing what everybody else wants you to do and start doing what you want to do, is what we call a nervous breakdown. Helen was hospitalized for a while, as pale and lifeless as she had been out on the concert stage. She was at a moment in her life when she didn't know what she wanted to do. She just knew she didn't want to do *that.* I came home from college a couple of weeks to be near her, visited her constantly, but we didn't talk about anything of consequence. We listened to opera on the radio, and to the Pirates games.

Her first show of strength came when she said she wanted to stop seeing her male psychiatrist and start seeing a female one. This request caused my parents enormous consternation. Dr. Blippetyblop was *such* a well-known person, and he had put *so* much into this case, and he felt they were making *real* progress (however slowly) and that it would be a terrible mistake to change doctors at this time. (Of course he did. That cunning little bastard knew a meal ticket when he saw one.) Helen was adamant. She didn't criticize Dr. Blip. She just said she wanted to see a woman.

Almost as soon as she got a female therapist—as if winning the argument were the important thing—she got much better. She left the hospital, got a job at the university library. She moved out of our parents' house and got her own apartment. She began to make a new set of friends in Pittsburgh. She decided she wanted to go to graduate school and become a therapist herself. I myself could have attested to her talent in this field; she had kept me together as an adolescent. Our parents took a dim view of these plans—she had had *such promise* as a musician—but by then Helen was strong enough that nobody was going to stand in her way.

I was glad to see my sister get better, but it was also true that her new life was pulling her away from me. For several years we weren't close. I was hurt, and didn't understand. I was afraid I was losing her forever. But she was taking on a new identity, and had to separate from the old one. In time she felt strong enough in what she had become to reconcile herself with what she had been. A few years later, during that period when Sara and I were living in Pittsburgh, she had me to her apartment alone, cooked her famous spaghetti sauce and opened a couple of bottles of Chianti. She explained what had caused her crisis, talked about what she'd been through for the past few years, said she was sorry she'd had to desert me that way, that she wanted to be my sister again. She'd wanted to all along, but there was a time when she just couldn't. "It's hard for me to tell you some things because I don't know what you'll think of them," she said. "I love you so much. It's very important to me that you approve."

"I'd approve of anything you did," I said.

"I bet you didn't approve when I deserted you."

"It wasn't that I didn't approve. I was sad. I missed you."

In our nervousness we had both gone a little hard on the Chianti, and were a trifle maudlin. Helen had tears in her eyes through much of the conversation, and even I, who never cried in those days, was on the verge.

"You don't know that you'd approve of *anything*," she said.

"Yes I do."

"You have no idea what I might tell you."

"It doesn't matter."

"I have one more important thing to say."

"So say it."

"You're the first person in the family I've told."

I knew what it was, of course. We hadn't been close for a few years, but I had seen who she was. I had seen whom she spent her time with.

It was so momentous a fact to her that she felt it must be an earthshaking revelation to her brother.

"I don't know how to put this," she said.

"Just say the first thing that comes to mind."

"I love women."

She had taken a wild stab and scored a direct hit.

"So do I," I said.

This remark, for some reason, brought gales of laughter from Helen. Tears poured from her eyes. She had to put her head down on the table. It must have taken her five minutes to quiet down.

I did, at that point, have one piece of advice for her.

"I think you should be careful how you tell this to our parents," I said.

As it turned out, there probably wasn't a good way to tell them. They were horrified at this news, at first disbelieving it, then totally rejecting it. "We should never have let you go to that woman," the Duchess said, referring to Helen's shrink. For a while they seemed to hope that Helen's lesbianism would blow over, like a bad cold, and that she would start seeing men again. Then they apparently resolved to ignore it. They didn't bring up the whole subject of romance with Helen. They never spoke of it again.

The Duchess's mother, who was bedridden at this point, and would die a couple of years later, had just one remark when she heard this news.

"Oh! And she was such a cute little girl."

Helen and I met at her house, but went almost immediately to a small Chinese restaurant that opened a few years ago in her neighborhood. It has marvelous food, but an even worse decor and atmosphere than most Chinese restaurants (if that is possible). A maroon carpet scattered with bits of those strange little chips they serve with the soup. Nothing at all on the walls. They haven't bothered to build any booths, or hang one of those dragons somewhere. The place isn't crowded on weeknights, so they leave you alone to drink your Chinese beer, eat the enormous portions of food they serve, then sit over a pot or two of tea afterward.

I'm afraid I've given the impression—contrasting her with her mother—that Helen isn't an attractive woman, or that she doesn't dress well, and those things don't begin to be true. It is true that her clothes are on the informal side, especially when she isn't working, but around the office she looks fabulous. Tonight she was wearing a blazer over a pale blue turtleneck, and some fancy jeans. She had on dangly silver earrings. She still doesn't wear makeup, but ever since she entered her thirties has had the kind of vibrant face that doesn't need it. Years ago, when there was that major thing she hadn't discovered about herself, she looked out on the world as if she couldn't quite figure it out either. Now her gaze is still frank, but not curious and distant. It is warm and alive. She is obviously a dyke—she has taught me to recognize this fact—and a very good-looking one. If I were a woman I'd be all over her.

"So," I said as we sat at the table. "Have you seen him since he got out of the hospital?"

"Twice. I went up there." To the apartment, she meant.

"How does he seem?"

"I'm still worried."

Helen was nothing if not honest. That wasn't the answer I'd wanted.

"Should I have come sooner?"

"I'm not worried that way. Like it's some urgent thing. Like he's going to die." Everyone had assured us that wasn't the case. "I'm worried about something bigger. I'm worried about him as a person."

There had been a great deal of ambiguity about this whole situation. A heart attack but not serious. They wanted me to come but not right away. There was also my own deep ambivalence about my whole relationship with my father.

Helen had been telling me for weeks that she was worried about him. Other changes had preceded his heart trouble and seemed to go right along with it. The Senator had always been first and foremost a face man. A glad hand. A broad smile. That immaculate Brooks Brothers suit. The conversation might not go deep, but he was always right there with it, reacting expressively, frowning and smiling at the right times.

Lately, however—and for a matter of months, according to Helen—he had been different. Grumpy. Preoccupied. He might walk right out on a conversation, or be absent while he was sitting there. The face he turned to you had no idea what the hell you were talking about. It was his appearance that worried Helen the most. He seemed deeply fatigued. Really quite changed. For the first time ever, he looked old to her. This had happened virtually overnight.

"Both times I went to see him," Helen said, "they came to the door together. As if that were very important. To show me things were just the same. But things don't begin to be the same. He moved at a snail's pace. He walks with a cane."

"He walks with a cane?" This fact disturbed me more than anything else I had heard.

"He fell in the hospital and hurt his knee. He says it's still a little weak. But it looks like more than a little. He seems to have lost some weight, which would be fine under other circumstances. But he wears this big smile as he comes to the door, as if everything's great. On a face that doesn't begin to look the same. It's kind of ghostly."

"He's always done that. Smiled through everything."

"But why pretend to something that just isn't so? We sit down to talk and I might as well be alone. I ask him something and I have to say it twice. I have to say it three times."

"He just had a heart attack."

"He was this way before the heart attack. He'll say things right out of the blue. Right in the middle of a conversation. At both visits he asked when you were coming."

"Why didn't you call me?"

"Because you *were* coming. There was nothing urgent about it. But don't you find that strange? Him asking for you?"

"Hell yes."

In the past I was the last person he wanted to see.

"The second time I visited, he went off for a nap. So I got to talk to Mother alone. I told her I'd been worried about Father for weeks, long before he'd had a heart attack. That he seemed tired to me, worried, suddenly older. I asked her if anything more was wrong than what she'd told me. She said no, just this problem at work, but it was continuing to trouble him. He did seem terribly concerned.

"I asked if she knew what the problem was and she said there was some supposed impropriety at the law firm. Some conflict of interest. I asked if it concerned Father directly and she said she didn't know. He would be just as worried in any case. I said didn't she want to know, wouldn't it be better for them to talk it out, and she got very cold, angry and cold. She said I had this way of coming on like a psychologist, and it infuriated her. I sounded so smug and superior. She said they had been married for many years and had worked out their way of handling things. If Father kept work-related things to himself maybe that was the best way for him. He told her what he wanted to and he always had. It was none of my business anyway."

The Duchess wasn't the best at taking criticism.

"All that didn't make me any less concerned. Father looks to me like a person who needs to talk to somebody. Who needs to get something off his chest. And I don't think, for whatever reason, that he feels he can talk to Mother."

"So that's where things stand."

"With them. But I was still curious, so I asked around among some lawyer friends. I found somebody from another firm who could tell me all about it. She knows the other lawyer. The one who's bringing the suit."

"Father's going to be sued?"

"Not necessarily. Not yet. It *could* result in a suit, if it gets that far. Anyway. Does the name Frank Weyland mean anything to you?"

"Not a thing."

"It would if you lived here. He's a big developer. Quite notorious. He's built these lavish shopping malls. In old existing buildings, or on huge tracts in the suburbs. People love him or they hate him. The business community says he's great. He brings in all kinds of money. Which undoubtedly means he brings it in to them. Other people think he's ruining the city. Destroying its old ethnic character."

"What do you think?"

"I could go either way. As malls go, his are pretty tasteful. Stylish. On the other hand, they're not the corner drugstore. They're full of all these national chains."

"There's a guy like him in every city."

"Father's his lawyer."

"Shit."

"What would you expect? Weyland wants the best."

"Yeah."

"He also probably wanted an established firm. One that was well represented in the city. Since he was coming here from Cleveland. Anyway. The case in question goes way back. Years back. To this time when he needed a zoning change. He was tearing down some old buildings. Putting in one of these huge malls. Now it just seems like a part of the landscape. But at the time it stirred up a huge controversy. It would greatly increase traffic where they were building it. Change traffic patterns. It would drastically change a couple of neighborhoods. People were up in arms. They came to the hearings in droves. Signed petitions. Got on the news. It was a big deal."

"It always is."

"He got the change."

"Those people always get the change."

"Apparently Father didn't appear at the hearings himself. Mr. Harrold is better at that."

Mr. Harrold was an old partner in the firm. We'd known him all our lives. He was a dry thin bespectacled man. Very deliberate. He looked like a high-school civics teacher.

"But Weyland was mainly Father's client," Helen said. "Anyway, at the same time, the firm was handling a divorce case involving the chairman of the zoning commission. They were representing his wife."

At this point, when I've been over the whole thing countless times, it seems obvious what the problem is. But when Helen first told me I didn't understand.

"That's where the problem is," she said.

"That's the big crime?"

"It's not a crime in itself. But that's where the possibility exists."

"I don't get it."

"You've got to picture the people. Frank Weyland is going in front of the zoning commission. Trying to get this zoning change, from which he stands to make piles of money. Mr. Harrold is standing there beside him." Looking as if he might break into the pledge of allegiance at any moment. "In the meantime, off in a courtroom somewhere, the zoning commissioner's wife is divorcing him. Trying to get a fair settlement. And a lawyer from the same firm, from Father's firm, is standing beside her."

"You don't know who?"

"Somebody who's not there anymore. But what if this lawyer looks over at the zoning commissioner, gives him a little wink, and advises the wife to accept a pathetic settlement. Much less than she should have gotten."

"This would happen right there in the courtroom."

"It probably never got to a courtroom. I'm trying to make it clear. Using a visual aid. For someone who doesn't have the sharpest of legal minds." She reached over and patted me on the head.

"Thanks."

"My lawyer friend did the same for me. Anyway. The zoning commissioner goes back to the hearing, walking with a new spring in his stride. He just saved a pile of money. He also, so to speak, just screwed his wife for the last time. He winks at Mr. Harrold and grants the zoning change. To the same firm that just gave him a break in divorce court."

"He can do that? By himself?"

"He has a lot of influence. He's the chairman. He can enthusiastically support the change. Talk to other members of the commission. He also runs the hearings. He can favor one side or the other. Control the debate."

"And that's what happened?"

"That's what the wife says. She says she didn't get nearly the settlement she should have."

"That doesn't mean all this other stuff went on."

"No. But apparently the settlement was pretty bad. My lawyer friend was shocked to hear it."

"How did she hear?"

"She knows the lawyer who's bringing the suit. He's apparently kind of a loudmouth."

A lot of people probably knew. At least a lot of lawyers. They were a gossipy community.

"All this was years ago," I said. "And nobody noticed until now."

"There was nobody to notice. Everybody else was happy with the way it came out."

"So what happens?"

"Well. At first it looked like a simple case of malpractice. This woman's lawyer didn't get her enough money. That would have been settled quietly, especially because it happened so long ago. But if it's this other thing. If Father saw to it that the woman got less so he could help out Weyland.

That's something else altogether. Conspiracy to defraud. That would be very much alive in a court of law. And it's a much more serious charge. A lawyer who did something like that would be in deep shit. Subject to disbarment. Maybe criminal prosecution."

"God."

"For a while it looked like they were just pursuing the malpractice case. A small settlement. Then they started to talk about this larger thing. That's when Father got sick. His illness has delayed proceedings. But sooner or later they'll go forward."

"I wonder how things stand."

"This loudmouth lawyer claims to have a great case."

"They all say that."

"I suppose. But the fact that this is such a large and respected firm. And that Weyland's a part of this suit. It's bound to get a lot of notice."

It was frustrating. Knowing this much, and no more.

"What do you make of it?" I said.

"I don't know."

"Do you believe it?"

"I'm not sure. Although I must say. As my friend was talking to me. Telling me this long involved story. She seemed to believe it."

"She works for a rival firm."

"True."

"I don't think the first thing to assume is that he did it. Maybe that young lawyer just screwed up. Maybe *he* had something to do with the zoning commissioner. Maybe Mr. Harrold did it."

"I know. I'm not saying I believe it. That wasn't my first concern. But from hearing my friend talk. The way she went on and on, almost in spite of herself. There's a certain amount of juicy gossip to it all. A certain amount of scandal."

"Yes."

"I think that's what would bother Father. Not some difficult lawsuit. He's up to that. But if his honesty is being questioned. By other lawyers. That's what it would be if he got disbarred. He's always been so proud of his profession. Felt such a solidarity with lawyers."

"He has."

"To think that people were talking behind his back. His old friends. I think that would be disastrous."

Helen had a way of focusing on the most important point.

"I've thought all along we should bring it out in the open," she said. "Talk about it with Father, so there's not that strain of keeping a secret, and he knows we're all behind him. His family's with him, if nobody else is. He doesn't seem to want that. And Mother won't hear of it. But if this lawsuit is filed, according to my friend, it'll be in all the papers. Everybody will be talking. Even Mother won't be able to keep it quiet."

"She'll try."

"She won't have a chance. We'll be able to talk at that point. Until then I think we should just wait."

It seems strange, as I look back on it—especially the way things turned out—that we would just wait, that we would do nothing, at least that I would do nothing. What Helen had told me that night was deeply disturbing. It would occupy my mind—at least the back of my mind—for some time. It certainly occupied my thoughts during the bus ride home that night, which I took with a single other passenger, a slender elderly black man who kept shaking his head and blinking, talking to himself. But there were other things on my mind that night too, just the question of how the Senator and I would get along, whether Helen was right that he seemed to want to talk to me, whether we would be able to talk in a new way. Those things seemed of more present concern than the particular problems he was having. It was also true that his problems at work weren't especially pressing. He hadn't been to work for some time. We were far more concerned with the state of his health.

It wasn't late when I got back to the hotel. Helen had had some work to do, and we knew we'd be seeing each other again. I was full of the conversation we'd had, but also full of energy, which was just as well. There was a note waiting for me at the desk. "Charles. I'm having a drink in the lounge. Love for you to join me." It was signed, with a flourish, with a capital A.

The Other Charles

In my seventh year, when the third of my family's five children was born—a classic moment—I suddenly got fat. Until then I had been a positively skinny kid, staring up in photographs with a gooney, silly look on my face, but in that year, as if something terrible had happened that caused me to undergo a grotesque transformation, I got fat. My skinny little face puffed out into a much larger, older boy's face. I grew two chins, three chins. My torso took on a hefty layer of flab. I had a big soft belly with thick rolls of flesh, tits like a twelve-year-old girl's, huge soft thighs.

If you had been a casual observer, if you had watched the whole thing on time-lapse photography (the way Walt Disney used to show a caterpillar changing into a butterfly), you would have said, How could a thing like that happen?

I honestly don't know. I have no memory of it. I must have *done* it (something like that doesn't *just happen*), but I don't remember doing it. I must have done it while I wasn't looking.

Why did I do it? It was as if I were taking revenge on somebody, as if I said, All right, I hate this kid so much I'm going to turn him into a grotesque bag of flab, and the person I did it to was ... myself.

The family joke—mention of this product still brings a roar of laughter from my brothers—was that I had discovered a substance called Nestlé's Quik and gone absolutely apeshit, blowing myself into a blimp with that single product. That can't be true—it takes more than a little chocolate powder to manufacture all that blubber—but it isn't a bad symbol for the whole process. It takes the most basic of foods, one which people consume out of a real need, and turns it into the kind of sickeningly sweet confection that you might crave and drink too much of, and that fills you like lead. When I was playing ball and got thirsty, I ran inside for a glass of Quik instead of a glass of water, satisfying my thirst with 300 calories instead of none. I mixed it at the kitchen counter and threw it back in a couple of gulps, the way a drinker pops into a bar for a quick one. In the same spirit, if I was having a bowl of ice cream, I covered it with chocolate syrup, threw on peanuts, whipped cream, and a cherry, and grabbed some cookies to go with it. The guiding principle behind all my eating was, I want more! If I can't have what I really want (passionate physical love from my mother), I am by God going to have this (enough calories for a family of five). The expression on the face of such an eater is not pleasure. It is resolution. It says, I'm going to do this! Nobody's stopping me!

I can still remember the day, over thirty years ago, when what I had done really came home to me. Until then I hadn't noticed the blubber all over my body, the way you don't notice a fly settling on your arm, but in third grade the school doctor—a tall elderly gent with a look of barely restrained anger on his face—came for his yearly visit, and we all got weighed. I was one of the three heaviest kids in the class. It was a dead heat. We all tipped the scales at eighty-three pounds.

I can still remember what I felt as I stepped off the scale, a kind of breathless sensation, flushed in disbelief.

Holy shit! I thought. I'm fat!

There seems no doubt that the changes in my body had something to do with my brother's birth, though I don't remember a particular loss of love from that time. My memory is that I had never gotten much physical affection from my mother. Perhaps that moment just brought the fact to my attention. In the same way, being fat brought out an aspect of my personality that I believe to have been there all along (there was a fat person struggling to get out of my skinny person). I feel sure that on the day we were weighed, countless jokes were made at the fat boys' expense, but though the other boys went off and sulked, maybe pounded their tormentors on the playground ("Sit on him! That'll teach him!"), I went along with the jokes and made more at my own expense. I had become the kind of person who is automatically funny, just by his appearance, and who makes himself agreeable by going along with the joke. The kind of boy who eats—along with everything else he is eating—shit.

I wanted everyone to be happy, everything to be harmonious, and if that meant I had to listen to jokes about being fat, if it meant I had to make jokes about myself, if I had to get fatter so the jokes would be funnier, so be it! I'd make the sacrifice. I'd make a complete ass out of myself if it would make the world happier, if it would avoid conflict (if it would avoid real emotion). If fat hadn't existed, I'd have had to invent it. I became a person who felt he was physically unattractive, who spent a great deal of time dwelling on that belief, who thought his life would be better—everybody would love him!—if he just weren't fat (and thereby had a pat excuse for why his life wasn't good). I became a person who defined himself by his appearance. If you had asked me, that was the first thing I would have said. I was fat.

All of this brings to mind a certain kind of comedian—Fatty Arbuckle, Oliver Hardy, Lou Costello—who is funny because of the way he looks, who makes capital of his appearance by putting himself in situations that accentuate it (squeezing through a narrow doorway, dancing with a dainty woman, chasing a midget). I think in particular of Costello, a pathetic little fat guy who always fucked up, who was always being put down and who always put himself down, who admitted *ad nauseam* how worthless he was. Costello was likable not for his good qualities but because he was so pitiful, like a droopy little basset hound that you periodically have to whack the living piss out of with a rolled-up newspaper. Costello had a girlfriend—a blond bombshell by the name of Hillary

Brooke—who was considerably taller than he, sexy and beautiful, but their romance was obviously part of the joke. She knew Costello was a hopeless little bastard and often admitted as much to Abbott, who was probably screwing her on the side (while Costello was off eating a lollipop). To a sensibility like mine, which at that point couldn't imagine getting a girl any other way, the idea had a certain appeal. If you were really a royal fuck-up, you might get a girl. Maybe I just wasn't pathetic enough!

I think of the amounts that I ate in those days—especially as I moved out of childhood into adolescence—and am astounded. Massive platters of fried chicken were served at our table (the children *were* eventually allowed to move out from the kitchen), and, as soon as they were, I was looking for the seven pieces I was going to take. Start with two breasts. Be sure to get the biggest ones. Blobs of mashed potatoes the size of softballs, drowning in thick chicken gravy. Mountains of peas. That was the fateful period in my life when the Sara Lee cake was invented, an incredibly concentrated food that seemed to cram the ingredients for a regular cake into one about half that size. A piece of that cake could turn your face on like a neon sign. I used to take about a third of a cake, buried in ice cream, then have a second helping just like the first. I must have consumed a thousand calories at dessert alone. I can remember nights when we had lasagna, heavy blocks of enormously rich (and extremely delicious) food. I would have had one helping twice as big as anyone else's, a second helping just like the first. I'd pick up my plate for a third. I wouldn't be hungry at that point. I hadn't been hungry since the first few bites of the first helping. I was stuffed, in fact. I could hardly move. But I was reaching for more. I'm not talking about an irrepressible adolescent here, the proverbial bottomless pit, who could eat enough for three at dinner and then rush out—with a loud effortless belch—to play ball with his friends. I'm talking about a big slow heavy boy, burdened by his life, who sits at the table as if at some enormous task he has to perform, turning his body into a giant redwood tree. Huge and petrified. He might as well have been shoveling cement into his mouth.

This is the dark side of being fat, the side Dom DeLuise never tells us about, the big blubbery fifteen-year-old waddling through the locker room with his tiny little dick. Why does nobody ever bring that subject up, the single most obvious fact about fat boys? What's the problem here? Is it just that, in comparison with his enormous body, his dick looks small? Is it that the fat hangs down and obscures the first few inches (until, in moments of passion, it comes burrowing up out of its hole like a groundhog)? Is it that he has somehow diverted his libido into eating (it took a wrong turn at that fork in the road), so that, instead of producing a big dick and a healthy pair of balls, it has produced rolls of blubber instead? Or is it what a friend of mine once suggested, that your dick is a barometer of how you feel about yourself as a man, so that if you're feeling good it hangs like a hammer, but if you're not (and what fat man ever is?) it shrivels into a stump? A fat boy has a small dick because he doesn't feel like a man. He also has tits like a girl's, wide suggestive hips, balls that have beaten a hasty retreat up into his body until they resemble nothing so much as . . . a pussy!

Fat boys are girls. That's the real problem.

The Duchess, to her eternal credit, never said a word about my being overweight. "Charles isn't fat," she would say, with absolute conviction, to anyone who used that word anywhere near me (usually my comedy team of younger brothers, Mo, Larry, and Curly). This extraordinary ability to deny an obvious fact must have been something she learned through years of consorting in society. The Senator was another matter. He was overweight himself; he too had been fat as a kid, though he had slimmed down in the army before prosperity blew him up again. He was in the delicate position of seeing one of his major flaws duplicated in his son ("This *must* be Charles," his friends would say, picking me out of a throng of thousands), and naturally wanted to correct in me what he was helpless to change in himself. He sometimes—in a blunt, hearty, masculine way—kidded me about my weight, something which I found deeply humiliating. He spoke to me more seriously at times of lean red meat (they used to think that was good for you), leafy green vegetables, skim milk, carrot sticks for a snack. He spoke of vigorous physical exercise, which in those days meant ten push-ups and twenty sit-ups. More than in anything he said, though, I felt his disapproval in his attitude toward me. His wish that I should be otherwise. That I should be another person.

But I have often thought that, at some deeper level that he may not even have recognized, my father wanted me to stay as I was. He humiliated me about being fat so I would stay fat (humiliation not being renowned as a spur to change). He wanted me to stay as I was so he could stay annoyed at me, a heavy bland obedient boy—like a dumb ox, or a dray horse—who would never rise up to challenge him, who would never look up from the beaten path he was slowly treading.

The same dull heavy feeling that hung over the meals I ate (I think I'll have just *one* more helping of lasagna) hovered over everything I did. My father was a prominent partner in a major law firm. Mahogany desks, plush leather chairs, silver decanters of ice water. I admired him. I honestly did. But there was an assumption from the moment I was born that I would follow him into that firm just as he had followed his father, that I might as well acquire that portly girth so I would have it when I got there. As if I could already see those legal tomes ranging in front of me, feel their weight and dryness, the whole world seemed that way to me. Modern European history. American history. The front page of the newspaper. Political discussions at the dinner table. *U.S. News and World Report.* Only in English class did I feel some lightness and ease, a spark of real interest, but in my father's world—and at the boarding school he sent me to—literature was a minor pleasure, about on a par with the bridge club, or with classical music. Something for the women to do. (Have another slice of this beef, son.)

My brilliant sister, who could do all the things I couldn't, seemed a miracle of nature. I couldn't imagine how her mind could be so quick and agile, could operate with such ease in the midst of all that dryness and weight.

I look back on that young man—young Charles, wearing the neat little crewcut his mother liked on him so much, tipping the scales at 204 at his height of 5'8"—as a brother of mine, a long lost brother, as if he is still off somewhere eating chocolate sundaes and trying to make his way through that American history textbook, trying to do a chin-up, whatever. He is who I was when I became a man, and at low moments I can still see myself as him. I can still feel slow and stupid, heavy, sweaty, shy, unattractive to women, inadequate as a man. I can still think my dick is small. Most of all, I can feel fat. I can eat one piece of cake and feel like an enormous tub of lard who has had his seven pieces of chicken and is about to have his second piece of cake (throw a little ice cream on there, would you?). I can look in the mirror and see myself as that other person. I can feel that weight on me. And when I do that, I try to face that other self and say—for the thousandth time—good-bye to him, not angrily, but as an old friend with whom I went through a lot but whom I need to leave behind. It is a sad farewell in a way. He and I were so close. I learned a lot from him. It is a farewell that I never quite succeed in taking.

When I actually did take that farewell, in real life, it happened over a period of months.

I went to college in the South. I had failed to get into the Senator's *alma mater* or any of the other Ivy League schools I had applied to. I wound up attending my fifth choice. Seldom in my life had I felt bigger and slower and dumber. The Senator had advised me to have a spectacular first year and transfer. He still thought I was in the running (though way back in the pack) for the prize that he had decided I was seeking. I felt like a big bludgeoned ox, exiled to a foreign pasture. I blinked a few times, opened my heavily lidded eyes, and looked around.

I have always said I was more influenced by the sixties than anyone I know. People who knew me then (guys who grew beards, smoked dope, fucked around, protested the war, and are presently working for General Motors) don't know what I'm talking about. It looked as if I hardly entered in at all. But slowly, not very noticeably, everything about me changed. I was not, and am not, a political activist, but I gradually absorbed the political climate and acquired a kind of skeptical anarchism that has remained my politics to this day. I didn't grow a beard, I didn't fuck around (I *did* fuck), I didn't do any drugs other than beer. But something in that whole atmosphere, that upsetting of the applecart, was very liberating for me, probably necessary. If I had grown up twenty years later I would be headed for law school. That minor, apparently worthless interest I had, in literature and writing, suddenly—at a time when nobody believed in anything—blossomed. Might as well do that as something else. When I let myself touch that interest, it became everything to me. I realized that I wanted to write, that I had always wanted to write, that writing was the one thing I did with interest and ease. I started hanging around with the literary crowd; I joined the arts section of the newspaper; I lost my virginity to an intense and histrionic woman poet whom I profiled when she visited the campus, and who was my first (and most demanding) instructress in oral sex; and I took off, with about the same effort with which you'd take off a jacket (Jesus, it's hot in here), forty pounds. I just didn't eat in the old way anymore. I didn't use food for the old things. That weight hadn't belonged to me.

All this in my first year in college.

The reverberations at home were enormous. Those were the days when everyone was rebelling, all the young men were coming home with long hair and beards and new political sensibilities. Some of that would probably have been tolerated in my household, which was intellectually (if not politically) liberal, but as the years passed, as it became clear that I wasn't going to get over this adolescent silliness and go to law school, the Senator grew livid.

His arguments were predictable. I was taking up an occupation that wasn't a true profession and that wouldn't use my talents. I would tire of it in a few years and want to do something else. I wouldn't make any money. I wouldn't be able to support a wife and family in comfort. I was not only abandoning a traditional family occupation—our men had been lawyers for years—but I was in effect abandoning the family.

He would never have admitted it, but it is obvious that—more than anything else—his feelings were hurt. He had always believed his eldest son would come into the law firm with him. When I didn't, it shattered a dream. He took it very personally. He felt he had lost me as a son.

I think that he must also have been resentful. Hadn't he in some way, years before—when he had come back from the army, say, all trimmed down and ready to resume civilian life—rejected the choice I had made, not to follow his father into the same old profession and the same old firm, but to

DAVID GUY

take up some life of his own? Did he look back on that moment and wonder what might have been?

I certainly do. I'm not pretending that I know I made the
right choice. I could comfort myself that I was living out my
interest (and I do love my work), that I was living in my body
in a way that a fat man never does, that I was in many ways
healthier than I might have been. But I was also—and these
things weren't disputable; they were facts—returning to
Pittsburgh at the age of forty with no real home, no family,
no human center to my life, a profession that would always
be perilous. Off in some other world was the boy I had left
behind, who had come around after a few years and gone to
law school, joined the firm and endured a certain amount of
drudgery in the certainty that he would someday be a partner, consoled himself at lunch with the small fillet and the
lyonnaise potatoes and the deep-dish apple pie, gone home in
the Chrysler to the wife and kids in the big brick house, at-
tended the major social functions in the city, become an elder
in the church and a bulwark of the Republican party. It didn't
seem a bad life. It had its satisfactions. It seemed to offer a
kind of certainty that my present life didn't.

Years ago, I had rejected that life for another one, and, in
so doing, had chosen another body as well.

FIVE

The bar was a dim quiet lounge, with padded bar stools, small tables along the wall with miniature easy chairs. Andrea was sitting toward one end of the semicircular bar, the side nearest the door. She was wearing a cream-colored silk blouse, a pale gray skirt. Those colors looked great on her. I am tempted to say that any color looked great on her, but the truth is that she knew what looked good and only wore that. Anytime I saw her, even if she was just wearing jeans and a shirt, she looked smashing.

"I was going to give it another ten minutes," she said. "Although I must admit I've already done that twice."

"How long have you been here?"

"An hour and twenty minutes. One vodka tonic and two Perriers. Three guys have offered to buy me drinks. I told them I was waiting for someone. The next guy was going to get a second look."

"You must really want to see me."

"I must."

That was an odd, arrogant thing for me to say. It wasn't

like me. I wasn't myself. I was surprised that Andrea was there, flattered, slightly flustered.

I wouldn't have said that Andrea looked angry, but she did seem in the grips of some strong emotion. Acute impatience, perhaps. Her color was heightened. She looked as if she were about to jump up and scream.

"You could at least look glad to see me," she said.

"I am glad to see you. I'm very glad. I'm stunned."

"Don't take it too far. There wasn't much on TV."

Maybe I wasn't so flattered.

"Do you want a drink?" she said. She took my arm and looked deeply into my eyes. "I hope you don't want a drink."

"You hope I *don't* want a drink."

"You could have something sent up. Oh hell." She put her head in her hands. "I'm so far ahead of you. What *took* you so long?"

"I didn't know you were here."

"I know. I know. I'm not being reasonable." Her face quieted, then took on a pleading look. She often, when she asked me something, looked afraid, or sad. "Could we go to your room?"

"Sure." I answered automatically.

"I'm not this forward all the time. Really. But a person can go crazy in a place like this. I had a sudden impulse to come down here. I'd had such a nice time talking to you this afternoon. It was the first conversation with a man I'd enjoyed in months. Then I got here and I didn't know if you'd show up. Maybe you'd decide to stay with your sister. I didn't know if you'd want to see me if you did show up. Maybe you'd read my note and go to your room. None of this is *your* fault, of course. But I can't sit here and have another Perrier. I don't even like Perrier. I can't sit around wondering if this whole thing's going to end with a handshake in the lobby."

As she said all this, she stood, picked up her pocketbook, took my arm, and headed for the door. We walked across the lobby. The night clerk and bellboys were watching us. We stepped into the elevator.

"What floor?" she said.

"Six."

She pressed the button.

Not that she was taking charge or anything.

I hate to sound stupid, but I hadn't figured out what was happening. It had gone by too fast. I hadn't attached any particular significance to the fact that Andrea wanted to go to my room. I thought she was just tired of the bar.

I'd have caught on sooner or later.

As the elevator doors closed, she turned and stood in front of me. Her eyes were full of sympathy, as if she really felt for me in this situation.

"I'm sorry I'm so crazy," she said.

Then—in that small silent space, where we were utterly alone—she wrapped me in her arms, and kissed me.

What *is* sexual attraction? That's the question.

After Sara and I split up, after the first dark numb weeks when I sat around staring at the walls, I started going out. I asked women for dates. There was a part of me that immediately felt as if I were in high school again (that meant, of course, that I weighed 204 flabby pounds and had a half-inch dick), a part that felt the same awkwardness and stupidity and shyness I had felt back then. Even so, I did all right. I was a free-lance journalist who had traveled all over the country and met fascinating people; I loved reading, music, dance, all the arts; I was a good listener (it was my job!); I wasn't bad-looking; I kept in shape. There were a number of women in their thirties and forties who were happy to go out with me.

It took me a while to figure that out.

I felt as if I'd been thrown headfirst into an alien culture. Dates began with a long series of questions: how my marriage had gone wrong, how things stood between my wife and me, what we wanted for the future, what I wanted for the future, what kind of relationship I was looking for, whether I'd been dating a lot, whether or not I intended to be monogamous, whether or not I intended to get married again, why Sara and I hadn't had children, whether or not I wanted to have children now, and—of course!—whether or not I'd ever committed a homosexual act or used intravenous drugs. I don't mean to suggest that these weren't good and interesting questions. But they were unexpected—the girls hadn't asked them in high school—and I didn't have answers to them. (I could make up answers, of course. I'm a writer.) The women

I went out with had detailed answers to all these questions, and in fact gave the answers without being asked the questions. They had all had extensive sexual experience, a fact that for some reason they wanted to make clear right from the start. I often heard stories of five or six lovers before dinner was over. Some expected me to pay for this meal; some expected to share expenses; and some wanted to discuss this question for a very long time. Some assumed, if I kissed them, that we were going to bed. Others wondered what I meant by a kiss. Some were offended that I kissed them so soon, since they assumed that meant I wanted to go to bed.

I just wanted to hug and kiss a little. Know what I mean?

I did have sex. After one of those extensive interrogations, the eight hundred questions to which I'm sure I didn't give the right answers, some women nevertheless took off their clothes and got into bed with me. (This singles' life. It's the greatest.) I did fine. My penis stood up. (It remembered!) It performed quite admirably. The women looked great. They smelled wonderful. They really did have fabulous sexual techniques. (All that experience hadn't been in vain.) It was very interesting. I was very interested. I was an interested observer.

I wasn't a *participant.*

I can remember when I was in dancing school, eleven or twelve years old, that dancing with some girls was like dancing in a dream. Our bodies fit right together; my every move was hers; we floated around the room as if on a cloud. If I tripped and fell flat on my face she tripped and fell flat on her face, smiling at me the whole time, as if I had just done the cleverest thing. There were other girls, though—and this had nothing to do with how they looked, or how I felt about them—whom I seemed to be dragging around the floor, hauling around the floor. Dead weight in my arms. If I went one way, she went the other. Sometimes we got crossed up and crashed into each other, often with astonishing force. (This must have been how slam-dancing originated.)

Having sex after my marriage ended was like dancing with the wrong girl.

The problem was that I wasn't feeling anything. I'm not referring to my emotions. I'm referring to my body. My penis was numb.

Among the sexually athletic women I was seeing, of course, that was considered an advantage.

Eventually I decided that the problem wasn't with the women, it was with me. Though I wanted company, I wanted affection and sex. I was in a strange limbolike state—learning to be alone—that I would have to assimilate before I went on. And the only way to learn to be alone is to be alone. There's no detour.

Part of learning to be alone involves dealing with the—sometimes overwhelming—wish to be with somebody. You can easily mistake that wish for something else. You can convince yourself that it means your time is up, that you have learned to be alone and are ready to move on. But it doesn't mean that. If you hook up with someone too soon, you will never learn to be alone. You'll live for the rest of your life in that state of limbo. You'll spend the rest of your life dancing with the wrong girl, no matter who the girl is, or how many girls there are. Because to dance with the right girl, you first have to learn to dance with yourself.

So: a major part of sexual attraction has nothing to do with the other person. It has to do with the state you are in. Whether or not you are ready.

At various moments that afternoon with Andrea—the first time she hugged me, the little kiss she gave me when I left the second time—I had an intimation, like a far-off echo, that I might be ready to move on, I might be ready to be with somebody. But I'd had that feeling so many times before that I immediately dismissed it. Such a feeling is often just a wish.

When she kissed me in the elevator, however, I knew: I was dancing with the right girl.

Her arms came gently around my shoulders, and her body was soft against mine, but then she held me hard. Her belly pressed against me. That hollow aching place inside me, which will never be healed (and which I have tried to soothe with mountains of food and the embraces of countless women) felt touched, and warmed. I felt suddenly bigger. I could breathe easier. She did not—as many women do—hold back in modesty, but immediately pressed her pussy up against me. I felt a throbbing there. ("The moment you stepped into the bar," she told me later, "I got wet.") Our mouths fell open. Our tongues fluttered together. It was as if we had kissed a thousand times.

My penis leaped to attention.

When Andrea pulled back from that kiss, she looked slightly breathless (as if *I* had kissed *her*), slightly eager, but also calmed, and at ease. She didn't look like the cat who had swallowed the canary. She looked like the cat who was about to swallow the canary.

We kissed again.

I'm talking about a woman who had lines of sadness at the sides of her eyes (when I met her mother, she had the same lines, only much deeper; the women in that family had looked on something horrible); who had freckles all over her face, like a little kid; who most definitely did have too large a mouth. She had a decent body, but not an exceptional one; it was soft, with a small protuberant belly and the saggiest most deflated tits I had ever seen. Her thighs were too thick. She had a plump chunky bottom.

Yet for a time to me she was the most beautiful woman in all the world. I didn't want to look at another woman, much less touch one. I was far gone.

What *is* sexual attraction?

I loved the tone of her skin, its pale shade, its softness. I loved those wrinkles beside her eyes, the way her face had been etched by experience. I didn't want a woman who hadn't been touched by the world. I loved the sad, hollow expressiveness of her eyes, filled sometimes with fear. (I wanted to remove that fear.) I loved her burnished red hair, straight and soft on her head, bushy under her arms and between her legs. I loved her low husky voice, her quiet laugh. I loved the way she smelled.

Are those things sexual attraction?

I don't think Andrea particularly knew what I wanted or figured me out. I think she just had good instincts, acted the way she usually did, and hit the jackpot. I think it was important that she cried when she did (nothing draws me to a woman more), put me in touch with her pain, made me *feel* for her. I think it was important that, right from the start, she was emotionally intimate with me, since my recent experience (including the last years of my marriage) had lacked intimacy. I think that the way she had dumped on her husband, dumped on all men—which should have warned me off—lured me on. I wanted to change her mind. It was important that she wanted me, that she had so obviously wanted to see me, that she wasn't shy about showing that.

She was the woman—I had been waiting for her all my life—who had come to me and kissed me.

Then there was her manner once we got to the bedroom. I believe the word is blatant. By the time I had turned on the lamp, closed and locked the door, taken my jacket off and hung it over the back of a chair, she had—I was watching—kicked off her shoes, unbuttoned and stepped out of her skirt, thrown off her blouse, yanked back the covers of the bed and reclined on the sheets. She was leaning on an elbow. One leg was flat on the bed, the other up and bent at the knee. Her legs were open. She was naked.

"You forgot to wear underpants," I said.

"They just slow me down."

"You could use a little slowing down."

"Am I going too fast?" She asked this question with an air of utter innocence. Three minutes before we had been standing fully clothed in the bar, and the subject of sex hadn't been mentioned. "I could put my clothes back on. We could head back to the elevator."

"I'm kidding. I like it."

"I was so turned on by that kiss."

She had been turned on before the kiss. She had been turned on before I arrived at the bar. She had probably been turned on before I got to town.

This woman was ready to fuck.

There was also the way she spread her legs. Women in this culture (probably most cultures) have been taught to keep their legs together for so long that they have trouble bringing them apart. It is the same way we stifle our rage until we can no longer scream. But there is a kind of woman who has rebelled against the mores of this society. She has been a bad girl all her life. She has been a bold girl all her life. Her legs fall open like an old book. They are always partly open. When Andrea spread her legs for me later that evening, when she really did it, she put one foot on *this* side of the queen-sized bed, the other foot on *that* side. Her cunt opened like an oyster.

As she lay there now, in that relaxed easy pose, her whole posture focused on her pussy. She knew you were looking at it. She wanted you to look at it.

I stepped toward her.

"Aren't you taking your clothes off?" she said.

"In a minute." I knelt beside the bed. "There's something I'm going to do first."

"Oh." She sounded pleased. "I see."

The last thing about Andrea and me is that we were extremely compatible. What one of us liked to do the other liked to have done. We delighted in each other's pleasure.

I slung her thighs over my shoulders. Her bushy red hair grew in profusion, all over her pussy, in a narrow trail up her ass. She had a mild smell, a strong taste. I settled between her legs as if, after a long journey, I had found my way home. Her pussy was soaked. She lay with her eyes closed, her fingers in my hair.

I don't think it is giving away too much to say that the thing that feels best ("Just *what* were you doing down there?") is a sort of slow soft steady licking. Don't get excited; you go too fast. Don't show off. There is a way of making your mouth small and sucking on a particular place. (The woman groans.) There is a way—once you have sucked gently in—of running your tongue quickly over that place. (The woman yelps!) Some women like a finger or two inside them once they have gotten excited. Andrea seemed to like that. I was stunned at how big she was. I had two fingers inside her and plenty of room to wiggle around. I could feel her pussy gently throbbing. Finally she groaned, clutched my hair in her fingers, and—with little convulsions—lifted her torso slightly off the bed. Ripples passed over her belly like a breeze over a lake. Her pussy tightened on my fingers, and released.

"Christ," she said.

When she lay back, the look on her face—you rarely saw this look on this face—was bliss.

"You are great at that," she said. *"Great."*

Aw, shucks.

"I've never had it better, Charles. And I've been with women."

This remark would find its way back to Helen.

"You look sleepy," I said.

"I'll wake up. Take off your clothes. I don't like being the only one naked."

When I had undressed and come back to the bed, she reached over and took a box of condoms out of her pocketbook.

"Would you like to wear one of these?" she said. "Or wait for a blood test?"

"I'll wear one of those."

"I can see where we'd find most of your blood right now." She reached up and gave this place a squeeze.

"Do you think these will fit?" She opened a package and started to roll one on. "I should have gotten the extra large."

This woman knew the right thing to say.

"I only have three," she said. "I hope that's enough."

"If you do it right," I said, "one's enough."

I wasn't quite up to doing it right, as it turned out. It had been months since I'd fucked a woman, much longer—probably years—since I'd been satisfied by the experience. There are certain bodies that fit right together. Rhythms that blend right in. That first time I felt my excitement build much faster than usual, and I just let it, it seemed so right. There were—in my loud shout at the end—months of tension and frustration. The second time, as it turned out, would be better. It would go on much longer, fiercely, violently, until we both collapsed in a sweaty heap, and slept like the dead.

Between the first and second times, I had gotten up to turn off a lamp. One was still on. We lay there talking for a while, or just being with each other. She caressed my chest with her fingertips. I gently scratched her back.

"Could I stay here tonight?" she said at one point.

"Sure."

"It's so luxurious."

"For me too. I'm not used to this. We'll have to have break-fast sent up."

"You can eat me for breakfast."

"That too."

She went so well with a little maple syrup.

"I don't want to interfere," she said. "What time do you have to see your father?"

"Whenever. I'll call first."

"Are you nervous about seeing him?"

I took a deep breath, let out a sigh.

"Say no more," she said.

"Things have always been tense between us," I said. "Since I went to college. It's never been easy."

"What's the tension about?"

"Lots of things. The way I live. I disappointed him. Didn't become a lawyer."

"Jesus. Pardon me for living."

"Now he's had a heart attack, which certainly adds to the tension. I'll be worried about that. And my sister thinks something else is going on. Some crisis in his life. She thinks he wants to talk to me."

"That could be a good thing."

"It could."

Somehow I had my doubts.

"My father's a crook," Andrea said.

Her hand was still on my chest. I could feel it, as she said those words, simultaneously go cold and begin to sweat.

"He was, anyway," she said. "Embezzled money from the company he worked for. He did it for years. My mother didn't know at first, then he told her, just to make her a partner in it, I guess. She didn't do anything about it. She had children by then, didn't see a way out. She did eventually tell me, though. I was the oldest. She said it had to be our secret. I understand why she did that. She needed somebody to confide in. But it was hard on me. It was a hard thing to know."

"How old were you?"

"Twelve."

I couldn't imagine a more difficult age to hear such a thing.

"Then when I was sixteen he got caught. It was a big story, in all the papers. He was tried and sent to prison. I was right at the age when you're terribly worried about what people think. They didn't say anything, my friends, but they all knew. I was sure they were talking among themselves. I could feel them staring at me."

Andrea had started to cry. Tears poured from her eyes. I could feel them hot on my chest as she continued to speak.

"By the time he got out of jail I had gone to college and moved away. My mother had gotten a divorce and remarried. He wanted to see me again, but I wanted no part of that. I wanted that in my past. I told my brothers to tell him. Even so, he wrote me, tried to call me. I hung up as soon as I heard his voice. He finally got the point."

Andrea was crying hard now. Even in her deep grief, her body didn't shudder as convulsively as mine. It was used to crying.

"Sometimes when I was a girl I wanted to kill him. I really wanted to kill him. I wanted to take a knife and rip him up."

Andrea's anger with men wasn't really about her husband. It ran much deeper.

My chest was soaked. Tears, for some reason, have always excited me. They bring the woman close. I held Andrea in my arms to comfort her, and as I did I had a tremendous hard-on.

The hand that reached down to clutch it was like ice.

"Can you do it again?" she said.

"Sure."

"I want you to do it my way. I want you to do it for me."

"I will."

The hands that put on the rubber this time were rapid and determined. They pushed it down in little strokes, then, when it was on, squeezed my cock hard.

She sat beside me and looked into my eyes.

"This isn't me, Charles," she said. "Please don't think this is me."

"All right."

"And it isn't you. It isn't quite you I'm talking to. Do you understand?"

"Of course."

The hand that had been resting on my thigh flashed up and slapped me. It slapped me hard. I saw stars.

"Fuck me," she said.

She rolled over on her belly and raised her ass. Without thinking—my ears were still ringing—I took a full swing and smacked it.

"Fuck me!" The face that she turned to me was furious. "I told you to fuck me."

I grabbed her ass and rammed into her. "Oh!" she shouted. I pinned her to the bed and did it to her.

"Bang me," she said. "Do it hard. Make me forget."

I could see my red handprint on her ass. I smacked her again.

"Yes!" she shouted.

Her groans, as we continued, were hoarse, and full of rage.

Finding Comfort

We went every year for our summer vacation to a rickety Victorian inn in Connecticut. It was a charming structure, though its facilities weren't terribly up-to-date. By the time I was twelve, we were renting a suite with four bedrooms, a living room, a couple of bathrooms. All three of my brothers had been born at that point, though the youngest—Curly, or was it Shemp?—was just an infant.

One afternoon that summer I was sitting in the bathroom daydreaming. That was one of the few places where I could find any peace. It was also one of my favorite places to read. I knew about sex at that point, knew about the act of intercourse, but not much more. I didn't have an especially clear picture even of that. But I thought about it often, pondered the mystery, and as I sat in the bathroom that day I made a circle of my hand and put it around my penis. *That* was how it would be in intercourse, I decided. I moved my hand up and down. I hadn't had a hard-on when I started, but I continued to move my hand because it felt good, and began to get the kind of half-erection I got in those days. I moved my hand faster and faster. The sensation spread down into my thighs, up into my belly. I fell back against the toilet and threw my head back. The pleasure was so intense it made me dizzy. When I looked back down I saw a small discharge. At first I was frightened, but then I realized what it meant. I realized what I had done.

That must have been what my friends meant when they talked about jerking off.

My first feeling was one of delight—this *really* felt good—and of pride, at having discovered it myself. I had not, in the classic way, been shown by an older boy, a scout leader or somebody. I had discovered it on my own, the way Adam must have (before he lost that rib). I wonder what *he* made of it.

It is important to picture the boy who made this discovery. As he sat on the toilet, his heavy thighs spread over the seat and rolls of blubber hung down from his belly. He was sweating a little. He always felt fat, sitting in the bathroom. (He felt fat nearly everywhere.) He was, in some ways, a shy boy, but also a good-natured one, popular among the boys, re-nowned for his jokes (especially those great ones about being fat). He wasn't at the center of the popular crowd, but he was solidly at the periphery, a kind of court jester. He was not, however, popular among the girls, at dancing school and at the boy-girl parties they were starting to have. He lost his confidence around girls. He was the fat kid at those parties, but worse than that he was the kid who felt fat, who felt stupid and awkward (who was secretly hoping that, if he looked wistfully pathetic, a tall blond named Hillary Brooke would take pity on him, see that there was a good heart be-neath all that flab and make him her boyfriend). He felt ter-ribly shy about approaching girls, especially because the girls in his social set—even at the age of twelve—already seemed mature and sophisticated. He had tremendous longings—they were written all over him—for hard hugs, passionate kisses, but he could not bring himself to seek them. He stifled his longings by stuffing himself with food, and—from that day in the bathroom on—all of his sensual and sexual expression was confined to one small part of his body.

Can you imagine the pressure that put on such a delicate piece of flesh?

The fact that I am about to mention is probably the strang-est of my whole strange life. I tell it with no idea whether it will meet with a sympathetic response anywhere in the world.

It also seems a central fact of my life. It sums up my whole adolescence.

From the time I was twelve, for two years or so, I masturbated nine times a day.

My masturbating was like the way I ate, the seven (count 'em) pieces of chicken I ate every time we had chicken, the enormous chocolate sundae (with a side of cookies) that I fixed for myself every evening without fail. I didn't do those things because I wanted to. I did them because I had to. The day wouldn't have been complete if I hadn't. Something would have been wrong.

In the same way, for something like the same reason, I masturbated nine times every day.

I would sit in the bathroom, or lie on my bed—if I was sure I wouldn't be disturbed—and take my penis in my hand. I didn't caress it into a hard-on. I didn't know to do that, and I didn't have time. I was too nervous. I just grabbed it and started yanking away. My prick would get hard, but not terribly so. I would come once, twice, three times, softening after each orgasm, then hardening up again. I wouldn't come much. It was mostly—and more and more after each orgasm—translucent semen, very little white sperm. Having done it three times—I *had* to do it three times—I would clean up and leave.

The expression on the face of such an eater—as I said about food—is not pleasure. It is resolution. It says, I'm going to do this. Nobody's going to stop me.

I didn't masturbate happily, probably not once in those whole two years. I masturbated furtively and compulsively. I stole away from the bathroom as if from a crime. I wasn't loving my penis. It was more as if I were punishing it.

I remember riding the bus to school in those days—I would already have masturbated; I had "been to the bathroom" after breakfast—and thinking how strange I was, that if my friends really knew who I was, if they knew what I did, they would think I was the weirdest guy in the school. This was the great dark secret of my life. I was terribly sad about it. I thought there was something very wrong with me. The times were enlightened enough that masturbation was not considered an evil practice. It was no longer believed to cause insanity. What the books said was that "most" boys masturbate

(I felt that my friends were the exception to this general rule. Maybe some of the pimplier weirder guys jerked off, but most of my friends seemed too well adjusted), and that it was "all right" (nobody mentioned that it might be fun, or ecstatically pleasurable) if you didn't do it "to excess." The books didn't say what excess was, but there was no doubt in my mind that nine times a day qualified, and that my masturbating was therefore not all right. A friend told me about a sex maniac he had read about in a cheap novel who had to have several women every day; some thugs locked him up and he nearly went crazy, was finally reduced to masturbating, and he ejaculated blood. I was convinced I would see blood spurting out of my dick any day. In fact, I didn't know about lubricants yet, about the soothing properties of baby oil (I have since come to believe they should affix a small label to the bottle, 'Great for Hand Jobs Too!'), and I had a permanent sore spot on the underside of my cock. It often bled. I could see I was rubbing my penis raw, but I couldn't stop. I was a masturbation addict.

It is obvious that both eating and masturbating had moved beyond simple sensual pleasures for me and become rituals, compulsive acts (the obsessive numbers gave it away). Like all compulsive acts—like religious rituals, for instance—they were warding something off, attempting to control a mystery. They held certain appetites in check (actually, they beat the living shit out of them), so I wouldn't notice them, wouldn't notice what was behind them. I wouldn't notice the longing for love that lay behind my yearning to be touched. I wouldn't even notice the yearning to be touched. I made my penis ache so I wouldn't notice another, larger, ache.

Does such a boy become a man who isn't sensitive to his body as a whole, who only—as the expression goes—cares about his dick?

I had continued to fantasize about sex; the fantasies played into the masturbating, and also served something of the same purpose. I thought about sex in moments of idleness, moments of solitude, because it produced a bright image and distracted me from other things (the vast spaces of the empty universe, for instance). The fantasies I'd had since childhood had not changed, but I had changed in them. I had gotten older, so they were not as ridiculous as they once had been, or they were ridiculous in another way. Instead of coming to a five-year-old and kissing him, a woman was coming to a fat, shy fifteen-year-old. As I learned about sex, the fantasies moved beyond kissing, but the woman still came to me. I had done nothing to earn her favors. It was still an image of unconditional love. But now she put me on my back and blew me.

The summer I was fourteen, I was going with some friends to a summer house that one of their parents had in Maryland, and I resolved not to masturbate at all. I certainly couldn't have kept up my nine times a day habit. The trips to the bathroom alone would have been out of the question. I was desperately afraid of being exposed as an obsessive jerk-off artist. We were very active, swimming, waterskiing, sailing, climbing cliffs, so my time was taken up; we were also sneaking off to drink beer and smoke cigars, so my dark side was being fulfilled. I was greatly relieved to discover I wasn't irrevocably hooked to one vice. I held out until the last morning, when I had a few minutes alone in the bathroom and figured what the hell. I was fully mature by then, in a way that I hadn't been two years before; I was genuinely horny in a way that I had probably never been in my life. I was amazed at how big and hard my dick got (I had barely touched it!), at the copious gush of white sperm it produced (those cells produce *babies*, I thought), and, above all, at how wonderful it felt. I resolved at that point to masturbate less, not because the amount I did it was strange (that had never stopped me before), but because it felt so much better if I did it less.

From then on, for years, masturbation was a habit I fought. I loved doing it, but I didn't want to do it too much. It was certainly a nightly temptation, a many-times-a-day temptation, which I resisted much more than I gave in to, but I still did it all the time. It is hard to remember the incredible sex drive of adolescence, when you can be horny twenty minutes after you've come (as if you'd just eaten Chinese food). Given a free afternoon, I would head for the library, head for a bookstore, and spend two or three hours looking for sexy passages in books. I had a tremendous curiosity for everything having to do with sex, not only what people did but what they thought and said and felt. At the end of the afternoon I'd rush home to masturbate. Sometimes I couldn't wait, and did it someplace else. I jerked off in the stalls of public bathrooms, in the dank basement of a bookstore where I once worked, standing behind a tree in the woods, sitting on a deserted street in the front seat of my car. I spilled my seed all over the city.

What I believed was that masturbation was not real sex; it was what you did while you were waiting for sex, when you were too shy and pathetic to have a girlfriend. When I did have a girlfriend, when I got married, I stopped masturbating for a few years. I didn't need *that* anymore, I thought. What a relief, finally to get that monkey off my back. But in time I came to realize that I was missing something by only having sex with a partner. I missed the days when I could lie quietly and let my fantasies range wherever they wanted; when my orgasm was strictly my own, not a gift to somebody else; when I could lie there and play with the come on my belly, admire it. I was finally at ease with the practice, doing it not because I had to, but because I wanted to. It is an odd fact, but a true one: the time in my life when I most enjoyed masturbation was as an adult, when I was married.

SIX

A ndrea and I didn't speak the next morning of our violent second sexual encounter. We never mentioned it again. We woke up around eight thirty—late for me—feeling rumpled and drowsy, relaxed. We hugged for a while, tickled each other's back. Andrea never wore any makeup, and had that long straight hair, so she looked about as good first thing in the morning as any other time. In a way she looked better, sleepy and placid. We ordered breakfast. I shaved, and we took a shower together. I went to the door in my robe to intercept room service; Andrea had nothing on. We ate in bed together, fresh fruit and French toast, delicious coffee. We got a little silly with the syrup, wound up making love again. We took another shower (that syrup is sticky). I called my parents with a rough estimate of when I'd be there. It was nearly 10:30 by the time Andrea and I were dressed and ready to go.

"I hope things go well with your father," she said, kissing me good-bye.

"I hope so. Anyway. I feel better than I did."

"Good."

"I'll call you."

"Do that."

It was the kind of day I love in Pittsburgh, or anyplace else for that matter, perfectly clear and stunningly cold, the arctic air a palpable presence that you step into. No wind to speak of, no moisture in the air. It was the kind of morning that clears your head in about thirty seconds. I took the same bus I had taken to Helen's, which left me a long walk, but I like a walk. I was wearing a heavy topcoat and scarf, thick gloves and a cloth cap with earmuffs. There was hardly anyone on the sidewalks. Traffic was light.

It has always been one of my great pleasures to come back and walk through those old neighborhoods—Shadyside and Oakland—but coming home has not been an unsullied pleasure. There were the hard times when I was in college, and the years immediately after that, heavy with tension, since the Senator was always certain, on any given visit, that *that* was the time he would convince me to go to law school. I especially felt that pressure in the early years out of school, since I didn't have much I could say I was doing. I was bumming around, taking various jobs, trying to write fiction, while Sara was the major breadwinner, working as a waitress. It was a hard time as I look back on it, but we were fresh out of college, and in love, and I was just happy not to be sitting in a rice paddy in Vietnam. (I'd drawn a high number in the lottery, but we hadn't been sure what that meant at first. We thought maybe Nixon was just lulling us into a false sense of security.)

After that came our Pittsburgh period, when Sara had come back for graduate school and I—after my fiction hadn't panned out—became a political and arts reporter in the underground press. We thought living in Pittsburgh was a good idea because we had connections there, and we knew we wouldn't have much money. We hadn't realized how hard it would be living near my parents. After beating her brains out for three-and-a-half years, Sara decided graduate school wasn't for her. I was getting tired of reporting, so we took off, I to write the novel that I had felt building in me for years, Sara to do something, anything, that was new. We wound up back in North Carolina, where we had gone to college. Things were rough for a while, but she went into graphic design, which she had a natural flair for, what with her background in art. She started a business with two guys, both of whom had been trained in design, and within a year and a half it was flourishing. I, in the meantime, had drifted past page three hundred of my novel with no end in sight. I'd started with great energy, but what I'd written didn't seem to be coming together. I had thought it would take on a form of its own, but that didn't seem to be happening. For months I had been completely adrift.

Somewhere in there saw the commencement of my zombie period. I had always believed I would be a novelist. That belief had given my life meaning. When it turned out I wasn't, I was shattered. For months I was deeply depressed. I didn't *know* I was depressed. All I knew was that I was carrying a cement block around in my chest. Sara, in the meantime, was happier than she had ever been, fulfilled in her work, spending nine or ten hours a day in the presence of other men. One man in particular.

What I had to discover about myself was that I am a writer of limited imagination. I had strong instincts and intuitions, a deep interest in the human psyche, reasonably good powers of intellect, but I didn't have whatever it takes to create a whole world out of nothing. The best novelists do. (Fuck them.) Given a real situation, the kind of feature story a reporter does, I could put enough of myself into it to make it exceptional. I just couldn't start from scratch. I belonged in an odd gray area between reporter and novelist. Reporting ultimately bores me. Writing fiction ultimately terrifies me. But there is a certain kind of feature journalism that I am ideally suited for. I just had to learn that fact. I had to accept it.

I'd also finally had it out with the Senator. I'd heard about law school one too many times. I told him that this thing just wasn't going to happen, that he had to drop the subject. He did drop it, but that left a gaping hole in our relationship, partly because he didn't know what else to talk to me about, partly because there was a lot of unfinished anger between us. There was an emptiness between us that we just couldn't fill.

There was also a bizarre gap in our family. It was as if there were two different families. You had Helen and me, who had turned out so differently from what everybody had hoped. A hack free-lance writer and a lesbian psychotherapist. There was that strange seven-year lull during which the Senator and the Duchess had given up sex or something. ("He musta been shootin' blanks there for a while," the family gardener once said to me.) Then there was the sudden appearance on the scene of Mo, Larry, and Curly. Far be it from me to make light of them by not giving their real names, but all through my youth they were just like a comedy team, running into a room to bop me on the head, poke me in the eye, then, when they came of age—perhaps because they were reacting against Helen and me—they became the offspring that the Senator and Duchess must always have dreamed of. They were the three preppiest guys you ever saw in your life, good-looking, trim (the little bastards), appropriately witty. They did all the right things with their schooling, then Mo and Larry topped it off by joining the Senator's law firm. Curly got original on us and became a brain surgeon. They also became, in my humble opinion, three of the dullest human beings on the face of the earth. Their choice of careers did take the heat off me. By the time I was in my thirties, I was going back to a family that seemed totally alien. I had nothing in common with them. I was, by their standards, the black sheep.

It didn't help any that my marriage had ended. My brothers were accompanied at all family gatherings by their diamond-bedecked wives. Mo and Curly had children. Their families looked as if they had just stepped out of the Land's End catalog.

But the Senator, when he was sick, wanted to see me.

There's something about the eldest son. A primal connection with the father. The others can join the law firm all they want, it doesn't make any difference. It was also true that, in talking to the others, the Senator might as well have been talking to himself. They had made themselves over in his image. I didn't think they were especially good replicas. What the hell, they were still young.

I eventually made it to the Hall of Fame, a trek that involved, at the end, a climb up an incredibly steep driveway. That driveway, incidentally, never has any snow or ice on it. The people in the Hall aren't paying that kind of money to have trouble getting their Lincoln Continentals up into the garage. I think they hire a bunch of little guys to run out and catch the snowflakes as they fall.

I stepped into the vestibule and waited for the two doormen to decide I was fit to be admitted. You enter a small ornate lobby—there is, literally, a red carpet rolled out for you on the marble floor—then walk to one of the two wings of the building, where a doorman takes you upstairs in an elevator. He didn't ask where I was going. Those guys are paid to remember what their tenants' offspring look like. There are four apartments on each floor, two in each wing. This is not a small building. These are not small apartments.

I rang the doorbell and waited.

I will never forget how the Senator looked when he came to the door that day. I don't know how long he had been waiting, anticipating this meeting. He was leaning on his cane, looking slightly winded. But the man looked great. He was wearing a yellow cardigan over a blue oxford cloth, gray slacks, tasseled loafers. He still had part of a tan from the couple of weeks that he and the Duchess had spent, earlier in the winter, in Florida. His eyes were bright and alert. He looked straight at me as he opened the door, and beamed.

"Charles." He took my hand with the same bone-crunching grip he'd always had. "It's good to see you."

The Senator was still a big man. Huge shoulders, a barrel chest, steel gray hair, a wide handsome face. He has a big belly to go with that chest, but he doesn't look fat. He looks solid.

"It's good to see *you*, Dad."

The Duchess stood in the background, watching us.

This was a man who knew how to present a face. Moments after his heart attack, I swear to God, if he'd had to look good for somebody—if he'd had to meet a judge—he could have done it. Pain wracking his body. I had the feeling that, at the moment when we met at the door, he'd never wanted to look good for anyone as much as he wanted to look good for me.

I stepped into the apartment and greeted my mother. We walked through the little minuet of an embrace that we always do, barely touching. The Senator gave me a surprisingly forceful whack on my back. "Take off your coat, son," he said. "Stay awhile. It's cold out there. Bitter cold."

I hung my coat in the closet, and we moved toward the living room.

Straight ahead was a huge window with a wonderful view of Oakland (especially at night). The carpeting was a snowy white, the couches—one along the side wall, another at right angles to it, behind a coffee table—were cream-colored. There were two small Oriental rugs, a variety of art works on the walls. Two easy chairs along the wall opposite the couch. A grand piano in the corner.

"You look great, Dad," I said. "You really do. Nobody told me you looked this good."

"Oh, your sister. Your mother. They worry about every little thing. There's nothing wrong with me. Most men my age have a heart attack now and then."

"You just be careful, Bruce," the Duchess said. "Go slowly."

Our progress toward the living room was not as comfortable as that initial meeting. The Senator was moving slowly, leaning heavily on his cane. He seemed to be concentrating hard, as if he had to keep reminding himself to be deliberate.

"When did I ever go any other way," he said, "than slowly?"

I could remember a time. I could remember when the Senator had never moved at less than a jaunty clip, almost a dance. He was light on his feet for a big man. Seeing my father move this way was starting to bother me, to fill my chest with an ache, however prepared I'd thought I'd been.

"Your mother looks good," he said. "Doesn't she?" We had to fill up this journey with words.

"Mother always looks good," I said. "She's a good-looking woman."

"Honestly," she said. "At my age."

Even at her age. The woman looked good.

We finally got to the couch. The Senator plopped down. He seemed, even after that short walk at a snail's pace, slightly fatigued. He held his cane in front of him.

"How about a drink for this man?" he said.

"*Bruce,*" the Duchess said. "At this hour."

"I'd have a drink at this hour," the Senator said, "if I were still a drinking man. It's an occasion. Besides. A beer in the morning gives the world a certain glow."

"Maybe I'll have one," I said. "I could use a certain glow."

"You'll spoil your lunch." The Duchess shook her head as she stood.

"One beer," the Senator said, "never spoiled a man's lunch."

I should say at this point—something that hasn't come through in my intricate analysis of the past—that I loved these two people. Helen did too. Quite apart from what we perceived as their shortcomings. If I hadn't loved them, if my attachment to them hadn't been so strong, all that they said and did wouldn't have been so important to me. I should also say that they were two rather interesting and charming people. The Senator in particular. I had never wanted to be a lawyer with him, but he could tell you some stories about the law, and about political shenanigans in the city, that would make your hair stand on end. Or keep you laughing for hours. Whichever you wanted.

The Duchess came back with my beer (a Beck's; the Senator didn't fool around) and a tonic water and lime for the Senator. She brought nothing for herself.

"Your mother is going to be leaving us for lunch," the Senator said. "Getting together with her women friends."

"Your father wanted me to leave," the Duchess said. "He wanted some time alone with his son."

"She prefers to leave. I know that. You know it. These women like to get together in the middle of the day. Have a little too much sherry."

"Too much whiskey is more like it," the Duchess said. "These women."

"But she's left a lunch for us. Breast of chicken for me. A dish that I've had God knows how much of in the past few weeks. I had her make it into chicken salad for you. A little curry powder. Some grapes. A hunk of French bread. I'd hate to condemn you to my meals."

"Sounds fabulous."

"The refrigerator's full of beer. We should have a hell of a time. I can't drink, of course, but I get a certain pleasure out of watching. A single glass of white wine is all I'm allowed."

I was overwhelmed by the attention the Senator had paid to all this. The fact that he wanted to have lunch with me at all. Just the two of us. In the past, he would have been at work when I was at home, or out on the golf course (same thing); he might have invited me downtown for lunch. But he was always surrounded by his cronies down there—his cronies eventually included my brothers—and I just stopped going.

Nothing, however, surprised me more than the next thing he said.

"So. Tell us what you're working on."

The Duchess had also turned to me, as if that were the most natural question in the world.

The Senator had never asked me about my work in his life.

"What I'm working on?"

"Are you doing a story for somebody?"

Well, yes. But don't you want to hear about the last fifteen years of stories first?

Once I had recovered from the shock, I told them what I had going at the moment. I had a couple of book-review assignments pending. I do a weekly column for a newspaper down where I live. But my major project at the moment was a profile of a writer that I was doing for a national magazine. I prefer to do articles on artists, especially in the arts that I follow, so I've done a number on writers and jazz musicians. I also like eccentrically religious and sexual types, gurus and lunatics of all varieties. I like people who have taken an obsession and run with it. The smaller and weirder the obsession the better. I am especially interested in people who have made a bizarre obsession the cornerstone of their lives.

I don't want to identify the writer I was working on, so I won't be specific about the part of the country he lived in. It was not North Carolina, where I lived. He was a writer whom I had admired for years for the richness and eccentricity of his voice. He had the courage of his rhetorical convictions, followed his rough-hewn sentences wherever they led—and they wandered down some pretty strange paths—but he was never uninteresting. He took note of odd details that other writers ignored, made them coalesce into a unique and beautiful vision. He has always had a cult following, and in recent years the cult has grown enough to make him a comfortable living, what with some journalism and the occasional screenplay. He doesn't teach, but he lives in the vicinity of several universities, and he seems—despite his physical ugliness—to attract a certain kind of young literary woman. I had the impression he was consorting with two or three of them, but he also has a wife and two teenage children. How he walked this domestic tightrope I didn't know. (My next interview was with his wife.) At that point I had talked to only a few people who knew him, I was making my way through his books for the second (sometimes the third) time, and I had spent a lot of time talking to him. At first—in the best Hemingway tradition—he had been surly and uncommunicative, but gradually he seemed to be loosening up. The question I was ultimately trying to answer was where he had gotten the courage to write his strange and ragged little books, so far out of the literary mainstream. He was actually an intelligent and sensitive and sophisticated man, not the literary primitive some people took him to be. But he didn't care for literary fashion. He didn't give a shit if people liked him or not. So naturally people liked him a great deal.

I sketched all this out for the Senator and the Duchess. I can get pretty involved when I'm talking about my current project.

"Sounds like quite a character," the Senator said.

"He is."

"I'm not sure I'd like to *meet* him," the Duchess said.

No. She wouldn't. He smells, for one thing.

"Maybe the best place to meet him is in the pages of a magazine," I said.

The magazine in question certainly smells good. It has two or three perfumes in every issue.

"You're getting good money for this," the Senator said.

"Pretty good."

I command top dollar in the magazine world. Less than what the Senator makes on a halfway decent day, but still.

"Well," the Senator said. "I think it's about time for the men to have lunch. And the women to retire."

"I'll retire," the Duchess said. "But I want the men to promise"—she was staring straight at me—"that they won't get wrought up. They'll stay off dangerous subjects." She turned to the Senator. "Like who should have gone to law school twenty years ago."

"I haven't said a word," the Senator said.

"It's time for us to put all that to rest," the Duchess said. "To leave our differences alone. Those subjects are too dangerous now."

"They were always too dangerous," I said.

I was glad we were putting all that to rest. I was sorry we'd had to wait for a heart attack to do it.

The Duchess was still, in her mid-sixties, a lovely woman. She had put on some weight, but not much, and she was an expert at dressing so it didn't show. If anything, she was more finicky about her clothes than before. She still had a beautiful face, which was carefully and tastefully made up. There was gray in her hair, but only an amount that graciously offset the brown. Her eyes and brow still somehow had a youthful look, though her mouth could seem drawn and tired. But there was definitely a change in her manner toward the Senator. You wouldn't quite have called her nervous, but she was definitely on the attentive side. She seemed to be more watching him than participating in the conversation. She had never been a woman to hover around her husband, but I had the distinct impression now that she was reluctant to leave.

"We'll be careful," I said. "We won't talk politics. That cadaver in the White House."

"That great American," the Senator said.

He was being ironic. He was well aware of the limitations of our president. Not that he hadn't voted for him enthusiastically twice.

"*Don't* talk politics," the Duchess said.

"We won't. I promise."

The Duchess saw to it that we got settled. She got us out to the dining room—another agonizing trek—and got us seated, served the Senator his breast of chicken and his lettuce leaves with vinaigrette, got me my chicken salad, a small loaf of French bread with garlic butter. A second beer for me, a glass of wine for him. She waited until we got started and made sure everything was all right. Then she made her exit.

"How I wish this were a good red wine," the Senator said, after she'd gone.

"Wouldn't that be all right?" I said.

"No. Because to go with the red wine I'd want a bowl of beef stew. A thick fragrant gravy. Big hunks of potato and celery. To go with the stew I'd want a loaf of French bread, soaked with butter. I'd want a piece of cheesecake for dessert. I'd eat all that and die."

"Maybe you'll develop a taste for breast of chicken," I said.

I can't say how strange it was to be sitting alone in that apartment with the Senator. It was first of all strange that he was living in an apartment, not our enormous old house. It was strange that more family wasn't around, that servants weren't around. (The Duchess still had some help, but not full-time. That got to seem too crowded in the apartment.) I couldn't remember when I'd been this alone with my father.

"So how are you, Dad?" I said. "Really."

"Oh. I'm all right."

"Are you?"

"It wasn't that bad a heart attack. Not intense pain or anything, the way you see it in the movies. More like a bad case of indigestion." The Senator had had some monumental cases of indigestion. "But it was frightening. This thing happening to your body that you have no control over. Your body doesn't seem to be you anymore. It seems to be your enemy. And you know afterward that it could happen again. I feel fine now, but that thing is out there waiting to happen. It's terrifying."

"It is."

"I'd been under some stress. But I'm taking it easy now. I'm going to take it easy."

"You really are?"

"I really am."

"That's good. I'm glad to hear that."

The Senator shifted in his chair. "We've been worried about you."

"You've been worried about *me?"*

"Your mother and I. Your sister. She hears from you some. Your mother and I don't. We've wondered what was going on."

"I didn't know you wanted to hear from me."

"Of course we want to hear from you."

"You never heard from me much before."

"Oh. You know how that is. We figured you were down there writing. Down there with Sara. We figured everything must be okay."

Being married is hardly a guarantee that everything is okay.

"So how do I look?" I said.

"You look fine. You look great, actually. Your sister keeps us apprised. She says you aren't seeing anybody. You haven't been seeing a woman."

"No."

"Are you bitter?"

"I just haven't wanted to. I wanted to be alone for a while."

"You don't want to be *too* alone."

I was touched by the concern my father was showing.

"We were worried when you didn't come home for Christmas," he said.

That had been a first, I had to admit. I hadn't come home for the Christmas that had just taken place. The year before had been the first Christmas after my marriage had ended. It had also been the first Christmas that my parents had been in their new apartment. I hadn't wanted to stay there. Too tight. I could have stayed with Helen, but Curly—the out-of-town brain surgeon—had gotten his request in first, so the Senator had put me up at one of his clubs. That had been a generous gesture, but the whole thing was rather depressing. The place was populated by a bunch of guys the Senator's age, grizzled veterans who popped their teeth in every morning and staggered down to the dining room for some milk toast. I pictured myself doing the same thing in a few years. I also felt like the black sheep of the family, old Uncle Charles, that wasted old duffer who's staying down at the club with the World War I veterans. Nobody had much of an idea what to give me for Christmas. Two of my brothers gave me bottles of bourbon, which gave me something to do back in my shabby little room at the club.

I hadn't been able to bear the thought of spending another Christmas like that.

"I was busy," I said.

"Nobody's that busy. Not me at my worst."

"I had a deadline. I was working hard on an article."

"What did you do on Christmas Day?"

"I celebrated with some friends."

I was lying. I had cooked a small chicken and eaten by myself. A mashed potato. Some cranberries.

"I don't want to pry into your private life," the Senator said. "I've never wanted to do that. I hope you won't let me do it. But I can't help wondering what happened between you and Sara. What went wrong."

The only previous change in my relationship with the Senator, the only thing that broke the ice that had formed back in my college days, occurred when Sara and I split up. My parents—though very discreet—had been genuinely sympathetic, the Senator in particular. (I do think the Duchess considered it a bit of a disgrace. This was the first divorce that had ever happened in our family.) The Senator—comforting me in the way that he could—took me aside and spoke of the legal aspect of it all, said that of course he couldn't be my lawyer but that he would help in any way he could. All that hadn't really applied, because Sara and I had broken up amicably, neither of us wanting—so to speak—to screw the other. We followed the Senator's first rule of divorce, which surprised me a little, considering the source. "The more you can settle yourselves," he said, "the better. Whatever you can do to keep a lawyer out of the proceedings, you should. Because as soon as you have a lawyer involved, things get complicated. He starts performing his function, quite apart from who he's working for. Things get messy."

What do you tell your father, when he asks such a question? About what it was that ended your marriage.

To no one in the world do you tell the truth. The whole truth. You wouldn't if you knew it (which you don't). You tell whatever part of the truth you think that person can take, or what you want that person to know, or what you feel like telling at the moment. Or you lie.

Things were so much different with my father that day that I wanted to be as honest as I could, within the limits of what I knew.

"It was a lot of things," I said. "It was complicated."

"I don't mean to pry," he said.

"You're not. I don't mind your asking. I'm glad you asked."

It was better to have things out in the open.

"I think we'd just become different people," I said.

"Yes. Well. Everybody's different."

"I don't mean different from each other. I mean different from what we'd been. When we got married."

"That also happens."

"Dad. You've got to let me tell this. If you want to hear it."

"I'm sorry. I'm treating this like a courtroom." He shook his head. "I tend to do that."

No kidding. Then I wasn't wrong all those years.

"Things were so difficult when we got married. The world was so difficult. It was a horrible moment in history. The war going on. The draft. Violent protests at the colleges. Bombings and assassinations. It was a frightening moment to be stepping out into the world. I think that, at another time, we might not have gotten married. Not that we didn't love each other. But we would have waited awhile. But things were so bad then that we wanted to face it together. If we weren't tight together we might get blown apart."

If I was going to Canada I wanted Sara to go with me. And she wanted to go.

"I didn't know what I wanted to do," I said.

"I could have helped you with that," the Senator said.

"But we're not going to talk about that. You promised your wife."

"I know."

"You might as well have that beef stew if you're going to talk about that. You might as well have the cheesecake."

"Don't tempt me."

"Anyway. It took us years to decide what we wanted. To decide who we were. To grow up, I suppose you could say. It took me years to find out where I stood with my writing. By the time I did, Sara was a different person. She started out as this young woman who didn't care what she did. That was the woman I married. Then she went through a period in graduate school where she started to believe in herself, she gained in confidence, she believed in her intellect and her abilities. She was doing that with a whole new set of people, who she got very close to. That tended to draw her away from me. But graduate school wasn't right for her. Academia wasn't right. It was when we moved again, and she got in on that business, that she really found herself."

"I don't see what all this has to do with marriage."

"It just made things more complicated. When she spent her whole day just waiting tables or something, things were fine. She came home and wanted to be with me. She loved me just the same as ever. But when she got new interests, when she got around people who shared those interests, when she got passionate about those people and those interests, things changed."

"Couldn't she do that and come home to you?"

"She could have."

"I sure as hell did. For years. Worked all day and came home to my wife."

I wasn't telling him something. A fact absolutely central to the story. That when she came out into the world with those passionate friends, when she started that business, she found a man who wanted to do all that with her. Who shared her interests and shared her passion. Who fell in love with her. I, by some coincidence, was in my zombie period, staggering around trying to finish a novel that would not finish. It was one of the dark moments of my life. Sara asked me, in the midst of all that—trying to save herself, I imagine—if I didn't want to join the business with her. My writing wasn't working out, so why didn't I do that? She could teach me. She didn't understand that I had this thing about writing, I had to discover a way to be a writer, I wouldn't be *me* if I couldn't be a writer. My depressed state was like a hopeless bog to her, the same swamp she had escaped when she fled graduate school. She didn't want to go back to that, even vicariously. She thought I was sinking and wouldn't take the hand that she held out. So she fled into the arms of another man.

I didn't want to explain that to the Senator because he would hear it another way. The only detail that would catch his attention would be the other man. He wouldn't understand what I really believe to have happened, that Sara had become a different—healthier—person and was afraid of falling back and becoming the old one again.

"Women are different," I said.

"Honey, ain't that the truth."

The Senator liked to repeat the expressions of our cleaning woman.

"When they find something like that," I said, "something they're really passionate about, they want the man to do it with them. They want their whole world to go together."

"Has she found someone like that?"

"I don't know. I think so. I'm not really sure. I don't especially like to keep up with it."

That last part, at least, was true.

"Had she found somebody back then? Before you split up?"

The Senator wasn't going to let me off the hook.

"No."

"Had you?"

"What?"

"Did you have somebody else?"

"No." I took a deep breath, slowly let it out. "No one person. I fooled around some. I don't want to make myself sound blameless."

"You're not. You're making Sara sound blameless. You're making the whole thing sound as if it just happened. Nobody did it."

You couldn't get too much past the old man.

"It's such a different world you present me with," he said. "Women going out and having jobs. Being passionately involved in them. Wanting men to do that with them. I'm not saying there's anything wrong with that. But in the old days marriage was the sacred thing. It was the rock everything else was founded on. People changed and became other people, just like now. That's not new. Men and women met and got involved. That's been happening since time began. But you didn't let that affect your marriage. Marriage was the backdrop for all of that. It's not such a high priority anymore. It's one thing among many things."

The man had a point.

"People seem to want so much these days," he said. "Women want their whole lives to go together, you tell me. That's a wonderful wish. It's a nice idea. But it just doesn't happen. We live in a real world here."

Try telling that to one of those women.

"I wasn't a real good husband all the time," I said.

"Who is?"

"I was depressed a lot. Really down. Hard to be around."

"Everybody is. We stick with each other through those times."

I was touched by the way the Senator was standing up for me. He'd never done that before.

"And the sex," I said. "The sex wasn't good." I wanted to be as honest as I could. I wished I could be *really* honest. "We were pretty different."

"Yes. Well. It's not always a good match. I understand that."

I bet he did.

"Even that, people make too much of," he said. "How important is sex, anyway? Do you want to let it run your life?"

"I don't know. To me it was pretty important."

One of the great understatements of the twentieth century.

Married Love

I met her at the airport while we were waiting for a flight home at the end of the school year. I had noticed her around campus. She always wore a sweatshirt and jeans, and looked—with her short compact body, her curly black hair cut short—a little like a boy. She also carried herself like a boy, shoulders hunched and hands stuffed into her pockets, a funny little swagger to her walk. She had a beautiful olive tint to her skin, a hopeful expression in her wide brown eyes. In a crowd she would always be gazing around, as if hopeful of finding a friend, but if somebody met her gaze she always looked down. She was gazing around that day at the airport, but was wearing—somewhat to my surprise—a bright red jumper. She looked like a different person. We got to talking, and arranged to sit together on the plane.

She told me she had just broken up with a guy, a graduate student in her field—studio art—who had been a mentor for her but had treated her badly. He'd had several other girlfriends while he saw her and was very condescending and controlling. He'd fool around with her when *he* felt like it but would never actually screw her because she was a virgin and he was afraid she'd get hopelessly attached to him. (There was an old sexual myth to that effect.) Finally she had given up. Her ambition now was to learn about sex and become a great lover, go back and give him a taste of what might have been, then dump on the stupid bastard. She seemed genuinely unhappy about what had happened—I realized now that she had looked crestfallen around campus in recent weeks—but she had such a whimsical way of talking about it that you had to laugh. I told her I would be writing stories that summer, working in a factory to make some money. She said she was going off to California to live with some friends and find a summer job.

It occurred to me to wonder if I might be able to help her in her ambition.

In August, before school started, she called and told me her father had given her a car over the summer, asked if I wanted a ride down with her. I said I did, and asked her out to dinner. That was the night of the kisses on Mellon Square, spray from the fountains blowing over us in a gusting wind.

Back at her house, we built a fire against the early autumn chill, then sat and watched it, her head on my shoulder. Her hair, after a while, smelled like smoke. Her face got all ruddy and hot. She smiled and closed her eyes as I covered it with kisses.

My dorm room was a tiny single, virtually filled by a bed, a desk, and a dresser. Sara and I had to sneak in, since women weren't allowed in the men's dorms, but my room was on the first floor, next to the entrance. At night, with all the lights off, we could open the curtains and illumine the room by the lights on the quad. Nobody could see in. We would latch the door and ignore what went on around us. We didn't even answer a knock.

My only real sexual experience at that point had been with that blowsy, boozy woman poet, who had taken me back to her motel room after her reading. Her body was saggy, her kisses wet and tonguey, tasting of scotch and tobacco. She had been very funny, made me suck her tits for what seemed like an endless time, gave me explicit and detailed instructions in oral sex, but we'd had only the most perfunctory of couplings. She must have sensed it was my first time but was nice enough not to say anything. She praised my performance and my body, told me I was a beautiful boy. "You know, lovey," she said. "I really do like tongues better than cocks. And girls better than boys. But it's so hard to pick up a girl at a place like this. They're all so uptight. They don't know what you mean."

She's telling me.

My night with the poet had done nothing to prepare me for the experience of Sara's body.

For a long time Sara would get naked only down to the tights she wore under her jumpers. She liked what we were doing but didn't want to hurry the process. After seeing her only in a sweatshirt and jeans, or in one of the shapeless jumpers she wore on our dates, I couldn't believe what a beautiful body she had, with that olive tone to her skin, the smooth shapely muscles in her shoulders and arms, her flat taut belly, small breasts that were nevertheless beautifully shaped, with lovely brown nipples. She looked like a ballerina in her tights. We would hug and kiss for hours, bare skin to bare skin. I would kiss her breasts, but gently, because her nipples were extremely tender.

It was all right for me to get as naked as I wanted. She loved bare flesh, and had a particular thing for my penis, an organ with which she hadn't had much experience but that she liked for its novelty. She must have thought for a while that they were perpetually erect, because in those days my cock stayed that way—a huge red throbbing erection—by the hour. She was skittish about being asked to do anything in particular with a penis. She wanted to do what *she* liked. One night, when we were locked in an embrace, I started to move rhythmically against her tights. I couldn't help myself. "Is this all right?" I said, and she said it was, though I don't think she knew what I meant. In a few minutes I had the kind of copious gushing orgasm that you have when you're twenty. I got up and fumbled around for a towel.

"I'm sorry I got your tights wet," I said.

No I wasn't.

"It's all right," she said. While I wiped her off she looked at me and smiled. "It got small."

"Yes." Not for long.

"It's cute."

Not the word I would have chosen myself, but I'd take it.

"You know," she said, "I didn't really get all this before. How it was done, exactly. But now I do."

"It's kind of a mess," I said.

"It is. But I like it."

In time the tights came off. Her ass was as smooth and shapely and firm as her breasts. The hair between her legs was a brilliant black, shiny and abundant. I taught her to touch me with her hand, so it was my belly, not hers, that got splattered with semen. (Mine was used to it.) We waited to do more until she felt perfectly ready, and until it was a good time of the month. I couldn't believe, when the night finally came, the incredible intensity of entering her. I came in about five strokes, one of the most satisfying orgasms I'd ever had. She could feel it happen, she said, in my back. Where her hands rested on my back.

"It's so powerful," she said.

"Is it?"

"It's amazing. I've never felt anything like it." She was wearing a huge smile. "So manly." I lay on my back, and she traced her fingertips across my chest. "I loved it," she said. "It didn't hurt or anything." She laid her head on my chest. "I can't believe we finally did it."

I had not had much experience with sex, but I'd read up on the subject avidly and with great interest. Probably no one my age in the world had a greater theoretical knowledge of sex than I, though, as any student of biology knows, theory and practice can be far apart. I knew about the magic little button of flesh on a woman ("The good feeling spot," as a little girl of my acquaintance once described it), and I would gently touch that place with a finger during foreplay, to make Sara wet. One evening when I was touching her, before we made love, she said, "That really feels good tonight. It *really* feels good. I want you to do it for a long time."

Up until then, when we had made love, I would sometimes feel a little flutter in her, or a brief contraction, and say, "Is that an orgasm?" She'd say, "I don't know. I guess so." I knew that this phenomenon existed. I had read about it in any number of places (though some of the older books claimed that, while a man had a spine-snapping orgasm during intercourse, a woman just got a "warm glow" out of the experience).

On this particular evening, while I was touching Sara in a relaxed and desultory way, I could tell that something more was happening than had ever happened before. She was going to a deeper place. Her eyes were closed, and she seemed to be less present with me, more inside herself. She seemed, in fact, to be utterly oblivious of me, making quiet little moans and groans. Her cunt was flooded with moisture. It was all over my hand. Her body seemed to grow tense, like a spring that is being wound tighter and tighter. It felt as if she would snap. Suddenly she went into convulsions. Her hips bucked off the bed; her body jerked all over the place; every muscle she had seemed to be expanding and contracting at once. She had shouted when it started, now made a muffled shrieking sound. I got scared and took my hand away, but she shouted, "Don't stop!" The convulsions went on—though eventually growing milder—for twenty or thirty seconds. Finally they ended. Sara's face was drained, and she was breathless. She looked at me with startled eyes.

"I don't think those other things *were* orgasms," I said.

"No."

"Because I think that was one."

"Yes."

It sure as hell wasn't a warm glow.

A man's orgasm to that was like a pop gun to a cannon. And she had told me mine was powerful.

"What a neat thing," she said.

Sara never did come to like the big wet raunchy kisses that I liked. Her ideal kiss was a gentle one, just the tips of our tongues touching. Her nipples were extremely tender, so it was only with great care that you could suck them. You couldn't do it with passion. She didn't like me to go down on her; she thought that was dirty, and didn't like the sloppy wet feeling of a tongue down there. She didn't like that smell on my face and mouth. She also didn't like to blow me. She said my cock tasted like pee, and that the size of it gagged her. She wouldn't think of letting me come in her mouth, but there was no chance of that anyway, since she would only suck me for a few seconds. She also said, repeatedly—in the kind of whimsical way that was meant to convey an important truth—that if I ever touched her asshole she would leave me.

We would often, in those days, have elaborate and lengthy dates on the weekends. We would go out for dinner and have an enormous meal, half a young spring chicken, fried, with french fries and biscuits. Cheesecake and coffee for dessert. We'd take in a nine o'clock movie. Then we'd go to my room and make love three or four times, with long conversations in between, and still get to her dorm for the two o'clock curfew. It was nothing for us to do all that. We often did it on Friday and Saturday nights. Six or seven acts of intercourse per weekend. By Monday we were ready to dash off to the dorm for a quick one.

Back home we lived forty-five minutes apart, and it was much harder to find privacy. I would visit her house in the country, but in the daytime her mother was around, in the evening both her parents. We were always incredibly hot for each other, would get behind a door and kiss like a couple of maniacs, feel each other up. Once we went for an afternoon drive and stopped by a grassy meadow, perhaps a hundred yards long. It was an out-of-the-way spot, largely surrounded by trees, but the place we walked to was clearly visible from the road. Nevertheless, we took off our pants and did it, humping away fiercely, with only our pants as a blanket against the wet ground. Another time we lay down in the grass behind the garage at her house. The spot we picked wasn't visible from the house, but if Sara's mother had come out to get in her car she would have caught us in the act. She would have been about ten feet away. The long grass tickled our legs. The dog ran around us and yipped. Afterward we pulled on our pants and lay on our backs for a while, staring up at the sky.

We had gotten together as friends—barely acquaintances, actually—who wanted to fuck. Sara wanted to lose her virginity and become a virtuoso lover, and I was more than happy to fuck my brains out. But in the midst of all that fucking, something else happened. We spent all that time in bed, in intimate connection. We were also inseparable out of bed, eating our meals and studying together. We became vital parts of each other's lives. Best friends. You wouldn't have said we fell in love, but we came to love each other, and when it was time to step out and face the world, we wanted to do that together. We hardly had to talk about it. We just knew. I wasn't the love of Sara's life, and she probably wasn't mine—that wasn't a concept I'd given much thought to, since I'd never expected to be loved anyway—but in the world we saw around us, what we had was good. We didn't want to lose it.

Married life was hard. Neither of us had any money from our families at that point, and I don't think we would have used it if we had. We wanted to make it on our own. We lived in a tiny boxlike four-room house, with a cat. Sara worked in a restaurant, I at various places—a library, a bookstore, a bar—where I could keep odd hours and have my mornings for writing. Often at night we would hardly have seen each other by the time we got into bed. We were wrung out and exhausted, too tired to make love, too tense to go to sleep, so we got into the habit—a funny little habit, when you think of it—of just touching each other with our hands. It seemed an activity of about the right intensity for the shape we were in. I had gradually learned from Sara, and no longer touched that one little spot, with my finger, but slowly rubbed the whole area with three or four fingers, moving in a little circle. Sara had gotten as expert at handling a cock as a thirteen-year-old boy. She could stroke it smoothly, intensify what she was doing as she felt the pressure start to build, put pressure on the glans and release it just as I was about to explode. We did it almost every night, right after we went to bed, often without saying a word. It was a nice thing to do for each other, a friendly gesture, like a back rub. It was fun to lie on each other's shoulder and feel the excitement start to build, hear the happy little gasp as it was released.

When I think of the early hard exhausted years of my marriage, I think of that one thing, lying in bed and making each other come so we could go to sleep.

When you are young you have so much energy, your dreams are so fresh and strong that they can take a terrific battering.

They cannot take an endless battering. The realities of life wear you down over time. Time itself wears you down. I had written dozens of stories that had been rejected everywhere; I had written for that little newspaper that had a narrow prestige and almost no money; I had poured my heart into three hundred pages of a novel that wound up going nowhere. As I gradually, over the course of two or three months, saw that project dissolve in my hands, I found myself standing at the edge of an abyss. I looked into my future and saw an endless blackness. I felt tiny in the face of it. I felt it would swallow me up.

If you stare long enough into that abyss, you undergo a change. It isn't that you see something emerge. It is that you accept the emptiness. You realize that the emptiness is what *is*. It isn't supposed to be some other way. You really are tiny in the face of it. You are minuscule. But it doesn't swallow you up. You remain what you are. A minuscule being in the face of an endless blackness.

The trick is not to go out of your mind before you have that realization.

I grew a knot in my chest, just beneath my breastbone. It felt as if someone had reached into my chest and gripped the muscles there, not terribly hard, but persistently. Sometimes, in moments of stress, it tightened into a burning. Sometimes it diminished until I could barely feel it, just one finger, or two, pressing beneath my breastbone. But it never ended.

Who is this guy who has ahold of me? I thought. What does he want?

I saw several doctors, who had various names for what I had, various remedies. They filled me with medicines and put me on diets. One went so far as to take an X ray, which involved elaborate machinery and hours of time. I lay strapped to a motorized table that moved around, tilted me at all kinds of bizarre angles, while doctors in another room looked at my insides on a screen. They sat forward in their seats and stared, looking for what was wrong. They saw nothing.

I was suffering from rage at the world. It doesn't show up in an X ray. I'd had a dream of the way my life was supposed to be, and the world had betrayed me. It had broken my heart. What I needed was to roar and breathe fire, shout out my rage, beat the living piss out of the world. I could have used a shovel or something. It wouldn't have done the world much harm, and it would have done me a great deal of good. But I didn't know that then. I didn't know I was full of rage. I thought I just had a stomachache. I thought I had no right to be angry (anger doesn't ask about its rights), that I was just another lousy writer with delusions of grandeur. In order to quiet my rage, which was boiling beneath the surface like a volcano, I had to hold it in. I had to cut it off precisely at the spot where it would emerge, at the top of my stomach, beneath the breastbone.

I was the person doing the gripping. I was gripping myself. Why didn't I let go?

The knot in my chest sometimes kept me from sleeping. It woke me up early (which left me tired and increased my stress and tightened the knot). One morning, as I lay beside Sara with all the ease and flexibility of a concrete slab, she opened her eyes and was immediately awake. I had been awake for hours. She had just had an incredibly sexy dream, which she proceeded to tell me in glowing detail while she threw off her nightgown and turned my way. We often made love in the morning. It was in many ways our favorite time. Sara felt so good in my arms, and the morning felt so good—a spring breeze drifting in the window—and I wanted so much *to* feel good, that I pretended I did. I pretended I was there in my body, which I wasn't (I had retreated up into my head, away from the pain). As I rolled over on Sara, I pretended that my three-quarters erect penis, which looked roughly like a real erection, actually had some feeling in it, which it didn't. I wouldn't have wanted to disappoint her, after all. I wouldn't have wanted to let her down sexually. I wouldn't have wanted her to know how much pain I was in. That might have scared her. (I tried to spare my wife from the pain I was going through. I felt I should be able to take it by myself. I thereby cut her off from the deepest part of my life.) So when I slipped inside her and felt myself immediately start to come, when I felt myself coming and getting smaller at the same time, I thought, *What* is *this*? I came not with that enormous surge that roars through your body, like a wave crashing against the shore, but with a tiny little ripple, way off in some distant part of my body (did a pin drop?). As I hovered above Sara, I felt myself flush, sweat popping out all over my body. I wanted to hide my head. I wanted to crawl into a hole somewhere. I felt shame.

"What's wrong?" Sara said, an air of concern in her eyes. She meant, What's wrong with you? With your spirit? What's this sudden flush, sweat popping out on your body?

I thought she meant, What the hell happened to your cock? I collapsed beside her. "I don't know."

This phenomenon is what the world calls premature ejaculation. It is about two steps up from the basement floor. The basement floor is impotence.

I thought: I can't write, I can't eat what I want, I can't sleep. Now I can't even fuck.

A man in this situation thinks, What happened to my penis? The answer is: Nothing. Your penis is the center of your body, and your body has a wisdom that your brain doesn't. It knows things that your brain hasn't noticed. ("He thinks with his dick" should not be an insult, if a man is whole.) My rage was coming between me and my cock, and I kept trying to go around it, function as if the rage didn't exist. My cock was saying, You can't do that anymore. I won't let you do it. I don't need the whole person with me to function, but I sure as hell need more than this. I can't do anything when you're huddled off in your head, hiding from your pain and your rage.

Accept your rage, my body was saying. Acknowledge it. Let yourself feel it. But I was afraid to do that. It felt like pain, for one thing. Nobody wants to feel pain. I was also afraid of what it might lead me to. I was afraid of what I might do. I was afraid that if I started to roar I would never stop.

A man whose penis isn't working, who is cut off from his sexuality, will do anything to get that feeling back. He will go through any contortion. His penis is *him*, as he knows at some deep level. If he doesn't have that, what does he have? A man also, at difficult moments in his life, has a way of getting things confused that don't essentially have anything to do with each other. If he can't succeed in *this* (his career), if all his hopes and dreams have been shattered, he will by God succeed in *that* (the sexual realm—he will become one of the great fuckers of women on earth). He takes energy from the one and uses it for the other. It is also the case that, if he is feeling rage in his body but doesn't want to admit its true source—doesn't want to admit (it's so humiliating!) that the world has shattered his hopes—he may direct that rage toward other people. Writers who have succeeded, for example. Those crummy bastards who have kept him from getting what he wants. Or people who are close to him. Easily accessible objects of anger. His wife.

"I want to eat you," he said.

In anger, in fatigue—for the thousandth time—she closed her eyes. "No."

"Why can't we at least try it?"

"Because I don't like it. I've told you a million times I don't like it."

"Everybody else likes it."

"I'm not everybody else."

"I wish you *were* everybody else."

How had he wound up with the one person in the world who wouldn't do this thing he liked so much?

"When you want to do this," she said, "you're not really here with me. You're off in your head with one of your dream women. If you were really here with me, if you really wanted to be with me, you'd want to do what I want."

"I want you to be my dream woman for a while. That would be so wonderful to me. I'd love you forever if you'd do that."

"I'd like you to love me for what I am."

"Couldn't you do this for me? Out of love?"

"That wouldn't be love. That would be make-believe. I'd be a whore."

"What's wrong with a little make-believe?"

"I want you to be *here*. With *me*. I never feel you here with me. If you could do that, if you could be more with me, it might be more like you want."

Bullshit. It would never be like what he wanted.

"Besides," she said. "If it weren't this it would be something else. I'd do this and you'd go to the next thing. You'd find another thing I don't want to do. And you'd harp on that. You'd keep going until you found something. You want to have something to be angry about."

He honestly believed he would be happy if he got that one

thing. Or maybe two things, on the outside. He couldn't understand why she wouldn't at least try. Was he never going to have anything in this world that he wanted?

A woman feels love and wants to have sex. A man has sex and comes to feel love. In the normal course of things, this delicate distinction gets blurred over. It all just kind of happens together, love and sex. But if a man and woman grow too far apart, the distinction looms larger. There is no way to get them back together. It is what you call a Mexican stand-off. Nobody moves.

You can't suck her tits you can't eat her pussy you can't so much as brush by her asshole she won't suck your cock. What else is there? What's left?

Those long nights in the dorm room, the curtains open, moonlight streaming in on the rumpled bed, the endless conversations, quiet laughter, all that happy fucking. What happened?

When you are fucking a woman who no longer loves you, who doesn't want to fuck you, who doesn't want to be there beneath you, you can feel it. You can feel the boundaries on her body. Touch the wrong place and she goes dead. You can feel the body's profound uneasiness beneath you. It squirms. It sweats. It would like to throw you off. It would like to throw you through the roof. You are using this body. You can feel that you are using it. You are not fucking a person. You are fucking a hole in the middle of a body. You work hard above it—sweating, groaning—trying to finish so you can get off and leave it alone. You have gotten the message. Finally you gasp at your climax, and you hear the body beneath you heave a large sigh. It is not a sigh of pleasure. It is a sigh of relief. It says, Thank God *that's* over. I don't have to do *that* anymore.

Such an act does not bring you closer to someone. It drives you further away. Until finally, one day, she is gone altogether.

When my marriage had ended, when Sara had been gone for about three months, I met my therapist late one afternoon when everyone else had left the building. I'd been seeing him at that point for almost a year. He closed the doors; I loosened my clothes; he handed me a foam-rubber encounter bat. For the next forty minutes, while he urged me on, I beat the living piss out of his office. I roared. I screamed. I stomped the floor. I shouted out all my irrational hatred and bitterness. I shouted at him. I shouted at the world. I tore into it. When I finally finished, my voice was gone, and every muscle in my body was exhausted—I could hardly stand—but I also felt, for the first time in years, utterly relaxed. I felt whole and together. My body was mine, in a way that it hadn't been for as long as I could remember. And my cock felt heavy. Hanging there like a slab of meat. There was much more to do. There were many more feelings to explore, over a long period of grief. But they all started in that blind wordless rage.

SEVEN

I once contemplated divorce," the Senator
said.

Lunch was over. I had taken the dishes
out and put them in the dishwasher,
cleaned up the kitchen. ("I'll just sit here and take my pills,"
the Senator said. "You'll probably be done before I will.") We
made the slow trek from the dining room, but this time went
to the Senator's study, which also serves as the spare bedroom, since the couch folds out. It was a large, crowded, comfortable room, with floor-to-ceiling bookcases, the Senator's
cluttered desk against one wall, a huge television, a state-of-
the-art stereo system. There was even a small bar in one corner. The Senator insisted I have a cognac after lunch, though
that is hardly my practice. (I usually have bread and cheese
and fruit for lunch. Water to drink.) I sat there in the kind
of pleasant stupor I'm in whenever I have alcohol for lunch.
Then he dropped that bomb on me.

I tried not to blink or wince or anything. I tried not to fall
out of my chair.

"When was that?"

"Oh. A few years back. Ten or twelve. Maybe fifteen. When

DAVID GUY

all the boys had gone off to college. We were in that big house
alone."

I was not unaware that, a few minutes before, the Senator
had told me his generation didn't do divorce. Marriage was
the bedrock for the other aspects of their lives.

He was sitting on the couch holding his cane in front of
him, looking perfectly matter-of-fact.

"It was a strange moment for me. A difficult moment. I
know I'd never been all that active a father. Home all the
time playing with the kids or something. Being a boy scout
leader. It wasn't that I didn't want to. I just didn't have the
time." He'd been pretty good, as fathers go. He used to schedule his appointments around our activities. Games and recitals. "Certainly, by that time, there wasn't much to do. Big
teenage boys. But I'd always loved the bustle of a family. The
confusion of it. Coming home to a big house and never knowing who might be there. Who was over for dinner. Shooting
pool or playing Ping-Pong. Shooting baskets out back. I loved
being around all that. I really missed it as it diminished. Just
two boys, then one boy, in the house. Then none. I knew they
had to go. I wanted them to go. But I missed them.

"I guess this is an awful thing to say. I wouldn't say it to
a whole lot of people. I don't think I'd even say it to your
brothers. But I always hated the nights everybody was gone,
and I was home alone with your mother. Especially at the
dinner table. It was always so easy with the boys around. We
could talk about sports or girls or something. School. But
when it was just your mother and me, at that huge dining-
room table. It was as if we'd lost touch with each other, in
all those years of having the family around. She didn't want
to hear about my work. I wasn't interested in what she was
doing. Whatever in God's name that might have been. We
couldn't have a social engagement every evening, though we
sometimes tried. So we'd sit there trying to think of something to say. After thirty years, or whatever it had been. The
silence was palpable. It filled the room. I sometimes thought
it would drive me out of my mind.

"Then when Todd was gone. Off to Dartmouth. And nobody
was left. All I could think of was that every night was going
to be like that for the rest of my life. Until I died. I'd be
sitting in that dining room trying to think of something to

132

say. To a woman who had already heard everything I knew. And with whom, at that point, I wasn't all that interested in communicating." He looked up at me. "Does this sound awful?"

"It sounds natural."

"It doesn't mean I didn't love your mother."

"I know. It also doesn't take thirty years to happen. Four or five can do it."

"But at that point you have kids. And the kids take up the attention. The kids make the noise."

Some people have kids.

"There were times," the Senator said, "I swear to God, when I'd have done anything not to face that prospect. I'd stay downtown and pretend to work. Eat in a restaurant by myself. I have no doubt your mother felt the same way. You could feel the tension in that room. And after Todd was gone, there was a period of time when it seemed so bad that I would have made a major change. I would have ended my marriage. Thrown the whole thing off. Just so I wouldn't have to face that silence for the rest of my life."

Those are the times when another woman begins to look good. It isn't just that she's younger or prettier. It's that she hasn't heard all your conversation. You're starting from scratch.

She'll be so impressed.

"I think this is why I wanted you to come back," the Senator said.

"What?"

"Why I wanted you to come back and live here. Be an attorney."

"Wait a minute. When was this?"

"I don't mean just at that moment. I'm not talking about a specific time. I'm talking about that wish in general. Anytime I felt it."

He thought *I* was going to come back and sit at that dining-room table with the two of them? He was nuts.

"The way things are set up these days is all out of whack," he said. "Society in general. It's strange to this century, to say nothing of human history. We keep kids around too long for one thing. Any other culture in the history of the human race, you're a man when you're thirteen or fourteen. Even in my father's generation, not too long ago, a lot of men were out working by then. Nowadays you've got to go to graduate school. At least one. You're not on your own till you're twenty-five or thirty. On the other hand, in the old days, and I swear to God there's some connection here, people didn't go so far when they did leave. It wasn't so hard to break away, maybe because you hadn't been there that long. You didn't have to go to California or something. A man had a farm, say. His son settled down and farmed with him. They'd build him a house. Or in the city, a man had a hardware store. Jones Hardware. Pretty soon it was Jones and Son."

We were treading right on the edge of a dangerous subject.

"What if the son didn't like the hardware business?" I said. "What if he wasn't good at it?"

"That's a different thing. I don't mean that isn't possible, or that it couldn't have happened. I'm just saying that what I wanted was natural. To have my son around. My daughter. Maybe some grandchildren, for God's sake. Everybody kind of huddled together. Seeing each other a lot. So there aren't just two people in the dining room. Or at least that isn't always the way it is."

Then what he got was a son who never wanted to see him. A daughter he didn't especially want to see.

"I always felt you wanted me to *be* somebody else," I said. "Some other person. The man I had become wasn't good enough."

"I didn't mean to make you feel that way. I don't think I really meant it that way. I'm sorry."

There were some unprecedented things going on that day. An apology, yet.

"I think I just wanted a family around me," he said.

"So what happened?" I said.

"When?"

"Back then. When you were contemplating divorce."

"Oh. Yes. Well. I don't know if you'd say I was contemplating divorce."

"That's what *you* said."

"I suppose it is." The Senator rubbed his chin. "And I suppose that is the truth of the matter. It just startles me. Even me. To hear it."

What I really wondered was whether there was more to

this story than he was telling. A woman in the picture. But that was something—even on a day when we were being so frank—that I couldn't bring myself to ask.

The Senator heaved a huge sigh. "I suppose you'd just say I got used to it. I think it was actually a larger anxiety I was facing. I wasn't really worried about making conversation at the dining-room table. I was worried that my life was over. No more people around. No warm family feeling. That dining room was like a tomb. There was some truth to all that of course. Part of my life *was* over. I can see why men go a little crazy in that situation. Run after a new woman. Try to start over. I guess the thing that saved me was trying to picture an alternative. Moving to an apartment. Living in one of my clubs." Jesus. "It all sounded so sordid and depressing. It sounded worse than what I had."

"Did the feeling get better?"

"I'm not sure something like that does get better. It just gets numb. The thing that once looked so terrifying becomes banal. You grow accustomed to the silence. And as it turned out, of course, the boys did come back. Two of them, anyway. I'm certainly glad at this point that I didn't do anything foolish. Your mother's been a tremendous help during my illness. I don't know what I'd have done without her."

It was an interesting question, whether having someone around during your illness was worth what had happened earlier. Enduring a silence, which led to a numbness, which killed whatever feeling you had left between you. So you lived without feeling. Was that a life worth living?

That was the question.

My parents did seem different together now, in the little I'd seen them. Closer, and more at ease.

"Was it lonely for you?" the Senator said. "Being without a wife all of a sudden. After all those years."

"It was."

"How did you handle it?"

Badly.

"It's like what you're saying," I said. "It doesn't really get better. You get used to it."

"Is it what you want?"

"I want to be able to handle it. So I don't *have* to have somebody."

The Senator and I had never talked so frankly. He wouldn't have asked me about such things even a few months before. His illness seemed to have changed him.

His new attitude made me bolder.

"What is it that's going on at work?" I said.

"What's that?"

"Helen says you've had a problem there. Some kind of stress. She thinks it might have had something to do with bringing on your illness."

"Oh, I don't know. I don't think that. It's kind of a minor thing. A supposed conflict of interest. One case we were handling, or at least one client, supposedly compromised what we were doing in another. It's the kind of thing that happens in a large firm. Your right hand doesn't know what your left is doing. At the most it was an impropriety. Something we should have noticed but didn't. I can't be sure how the Bar will see it. But I don't think it amounts to a hill of beans."

The way the Senator was speaking undercut his words. Ever since I'd arrived that morning, he had been different with me than ever before, at least in recent memory. More human. Man-to-man. It is the way someone becomes who has been through a life-shattering experience. He strips away the bullshit and gets down to the real person. But in talking about work—perhaps *because* he was talking about work—he had slipped into that blustery, tough, everything's-under-control manner that men have. Lawyers especially. I don't mean that what he was saying wasn't true. But there was something funny about it.

Almost immediately, though, he changed back.

"Why don't you stick around a while?" he said.

"Today?"

"Not today. I'm supposed to take a nap about now. I don't miss that nap. I mean in general. Stick around in Pittsburgh. I don't think you want to stay *here.*" He gestured around the room. "It's not that comfortable. But I could put you up at a club. Or maybe Helen would have you. One of your brothers. Someplace you could make yourself at home, and do your writing."

I'm fairly flexible in that regard. When I *can* write, I can do it almost anywhere.

"I've got some time now," he said. "I hope to go back to

work eventually, though probably not full-time. But I'm not going in at all at the moment. We have a chance to talk, which we haven't had for years." To say nothing of the fact that we hadn't wanted to. "We might not have this opportunity again. You can see your mother now, see your sister. You can see the old hometown. You've got nothing pulling you anyplace else, at least not that you've mentioned. It's a perfect opportunity."

It did seem a unique moment in our lives, most of all because—if that afternoon was any indicator—we were getting along in a new way. I was pleased, and touched, that he had asked. But I must admit that, when he did ask, the first thing I thought of was that, if I stayed, I would get to see Andrea again. She had been at the back of my mind all day, like a faint scent of flowers drifting in a window. I had hardly expected to come up to the city and run into someone I'd be so attracted to. I hadn't been looking. I wouldn't have expected to find someone who was not only available but—how should I put this?—ripe. Eager. Most surprising of all, though, so surprising that I hadn't quite taken it in yet, was a deeper feeling I got from her, of freedom and abandon. There had been a time in my life when I had looked for that feeling desperately, in all kinds of impossible places. I had done everything I could to find it. Finally I came up against the hard truth that I wasn't going to find it, that there was something in the way I was looking—or in looking at all—that made it all hopeless. I wouldn't get that feeling from a woman. I would have to find it within myself. I had lived with that truth for months, lived by myself for months, peered into the nooks and crannies of who I was and examined what was there. Now that I had done all that, now that I had given up on finding what I was looking for in a woman, I had found it. There was a certain irony—also a deep truth—to all of that. I had once thought my heart would break if I didn't find that feeling. But I didn't find it until I didn't need it anymore. I didn't find it until I stopped looking.

"Helen's been talking about this possibility too," I said. "She said she'd put me up."

"Sounds perfect."

"I *will* have to see if I can write."

"Of course."

I was leaving myself an out.

"But I think I would like to try it. I think I'd like to stay here for a while."

"Charles, I'm delighted." The Senator beamed. "I think this is a wonderful chance for us."

"I do too."

He held out his hand, and I took it. We smiled at each other for a moment, gripping hands.

"It also makes me feel less guilty now. Because I'm really enjoying this visit. But I've got to take that nap."

"No problem. I've got things I can do."

"Maybe we can have lunch again tomorrow. Or dinner. Something."

I stood first, and hoisted him from the couch. That was no easy task. We made our way slowly into the bedroom. He took off his shoes and lay down on the bed, closed his eyes. Anyone, it seems—no matter what his size—looks a little like a child, helpless and vulnerable, when he gets into bed. I pulled a blanket up over him. I had never put my father to bed before. Almost immediately, before I was even out of the room, he fell asleep and started to snore, loud enough to bring the walls down. I'd had no idea he snored that loud. At least I didn't have to tiptoe away.

To get out of that building, you press a button by the elevator. A buzzer starts to ring and doesn't stop until one of the doormen heads up. I had collected my hat and coat by the time he arrived.

Down in the lobby, the Duchess was waiting for me, in a little alcove with a couch and some chairs. She still had her overcoat on. She seemed just to have gotten in. She smiled as she saw me, what you would call a polite smile. No real spirit behind it. I went in and sat across from her.

"Did your father get down for his nap?" she said.

"He did."

That must have been how she knew I'd be coming down.

"How does he seem to you?"

"He seems great. Maybe just because I was expecting something worse. He does move more slowly."

"He's being cautious."

"But he looks good."

"This is a good day for him. He doesn't always look so well. He's really been looking forward to seeing you."

The Duchess herself didn't seem terribly happy to see me. Maybe it had nothing to do with me. There were new lines of worry around her eyes. She seemed tired in a way that I hadn't seen her before. The Duchess rarely looked tired. She also seemed distracted. Fidgety. Moving around as she sat, and fiddling with things in her pocketbook. She avoided my eyes.

"There's one thing I wanted to talk to you about," she said, "before you see your father much more. It's something I have a difference of opinion about with Helen. An honest difference of opinion. I know she means well, and that she wants only the best for your father. But I think it would be best if both of you, and I've mentioned this to her, don't ask about problems he's having at work."

Another reason to think they were more serious than he was letting on.

"Helen seems to have the idea that everybody needs to talk about everything. That if you just talk about something you'll make it all better. I'm sure she's right about some things, though I personally have never been one to bare my soul." Truer words were never spoken. "But I really think in this case. Since he's staying home from work expressly to get away from all that. That it might be better if we didn't bring it up."

By we, she meant Helen and me.

"I understand," I said.

"It isn't as if he wants to talk about it."

"I hadn't realized it was such an issue. I asked about it, but I didn't press him. I won't ask again."

"Thank you, Charles." She stood. "I knew you'd understand." She gave me a little kiss on the cheek. "We're so glad you came for a visit. We hope you'll stay a long time."

"I think I will. A while, anyway."

"That's wonderful."

As long as I didn't bring up the thing from work.

I must admit to a little impatience at that point. I do love the city, and I had loved my walk that morning, especially because it had cleared my head and refreshed me. I probably needed my head cleared again, what with all the alcohol I'd

DAVID GUY

had. But now that things had gone so well and I'd decided to stay, now that I knew I'd be seeing Andrea again—or at least that I wanted to—I didn't want to take a leisurely walk. I didn't want to stroll through the old neighborhood. I wanted to get downtown as fast as I could.

I had the doorman get me a cab, a rare extravagance for me. And I didn't take it back to the busway, as I could have. I had it take me straight downtown. Not to my hotel, but to Andrea's store.

I stopped outside the door for a moment to look in on her. The weary discouraged woman I had seen the day before, with her fuck-you posture, now looked relaxed and at ease. There was color to her face, a certain contentment just in the way she held her body. She was apparently wearing contacts, or at least not wearing those large-framed spectacles. She also had on a bright turquoise sweater over black pants.

When I stepped into the store, though, and she saw who it was, a look of fear came into her eyes.

"You're leaving," she said.

"I just got here."

"I mean leaving town. I'm not surprised, after all you told me. How hard things are with your father. I'm only surprised you stopped in to see me. You wouldn't believe how many men wouldn't do that. They not only don't send flowers the next day, they don't call. Ever again. Just think how *that* makes a woman feel. After she's given her body to this prick."

I'm fine, how are you?

We were in our anti-man phase again. Once again proving that the best defense is a good offense.

"I'm staying," I said.

"What?"

"I'm not leaving town. I'm moving in with my sister."

"For how long?"

"I don't know. As long as she'll have me. As long as I feel like it."

Andrea had brightened. Her face relaxed. She still had a trace of fear in her eyes.

"When did you decide?" she said.

"About twenty minutes ago."

"When you were back with your father."

"Yes."

"And you came right away to see me."

"I haven't even told my sister."

"Charles." She threw her head back and looked at the ceiling. When she looked back at me, her eyes had softened. She looked as if she were about to cry. "You are one in a million."

She walked to where I was standing in the middle of the store, threw her arms around my neck, and kissed me. This was a wide-open store, with a huge display window, in the middle of a city. And this was no small kiss. It was a long wet sloppy kiss, her arms tight around my neck, her tongue darting everywhere.

By the time she had finished, I was breathless.

"I'm going to close the store for a few minutes," she said.

"Why?"

"So I can take you upstairs and blow you."

I only hoped there weren't any customers lurking in the magazine alcove.

"That's because I don't have any rubbers," she said. "If I had any rubbers I'd fuck you."

"I could get some."

"No. I think you deserve this. Something all for you. A woman on her knees."

She walked to the door, flipped the sign from "Open" to "Closed," and latched it.

"You're sure I deserve it," I said. I liked that concept.

"Absolutely."

"Why?"

"Because you came back to see me. I'd have blown you if you were taking the next plane out of town. Just for coming back. Because you made me feel good last night. Attractive and sexy and wanted. Because I've been waiting all morning to set eyes on you again. Your pretty little face. Because I've felt terrible for months, sad and depressed and in pain, and now I feel hopeful again. Back in my body. You put me in my body." I also put *me* in her body. "Because you decided to stay in town, and came to tell me. Because you looked so happy to see me. Because you have such a magnificent cock. Who *knows* why I'm going to do it. I just have a strong feeling it's going to happen."

Saying all this, she had walked up a stairway to a tiny attic and was stooped under a low ceiling, moving empty boxes around to make a little space on the floor. "We've got to improvise a little here," she said. I had taken off my coat and sportcoat, my hat and scarf.

"This place isn't even big enough to stand up in," I said.

"You're not going to stand up." She looked back at me. "Unless that's the way you've got to have it."

"No."

"Then I'm going to put you on your back. Make sure you're good and comfortable. And take you on a trip to heaven." She had guided me back onto the floor. "I'm very good at this," she said.

"I bet you are."

"It's just my little way of saying thank you."

It isn't always better to say it with flowers.

Illicit Love

The building caught my attention the first time I saw it, sitting out in the scrubby Carolina countryside, down a two-lane road from a gas station and a diner. "Massage," it said, on a battered sign out front. "All Girl Staff." There was something terribly ordinary about it, a cinderblock building ten minutes from town. There was also—to my mind at least—something fascinating about it. The small door to that building led into a vast wicked world that I'd always wondered about. I couldn't believe it was sitting so matter-of-factly out on that little country road.

The woman who met me at the door looked barely twenty. She was tall and thin, had a plain narrow face and dirty blond hair, a long hooked nose that had been badly broken. She wore sandals and a skimpy bathing suit and was extremely shy, averting her eyes the whole time we spoke. She told me the prices for various services—a topless massage, nude massage, two-girl massage—none of which mentioned sex, though they all suggested it. I chose the twenty-minute topless session, the cheapest. She took me into a small room with a king-sized bed, told me to get comfortable. Beside the bed was a small table with a can of talcum powder and a bottle of oil. The walls were lined with mirrors.

When the masseuse came back—I was lying on my stomach on the bed—she had me move over and knelt beside me. I could see her best if I watched in the mirror. She pulled down the straps of her bathing suit and lowered it to her waist. She had tiny but shapely breasts, a flat hard stomach. Her ribs stood out. She sprinkled me with powder, went over my big muscles hard, with her hands, then gently, with her fingertips. She knew all the right places to touch. Eventually she had me spread my legs and knelt between them, concentrated on a small space from my ass down the insides of my thighs. Her fingers would tickle and probe between my legs and along the cleft of my ass. She had a wonderful way of prickling with her fingernails. She would reach carefully up under me to caress my balls. The whole time she touched me, her eyes—I watched them in the mirror—were lowered, as if modestly.

By the time she had me turn over I was terribly excited, my cock throbbing and twitching. She still didn't raise her eyes, slowly went over the front of my body as if she hadn't noticed my excitement. She spent a long time on my nipples, brushing them with the flat of her hand, tugging and pinching. A woman had never touched me there before. I didn't know what was going to happen, whether she was going to get up and leave me that way, whether I was supposed to say something, but when she had finished with the rest of my body she reached for the oil and poured some into her hand as matter-of-factly as she had done everything else. She glanced up into my eyes—for the one and only time—as she rubbed the oil onto my cock, then looked back down again. She tickled my balls with her fingernails while her other hand stroked me. I stared in fascination at her impassive face. As I groaned and was about to come she heaved one huge sigh and flushed, as if finally, briefly, excited. She kept stroking until I was finished.

Afterward I asked if I could have touched her and she said sure. Most guys just did it. She said that if I got a nude massage I could touch anywhere I wanted. I asked if she ever did anything besides massage and she said no. She didn't know about the other girls. I asked her name and she said it was Becky. She hoped I would come and see her again.

As I left I told her my name. I thought it strange that she hadn't asked.

In the university library where I worked, there was a woman named Peg who had the same day off I did—we both worked Saturdays—and a similar love of books. She was an amateur sculptor, with a large strong body, a bright friendly face, what seemed like boundless energy. Anyone who could remain cheerful while filing call slips had to have something going for her. She had been divorced a year before, was five or six years older than I. We took to meeting for coffee on our free afternoons, after I had written and she had worked at the studio, then I would walk her home to her little duplex. We started off talking about books and art, eventually got into more private matters. She talked about her divorce. She seemed remarkably cheerful for someone who had been through such hard times. She often said how wonderful and unusual it was to have found a man friend who was interested in the arts. At the end of the afternoon she always gave me a big hard hug, in what seemed an overflow of high spirits. She felt strong and passionate.

One afternoon it was raining when we got back to her place, and we stepped inside for a moment. At the end of our hug, without really thinking what I was doing—though I had often fantasized such a moment—I kissed her. We looked at each other—startled—then kissed again. Her mouth opened wide and sucked in my tongue. We stumbled back into the living room, our mouths still pressed tight together, and fell onto the daybed. I had grown instantly excited, shoved myself against her; she grabbed me through my pants, then pushed me away, pulled up her skirt and took off her underpants. I took off my pants and, without a word, plunged into her. We fucked like crazy, groaning and shouting. I finished quickly and fell onto the bed beside her. We were both breathless. "God," she said after a while. "I don't believe I did that." I had to get up and leave almost immediately. She was flushed and beaming as we said good-bye at the door, gave me a long passionate kiss.

The next day at the library, though, she was red-eyed and teary, would hardly speak to me. It took most of the day to get her off alone and ask what was wrong.

"I can't see you anymore," she said.

"Why not?"

"For the obvious reason. You're married."

"That didn't seem to bother you yesterday afternoon."

That was a mean thing to say. I was hurt.

"I forgot myself," she said. "I don't know what happened. I just wanted it so much."

"Why should it bother you if it doesn't bother me? That I'm married."

"It puts us in an unequal situation. You have someone to go home to. I don't."

"You had me for the afternoon."

"That didn't help me any last night. When I was all alone."

"Isn't it better to have somebody some of the time?"

"No. It just makes me feel lonelier. It makes me notice what I don't have."

"But it was so much fun. It was wonderful."

"It *was* wonderful. But it can't happen again."

"We don't have to make love. We could just get together and talk."

"You don't really mean that. Even if you think you do. You'd still want to do it. I'd still want to do it. We'd wind up doing it. You don't go back from this."

"Would that be so bad, if we both wanted to?"

"It gives me pain, don't you understand that? I'm not going to give myself pain." She sobbed. "This is hard for me. I liked our afternoons so much. And I want a sexual relationship. I want one terribly. But this can't be it."

"I don't get it."

"Someday you will. Someday you'll understand."

At the bookstore where I worked, a woman named Denise Morris often stopped by late in the afternoon. She taught music and gave piano lessons at a local college. She was a slender blond woman, quiet and demure, but very much at ease, very friendly. She read avidly but on a limited income; she only bought mass-market paperbacks, but would buy the hot titles as soon as they came out. She was the kind of reader I loved to talk to, intelligent and enthusiastic, but utterly unacademic. She must have read rapidly, because she bought books two or three times per week. One evening we walked out together and wound up having coffee. After a while that got to be something we did regularly.

She asked if I did any writing myself. I was at a point in my life where I rarely spoke of my writing—it was too embarrassing—but she seemed a safe person. I told her about everything, the countless unpublished stories, the novel in which I had passed the two-hundred-page mark. She didn't say something stupid, like that she was sure I would publish something someday, just listened sympathetically. She told me she had composed music for the piano, but had never performed it. Performing, in fact, was a phobia of hers; she hadn't done it for years, and even got someone else to accompany the school chorus. I told her of Helen's music career, and of its abrupt end. She said there had been times when she'd wanted to give up music too, but there had never been anything else she thought she could do.

She said she would like to read something I'd written. I told her I didn't want to give her anything unfinished, but might show her a story or two. I said I would like to hear some of her music. She said that was very scary for her, but thought about it for a minute and said that if I was willing to take the risk maybe she would too. She ought to be able to handle an audience of one. She'd probably want to start with somebody else's work, then move on to her own. She did say we'd have to schedule it when her housemate wasn't there. Her housemate was an old friend from graduate school. They'd lived together for years.

I began, on my visits to that little building in the country, to get a longer, slightly more expensive massage, where Becky was naked and I got to touch her too. However lean, her body was lovely, with a hard narrow back and muscular legs. She had a small ass, flat as a boy's, soft as a baby's. I would try to massage her as she had massaged me, hard at first, then gently, with a delicate touch. "You don't know how good that feels," she would say.

"Yes I do," I would say.

She wasn't in the least bit squeamish about how, or where, I touched her. As she lay on her stomach I would spread her legs and kneel between them, touch however I wanted. "It's fun just to look," I'd say.

"Yeah," she'd say.

When she turned over I would suck her tough little nipples. She would work on mine too, tugging at them roughly, digging in with a thumbnail. Thrills of pleasure ran down my body. Eventually we would lie in a close embrace, her long limbs wrapped around me, and she would work a slippery hand down to my cock. She had a way of making me come violently, so my body jumped against hers. Beside my ear, she would gasp. My semen clung stickily to our bellies.

When my stomach hurt, for the two years that it hurt nearly all the time, the only thing that made it feel better was a woman's embrace. Any woman's. When I held her against me, pressed her body to that place, the pain disappeared, as if she had absorbed it. Sometimes I wished I could spend all my time in a woman's arms.

I had a special liking for Mozart sonatas, so that was what Denise prepared and played for me. She was genuinely nervous; her whole manner was different, and she had to sit at the piano for a long time that afternoon before she could begin. I felt about her playing the same way I had felt about Helen's, years before; it was technically excellent, sometimes almost perfect, from what I knew of the particular sonatas, but it somehow lacked fire, or panache. Out of a kind of modesty, I think, she tried to keep herself out of the piece, make it all Mozart, but in leaving herself out she was leaving out some of Mozart too. Still, the music was beautiful, and it was terribly intimate to sit in that room and listen to her play it. It brought us closer than any conversation could have. I wondered how she sounded when she was alone. It must have been frustrating to have such a talent but not be able to show it to anyone.

One evening her housemate came in as I was leaving. She seemed just like Denise, demure and quiet, very sweet. She was a pediatrician. They didn't especially seem to be lesbians, though Helen had told me many times that you can't tell by a woman's appearance, or by the way she lives. She claims she can always tell, just by being in a woman's presence. A thirty-second conversation will do it, she says. Every time.

* * *

Once when Becky was lying with her head on my chest, caressing my balls—she had been doing that for three or four minutes, not saying a word—I said, "Would you touch down a little lower?" She began to use her fingernail on that sensitive piece of flesh just beneath my balls. "How about a little lower?" I said.

"I'll get some oil," she said.

I thought she was refusing me, or didn't hear, but when she got the oil she reached down to rub some on my asshole, then gently slipped her finger in. I hadn't asked her to do that; she just knew. She worked it slowly in and out. Somehow, still pressed against me—the woman must have been a contortionist—she got her other hand down to my cock. Just before I came, she shoved her finger all the way in, then yanked it out. The pleasure was so intense I screamed.

I gave a few stories to Denise. She was nice about them, and encouraging—"You really do write well," she said—but I could tell she wasn't exactly thrilled. There was something flat about my stories. Even I knew that. "I definitely think you should keep writing," she said. There was a poignance to that statement for me. That was just about at the moment when I was grinding to a halt on my novel. I would get up every morning and try to write, but it didn't go anywhere. It all seemed dead to me.

Denise started to play some of her music for me too, and, though I liked it fine, I didn't know what to make of it. I had followed music down to Stravinsky, and this was somehow past that, nowhere near as rich, of course, but more advanced musically. I tried to be enthusiastic, but I must have sounded the way she did about my stories. Still, the fact that she had finally played her music for someone was a big step for her, and loosened her up in general. She began to play the Mozart better, and continued to play that along with her pieces.

One afternoon I sat behind her in an easy chair as she played the slow movement from a Mozart sonata. She played it beautifully, and expressed more feeling—perhaps because the feeling was quieter—than with other things she played. The music seemed to hang in the air as she finished, as if we were still hearing it. She sat with her back to me for what

149

must have been twenty seconds. Then she turned to me and said—in a most uncharacteristic phrase; I'm sure she wasn't referring to her playing—"That was exquisite." We both stood, and stepped to meet in the middle of the room, and kissed. That was the first time we had so much as touched. We pulled back and looked at each other, kissed again. These weren't like the wild kisses I'd had with Peg, sloppy and out of control; they were deliberate, and willful. She had a small face, I suddenly noticed, and a tiny mouth, which barely opened as we kissed. I was thinking of that afternoon with Peg, and the way it had ruined our friendship. I didn't want to ruin this one.

"Playing this music for you is like making love to you," she said.

"I know."

"I'd like to really make love to you."

I swallowed. "You would?"

"I don't mean to be aggressive. I know you're married. That isn't a problem for me."

I kissed her again. This time her mouth opened wider.

"It's strictly up to you," she said.

We went up to her bedroom. She had a high four-poster bed that looked like an antique, a fluffy white bedspread, a glass-topped table with all those little women's bottles on it and a huge mirror in front of it. She pulled the bedspread down and carefully folded it over, just the way her mother must have taught her. Something about the quiet of all this, the delicacy of it, was making me terribly excited. I was being welcomed into the boudoir of a sweet shy virginal music teacher.

She turned to me and touched her hands to my chest. Just barely. "This is embarrassing," she said. "But is there anything you don't like?"

"No. I like everything."

"Good."

There was a footstool beside the bed, and she knelt on it while she undid my pants and let them fall, took down my underpants and—somewhat to my surprise—took me in her mouth. She started to caress me with her small warm hands. Her mouth was so small that my cock felt huge inside it, barely went in, but she was knowing and skillful, especially with her hands. The excitement was intense, and built much faster than I thought it would; before I had asked if it was all right I had come, a tremendous orgasm that left me gasping and shuddering as I stood there. I expected to have made a mess, but when I looked down there wasn't a drop anywhere. Her mouth wasn't even moist.

So much for the shy virginal music teacher.

"I want you to do that to me," she said.

She took off her clothes and I took off mine before she lay on the bed and I knelt on the footstool. She had a funny figure, a small upper body with tiny breasts, beautiful legs—I'd never seen nicer legs—and a huge round bottom that was all out of proportion to the rest of her. She held my face gently between her hands. "I love to be licked," she said. "But when I'm about to come I need to be sucked. Gently. I'll tell you when." I was expecting to lick for some time—it was okay; I was ready—but it was only about three minutes before she said, "All right. Suck me. Yes. There." She made the motions of an orgasm, but it didn't seem quite to happen. "Lick some more," she said. We must have missed it. The same thing happened again, and again. I figured I must be doing something wrong. Finally she pushed my head away. "Stop," she said. "I can't take anymore."

"Is there something wrong?" I said.

"No. It feels wonderful. I've just had it."

"Did you come?"

"Four times."

My mouth must have fallen open.

"I'm one of *those* women," she said. "We don't come as violently, but it all gradually builds. You can only take so much right on the spot. Then you need something else." She reached down and grabbed my cock. "Like this."

It was hard again. Even I could hardly believe it.

"I'm ready for something deeper," she said.

Her pussy was the opposite of Becky's. Very tight, and hard to get into. Fucking her was terribly intense. She seemed to be off somewhere, her eyes closed, the whole time.

Afterward—I had never been with anyone who did this, though it was the classic move—she lit a cigarette.

"I thought you'd be inexperienced," I said.

She laughed, in her throaty alto. "Hardly."

"You never speak of a boyfriend."

"I haven't had one for a while. That doesn't mean I never have."

"Do you miss it?"

"I put a lot of what I miss into the music."

That was the music I wanted to hear.

"And I masturbate a *whole* lot. If you want to know the sordid truth. But you've got to go now. I don't want Judith to find us."

"Would she mind?"

"I'd be embarrassed. A married man. It's so wicked."

That was why I liked it.

When you have lost touch with your writing, utterly lost touch, the realization is slow to dawn. You don't want to realize such a fact. At first it seems you have started a difficult chapter. Chapter 15. You can't make it come alive. You decide it's the first section that is really dull, so you cut it and rewrite around it. But the second section doesn't make a good opening either. You've got two versions now, and you can't decide. You go on to Chapter 16, but you realize you have to decide on 15 before you write 16, so you make an arbitrary decision and take the second version. Then 16 doesn't seem any good; it seems *it* would be better the other way, so you reverse your decision and write another Chapter 16, but that doesn't seem good either. Now you've got two versions of 15 and two of 16. None of them looks any good. You wonder if the problem isn't with Chapter 14.

"This is all so surprising," I said to Denise.

"How's that?"

She loved to smoke her cigarette afterward. She would lie on her back and blow smoke toward the ceiling, where we watched it gather in a huge cloud.

"You don't seem the type for this," I said.

"What *is* the type?"

"You seem so quiet. Dignified. A mild-mannered music teacher."

A few minutes before she had been draped across that high bed, her legs hanging down to touch the floor, while I took her from behind, and she came again and again. I had asked her to tell me when she did, so I would learn to recognize it.

"There," she would say, groaning and gasping. "Oh. God. *There.*"

"Maybe all the music teachers are out there having hot sex," she said.

"Do you think?"

"Maybe the world is much sexier than we imagine."

Actually, I would guess it's less sexy.

What was unusual about Denise—unprecedented in my dealings with women—was that she showed so little emotion about it all. She didn't go into raptures about how much she cared for me. She didn't ask a lot of questions about what all this meant or how long it would go on. She didn't express a shred of guilt about what we were doing. She just seemed to want to do it. She loved sex. She loved it as much as anyone I had ever met. Yet as far as I could tell from her conversation she hadn't had a man in months. Perhaps years.

"I'm teasing," she said. "I know what you mean. I think the truth is that you can't tell from the outside. I wouldn't necessarily have picked you for a terribly sexy person. I thought you were quiet too. Bookish."

"I am."

"But you're also sexy. People are different, that's all. Different from each other and different from what they seem. You can't tell from looking at somebody what's going on behind his exterior. You can't tell from talking to him. You have to get behind the exterior. To get hold of his body. You have to *feel* how he is. Who he is."

The great lesson of sex.

Sometimes when you're having trouble with your writing you walk out to the living room and turn on the television. A game show is on. You can't believe people watch that crap. But you get the first couple of questions. You get the third one, and no one on the show does. You're on a roll here. Maybe you could go on one of those shows and win a lot of money, quit your job. It would be great. You could write all the time.

One afternoon Denise had me lie just the way she had, my torso draped across the bed, my feet touching the floor. Then she knelt on the footstool and gently spread my ass, and licked there. She licked and licked. I had never felt such a tiny little pleasure grow to be so intense.

"You must think I'm weird," she said.

"I think you're wonderful."

She slipped a finger inside me. "That feel good?"

"It does."

She worked it further in. "Too bad I don't have a cock," she said.

After the game shows, *Perry Mason* was on. Some of the episodes I hadn't seen. Others I had, and they took me back to my youth. Those old shows were surprisingly well made. You could learn a lot from them about the structure of a narrative.

"You're early today," Becky said. The place had just opened. It was 10:00 A.M.

"I got the morning off."

I had never told her what I did. She had never asked.

"Haven't seen you for a while," she said.

"I've been busy."

After she massaged me for a while—she had turned me over and started to tickle my chest, tug on my nipples—I said, "Have you ever beaten anyone in here?"

"What?"

"Spanked them."

"Oh. Sure."

"Do you do it a lot?"

"It comes and goes. Sometimes it seems that's all you're doing. Then nobody asks for it for weeks."

"Do you think it's weird?"

"I like it. Hold on a minute." She went out of the room and came back with a small paddle. "I'm glad you brought this up. I've been thinking you needed a little discipline." She put me over her knee and gave me a whack. "Have you been bad?"

"I have."

"What have you done, you bad little boy?"

"I haven't been doing my work."

"Why you *stupid* little *bastard.*" She began emphasizing her words with smacks from the paddle.

"I've just been goofing off."

"You *prick!*"

"I sit in front of the television all morning."

"Is that why you haven't been in here?"

"Yes."

"It is *not!*" I screamed, she had hit me so hard. She grabbed my hair and pulled my face up. "You've got another girl, don't you?"

"Well . . . "

"Tell me."

"Yes! Becky, please. It hurts."

"It's supposed to. What's this bitch's name?"

"Denise."

"Sounds like a real slut. Does she suck it?"

"Yes."

"Does she swallow your stuff?"

"Yes."

"Shit!" She grabbed my hair and pulled my head up again. "Do you go down on her?"

"Yes."

"Son of a *bitch.* While *I'm* sitting *here* with *nothing* but my finger."

"Please, Becky. Please. I'm sorry."

"You're *going* to be, cuntface. Your ass is going to look like *hamburger.* Now." She held me by the hair and moved herself around, got my head between her legs. "Get to work. And if this isn't good—if this isn't the best I've ever had." She put the paddle down where I could see it. "You know what you're going to get."

If you own a VCR, you don't ever have to go to an adult bookstore. You don't have to avoid the guys trying to pick you up, or step through the come on the floor, or look down at the side of the booth and notice that there is a large hole there, and a hard red cock peeking through it, belonging to the guy in the next booth. You can watch in the privacy of your own home, with the curtains closed and the machine running. You can lie on the couch and watch dirty movies all morning.

* * *

"I think I'm weirder than you are," Denise said.

"You keep saying that. You don't seem too weird to me."

"I mean sexually."

"I know what you mean. I'm pretty weird myself. We haven't gotten into my weirdness."

"I guess I'm thinking of something specific."

"What's that?"

"I'm more anal than you are."

I looked at her.

"I'm more anal than most everybody," she said. "At least that I've run into."

"You haven't told me this."

"I keep dropping little hints. Doing things."

"It's just that I haven't done it much before. It isn't that I don't want to. Tell me what you like."

She reached over and grabbed my cock, which had gotten hard from our talking. "Why don't we just skip to the main event?"

I gulped. "Really?"

"Unless that's too much for you."

"Not if it's not too much for you."

"I think I can take it."

She took a tube of lubricant from the bedside table. She took her time putting it on me, caressing as she did. When I reached down to put some on her, her asshole felt tiny. I didn't see how I could ever get in there. "Try a finger," she said. It slipped right in.

"Now we'll try something bigger," she said. She rolled over on her belly and stuffed a pillow under her. "This is a profound experience for me," she said. "I won't quite seem to be here."

She never did. Sex took her far away.

"But I'll be back," she said.

She reached back and positioned me against her. At first I didn't seem to go in at all. She changed her angle slightly, moved me a little. Suddenly I plunged all the way in. "Christ," she said.

"Does it hurt?"

"Yes."

I started to pull out.

"No," she said. "I want the pain. It's the pain that does it for me." She gasped. "It's not really pain. It's intensity. Just go easy. Go slowly."

Her eyes were closed. Her face was buried in a pillow. With every stroke, this slender woman—the quietest of lovers—gave a long low groan.

The guy at the video store gets to know you. There aren't many customers in the morning.

"What do you do, anyway?" he said.

"I work in a bookstore. Second shift." I didn't mention that the second shift was just four hours.

"And all morning you watch movies."

"Yeah."

"Sounds like a good life. Kind of ass backwards."

"You get sick of those game shows."

"You ought to get cable. They got ball games round-the-clock."

"You get tired of ball games."

"Hey." He held up the video I'd just rented. "You get tired of blow jobs too."

Reading through Chapter 17 one morning, trying to get back into it after a week away, I couldn't see that it had anything to do with the rest of my book. I had no idea what I'd been trying to do with it. Or what I should do next.

I left the bookstore after work and Denise was waiting out on the sidewalk for me. It was dark already, and bitterly cold. She was bundled up in an overcoat and scarf. I smiled.

"I wasn't expecting you," I said.

"I know."

"This isn't really a night when I can get free."

"It's all right. That's the thing, Charles. That's what I wanted to talk to you about. I've decided I can't see you any-more."

I felt all the breath go out of me. For a moment I couldn't speak. I felt as if I might faint.

"I'm sorry to have to tell you this way," she said.

Her face was strained, and slightly reddened. She wasn't quite looking at me.

"I don't understand."

"I can't really explain," she said. "That's what's so awkward. It's just something I've decided."

"I thought we were happy together. I thought we were having fun."

"We were."

"This was the best love affair I'd ever had. The best sex."

"It was good for me too. Believe me."

"Did I do something wrong?"

"You did nothing wrong. You were delightful, the whole time."

"Is it because I'm married?"

"That never bothered me. I told you it didn't. I felt that was your business."

I didn't know what to say. Everything I said sounded stupid. I knew I looked stupid too. My face was falling apart.

"I just don't understand."

"I know. I'm sorry."

"Can we still see each other? Just to play music or something. Can we still be friends?"

"Eventually, I think. But not for a while. I think it will be better if we don't see each other at all for a while. It will be easier."

"Easier for who?"

"For both of us. Believe me, Charles. It's the best way. I'm sorry. I've got to go."

She didn't kiss me good-bye. She didn't touch me. She kept her hands in the pockets of her overcoat, in fact. She just walked across the street to the parking lot and drove away. She never came back to the bookstore again, at least not when I was there. When I called her house, her housemate always answered, and said Denise was busy. She said the same thing the two times I went to the door. I saw Denise out driving once. Another time I saw her at the shopping mall, about thirty yards away. She didn't seem to see me either time. When I got down to that part of the shopping mall I couldn't find her. I couldn't find her out in the parking lot either. I never spoke to her again.

We had been to bed six times.

A moment comes—and it comes pretty soon—when pornographic movies in the morning don't hold your attention.

They don't keep your mind off anything. They are like staring at a blank screen. You try regular movies. You try foreign films. A survey of the greatest masterpieces in film history. You begin to realize that the problem is the time of day. You're not supposed to be watching a movie at that hour. You're supposed to be working.

Whenever in my life I have had good sex and lost it, I have always been afraid I would never have it again.

I found the belt in a specialty shop in the mall. It was a beautiful soft leather, and so thick that it didn't fit my belt loops. Becky was never at a loss. She made me kneel on the bed with my head down and my ass in the air. She would whip me for five or six strokes and then yell at me for a while, tell me how much worse it was going to get. Now and then she would pick up my head by the hair and make me lick between her legs, fuck her with my tongue. It was just what I wanted: the rhythm of the whipping, the loud smacks, the pain—worse when she caught me with the side of the belt— but somehow it wasn't enough. It wasn't the blinding pain I was looking for. The oblivion.

"It's looking pretty bad back here," she said at one point.

"Just do it," I said, from where my head lay on the bed.

"I'm just saying. It looks pretty raw."

"Do your job, whore. You got paid."

"Don't call me that."

"It's what you are."

The next smack was the one I was looking for. She brought it from way down on the bed, over her shoulder in a high arc, then down on my ass with everything she had. For a moment I just gasped, I was so stunned. Then I got my breath and screamed.

She had stepped onto my back with her foot, whipped me again and again. She wasn't being careful, was cutting into me often with the side of the belt, hitting my legs as well as my ass. I scrunched up and tried to protect myself, shield my vulnerable spots. I was screaming and she was screaming. The pain was beyond belief. Suddenly the door burst open and the other masseuse was standing there holding a baseball bat, all the blood drained from her face. The three of us froze and stared at each other. "You okay, Becky?" the woman said.

She asks if *Becky* is okay.

"I'm okay," Becky said. "Close the door." The woman did.

Becky fell down on the bed beside me. "Jesus," she said. "I went a little crazy there."

I was trembling, lying beside her. All the little hot spots of pain on my body were flashing. Especially bad were the little tender places at the sides of my hips.

Becky lay beside me and took me in her arms. "I'm sorry," she said.

"I'm sorry for what I called you," I said. "I didn't mean it."

"I hate being called a whore."

"You're not a whore. I just said that to make you mad."

"I am a whore. That's the whole problem."

"You're not. You're wonderful, Becky. I love you."

I meant those words. I wasn't just saying them.

"It's okay," she said. "Listen. I'll suck you or something if you want. Do something special, to make up for it. You can screw me."

"You don't have to do that."

"But first I've got to get you a towel. You're bleeding."

It took me about ten minutes, a chapter at a time, to burn my book. I started with the two versions of Chapter 15.

One morning I had walked up to the video store but decided not to go in, was walking aimlessly along the sidewalk, when I ran into Peg. I had hardly seen her since I quit my job at the library, certainly hadn't talked to her. She brightened when she saw me, held open her arms—all was forgiven—and gave me a big hug. She pulled back and stared at me.

"You don't look too good," she said.

"I'm not too good."

"Want to go for a walk? I'm off today. Want to walk in the park?"

"Yes. I'd like that."

On our way to the park, I told her about Denise. How we had met in the bookstore, the interests we had in common, the long talks we used to have over coffee. "Just like us," Peg said. I told her how Denise had played music for me, how easily and naturally we had made love the first time, the way Denise had seemed perfectly willing to go on with the affair, how wonderful the sex had been. And the way it had all ended without explanation in thirty seconds one evening. I hadn't told those things to anyone, but I figured I had nothing to hide from Peg.

By the time I had told her about that last evening we were sitting on a bench in the park.

"Oh Charles," Peg said. "That must have hurt a lot."

I put my head down and sobbed. I wasn't much of a weeper in those days, but I was so worn down that morning, and it was such a relief finally to talk about all that, and to hear a word of sympathy. I must have cried for ten minutes, while she held me awkwardly, both of us bulky in our winter coats.

"Is that all that's wrong?" she said.

"Well. My writing went to hell."

"*You* went to hell. Your writing just tagged along."

She might have had a point there.

"How old was this woman?" she said.

"My age. Mid-thirties."

"And how long has she been living with the other woman?"

"Since graduate school. Ten years."

Peg sat for a while and gazed out at the trees. My sobbing had gradually quieted.

"Well," she said. "What I think. Not that it does you any good at this point. But I think they *are* lovers. Being together all those years. Owning a house. Denise being so sexy but not dating men. It all adds up."

"I suppose." I hadn't wanted to see that.

"I think they're lovers, but Denise also likes men, and because you're such an attractive man, and such a sensitive man, and maybe just because she wanted to get hold of a nice hard cock again, I don't know, she had an affair with you. That's why she didn't mind that you were married. You both had somebody else."

"Yes."

"But her friend found out. Or just suspected and confronted her. So Denise had to stop. Because that relationship is too important to her. It's who she really is. But they're closeted about being lesbians. One's a doctor and one's a teacher. So she couldn't tell you. Especially not you. A jealous and angry lover. She was in a bind. She had no explanation."

I sat and thought about it. It made as much sense as other things that had passed through my mind.

"I know this doesn't make it all better," Peg said.

"It helps. The whole thing would have been a lot easier if she'd given me an explanation. I felt cursed or something."

"I know."

Peg had her arm around me, was staring out at the park.

"You're in a hard situation," she said. "Not getting what you need from your marriage, trying to get it elsewhere. I understand why you're trying. I really do. You want to hold things together. But I'm not sure that ever works. It always gets messy. I think you've got to get those things in your marriage."

"I don't know if I can do that."

"I know. The wounds are hard to heal."

We sat in silence for a few moments. My stomach was killing me.

"I'm in such pain," I said.

"I know you are. I don't want to sound like one of those people who says this all the time. I'm not one of those people. And I don't say it glibly. I know what you're going through. More than I'd like to say. But I don't think you should do this alone. I think you need some help."

The first three times I saw my therapist, he hardly said a word. The first thing I talked about, for the whole first session and part of the second, was my writing. I told him about my marriage, my sexual adventuring, the pains in my stomach. From time to time I said, "Should I shut up for a while?" but he said, "No. I think this is to the point." At the end of the third session I finally ran out of steam.

"So," I said. "Am I crazy?"

"Yes," he said. "In the same way I'm crazy. And everybody else I know who's really alive."

"Can you cure me?"

"You can be cured. In the way that one is cured of these things."

"A couple of months' work."

"A couple of years."

I shook my head and smiled. "Sounds grim."

"Not as grim as the alternative."

I had the number because I had often called to make sure she was working that day. "Becky?" I said.

"Yeah."

"This is Charles. I've come to see you a lot. I don't know if you know my name."

I couldn't remember her ever using it.

"I'm not too hot with names," she said.

"It's all right. I just wanted to let you know. I'm not coming in anymore."

"You're calling to tell me you're *not* coming in."

"I just wanted you to know. It's nothing about you."

"Oh?"

"I don't want to do that anymore. But it was very important to me when I did it. And you were wonderful. Very sweet."

"But now you're getting married."

"No. I've been married."

"You're getting back with your wife."

"I'd like to. I don't know if it will work out."

"Yeah. Well. Thanks for calling."

"I just wanted you to know it had nothing to do with you."

"Sure. Listen, mister. Do *you* want to know something? Something you find out by working here?"

"What?"

"You'll be back."

I didn't say anything for a moment. I thought there must be more to the message.

"I know what you mean," I said. "But I really don't think I will."

"Lots of guys say they're quitting. Some of them while they still got their pants off. Their dick's still wet. But they always come back."

"I don't think I'll do that. But I wanted you to know how much you meant to me. I'll always remember you."

"Are you the guy with red hair?"

"No. My hair's brown."

She laughed. "That doesn't help me much. But you remember what I said, sugar. I'll be seeing you later."

She hung up.

PART II

PART II

EIGHT

From the window where I sat every morning, working, I watched March creep into the city and thaw it out from a bitter winter. I am an early riser, between six and six-thirty, so for much of the winter I was up while it was pitch black. Helen's first appointment is at ten, and she sometimes sleeps past nine, so I would tiptoe down to breakfast—a huge bowl of granola with all kinds of nuts and dried fruits—and take coffee upstairs with me in a thermos.

Helen has one of those tall narrow tan-brick houses in the city, with a not especially large but perfectly comfortable room on the third floor. That was where I stayed, with a single bed, a dresser, and a table that I moved over in front of the window and used as a desk. The window looks down on a cobblestone courtyard in the back, which fronts what used to be a carriage house that Helen has remodeled and rented out. Behind that house is an alley paved with bricks, and across the alley the rear ends of a whole string of houses. So from my third-floor perch, as I sat and sipped coffee, started to work, I saw that street of the neighborhood come awake, lights coming on in the houses as people took showers and got dressed, sat down to breakfast at tables in the kitchens. The kids would dash out their front doors to school. The parents, after a while, would step out the back to get their cars out of garages in the alley.

Through the end of January and nearly all of February it looked dreadful out there, dark and bitter cold (it wasn't exactly toasty where I was, up in that drafty attic with only a space heater at my feet). People walked with little bitty steps through the snow or ice, spun their wheels getting out, sometimes had to shovel or chip their way out of a bad spot in the alley. But in the early days of March the mornings were brighter as I came to my desk, the weather less forbidding. Toward the end of the month I saw a man step into the alley, look off at the blue sky at the end of it, and stop where he was to raise his arms and take a huge stretch. He seemed to be welcoming in the spring.

After I had made my original decision to stay in the city, I hadn't been as sure that it would be easy—or that it would even work out—as I had once been. I have a kind of work that transfers locales more easily than some, but that doesn't mean it transfers effortlessly. I put my own phone in upstairs at Helen's. I also hired an answering service in North Carolina, to take messages and give out my number when they thought it appropriate. I am in touch with a number of magazine editors—also a number of book-review editors—and it is important to get my number around. I didn't want to give up the column I wrote for a newspaper in North Carolina. For a while I wrote on vaguely national topics, but after a few weeks I came clean and admitted I was on sabbatical from the state, and was writing from a place that, as far as most North Carolinians are concerned, might as well have been Paris. The pieces apparently went over pretty well anyway. It was a personal column, with a personal voice. You either liked it or you didn't.

I finished the article about that writer. My editors seemed to like it, and it went into production almost immediately. They got some great pictures of the man hunting in the woods, pounding away on his little portable typewriter, eating one of his gargantuan gourmet meals. They even got a shot of him lifting a barbell.

I did ask his wife about the young women who were hanging around the place.

"He fucks them," she said.

She was a woman not unlike her husband, short and slightly plump, with a head of thick curly black hair and a rough ruddy complexion. She apparently liked the gourmet meals—and the wines—as much as he did. She was wearing a string of Indian beads around her neck, over a workshirt, kneading bread in the kitchen as we spoke.

"He does?" I was slightly startled by this remark.

"Sure. Wouldn't you?"

"I don't know. Is it all right with you?"

"I can wish they weren't around. But what do you expect of the man? After all those years of working so hard and getting no attention. Now he's got these little girls hanging around wanting to learn how to write. What's he supposed to do, give that away?"

I had thought that was the idea, yes.

"Anyway, he fucks me too. And I fuck better than they do. Ask him. They've got a lot to learn. Not just about writing."

I'm not sure I shouldn't have written the article about his wife.

Now I had started an article about a witch. Not an old woman with a hooked nose who cooks up potions in a caldron, but a ravishing young political activist who—as part of everything else she does—practices the pagan religions. I had been skeptical when Helen told me about this woman, but I read some of her articles, which have been published in various New Age and leftist magazines, and found her to be a brilliant intellect and a fine writer. I had traveled once to upstate New York to meet her. I talked to some members of her coven (are you believing this?). Now I was going over my notes, doing an exhaustive study of the woman's writings, trying to decide what to do next.

I am a creature of habit, but the only absolutely etched-in-stone habit I have is that of writing in the morning. I am an intense person when I write (also when I don't), and the five or so hours I spend are usually all I can take. I do other kinds of work at other times in the day—reading or note-taking—but I confine my writing to the morning. After that I want a little lunch—a very little, as I have entered middle age—and some exercise. Which is slightly harder to come by in the city than in North Carolina.

Fortunately, the downtown YMCA was offering a ninety-day membership. It is a beautiful facility, in a bright new building. I would mosey on down after lunch and take a swim or use the weight machines. All I really missed was the cycling I do to and from my gym in North Carolina. For a while I took a bus downtown, but in the middle of February I leased a car, so sometimes after that I drove. That was quicker and easier than the bus, but I had to deal with parking, which is much more expensive than bus fare.

I tended to see the Senator at odd hours. At first we just had lunch the way we had that first day, up in the apartment, except that the Duchess usually hung around. There were also evenings—obligatory evenings—when I went over there for dinner with Helen, and maybe one of my brothers came with his family. But it was also true that, more and more, he and I would be alone together, just the two of us, in a way that we had rarely been in our lives, at least our adult lives.

Sometimes I would go over and sit with him in his study. He might take me out to dinner, to one of his clubs, or to a favorite restaurant, where he knew people and could get food prepared the way he needed it. And sometimes—this was absolutely unprecedented in our lives—he would invite me over to the Hall of Fame, and we would go down to the garage and get his big Lincoln (about like driving a truck to me) and go for a ride. We might go to some familiar haunt, or just ride around aimlessly. He had a remarkable knowledge of the city, and took me through all kinds of neighborhoods where I'd never been. He would direct me past distinguished houses, telling me who had built them and who had lived there, who was living there now. He would tell me about buildings of note. But much of the time, with the stimulation of those places, or perhaps with no stimulation, just because he wanted to, he would speak of the past, sometimes a past I remembered and sometimes one I had never known.

He talked to me, for instance, about his early years as a father, those years when I remembered him and the Duchess going out all the time, dressed to kill. To all the world he looked like a man who had walked into a perfect setup, with a position in his father's law firm, a wealthy and beautiful wife, a huge house that had been in her family for years. But that situation was not all it had seemed. For one thing, his father hadn't wanted to show any favoritism, so the Senator had started at the bottom, working as hard as any other young man just out of law school, not getting paid any more. None of that bothered the Senator, but the truth was that he wasn't on a par with everyone else. The other young men knew that he was a partner's son and that, barring a colossal fuck-up, he would be a partner someday, while they might never be. They resented and probably disliked him, didn't treat him as one of the boys. He occupied a lonely position.

"I would never have done the same thing if you'd come into the firm," he said. "I didn't do the same with your brothers. They didn't start at the top, but they sure as hell didn't start at the bottom. Everybody knows they're the boss's sons. You might as well acknowledge it."

It was also true that he hadn't wanted to move into that big house as soon as they did. He'd had a much more modest place picked out when he proposed. It wasn't until later that he found out the Duchess's family had other plans.

"I understand what your Grandfather Morse was doing," he said. "He raised his daughter with certain advantages, and wanted to see that she continued to have them. He also wanted his house in good hands. So he gave it to his son-in-law, which on the outside looks like a wonderful generous thing to do. It *was* a generous thing. But it also guaranteed that his son-in-law would live a certain way. You've got to have servants in a house like that. Nobody keeps up a place like that alone. You've got to have certain amenities, a certain kind of wardrobe, a certain car. My family had always lived simply, big law firm or not. I never got a chance to do that."

The Senator told me these things while we were sitting beside the house in the Lincoln. It had finally been bought by the university. Nobody could afford a private residence like that anymore.

"It also meant another thing. Something I don't think your grandfather intended, but that was very significant for me all the same. It meant that in the early years of my marriage, for a number of years in fact, I didn't support my family. Not only had I not bought the house I lived in, but I couldn't decorate and keep it up. Not the way your mother wanted. We had to use her money from the start. This might sound stupid, but I'd have lived in a house I could afford, however modest. There I was working my ass off at the law firm, resented by the other men for who I was, and I was going home to a place I hadn't paid for. My whole life was like that. I didn't deserve what I had."

"Why didn't you turn him down?" I said. "Tell him you didn't want the house."

"I was too young. He was a hard man, your Grandfather Morse. He wasn't used to people refusing him. Certainly not a man in his twenties. And it was obvious that your mother wanted to live in that house. She wanted to live that way. I was about to become her husband. I wanted to give her what she wanted."

A certain kind of young husband tried to do that. Please his woman. Not always remembering to please himself.

The Senator heaved a huge sigh. "Your mother loved a party, Charles."

"Doesn't she still?"

"Not like she used to. Back in those days, she wouldn't miss one. It wouldn't have occurred to her to say we were busy that night, or that we'd been out too much lately, we needed a night at home. I loved your mother. God knows I loved seeing her all fixed up. I loved being seen with her. But I wouldn't have gone to all those goddamned parties. I'd have stayed home now and then."

I had started to drive again, just edging along. The Senator gazed at the place as we passed.

"It was a great old house," he said. "It holds all kinds of memories. But I honestly never felt it was mine until I could afford it. I never felt it was mine until I was into my forties."

By that time, I was almost gone.

Another afternoon we drove out to Fox Chapel to see my old school. The Senator had gone to the same school, though his campus had been elsewhere. We drove around campus, but the grounds were snowy, and there were students around, so we didn't get out, as we had planned. We wound up driving around that suburb, which was the poshest in the city, colonial and modern houses set back from the road by rolling expansive lawns. In my heart I probably disliked that place, and disapproved of the people who lived there, but it could certainly be beautiful on a winter afternoon, snow draping the golf course and the huge sloping lawns. The sunlight was almost blinding off the snow.

The Senator and I had ridden for a long time in silence. He must have been thinking of the young people he had seen back at the school.

"How is it that you and Sara never had children?" he said.

To his credit, the Senator had never asked me that before. He hadn't brought up the subject of grandchildren, though I'd always known he wanted them. Now he had some, from my brothers.

"Don't you think it was better," I said, "the way things turned out?"

"You could say that. Then again, things might have turned out differently if you'd had them."

That was a painful thought to me. Another life, which I'd chosen not to live.

"I don't think so," I said.

"But why didn't you?"

"At first because we didn't feel ready. All those years when we wanted to do other things. There seemed to be plenty of time. By the time our lives were more settled, we weren't getting along. It was out of the question."

Sara was pregnant now with her new man. I didn't think I'd bring that up.

"I certainly didn't feel ready to have children," the Senator said, "when I had them. People didn't think that way back then. You got married, and the children just showed up."

He was staring out the window at those luxurious houses, the rolling lawns. He seemed hardly to be seeing them. He was talking as if to himself.

"I always wanted to be a good father," he said.

"You were a good father."

"I don't mean that way. I wasn't abusive or anything. I wasn't mean. You kids were easy to raise. You and Helen, anyway. The boys were kind of a handful. But I would have been another kind of father altogether. Home in the evenings playing ball. Going for outings on the weekends. Whatever fathers do with their sons. Or dream of doing. I was so busy when you were young. If I wasn't staying late at work I was going out somewhere with your mother. I kept telling myself I'd spend more time with you. I'd find a way to do that. But the years just seemed to fly by. It all got away from me. My life got away from me."

I knew how that was.

"Did you resent it?" he said. "That I wasn't with you more."

"I didn't even notice it. You spent as much time with me as other fathers did. Kids I knew."

"That was why we waited so long between you and your brothers. I didn't have time for children. I was already way behind. Your mother didn't know what the hell I was talking about. She thought things were fine. She had nothing but time. But I didn't want it to be like that. Her being the only one around. We still had the boys before I was ready. But at least by the time they were older. Playing sports and things. I could give them some time."

I'd had no idea the Senator had been concerned with such things. I thought he'd done what he had just because he wanted to. Come to some J.V. football game, to see me sit on the bench.

"Helen was the one I worried about," he said. "Partly just because she came first. I always figured I'd get along with the boys. I knew boys. But I didn't know what the hell to do with a girl. I was stunned when one came along. I wanted to have something that would be my thing with her. Something your mother had nothing to do with. I picked music. I didn't know beans about music. Just that it was something little girls did. I knew more about music than ballet. For years it was important to both of us. I was so proud of her. But it certainly backfired in the end. We've never even talked about it."

"Helen was good at music because she'd be good at anything," I said. "She's just one of those lucky people. But it wasn't her life's work. She didn't have any real talent."

"You don't think? She always sounded fabulous to me."

"Yeah. And you just said. You don't know the first thing about music."

He laughed.

"She could have been a music teacher at best. Piano lessons or something. She's doing something much better than that. At least for her. She found the right thing."

"I suppose." The Senator shook his head. "I just wish I knew what that thing is."

The Senator didn't understand the idea of therapy. Treating the insane, maybe. But talking to people because they couldn't get their lives together. He'd have just kicked them in the ass.

He wore a troubled expression at the mention of Helen. He often did. It looked like disgruntlement, or anger. Probably it was just pain.

There was a long silence.

"Do you think . . ." He paused. "Do you think I had anything to do with her . . . With the way she is?"

"I'm sure you did."

"I mean that she doesn't like men."

I knew what he meant. He had choked on the question. But I wanted him to say it.

"I think she likes men pretty well," I said.

"You know what I mean."

"You mean that she's a lesbian."

"I hate that word. I hate even hearing it now. I hate to hear it used about my daughter."

The expression on his face was like the one a child uses to hold back tears, his mouth curled up, chin thrust out. It was the expression that, on an adult, we call indignation. It was well established on the Senator's face. No danger that this little boy would cry.

"I don't think Helen dislikes men," I said. "Lots of women do. Lots of straight women too. But Helen likes men. She just doesn't like to go to bed with them."

"I don't understand that."

"Why not?"

"It isn't natural."

"Who says?"

"Everybody. At least everybody I know."

"I'm not so sure of that. They might say it in a group, with other people around. Trying to go along with the crowd. But not if you got them alone. If you could really ask them. Nothing in sex is unnatural. These things are just a part of us.

I'm sure we get shoved this way or that when we're young. But after that it's just there. There's nothing we can do about it."

"That's what I'm asking."

"What?"

"Did I have something to do with that? Did I do part of the shoving?"

It was remarkable that the Senator was asking this question. He had come a long way to ask it.

"What's the difference? If what she is is all right?"

"I don't want to have hurt her. I loved that girl so much."

"She loved you. She still loves you."

"I wanted to be proud of her."

"You can be proud of her. She has a wonderful career."

"I just wish it were something I could tell someone."

"Well." This was all getting oddly close to home. "If what you mean is that you want her to do a certain thing. One of the four or five things your friends approve of. So you can tell them that and they can be pleased. You've got a problem. But if what you want is to be proud of her. Of what she's made of herself. I think you've got as much right as any father in the world."

The Senator didn't buy what I was saying. He still wore that bitter expression, though it seemed to have softened slightly. But it was a big change for him even to have brought this matter up. Even to have talked about what Helen was doing.

The most interesting conversation we had came later that week, when we drove back out to the school on a Saturday so we could walk around. The snow had been cleared off the walkways, and there was hardly anyone on campus. We toured the new gym, where some boys and girls were shooting baskets (the school had been all male when I was there), then, after driving up to the main quad, walked into the academic building. The Senator still had his cane, but was moving much better those days. I think it had been fear, in part, that had made him go slowly before. He seemed less fearful as time went on.

The lights were off in the main hallway, and we couldn't find any switches, but some light was coming in the windows at the front. The Senator was staring at some plaques on the wall, looking for names he knew. I don't know just what brought the subject up—perhaps a suspicion that the Senator wished my name were on one of those plaques—but some words popped out that I had always wanted to say. I was almost surprised to hear them myself.

"I always had the feeling when I was a kid," I said. "Also when I was older. That you wanted me to be smarter."

The Senator was leaning forward with his cane, squinting at a plaque. "You were pretty smart, weren't you?"

"I was no Helen. She was a straight-A student."

"It all seems pretty insignificant now. Who *were* the kids who got good grades? Names on a plaque you can't even see."

The man had a point. Even if you could see the plaque.

"I didn't get into a real good school," I said.

"You got into a good school."

"I didn't get into the one you wanted."

"What the hell. You got into a good one."

The Senator was rewriting history. Either that or—more astonishing still—he had already rewritten it. He had actually decided, through the years, that I had done well in school. He had changed his mind.

"I thought you were disappointed in how I did. That you always wanted me to do better."

"Yes. Well. Fathers are like that. When they're younger."

He didn't seem to remember.

"I mean you really thought I screwed up. Failed in everything you wanted for me."

The face he turned to me, in that dim ghostly light, was astounded. "Charles. I thought no such thing."

"Are you sure?"

"Of course I'm sure. I'd have remembered *that.*"

"Well. I was there. I got that impression. I didn't get it out of nowhere."

You had to wonder if I'd blown it up a little.

The Senator had grown pensive.

"I wanted you to do well. I'll confess to that crime. So things would be easier for you. You'd have lots of opportunities. I'd always screwed up in school, never got good grades, and when the time came for me to get serious I wasn't ready. I'd never done any hard work. I knew my father had pulled strings for me. Getting me into Princeton. Into law school. Then of course he brought me into the firm. That was kind of a messy feeling. I wanted you to earn what you got."

He could have saved himself the trouble. I didn't want into the fucking firm anyway.

"I always thought you *were* smart," he said. "I knew you were smart. A father knows his children. You were as smart as Helen."

"I never did as well."

"But you were just as smart. I was convinced of it."

It was interesting to hear that. It was only in recent years that I'd begun to think my intelligence was on a par with Helen's. She had always said it was. I certainly hadn't felt that way when I was younger.

"I was just in a fog," I said. "Things were too much. Helen was so bright and energetic and cheerful. Everything was easy for her. Nothing was easy for me. I didn't know where I was half the time. I didn't know what I was doing."

I was describing the strange haze of adolescence, those days when you have enormous nervous energy and also no energy at all, when you have deep yearnings but can't bring yourself to do anything about them, when you can masturbate nine times a day but picking up the clutter in your room looks like an insurmountable task.

"Sometimes I thought it was because I was fat," I said.

"What? That you were in a fog?"

"I thought you were mad at me because I was fat. You didn't like me because I was fat."

That strange statement seemed to be at the heart of what I wanted to say to the Senator. That he hadn't liked me because of how I was. Fat and dumb. To his credit, he didn't give some knee-jerk reaction to it. He didn't immediately deny it, the way another parent would have. He stood in that dim silent hallway, bundled in his overcoat, leaning on his cane—facing me now—and considered it.

"I suppose I didn't like it," he said. "Not that I didn't like you. I didn't like it that you were fat."

"I thought you didn't like me."

"I always liked you."

"That's not the way it felt."

"I suppose not." The Senator shook his head. "I couldn't help how *I* felt."

I was glad he had admitted this. I knew I hadn't been wrong.

"The thing of it was," he said, "I'd always been fat. Most of my life. I hated it in myself. Especially when I was young. The way other kids made fun of me. Maybe kids were crueler then."

"I doubt it."

"Anyway, I was very conscious of that. Afraid my kids were going to be fat because I was. You see these fat families and you think, look what those parents did to their children. They didn't just do it to themselves. They did it to their children too. I was always worried about that."

"Yes."

"You were such a skinny little runt when you were young. You and Helen both. Then all of a sudden you just blew up. Out of nowhere. Eating all this sweet fattening stuff. There seemed to be no way to stop it. I had no idea why you were doing it. It was like my worst nightmare. I could see you were making life harder for yourself, opening yourself up to mockery and pain, damaging your health, but there wasn't a thing I could do about it."

He was right. It was a choice I had made for myself—nobody was going to stop me—but a choice so far beneath the level of consciousness that I wasn't even aware I had made it. I certainly wasn't responsible for it. I was seven years old.

"All through those years I felt so bad for you," he said. "I knew what you were going through. I'd have done anything to help you." I had felt his wish to help—to change me—as disapproval. "Then you went to college and took it all off. I couldn't believe it. You came back a new man."

I came back my own man.

"You never told anybody how you did it," he said.

"I ate less."

"Ha! You expect me to believe that?"

We were standing in that dim hallway smiling at each other. We both knew what a mystery that whole subject was, how it was connected with everything else in your life but also seemed to stand apart, how it could seem the most mysterious thing in the world and also the most obvious. You ate too much, so you got fat.

"It's like the man said." The Senator started to walk toward me, thumping along with his cane. "Everybody talks about how much I drink. Nobody talks about how thirsty I am."

"Yeah."

"Anyway. I never disliked you. I might have disliked me a little."

"You shouldn't have. You weren't so bad."

All this pointed to the most interesting question of all as far as I was concerned. There was no doubt in my mind that I'd been two different people, fat and thin. Which one was me?

"Whatever it was you did down at college," he said. "If you could bottle that. You'd be a millionaire today. Hell. I'd buy a bottle myself."

He took my arm—he was doing that those days, at steps and on the ice—and we walked out of the building and back to the car. I was glad we'd had that conversation, glad for what he had told me, especially glad he hadn't tried to deny it all. We had both been wrestling with our demons back in those days, in that case wrestling with the same demon. He was a cunning bastard too.

By the time I had gotten the Senator into the car and walked around to my side, I felt another question coming on. It had nothing particularly to do with the last one—except inasmuch as all our questions are connected—but that moment of honesty, when the air between us was clear, seemed the perfect time to ask it.

I got into the car and put in the key but didn't start it. I turned to him instead. "Why did you marry Mother?" I said. "Not to change the subject or anything."

He was still huffing from the exertion of our walk, his glasses slightly steamed. He reached up with a finger to wipe them.

"I've always wondered that," I said. "All my life."

"Every child wonders that," he said, "sooner or later. I certainly did, about my parents." He turned to me. "Why? Don't you think I should have?"

"She doesn't seem your type."

"Really?" The Senator burst into laughter.

"At least she didn't used to."

"What's my type?"

"You were always such a physical person. Hearty and robust. She was so . . ." Distant. Forbidding. Cold. "Delicate."

"Women are supposed to be that way, aren't they?"

"Are they?"

"I don't know. They used to be."

He let out another roar of laughter. The Senator seemed to find this subject hilarious.

"All those things you told me," I said. "The way her parents made you live in that house. The way your tastes are so different. She wanted that luxurious life. Dragged you off to those parties."

"All that came later," he said. "After we got married. At least after I proposed. Those are the kinds of things that always come up. The compromises you make."

"Didn't you give up too much in all that?"

"I don't know. What's too much?"

"You gave up who you really are."

"I don't think so. I'm still me."

The Senator was far more relaxed with this subject than I was.

"I do think it would have been better if I'd stood up to them more," he said. "Made my life easier. But I couldn't do that. I was too young and unsure of myself. It would have taken a hell of a man that age to stand up to old Commander Morse."

"So I gather."

"There were things I could have done better. But I loved your mother. I was far gone on her. I adored her. I couldn't believe she'd have me."

I had never heard my father say such a thing.

"She's an attractive woman now. Even now, in her sixties. But she was a beautiful woman when you were young. I don't know if you remember." I remembered. "And before that. When I met her. She was the belle of the ball. The most beautiful girl I'd ever seen. So gracious and sophisticated and smart. A fabulous dancer. I suppose she is more delicate than I am, but that's the way girls wanted to be in those days. Maybe things are different now. Nothing wrong with that. But back then women were these distant elusive creatures who you were supposed to pursue and never quite catch. In some ways I probably never did quite catch her. But that didn't change my mind about chasing her. Nothing could change my mind about that."

The Senator spoke these words without a moment's hesitation. They just rolled off his tongue.

"I didn't care if she was my type or not," he said. "I was just glad to have her. I was in love." The old man was grinning like a boy. "Don't you know what love is?"

One thing I liked about going to the Y in the afternoon was that it was just a few blocks from Andrea's store. If it was an afternoon when she was working—she had a crazy work schedule, which it took me a while to learn—I could go over and talk to her after my swim, or nurse a beer in a bar somewhere and wait for her to get off. She might give me a ride home if I had come down on the bus, or we could go out for a drink or for dinner. She only lived ten minutes from Helen's, so it was easy for us to get together, but I especially liked meeting her downtown, where there were dim crowded bars and good restaurants (especially if we crossed the river to Mount Washington). After all my years in the South, I found something especially romantic about an urban romance.

Not that I saw Andrea every day, or anything like it. Her four-year-old son lived with her half the time, and while I liked Chris, and he seemed to like me, Andrea wanted some time alone with him. She hadn't decided how she felt about sleeping with a man while Chris was in the house, so that eliminated half the nights in the week right there. It was also true that I wasn't the greatest person in the world to spend the night with. If I was at Andrea's house, I was up at the crack of dawn, wanting to get back to my writing desk. If she was at mine—I just had that one room—I wanted her to be out of there so I could work.

So we tended to see each other at odd hours. Andrea was actually just in the store slightly more than half time, but she had her son to raise and was still extremely active politically. She also worked part-time for a local accountant, typing letters, and answered the phone for him a couple of mornings a week.

"Is she really that low on money?" I asked her business partner, a woman named Karen, who dropped into the store from time to time.

"No. But she worries about it a lot. Especially since her separation."

"She drives herself."

"She always has. Always too much to do. Always on the go."

At the store she was often on the phone talking politics while simultaneously ringing up a customer and unpacking merchandise. It was not uncommon to find two or three of her political friends there for an informal meeting during working hours. She never seemed to do one errand without doing four or five others, and many of the times we got together she had just been one place and was on her way somewhere else. She liked brief intense encounters, and hated to be pinned down in advance. "Call me around lunchtime," she'd say, if I asked her out for even the next evening. There might be some political event, or a meeting, and she didn't want to miss out. She also hated having an evening where there was nothing to do.

She had an outrageous, dramatic side, and especially enjoyed our public encounters. She would hang all over me in a bar, batting her eyes at me, nuzzling my face, and in the store would announce, at 5:50, "Closing in ten minutes. My boyfriend and I have a date in the stockroom." She loved getting dressed up for dinner, which she would do right there in the store, with clothes that she'd brought from home, and it was when we were going to the most elegant places that she pulled her most outrageous stunts. "These are too tight," she'd say in the car on the way to some posh restaurant, and reach under her skirt to pull off a pair of black panties. "Put them in your pocket. *Don't* mistake them for your handkerchief." Once, after a particularly good dinner at an Italian restaurant—and an exceptional bottle of wine—she made me take her into a restroom and screw her while she leaned up against the sink. Another time, while we were snuggled up in the corner of a back booth, she reached under the tablecloth, took me out of my pants, and fondled me while I tried to keep a poker face (and my cock got as stiff as a poker).

There was one afternoon every week, though—Thursday—that we both had free, for two or three hours. We had a standing agreement to spend it in bed, usually at her place, occasionally at mine. I would arrive first—she was chroni-

DAVID GUY

cally late—and get a beer from the refrigerator, take off all my clothes and get under her big down comforter. When she got home she would get a beer too, maybe turn on some music. She often liked to take a shower, in the bathroom beside her bedroom. I would prop my head on some pillows and watch her dry herself. In my honor she would pay special attention to the thick bush of bright red hair between her legs, sometimes fluffing it out with a little brush. She would pick up her beer and walk toward the bed. Once she stepped right up on it, came and squatted down until her pussy was just above my mouth.

"It hurts," she said.

"It does?"

"It kind of aches. Kiss it and make it better."

Andrea was perfect for me in that regard. She enjoyed all kinds of playing around, but the thing she always looked forward to, the thing she positively yearned for ("Is it too soon to be doing this?" I once asked, as I crawled down between her legs. "Never," she said.) was also the one I liked the best. That was the only way she could come, but she always came that way, and she liked me to do it before we fucked. That way she could be relaxed, and fulfilled, and let herself go.

Her dramatic approach that one day—walking up on the bed—was not atypical. As she had that first day at the store, that first night at the hotel, she tended to come on as the aggressor, leaping onto the bed to kiss me, moving her mouth around my body like a little vacuum, biting and sucking my nipples, attacking my cock like a vicious predator. She smothered me with her body as she kissed me, clutching me tight, sometimes—on a whim—turned upside down ("See anything you like?"). For a man who all his life had felt women were holding themselves back from him, not really embracing him, not giving themselves, this was heaven. She also liked to be on top when we fucked, sometimes with elaborate squatting postures, facing away or—especially—facing me. She liked watching my reactions.

We hadn't been to bed too many times before she said something about that.

"Is this the way you like it?" she said. "The woman on top?"

"I like it. I haven't done it this way much."

184

"You haven't?"

"I haven't been with a woman like you before."

The understatement of the century.

"I thought *you* liked it," I said.

"Don't you ever have an urge to get on top?" she said.

"It crosses my mind." I hadn't thought we'd been establishing a lifelong pattern. "Would you like that?"

"I might." She dug her fingers into my chest. A little smile came over her face. "You'd have to fight me for it."

What followed were some of the most titanic struggles I've ever had with a woman, in or out of bed. I learned to let Andrea start the way she always had, coming on strong. As soon as she felt the slightest pressure from me, her whole body went on alert, and a light shone in her eye. Once we'd started to wrestle, she'd do anything she had to, punch, pound, slap, kick, bite (my balls, I hasten to add, were out of bounds). I couldn't actually let her win, of course. I liked to let her think she had a chance. She exulted in her strength, and loved the struggle. But the real feeling of satisfaction came over her face when I put her on her back and pinned her arms down. She loved to be overpowered.

"All right, you bastard," she'd say. "What are you going to do with me?"

"I'm going to fuck you."

"Oh God."

"I'm going to fuck you until you can't stand up. Until there's nothing left of you."

"Jesus."

"But first. Just to really drive you crazy. I'm going to fuck you with my tongue."

She had lost the battle and won the war.

She was *there* when we fucked; that was the thing about Andrea. When I had her on her back, arms pinned to the bed, she still wore a glow, staring up at me; the little motor in her hips was rumbling even after I subdued her, and once I thrust into her, she gave a sigh of relief—as if to say, "At last!"—and started to move on the bed like a bucking (or fucking) bronco.

It was on the third or fourth of those Thursday afternoons that I had a little talk with her.

"There's something I need to tell you about," I said. "Something I like. It's a little kinky."

"Uh oh."

"You don't have to do it with me. I'd like it if you did. But I do have to tell you. You have to know."

She didn't seem at all bothered by what I told her. She didn't seem surprised by it.

"I've known people who were into it," she said. "I never have been myself."

"But you'll try anything once."

"I don't know if I'd be good at it."

She was good. Some people seem to have an erotic imagination and some don't. Some are tuned in to the interplay of power in sex (Andrea obviously had no problem there) and some aren't. She thought she might pull back from hitting someone. It turned out she didn't.

We nearly always did it the same way. It would come to mind when we were in the midst of our lovemaking and I felt the need for something more. She would roll us on our sides, or throw me off and drape me over her knee, or force me to kneel on the bed while she picked up a belt. She really had no trouble hitting me at all. I could make it go on and on ("You stupid bitch. I didn't even feel that") or end it rather quickly ("I'll be good. I swear I'll be good. I'll eat you"). There was always a great deal of verbal byplay involved, and as much laughter as there were screams of pain. The screams were somewhat exaggerated.

We would fuck like crazy after that, fuck like animals, groaning and shouting and biting each other, our bodies soaked with sweat. By the time we had finished we'd be exhausted.

Once, when we were at my place, Helen was there when we came downstairs. I didn't know how long she had been in the house. She kept a perfectly straight face as she said hello to Andrea. We chatted a while, and she didn't say anything to me until several minutes after Andrea had left. Then she said, "I don't want to get too personal here. But do straight people always make that much noise?"

I kept a straight face too, as I considered the question. "The women do," I said. "I think it's something about the penis. It drives them into a frenzy."

"I almost called the police," she said.

Andrea was more affected by her monthly cycles than any other woman I had ever met. They split the month right in half, and she got progressively more closed up and irritated in the second half until, by the end of the month, she was spoiling for a fight. She didn't want to whip me with a belt. She wanted to squash my balls with a sledgehammer. She also got progressively weepier, bawled her eyes out the last couple of days. But once her period had actually started—she was a heavy, heavy bleeder—we had incredible sex, which left the sheets, pillowcases, bedpad, mattress, and often most of our bodies, covered with blood. We looked as if we had just fought for the middleweight championship of the world. Afterward we would take a shower and watch the blood-stained water flow down the drain.

Once when we were talking about using the belt, she said, "Should I pull it out of my pants with a flourish, the way my father did?"

"He did that?"

"He made a big production of it. It was part of the punishment."

"Then he used it on you?"

I hadn't had any idea she'd been punished that way.

"He made you bend over wherever you were. Over a chair or something. Then he pulled down your pants. He doubled up the belt."

"Did it hurt a lot?"

She laughed. "Charles. No pain I've felt since has even come close. Not childbirth. Not anything. I'd scream until I couldn't make a sound anymore. I'd scream until I couldn't see. But you didn't dare move. If he had to chase you it was much worse. He didn't care where he hit you."

She was still laughing, as if to say, Look what I've been through.

"The man was incredible," she said.

A couple of weeks after I had told her mine, she said, "I have a fantasy too."

We were lying in bed, sipping beer and talking.

"I've never told it to anyone," she said.

"How come?"

"It was mine. It was private. I didn't want anyone else in on it. Especially not a man. Although it was a man I'd have to do it with."

"But you want to now."

"If you promise never to tell anybody."

"Why now?"

"I don't know. I feel different. I feel different with you. You're not like the other men I've been with."

We were with new types.

"Besides," she said. "You told me yours."

It has always been one of my theories of human relations that what brings you close to someone is not hearing a confidence but telling one. You have given the other person a precious part of yourself. You have entrusted him with it.

I could see why she hadn't wanted her fantasy to get around. This woman who was aggressive in so many areas of her life, who was domineering and controlling, who was one of the most prominent leftist and feminist leaders in the city—a tireless advocate of personal freedom—liked to be tied up. She liked—after we had wrestled for control, and I had won—for me to hold her arms down and tie them to the bedposts. After that I could pinch her, bite her, tease her, berate her verbally, anything I wanted. She liked me to make a show of her helplessness. But what she wanted eventually was for me to pull the bonds tight, really stretch her out, and use my mouth on her. Winding up in a particular spot. Her body always buckled when she climaxed, collapsed into a fetal position, and what felt fabulous was when she was restrained from doing that, held so tight at the thighs that she couldn't move. After that—immediately— she was ready to be entered, really banged. I loved to kiss her while we fucked, and mutter all kinds of things down at her, that I was never going to come, I was going to fuck her all night, that I was going to leave her tied up for days, I would have my friends in to look at her, I would let them do things to her, I would let them watch me screw her.

"There's nothing I can do," she would say, glowing at the very idea. "I'm helpless."

She was very much involved while we did it, but sometimes felt sheepish afterward. She had never done all this before. She wasn't sure of her right to do it.

"This is so weird," she said once, when I was untying her.

"No it's not," I said.

"It is."

"It just seems that way when it's over."

"Why do you think I want it?"

"You're in control all day. Taking charge. You more than most people. It's natural to want to let down."

"I suppose." She was rubbing her wrists.

"That's a big part of being spanked for me. The surrender."

"Yeah."

"I don't want people to beat me out in the world. Out in my everyday life. But I like it here."

She leaned up to give me a little kiss.

"Also," I said. "You just like the feeling. You like it when things are rough."

"Right. So the question is. What am I doing with a wimp like you?"

We laughed, but that question wasn't entirely in jest. In the past she had always hooked up with men who mistreated her in the relationship. Their battles weren't play. She had an undeniable attraction to such men.

"I guess I just love you," she said.

That was something she said to me often. Two or three times every time we were together. I sometimes thought she said it too much, as if she were trying to remind herself, or convince herself.

But I loved her too. I have thought back through all the things that made me feel that way, searching for what was unique. There was my wish to rescue her from unhappiness, always a deadly trap for a man. There was my wish to show her that a man could be kind and gentle, but still exciting. I have sometimes thought there were certain physical facts that were irresistible to me: Her low husky voice, the pale color of her skin, the smell of her body. There was the way our bodies went together—a perfect fit—and the wild abandon of our sex life, in which anything was possible and everything felt right. I was never sure just what it was. But I knew I loved her. I never questioned that.

One afternoon in bed she said something that did more to explain her ambivalent attitude toward sex, toward the things we did in bed, toward men, than anything else she had told me. I had been telling her about some things Helen had been seeing in her clients, how a father's early emotional demands on a daughter—especially when his marriage wasn't working—could be practically as damaging as physical abuse. In certain ways it resembled physical abuse. Andrea had been nodding in agreement. "They all fuck you over," she said. When I finished she was quiet for a while, staring at the ceiling. Then she said, "He used to touch me."

I didn't have to ask who.

"He did?" I said.

"He used to get me to sit in his lap when I was a little girl. Watching TV or something. He said he liked having a little girl in his lap. I liked it too, at first. It was so warm and comforting. He would rub me all over, my belly and my legs, my chest. Wrap me in his arms. It felt so good. But then one evening, when nobody else was there, my mother was out in the kitchen, he touched me in a different way. His hand just reached up and did it. I didn't know what the hell was going on. I knew nobody was supposed to do that to me, that I wasn't supposed to let anybody do it. But this was my father, for God's sake. The person I was supposed to go to if somebody did it. I was afraid to say anything. I tried to squirm away, but as soon as I did his arms tightened around me. I couldn't move. He just kept touching me, rubbing that place. Very lightly and softly. It felt good, that was the thing. It felt good, but I knew we shouldn't be doing it. After that I didn't want to sit in his lap anymore, but he made me. He made me all the time. He made a big show of it, telling me to come sit with him, saying I was his little girl. It got to a point where he was doing it while everyone else was there. Everybody with their eyes on the television. I'd feel his arms tighten around me, and I'd know it was about to happen. After a while he'd actually go into my underpants. Up under the elastic on my leg. His finger would go inside me a little."

"God."

The bitterness and pain were pouring out of her. My arm was behind her head, but I didn't try to touch her any more than that. All her vibrations were telling me to stay away.

"He did it to me all the time, all through my childhood. Come sit in Daddy's lap. I used to hate those words." Her hand was cold and clammy when it rested on my thigh. "It made me want to grow up. I dreamed of the day when I'd be too old to sit in his lap. I couldn't wait to get out of that house. Once I did, I never wanted to go back."

NINE

So," Helen said. We had ordered moo shu pork as one of our entrees, and she had offered to fix me a serving. She did it all with chopsticks and spoons, just the way the waiters do, and handed over a perfect taco, tightly folded, not even leaking. She must have spent some time in the Orient. "Are you in love?"

"Not to beat around the bush or anything."

"I think I've been very discreet. I've been discreet for a couple of months."

"You have."

"I can't help wondering."

The truth of the matter was that we hadn't had dinner— we hadn't really talked—for weeks. I had never imagined such a thing would happen if I moved in with Helen. We were wonderful as housemates, never got in each other's way, but either I was busy in the evening or she was. Often we both were. If her girlfriend Cheryl was around, and I wasn't doing anything, I might talk to them for a while or even have dinner with them, but that wasn't the same as talking to Helen. I also felt that I should withdraw discreetly after a while and leave them alone. Cheryl would often spend the night. Lying in bed later, reading a book, I would hear quiet laughter coming up through the heating ducts, soft moans, the rustle of sheets. It was music to my ears.

"I'm afraid I am," I said.

"You're afraid?"

"It's rather unsettling."

Helen smiled. "It's supposed to be."

I took a big bite of moo shu pork. One of the few adequate consolations for the pain of love.

"In a lot of ways it's ideal," I said. "I'd be the envy of most men. I even envy myself a little. We both have our own lives. We see each other when we feel like it. The time we spend together is usually good. It's always intense. I look forward to it all day, think about it for hours afterward."

"Sounds wonderful."

"The problem is that there's no background to what we're doing. No context. Neither of us knows how long we'll be together, or how long I'll be around, or what I'm even doing here. Even I wonder that. You must wonder."

"You haven't been a bit of trouble. Even less than I thought you'd be. You can stay forever as far as I'm concerned."

"When you come right down to it, I'm just hanging around with my father. There's no crisis anymore. We're just riding around in his Lincoln."

"What's wrong with that?"

"It's a funny reason to live someplace."

It didn't sound funny to Helen. The boys down at the corporate headquarters might have found it a little weird. The boys in the law firm.

"I've thought of moving back here," I said.

"Really?"

"What's keeping me in North Carolina? I have friends down there. All the things you worry about leaving. But it hasn't interfered with my work to be here. I just fly out of a different airport. Mail things from a different post office. I have so much here that I don't have there. Family, for one thing. For the first time in my life it's not a strain to be around them. Then there's this woman."

"I think it's the woman we're really talking about."

You couldn't put much over on Helen.

I thought I should get to what was really bothering me.

"There's this look in Andrea's eyes," I said. "A scared frightened look. You don't always see it. You have to sneak up on it. I know it comes out of her experience. I think I even know what it comes from. But when she's with me. Although she really wants to be with me. There's a part of her that's looking for the door."

Helen paused over what I had said. It didn't need a glib answer.

"I can almost see her trying to calm herself," I said. "Telling herself it's all right. Things are going to be fine. But there's this scared little animal in there that wants to bolt."

"I know the look you're talking about," Andrea said. "I've seen it in clients, when they're getting down to the real issues. The question is, does *she* know it's there?"

That was what I didn't know.

"A person can come to terms with that feeling," she said. "Bring it to consciousness and decide not to act on it. Although it's always there somewhere."

"The thing of it is, she always *is* running. Comes flying in and goes flying out. She's very intense when she's with me. I feel that she's really there. But she's always got someplace to go."

"She just got out of a difficult marriage. She's not sure how involved she wants to get. She needs time."

What I wasn't mentioning to Helen was something on my side, probably because I hadn't admitted it to myself. I honestly did believe that, when I met Andrea, I had come to terms with my past with women. I don't mean that I had resolved the conflicts—what would that be like?—but that I'd taken a hard look at them and seen where they'd come from. It seemed both ironic and appropriate that, after looking for a woman like Andrea for so many years, I had only found her once I had stopped looking. What worried me was the possibility that, in finding her, I was buying back into an old way of being.

Before I'd met Andrea I would have said, I don't need that anymore, by which I would have meant that I knew I couldn't get it, I couldn't get some physical affection from far back in my life that I hadn't gotten then. All the women in the world couldn't give me that. The question was whether, in embracing Andrea, a part of me was still trying to get that. Every time I felt a pang at one of her sudden departures, every time I saw that look of fear in her eyes, I wondered. As I lay in bed with Andrea, our bellies pressed together—her soft strong belly, which she was always so ready to press to mine—I felt that old wound of mine healing over, because I had an abundance of what I had once wanted, and I wondered: Would the wound open again if her body were ripped away?

"Have you talked to her about moving back?" Helen said.

"Not seriously. As something I actually might do. She sometimes says she hates the thought that I'll be leaving someday."

"That's a good sign."

"She says it in the context that I will be leaving."

"She'd probably be scared if you moved."

"Hell, I'd be scared. I don't think I'd want to connect it to her. Just do it for my own reasons."

Helen frowned, and bit her lip.

"There's something wrong with that?" I said.

"If it's connected with her it's connected. She should know."

"But you just said. It'll scare her."

"She's got to face that fear."

Helen believed in playing hardball. She was always trying to get people to define their fears and face them.

"All this sounds a little like Cheryl and me," she said.

"I was wondering. Now that you're getting so snoopy."

"I haven't tried to hide anything. You haven't asked."

"I'm asking."

"Well. We've been together a year and a half. Almost two years. I know that Cheryl cares for me, and I adore her"—Cheryl was a slender, blondish woman, younger than Helen, bright and attractive—"but actually getting together, living as a couple, has been a problem. She was married for a while when she was younger, probably too young, and she lost all her power in that relationship. Her husband went out and made the money while she stayed home and worked on her art." Cheryl did pencil and charcoal drawings and watercolors. "If she wanted money she had to go to him. He sometimes complained about how much she wanted. Even if he didn't complain she felt funny. It was like being a child again."

"This situation is not unheard of."

"There were other problems too. But when she got out of the marriage, it was a big deal for her to be out on her own. Making her own money. Living by herself. That was why she stopped seeing men. They all seemed to want to take her over. Her independence was more important to her."

"Sure."

"So she turned to women. Who she felt would understand her problem. And they do. But Cheryl just works in a frame shop. Does her artwork on the side. The problem with me is the same one she'd have with a man. I'm more successful in the world's eyes. More powerful. I have more money. I'm older. I tend to be the dominant partner anyway." It was hard to imagine anyone—male or female—outshining Helen. "She worries that, if she moved in with me, I'd take her over the way a man would. I'd take the power from her."

There was probably some truth to that.

"She wouldn't move, for instance, until we could split the expenses right down the middle. The house payment. Groceries. Everything. And she can't do that. Not even half of my expenses.

"I could move into a place she can afford. Some tiny apartment, like I lived in years ago. I can't bring myself to want to do that."

"No."

"In the meantime, I'd love to be taking her on trips. Buying her clothes. Lavishing her with expensive presents. I'd like to move her in here and spend the rest of my life with her. But I can't."

"Now you know how those men felt."

"Please."

"It's partly just the situation. It doesn't matter who the person is. The situation is difficult."

"I suppose."

"Do you ever stay at her place?"

"I used to. She wanted all that to be equal too. But it was so small and cramped. Even the bed was small. I couldn't get to sleep. And there wasn't as much to do over there. At my place we can watch a movie. Listen to music. Just go off and be by ourselves if we want. It's much more comfortable."

We were smiling at each other. There was a certain irony to all this.

"I thought you dykes had everything all figured out," I said. "Everything was smooth."

"I'm afraid not."

"You were my last hope."

She laughed. "It'll all work out in time, I think. Or it won't."

"It will. She's crazy about you." I could see that when they were together.

By that time Helen and I had finished our food, and the restaurant had largely cleared out. The waiter had taken our plates, stacking them right up his arms—I was always amazed at the way Chinese waiters could do that—and brought us a second pot of tea. I sat back and relaxed. Helen was still leaning over the table.

"There was something you were going to tell me," I said.

"It's more fun to talk about this other stuff. It's also easier." She poured a cup of hot tea, took a sip, and looked up at me. "I think things are about to get hard again for Father at work."

My heart sank as I heard those words. I had almost put it out of my mind that the Senator was having problems at work. It was much easier to ride around in the car with him and talk about his past, pretend his troubles didn't exist.

He had started back to work for a couple of days a week, just a few hours at a time. Sometimes, if it fit with my schedule at the Y—and he would arrange things so it did—we would go home together. He always seemed more tired after work than at any other time. Grumpy and disgruntled, or worse than that. Brooding. I said something about it once.

"Are you sure you want to be doing this?"

"What?"

"Going to work these days."

"Oh, probably not as much as I used to. I got out of the habit."

"You don't have to."

"Don't I?" He smiled.

"You have all the money you need. You could retire."

"That's been true for a long time."

"Do you ever consider it?"

"I never did before. I've thought about it some lately. But

even if I did retire, if I decided right now, there would be things I'd have to do."

"What if you didn't do them?"

"I have to do them."

"What if you couldn't do them?"

"I'd still have to do them."

"What if you died?"

He glared at me. "In that case, I suppose, I wouldn't have to do them. But if I don't die, if I'm lucky enough not to die in the next few months, they have to be done."

"They're not worth having another heart attack, is all I'm saying."

"I'm not going to have another heart attack."

"They're not worth making your life miserable."

That was the mood that Helen had kept seeing him in before he got sick.

"I'm just having trouble getting back," he said. "I'm not in shape. I'll get used to it."

I had the feeling that what Helen was about to tell me was not unconnected to the work he had to get done.

"That lawyer friend of mine called," she said. "She says this thing is heating up again. She wanted me to know before it's splattered all over the papers."

"That's going to happen?"

"Once the suit is filed. She says it's going to be big. There's no way it wouldn't be, considering who's involved."

"Why all of a sudden?"

"She doesn't know. That's the one thing her friend won't say. John Auerbach. The lawyer who's representing the other side."

I almost had to remind myself what the whole thing was about, so much time had passed. It had a way of slipping out of my mind. The ex-wife of the zoning commissioner, who had been divorced years before, claimed that she hadn't gotten enough money. A lawyer from the Senator's firm hadn't gotten her a big enough settlement. And now she had decided, all this time later, that the reason she hadn't gotten enough was that the firm had been giving the zoning commissioner a break. They had gone easy on him in return for a favor: that he would give another of the firm's clients, developer Frank Weyland, a favorable ruling on a zoning change.

"Up until now," Helen said, "it's just been one person's word against another's. Everyone agrees the woman didn't get enough money. That's apparently obvious on the face of it. And it's a matter of record that Weyland got the zoning change. But now this John Auerbach claims he can put the two together. He can show they're connected. And if he can, the firm's in trouble. Father's in trouble."

That was apparently what he'd been referring to when he talked to me. That no matter what, even if he retired, he'd have to do this.

"Who else knows about this?" I said.

"I assume our brothers do. At least the ones in the firm. It sounds like every lawyer in Pittsburgh knows. I assume Mother doesn't know. If Father hadn't told her before."

If anything, he would be more reluctant now.

"What can we do?" I said.

"I don't know. I don't think there's anything to do, with this lid of silence on it all. Father hasn't said anything to you?"

"Not really. He did speak, very indirectly, of some problems at work."

"He must be very lonely with this. But I just wanted to tell you, so you'd know how he might be feeling. And I still think, if it's about to hit all the papers. If it's going to be as big as my friend said. That we'll be able to talk about it then. We'll have to talk about it. And we can be of some help to Father at that point, if only to let him know he's not so alone."

I wish I could have felt the same way as Helen. Once she had decided what the limits of the situation were—what she could and couldn't do for the Senator—she was satisfied. I somehow wanted to know the truth. Not the truth of what the Senator might tell me, or even what the courts might decide, but the truth of what had happened. I wanted to know the truth of my father's life. I don't know why that was—it hadn't much concerned me in the past—or why Helen was different. She wanted to know how she could help our father. I wanted to know what he had done.

I could have gone to my brothers, of course. Two of them were in the law firm, and must have known something about that suit. I somehow didn't want to speak to them. For one thing, they hadn't seen fit to come to me with this information, or to Helen. They didn't seem to think we could handle it. They weren't treating me like a big brother those days, more like an uncle or something, and an increasingly bewildered and befuddled uncle at that. You had to humor this guy. He didn't have a wife. He didn't have a job. He didn't have a BMW or a membership at the country club. The poor old boy was on his last legs.

But there was no problem getting an appointment with Mr. Harrold, the lawyer in the firm who had worked with the Senator on the case. I had known him all my life, had seen him a couple of times when I went to pick up the Senator. I chose an afternoon when I knew the Senator wouldn't be in— he was seeing his doctor—and asked the secretary not to let him know of my appointment. This was between Mr. Harrold and me.

Mr. Harrold had always seemed the odd man out in the firm. He was a tall thin angular man, with wire-framed spectacles and short brown hair peppered with gray. He was quiet and deliberate, always wore dark, vested suits and carried a pocket watch. He walked with his arms straight at his sides, a slightly backward-leaning posture, and a careful tread, as if he were walking on eggshells. Helen, who had first noticed this fact, referred to him as Mr. Shells when she was a girl and once mistakenly called him that to his face. He had the curious nervous gesture of taking a folded handkerchief from his pocket and wiping his mouth, though his lips were always dry as a desert. He had been perfectly friendly with us when we were young, though he'd never seemed to know what to say. If someone had told me that his only job at the firm had been drawing up wills, that would have seemed perfectly appropriate. But the Senator said he had an incredible legal mind. He was an invaluable asset to the firm.

Like the other partners, he had his own wing in the offices and his own secretary, a massive battle-ax named Mrs. Barclay who had been with the firm almost as long as he had. I have no doubt that if a client gave him a hard time she would body slam the poor bastard and stomp him into submission. She showed me into Mr. Harrold's office, which was done over in brown—wouldn't you know—with a huge wide desk and plush comfortable furniture. He was doing some paperwork when I came in. You had the feeling he hated to be taken away from it.

He made the obligatory small talk after we shook hands—asked after my mother and Helen—then waited for me to speak.

"I wanted to ask you about this lawsuit against my father," I said.

The man didn't blink an eye. There was some advantage to being a living mannequin.

"I wasn't aware a lawsuit had been filed," he said.

"The one that's about to be filed then. Whatever." Already the man had caught me on a technicality.

"He told you about it."

"No. I don't think he's even told my mother. Helen found out."

"Helen?"

"From a lawyer friend of hers." A lesbian lawyer. They're out to get you, man.

"I suppose word of it is being bandied about." He smiled slightly and indulgently. This, you had the feeling, was a man who never gossiped.

"She says it'll be in all the papers."

"I'm sure it will. If the suit is actually filed."

"I thought maybe you could tell me if it's true."

He honestly didn't seem to know what I was asking him. "What?"

"Did my father do this thing? Screw some woman out of her divorce settlement so he could help a rich client."

He gave me that condescending smile again. "I don't think that's the way the suit will read."

"However it reads."

He was sitting with his fingertips touching, his hands in front of his chest. His gaze didn't meet mine.

"That's for the court to decide," he said. "If it isn't settled out of court beforehand. As I think it probably will be."

Maybe this hadn't been the right person to come to after all.

"Mr. Harrold. My father did this thing or he didn't."

"Why don't you ask him?"

"My mother asked me not to. That was the first thing she

said when I got to town. Please don't bring up this thing at work."

That wasn't the real reason. The Senator and I were getting along well enough that I didn't care what the Duchess thought. The truth of the matter was that I was afraid the charges were true, and he would have to tell me. Or that he would lie, and I would see the lie. I was afraid of losing all the good feeling that had built up between us during the last two months. I wanted to know the truth, but I didn't want to hear it from him. I didn't want to have that confrontation.

"She thinks it might impede his recovery," I said.

"Well," Mr. Harrold said. "I don't know quite what to tell you. I've worked with your father for over thirty years. I know him as well as anyone in the firm. I have no reason to believe he'd engage in any kind of wrongdoing."

It occurred to me that he might not know the truth. It might be better for him not to know.

"What can you tell me about the suit?" I said.

"I can tell you about the attorney involved. Robert Parnell."

"Which attorney is this?"

"The one who's named in it. Who handled the divorce action."

"I don't remember him."

"He wasn't here long. Three or four years, just out of school. He was the kind of person we always get. Top grades in school. Very competitive and successful. A good-looking young man. A hard worker. He'd be in his offices when you got here, and when you left."

That was what the firm expected from its young associates. Total devotion.

"If he had a problem, it was with personal relations. He could do any amount of paperwork. You just shoveled it into his office and it came out perfect. But there was something frantic about him. A slightly wild look in his eyes. It could be uncomfortable sitting in a room with him. He had so much drive."

A complaint no one had ever made about Mr. Harrold.

"Where is he now?" I said.

"At another firm in town. A smaller firm. Men his own age. It wasn't working out with us. He didn't inspire that feeling of calm and confidence that a client needs. You can't teach personality."

Living proof of that statement was sitting right before me.

"Is it true what they're saying?" I said. "That he didn't get enough money for the woman."

"I think there's no question of that."

"Why isn't she suing him?"

"She is. Him and the firm that employed him. It's standard procedure."

"And he's claiming it wasn't his fault."

"The charge is preposterous on the face of it. That the head of a large and respected law firm would come to one of his lowliest associates and advise him to engage in malpractice. But the situation is just tangled enough. Since it vaguely involves this other client, whom everybody is always attacking anyway. It might have a slight air of plausibility. To someone who doesn't know your father."

"Who decided there might be a connection?"

"I don't know. The wronged woman brought the suit. Anna Jennings. That's one of the situation's mild ironies. She's a waitress at Nino's. That used to be one of your father's favorite restaurants. Now he won't go there at all."

It was true. Nino's was a place he might have taken me in the past. He hadn't even mentioned it.

"I'm sure it isn't easy being a waitress," he said, "although they probably do all right at Nino's. But somebody, somewhere, must have told her she could have gotten more money from her husband. Maybe now she could find some other way to get it. So she wouldn't have to work so hard. I wish they'd told her years ago. It would have saved us all a lot of trouble."

"You were ready to settle the malpractice suit."

"We were offering something. Not a whole lot. The statute of limitations has long since run out on that. They wouldn't get a cent in court. You have to wonder if this conspiracy thing isn't just a ploy to get more money. The statute of limitations on that only begins when the supposed conspiracy is discovered."

"Will you offer more?"

"Probably. But not too much. That's like an admission of

wrongdoing. It's up to your father. I'm sure he'll do what's best."

It seemed obvious to me that this was the matter that had been bothering the Senator, accounting for his dark moods after work.

"Was there anything funny about this other thing? With the developer?"

"Frank Weyland. No. It was a much bigger matter, of course. An important moment for him, and he's been an important client for us. He was an important client even then. But we did what we always do. Prepared a careful presentation for the hearings, which showed how the development would benefit the community. Lobbied the zoning commission. Your father did most of that. He's better in a one-on-one situation. I'm better in a courtroom." The Senator could glad-hand you to death. "There was a public outcry, as there always is. People are so resistant to change." This from a man who still carried a pocket watch. "But I think that if you went to that community today, if you asked people their honest opinions, they'd tell you they like their shopping mall."

They probably would. The malls themselves have gone a long way toward diminishing public taste.

"So Father would have met with this man."

"Who?"

"The zoning commissioner."

"Oh, absolutely. I met with him too. Someone as important as that. We gave him all kinds of attention. That doesn't mean there was a conspiracy. That was business as usual."

Sometimes I thought business as usual was a conspiracy.

It was interesting how much clearer all this seemed when you could attach a few personalities to it. An ambitious young lawyer with a wild look in his eye. A waitress at Nino's.

Mr. Harrold took out his watch. Not the most subtle of gestures.

"I'm taking up your time," I said.

"Not at all. I'm always happy to talk to a member of the family." He did, nevertheless, get up to see me to the door. "I hope I've been able to shed some light on this for you."

"You've been very helpful."

"I know you'd like to discover the truth of this matter.

You're in a profession where people still seek after truth."
Journalism? Was he kidding? "But in the legal profession
things are much fuzzier. The truth is there somewhere, in
theory, but more important are the attorneys all around it.
Jockeying for position. The real question is which one of them
is smarter. Bolder. Stronger. Who will make the right deci-
sions. It's extremely interesting. It's exciting, especially when
there's money involved. It isn't necessarily a process that
brings out the truth."

He wouldn't get any argument from me.

"Your father's one of the best. I wouldn't worry about him."

It was because he was one of the best that I was worried
about him.

"There's a part of me that wishes he weren't handling this
himself," he said. "Especially since he's been ill. It's not really like him."

"What?"

"Taking something on himself. Trying to do it all. But he's
quite insistent. It's his reputation that's at stake, he says.
There's an old saying about that. To the effect that, a man
who acts as his own attorney . . ."

Holy shit. Mr. Harrold was telling a joke. One I'd heard a
million times, but still.

". . . has a fool for a client."

I choked out a brief laugh. "I'm sure there's some truth to
that."

"Not in this case, Charles. Not in this case."

TEN

Andrea's house—a funny little stone place in Point Breeze, on one of those little side streets up off Willard—had been bought by her in-laws. It was a way they had of helping out the newlyweds, who wouldn't have been able to afford a house (Andrea was still a reporter in those days, and Arthur had a modest salary as an associate professor). It was also a good investment for them. They had put a lot of money down, and Andrea and Arthur had paid the small mortgage payment as rent.

After she and Arthur split up, staying in that house became an obsession with Andrea. It suddenly seemed the one piece of stability in her life, and in her son's. She had put a great deal of work into it and wasn't going to let her sleazy prick of a husband walk out on her for another woman and get the house too. The first thing she told him when they broke up was that she was staying and he was leaving. It wasn't a negotiable point.

But the situation was delicate. It was, after all, his parents who owned the place, and her relations with them had always been stormy at best. The agreement about the house had

DAVID GUY

never been spelled out in great detail when Arthur was there. After the breakup Andrea felt that things had to be more formal. She eventually decided that the only way she could feel really secure was if she bought the house from them. She made Arthur go to them with such a proposition. It was a long slow process—they liked having the investment—but finally they agreed, and set a price. All Andrea had to do was get together a down payment that would leave her with a reasonable mortgage.

She had been so exultant when her in-laws agreed to sell the place that I was slow to see how much anxiety the whole transaction was costing her. She had never bought a house before, and—what with her persistent fears about money—it was no easy task. She began to work more hours for the accountant. The day when the appraiser came to see the house was a major trauma, as were her multiple meetings at the bank. She got her mother to make her a temporary loan so she would have plenty of money in savings; she made it sound as if her part-time jobs were much more substantial than they were, and she exaggerated the prospects for the store. She seemed to think that if she didn't manipulate this situation for all it was worth she and Chris would be out on their ears, though her business partner Karen told me that her financial situation was fine and that she would easily get the loan, which turned out to be true. The closing was on a Thursday, the day we usually saw each other. She still wanted to meet— we could celebrate, she hoped—but she didn't know when she would get there.

I didn't mind. Andrea's house had always seemed a sanctuary to me, and I felt perfectly at home there. It was removed from city traffic, off on a little side street. It was bright—with large wide windows and a huge picture window in front—and had shiny hardwood floors. It was a trifle underfurnished (the Duchess would have said it was empty), mostly from used furniture stores, but that also made it feel simple and homey. Andrea heated only with wood, so even in March the place felt chilly. I got the woodstove going and sat down with a beer.

I could certainly see why she wanted to stay in that place.

She came in at the back, as she always did, and when she first stepped into the living room I thought the deal hadn't gone through. Her face was hollow-eyed and drained of color. I stood to meet her. "Charles," she said, and rushed into my arms. Her body was actually trembling. She burst into tears. "Thank God I'll never have to deal with that son of a bitch again."

One other factor in her mood was that she was about to start her period. I kept my own records on that.

"What son of a bitch?" I said.

"Arthur's father. Do you know what that old cocksucker did, right there in the bank?"

"What?"

"He tried to have a clause put in the contract about seeing his grandson. How often he'll get to see his grandson."

I didn't understand. "In a real-estate contract?"

"He's sitting in the lawyer's office moaning and groaning over a house he's never even lived in, and he says he's afraid that if he sells it to me I won't have anything to do with him anymore, he won't ever see his grandson again. He tries to have some kind of visitation rights written into the contract."

"What did the lawyer say?"

"He was startled, to say the least. He tried to tell the old bastard it would hold everything up, it would be very complicated to word, it didn't belong in this kind of contract. Nothing would quiet the man, he kept raving away like a lunatic, said he wouldn't sign until the clause was in there. Finally I had to sit there, in front of all those people, and promise the old putz that he could see his grandson once a week for the rest of his life. I had to solemnly swear. I'd have said anything at that point. I'd have solemnly kissed his wrinkled old ass."

She had stood back to look at me. Tears still flowed from her eyes, but she was also starting to laugh.

"Is there any truth to this?" I said.

"What?"

"That you wouldn't let him see Chris."

"He can see Chris when Chris is with Arthur. He doesn't have to take up my time. The worthless bastard's his son, for Christ's sake."

"So what's the problem?"

"He must be afraid I'll take Chris from Arthur. Which I

would gladly do. To teach that two-timing cocksucker a lesson."

"But you won't."

"Who knows? Let them sweat it out. Let them sweat bullets over there. The poor old bastard's hysterical."

Look who's talking.

Andrea had stopped sobbing and dried her eyes on the handkerchief I gave her. She had an almost instantaneous recovery time from her crying fits. We sat together on the couch. She grabbed my beer and took a big slug.

"So everything went okay," I said.

"If that's your idea of okay."

"I mean, you got the house."

"The bank got the house. I get to give them some money every month and live there."

"Andrea. The deal went through."

"The deal went through. The deal went through."

"Congratulations!" I gave her a big kiss. It tasted slightly salty at that point.

"Oh Charles." Tears poured from her eyes again. "What if I can't make the payments?"

Shortest celebration on record.

Andrea never could put her mind at ease. There was always something to worry about.

"You can make the payments. You worked out a payment you can make."

"I hope I can make it."

"You know you can make it."

"It's so much more than I've been paying."

"You're making more than you've been making."

I knew what to say here. I'd said it all dozens of times.

"What if I lose one of my part-time jobs?"

"You'll get another." Andrea could pick up a job at the drop of a hat.

"What if the store fails? We move to Shadyside and go belly up?"

"That'll never happen. You'll make more money in Shadyside. Much more."

"We'll also be paying twice as much rent."

"It's the right business move. Karen won't let you make it until she knows you can."

Karen had a superb business mind. Andrea knew that.

"Small businesses go under all the time. It could happen to anybody."

"If that happens I'll help you."

"How?"

"I'll give you money."

"You don't have any money."

"I have some. And I can borrow from my father."

"What if you're not here when it happens?"

"What if I am?"

"What if you've moved back to North Carolina?"

"What if I don't?"

"I mean two years from now. Three years from now."

"What if I don't move back to North Carolina? I stay here for good. Not with my sister. I move into a place of my own."

That wasn't the way I would have brought it up. In the context of a house closing and her fury at her father-in-law and her premenstrual hysteria. But I had been thinking about this possibility for a long time, wanting to talk to Andrea about it, and suddenly, in the midst of that conversation, the words popped out.

"You're thinking of that?" Andrea said.

"I am. I have been for some time."

"Charles. That would be wonderful."

I believed that, in the moment Andrea said those words, she meant them. Her tears had stopped, and she was smiling. She wore a sudden flush of happiness.

"Everything's so much different than when I came here," I said. "My father's feeling good. We're getting along better than we ever have. Things aren't too strained with my mother. My work's going well. I don't even miss North Carolina. And there's a lot more to do here. So many more opportunities."

Her smile diminished just slightly. She touched a hand to my shoulder. "So you wouldn't be moving for me."

That was the crux of the matter. The very question Helen had raised. So much seemed to depend on it.

"Would you want me to?" I said. "Be moving for you?"

"I don't know. I hadn't really thought about it. I'd just like to know what's true."

I would never have thought of moving if it hadn't been for Andrea. It would never have crossed my mind.

"I wouldn't be moving *for* you," I said. "Because you need me."

"That isn't what I meant."

"Well. The fact that you're here has a lot to do with it, yes."

I love you Andrea I adore you I've never been so happy with a woman I want to stay with you forever.

"I don't want to put pressure on you," I said.

"I know."

"I don't want to make you nervous."

She moved from where she'd been sitting—close to me—to lean back against some pillows on the couch. She was still holding her handkerchief, but her eyes were dry. The smile was almost gone from her face.

"We need to talk about what kind of relationship we're going to have," she said, "if you do that."

I hadn't said all this in the way I felt it. My quiet reasonable tone was a lie. I also hadn't gotten the reaction I'd expected. I'd been hoping for unconstrained joy. I thought she'd rip my clothes off on the spot.

"What do you mean?" I said.

"Well. This has been wonderful. Some of the happiest moments of my life. Also some of the hottest. But it's been kind of a shipboard romance. It hasn't had a future."

"Do you want it to?"

"If we can decide how we want it to be."

I couldn't understand the change in her mood. I suddenly felt about a thousand miles away from her.

"We have to decide that right now?"

"Not all of it. Maybe some of it."

"Like what?"

"Like whether or not we're going to see other people."

I stared at her. I couldn't believe my ears.

"Since when has that been an issue?" I said.

"Since about two minutes ago. Since you said you were staying. This is wonderful news, Charles. But it changes things."

"When I came to Pittsburgh you weren't seeing anybody. You were acting like you never wanted to see a man again."

She smiled and shook her head. "I was a real zombie."

"Apparently things have changed."

"Would you have wanted them to stay that way?"

"Do you want to see somebody else?"

"I didn't say that. I said we need to decide in general."

Nobody ever decides that question in general.

We shouldn't have been having that discussion. We were on different wavelengths, talking from different places. If there had been a referee around, he'd have sent us off to different corners.

"How do you feel about it?" I said.

"I've never been in a monogamous relationship in my life. Not even when I was married."

This apparently startling statement should not, strictly speaking, have startled me. Andrea had told me bits and pieces of things she'd done when she was married. She'd told me, for instance, that she had resolved not to fuck other men—she must have really wanted this marriage to work—but had done everything but with a couple of men, friends of Arthur's (wonderful friends). She didn't get specific, but told me that she and the guy had both had their clothes off and had been satisfied, so I assumed—knowing Andrea—that she blew him. Thereby, in her mind, avoiding adultery. You've got to draw the line somewhere.

But the major involvement during her marriage had been with a woman. I had picked that up in bits and pieces too, hadn't put it all together (I still haven't). Andrea had made it sound like just another part of her political and feminist education. She had been hanging around some radical women—as she tended to do—and one of them, named Ceci, attached herself to Andrea and began to lecture her on the multifarious crimes of men. She told her that involvement with women was much different, more egalitarian and correct; you had to experience it to know what it was like. (This was, among other things, a great line.) No real feminist—no real woman—would let a man get on top of her and put that miniature warhead in her (and then let it detonate, for Christ's sake!). All this had been right out in the open. Apparently even Arthur had been interested. He was always fascinated by a new political viewpoint. In time, however, it began to drive him nuts. Not only was his wife fucking somebody else, she was fucking somebody who was telling her what shits men were. At least a man wouldn't have done that. It was Andrea who finally ended the affair. Ceci had wanted her to divorce Arthur and move once and for all into the world of women. Apparently Andrea just liked cocks too much. It was a failing in her.

The reason the marriage had ended, therefore, was nothing if not ironic. Arthur hadn't wanted to split up; he had simply wanted to have an affair. With another woman, just as she had done. He had thought she would see the essential justice of this proposal. At the first mention of it she threw him out on his ass.

I didn't actually piece all that together until months later, of course. When I did, I couldn't believe the nerve Andrea had, the way she had so casually rearranged the facts.

It wasn't that I thought that what Andrea was bringing up—or what she had done—was wrong. My own history was checkered enough that I tried never to judge someone else. We weren't dealing with a rational drive here. But I had never been so cold-blooded about it. I hadn't plotted it out beforehand. And I certainly wasn't hoping to behave that way again. I wanted to find what I needed with one woman.

"You mean like, with Ceci?"

"That's one example."

"I don't think it would bother me if you wanted to go with a woman."

The idea was vaguely exciting.

"That isn't what I meant. The lesbian community doesn't approve of that kind of moving back and forth."

Oh shit. We wouldn't want to offend them.

"So you're talking about men."

"That's what's left."

"Is there somebody you want to fuck?"

"I didn't say that."

"Is there somebody you have fucked?"

"I'm bringing up the general principle."

"Why bring up the principle if there's nobody you want to do it with? What are you going to do, go out and find somebody?"

"I don't have to find somebody. I meet men all the time. In my political work, or they come to the store."

"Like who?"

"Nobody in particular. I'm just saying."

"Then why bring it up?"

"Like Mitchell Dantry, then."

Mitchell Dantry was a friend from one of her political organizations. He had a son about Chris's age, and they all got together sometimes so the kids could play. He and Andrea swapped day-care.

"You want to fuck him?"

"You're so much like a man. All these accusations."

I am a man, you twit.

"So why are you bringing him up?"

"You keep asking for an example."

"Are you interested in him?"

"He's fucking two other women. Two that I know of. He's notorious around here. But that's the kind of person I run into. That's the kind of man who's around."

So what's the big attraction?

"You keep saying you love me," I said. "You've never met another man like me. You've never had this experience."

"I haven't."

"So why do you want to fuck somebody else?"

"I'm not talking about an emotional involvement. I'm talking about getting laid. I'm not interested in men. I'm interested in cocks."

"Oh?"

"I like the way it feels when they go inside me."

The truth of the matter was that Andrea wanted to know that men were attracted to her. Not that they liked or cared for her, but that they wanted her. That was very important to how she got along with them. And the only way she really knew that, the only way she believed it, was if that thing got hard and went inside her.

This whole conversation had an uneasy, sticky feeling to it, as if it were really about something else. I was angry that she wanted to fuck somebody else, and she seemed angry too, possibly—as I look back on it—at the fact that I hadn't said I was moving because of her, although I also felt sure that such a profession would have scared the shit out of her. There was an air of embarrassment around this conversation. There was something fundamentally dishonest about it.

"How did we get started on this?" Andrea said.

"You brought it up."

"I did?"

"After I said I might be moving."

"I was so surprised." She moved toward me and took my hand. "I had no idea."

"Would you rather I didn't?"

"Of course not. I'm delighted with the idea. I just need to get used to it." She moved closer. "This might not have been the perfect way to bring it up."

"I know. I shouldn't have. It just slipped out."

I should never have sat on it for so long.

"Do you want to leave?" she said.

"Do you want me to?"

"No. But let's not talk about this anymore. Let's defer the subject to another time."

"All right."

"I'm sorry I brought it up. To say the very least."

"Let me say just one more thing."

"Okay."

"When you fuck this other guy. This theoretical other guy. This cock." This dick.

"Yes?"

"Put a rubber on it."

All of this seemed much more serious because of the times we lived in. I'm not sure it really was. It had always been a life-or-death matter. Now we could see that fact more clearly.

"I will. But remember. It's still just a theoretical cock."

That, as it turned out, was the only actual lie she had told me in the whole conversation.

I decided to stop talking at that point. There are whole discussions that should be done not with words, but with growls and grunts. Words just get you in trouble. They lead down unexpected and perilous paths. Andrea and I should have been snorting like baboons at that point, howling like banshees, not discussing a matter important to our futures. We shouldn't have started on words in the first place, what with the mood she was in. She should have walked in that room and started screaming.

I did then what I probably should have done the moment she came in. I put a pillow on the floor at her feet, and knelt on the pillow, and pulled up the beautiful blue skirt she had worn to impress the people at the house closing, and pulled off her immaculate white panties. I spread those legs that were never reluctant to part and knelt between them.

I was angry at Andrea at that moment, far angrier than I was admitting even to myself. A part of me kept saying it had been a hard day for her, a hard few weeks, that she was about to start her period, she shouldn't be held responsible for her mood. Another part wanted to bite her head off. But I wasn't angry at her cunt. Even when I was angry at the rest of her, I loved her cunt. It was just so pretty, so pink and ripe; it had that beautiful head of kinky hair; it was so moist and funky, so down to earth. It didn't play games with me. It didn't pretend to want me when it was really somewhere else. It was just what it was.

After a few minutes, then, Andrea got her chance to scream, though she never really did scream, just opened her mouth and went through all the motions. Sometimes I wished she would. I felt she was holding back on me.

We went into the bedroom and took our clothes off, got into bed, but as it turned out my penis decided not to participate. That is such a strange feeling: your cock feels so small and far away, even though it is, so to speak, right there. You look down and will it to rise, you beg and plead, you grow angry, and as you do, a gaping chasm opens up between your head and your cock, between those two parts of your body. Once Andrea realized what was happening—or rather, what wasn't happening—she grew frantic, gave me the most passionate kisses she had ever given, tugged at my nipples, went down and sucked on that lifeless object, nibbled and licked my balls, tickled between my legs. She did everything she knew I liked, and nothing, absolutely nothing, happened. (Are you sure that's my cock down there? Maybe it's somebody else's.) Eventually I told her to give up. That just wasn't my day. We lay there and held each other for a while.

What I have come to believe about such moments is that the problem is rarely with your penis. The split that you feel in your body is not between your head and your cock. There is something inside you—and often it is anger—that you are trying both to feel and not to feel, and you can't do that. Your cock is letting you know. When you get yourself together, it is saying, I'll be here. In the meantime, I'm taking a rest. Wise little bald-headed philosopher that it is—proud father of the human race—it doesn't want you to tear yourself apart.

ELEVEN

I got to the Y late that evening, after leaving Andrea's, and took my time once I was there. I took a long slow swim in the pool (there were some young guys in the lane beside me, competitive swimmers, who were doing intervals and training hard, moving along stroke for stroke. It was like swimming beside a school of dolphins), then spent some time in the sauna, which I don't normally do. I sat in the lounge and read *Sports Illustrated* for a while. I walked to a funky little bar near Market Square and had a couple of beers, nursing them with some popcorn that the guy was popping right there in the machine. I was having dinner late, and didn't want to get too hungry. Beer and popcorn are superb appetite suppressants.

I was eating that night at Nino's.

I had called earlier to make sure Anna Jennings was working. I'd said I was an old friend, asked for a reservation in her section. The headwaiter told me they stopped serving food at 10:00, so I made it for 9:30, for two. I wasn't sure they'd take a reservation for one. I figured I'd tell them my date hadn't been able to make it.

Nino's was on the first floor of an Oakland apartment building, several blocks back from Fifth, right on the edge of a slightly gamy neighborhood. The apartment building was still nice, though, and Nino's itself was a classic Pittsburgh restaurant: low lights, a nice bar, thick white tablecloths and heavy silver. The menu featured seafood and Italian specialties, but you could also get a good steak. I suppose it was slightly out-of-date at that point—not exactly nouvelle cuisine—but it was still the kind of place that a Pittsburgher liked to take his wife. It was the kind of place that those beefy Oakland businessmen liked to go for lunch. Three or four lamb chops and a baked potato.

I'm not sure what I'd expected Anna Jennings to look like— some worn harried divorcée, I suppose—but I was surprised at what I saw. She was a short woman, just over five feet, and slightly plump, with not much in the way of breasts. She amply filled the rear end of her uniform. She had long dirty blond hair, which she wore in a single plait down her back, and she had, not exactly a pretty face—it was too broad, with thick lips and bold thick eyebrows—but a radiant face. She moved with a graceful stride, never seemed to be working hard, and wore a big bright smile. She didn't give you the feeling she was waiting on you—more that she was entertaining you at her house. Serving her best recipes. Absolutely delighted to have you.

I was half-starved by the time I sat down. I usually ate two or three hours earlier than that. I had a huge green salad, full of fresh vegetables, lightly dressed with oil and vinegar, and then—in honor of the place, which reminded me of so many restaurants I'd eaten in when I was young—had prime ribs and a baked potato. I hadn't eaten a meal like that in years. There was enough meat to feed me for three or four days. The potato was also huge. I ate everything, with a half bottle of wine, a hearty red wine that Anna had suggested. I took my time over the food. She stepped up to the table once I had finished.

"I think you should have some apple pie with that," she said.

"You do?"

She nodded. "It goes."

"I'm pretty full."

DAVID GUY

"I'll cut you a small piece. It's a light crust."

"All right."

"How about some ice cream on that?"

There was no stopping this woman. "I couldn't possibly."

"A small pot of coffee? Freshly brewed?"

"Please."

By the time I had finished dessert—the crust *was* light; she *had* cut a small piece—the place was thinning out. It had never been terribly crowded, since it was a Thursday. There was a piano player in the far corner, who had been playing, with short breaks, since I arrived. He played only slow quiet ballads. "Stormy Weather." "Autumn Leaves." A few people were still at the tables, a few at the bar.

When I had paid the check, and Anna had brought me the change, I said, "Would you have a drink with me?"

Her already large smile got larger, but her brow wrinkled.

"Aren't you a little young for me?"

"I'm older than I look."

"How much?"

"I'm thirty-nine."

"You are older than you look. Are you married?"

"Used to be."

"I get a lot of attention from married men, somehow."

I shrugged. "I'm not married."

She looked at the clock. It was 10:52. "I get off at eleven."

"I'll wait at the bar."

I took a seat at the far end of the bar, away from the other customers. Anna had gone somewhere and changed, came out in slacks and a bright white top, a long navy-blue cardigan. She had made her face up a little, combed out her hair. She lit a cigarette as she sat down—"Don't say a word. I only smoke after work. Never more than three cigarettes a night."—and ordered a Jack Daniel's on the rocks.

"What's your name?" she said, after our drinks had arrived.

"Charles."

"We're not supposed to fraternize with the customers. It makes the place seem cheap. But I checked with Hugo, the headwaiter over there, and he said it was okay in this case."

I had noticed her going to speak to the headwaiter. He was a big dark greasy guy who glided around the room with half-

218

closed eyes, spoke out of the side of his mouth, as if in a perpetual stage whisper. He nevertheless had a booming voice, which could be heard all over the restaurant, hoping people enjoyed their food, wishing them a pleasant evening.

"Since you're such an old friend of mine." She turned and gazed at me.

"He mentioned that."

"As soon as he got the call. He's got to be careful with stuff like that. We get the occasional nut in here."

I had been thinking, I must admit, about trying to make this seem a casual pickup, leading the conversation around to her life and seeing if she'd mention this lawsuit she was involved in. That had also sometimes seemed the stupidest idea in the world. I hadn't made up my mind.

"I've had a long and interesting life," she said. "I don't claim to remember every little bit of it. But I don't remember you at all."

"Maybe I should tell you my last name. I didn't tell Hugo the real one."

"Maybe you should."

"It's Bradford."

She bit her lip. "I'm still drawing a blank."

"We're not really old friends. You're about to sue my father."

"Oh." For the first time all evening, the smile disappeared from her face. "That Bradford."

"That one."

"I somehow knew this wasn't a friendly visit." She fumbled with her cigarettes. "If this is to make an offer you need to talk to my lawyer."

"It's not to make an offer."

"I doubt that I'm even supposed to talk to you. Are you one of those brothers?"

"I'm not with the firm. I'm not a lawyer. I didn't even know about this business until recently. My brothers didn't tell me."

"Your father told you."

"My father didn't tell me. He's keeping it from everybody."

"How is your father?"

"He's better. He's fine. He's been a little grumpy lately. Until a couple days ago I didn't know why."

"I didn't mean to make him sick."

A major transformation had taken place in Anna's face. She didn't look angry or bitter. She hadn't suddenly become the haggard divorcée I'd been expecting. But the loss of that smile had robbed her face of all its life. She was hardly even attractive anymore.

"I know it seems strange that I've come to see you," I said. "I'm sure your lawyer wouldn't like it. My father probably wouldn't like it. But it seemed the easiest thing to do. I don't get along with my brothers. I went to another lawyer in the firm, but he was just full of lawyer talk. I don't want to go to my father. I don't want to upset him."

"I can understand that."

"I just want to know what's going on. I don't know why I want to know."

I wanted to know the truth of my father's life.

"I doubt that I'm supposed to tell you," she said.

"You don't have to tell me any big secrets."

"I don't know any big secrets."

"You don't have to tell me specifically about the suit."

"All I know is that my lawyer's optimistic. He seems to think we're in a very good position." She turned to me with real sympathy in her eyes. "I don't think he likes your father."

"He probably just wants to win. Those guys are ruthless."

"I wish I'd been able to do this without consulting a lawyer."

It was true. You couldn't file a lawsuit without seeing a lawyer.

"I can tell you my part," she said. "There are no big secrets in it."

"I'd really appreciate it." Somebody who talked straight.

"I might need another drink."

"Of course." I signaled the bartender.

When he came back with the drink, he said, "You okay, honey?"

She didn't look too good.

"Sure, Carl," she said. "I'm fine."

He took a long look at me before he stepped away.

I had gradually become aware that he, the headwaiter, and

most of the other employees in the place were watching me. Keeping an eye on her.

The story she told me was an old one, the kind that's been told a million times. It's the kind of story that's told every morning on the television talk shows. She was a local girl, had grown up in the east end. She went through the parochial schools and was an excellent student at Sacred Heart before she went to Pitt. It was when she was a sophomore that she met a local businessman, Phillip Jennings, at a wedding. He was nine years older than she, incredibly attractive and charming. He'd swept her off her feet.

"You always knew where to find him," she said, "at a party or something. Just look for the people having fun. Look for the crowd of good-looking women. Laughing."

For a while they'd had a whirlwind romance, going to fine restaurants and fancy nightclubs, spending the night in posh hotels. It was a kind of social life none of her friends had, but she was bored by the party scene at college, ready for an older man. It seemed just right, what she'd always dreamed of. After five months she found out she was pregnant.

"I'd used a diaphragm," she said, "but not every single time. Sometimes we'd be out somewhere or something. He was the kind of man you took chances with. He was overwhelming." She obviously wasn't a terribly strict Catholic, but strict enough that abortion was out of the question. After a brief burst of anger when she told him, Jennings agreed to marry her.

For a long time everything seemed fine. He was a good provider, a virtuoso real-estate salesman. They bought a house in the South Hills, and she actually enjoyed being a housewife. It had been her lifelong dream to be a mother. She had a second child, then a third. All girls. As far as she knew they were a model family.

The first suggestion that they weren't—six years into their marriage—was when a woman came to her and told her she was having an affair with Phillip. He'd told this woman his marriage wasn't working, he was about to make a change, then after a few months had abruptly broken off with her. "I was a fool to listen to that crap," the woman said, "but I wasn't the only one. Just ask around." When Anna confronted Phillip he denied everything, stormed out of the house, as if she were at fault for bringing it up.

But she did ask around, and all her friends knew. They hadn't known how to tell her. He was notorious. Secretaries at work, women in bars, wives in the neighborhood. For some reason, at the same time she was finding out—perhaps because he felt guilty—he started to get more blatant, to be seen more openly. One day when he thought she'd be out shopping all afternoon, she came home and found him with a woman on the couch. "All their clothes off," she said. "Actually doing it."

She paused and took a long pull at her drink at that point. She had finished her second cigarette.

"It's hard to understand the mindset I was in," she said. "This strange victim mentality. But I was still trying to hold things together. Asking how I could be this woman he was looking for. I kept thinking if I knew what he wanted I could give it to him. But he never told me."

By that time he'd started to hit her. They were having arguments all the time, and she'd bring up what he was doing—that was what they were really arguing about—and he'd slap her. Sometimes the girls saw him do it. They'd be terrified, scream at him to stop.

"I don't think there was anything he wanted," she said. "Nothing I could give him. He had what he wanted. He wanted to be with one woman and screw a lot of others. When I finally realized that, it was like a religious awakening. I knew I'd had enough."

She made him move out, and on the spur of the moment he had her sign a little statement he'd written out, to the effect that the separation was by mutual agreement and that he wasn't abandoning her. That was certainly true at that point, although for all intents and purposes he had abandoned her years before. By the time she needed a lawyer, she was too depressed to do a big search for one. A friend of hers had gone to this Robert Parnell about some minor matter and liked him. And he was part of a big prestigious firm.

At the settlement, they'd said the house and the business were of roughly equal value, so she would get the house and he the business. There was some dispute about that, because the business had enormous potential, but it was new at that point and its actual value wasn't all that large. She got a reasonable amount of child support. But there was no talk of alimony, and her impression was that that was because of the statement she'd signed. "I don't remember Parnell saying that in so many words, but that was definitely what I thought. I was in such a fog back then. There are a lot of things I don't remember."

She turned to me. "You probably understand how guilty I felt."

"I do."

"I felt that I'd failed in the most important thing I'd ever tried. My whole life was a failure. I couldn't believe they were giving me what they did. My children, for one thing. I'd have died without my children. That beautiful house, and all that child support. I was so grateful."

But she still didn't have enough to live on, so she had to go to work. She had no marketable skills—she had always thought she'd go back to school when her kids were older—so she'd gotten work as a waitress. First at a little pizza place, then at a kind of family restaurant, finally at Nino's. It had been hard at first. She'd had to be away from the children at all kinds of times—especially mealtimes—when she'd wanted to be with them. They'd had to stay with a babysitter and then, as they got older, look out for themselves. But they'd done that, they had come together as a family, and in time they'd grown proud of what they'd done. They were especially proud of having done it without a man around. Now her two oldest girls were in college, and she was determined that they would never have to do what she did, enter the job market with no skills.

Her face had grown calm as she got to that point in her story. Sad, but calm.

"Anyway," she said, "my life changed, and the years passed, and I didn't think about all that anymore. It was like a bad memory, not even a memory, it was like a sad story you hear about somebody else. Until one day when I saw your father in here for lunch."

It wasn't unusual to see the Senator in there. She'd seen him any number of times. She'd waited on him. She was waiting on him that day.

"I knew who he was," she said, "because years before, when

I'd been in those law offices seeing Parnell, he'd said hello to me. He said how sorry he was for my trouble. That made me feel good at the time. I'd been feeling like the lowest thing on earth." The Senator could express sympathy with the best of them. "He didn't remember me, of course. I hadn't ever introduced myself. It hadn't seemed appropriate."

But it wasn't the Senator who bothered her; it was the man he was with. Part of the problem was the way they were eating, lavish appetizers followed by huge lobsters, two bottles of wine, cheesecake for dessert, coffee and cigars. For lunch! (The Senator really knew how to live in the old days.) But there was something else about the man, partly the way he was acting—wealthy and arrogant and rude—but also something else, which she couldn't quite put her finger on until she heard the Senator introduce him to someone. It was that developer. Frank Weyland.

"I knew who he was too. Everybody in Pittsburgh knew, but I especially did, because years before, right around the time of my divorce, I'd seen his picture in the paper with my husband." They were standing there with big smiles on their faces, Jennings holding up Weyland's arm like a prizefighter's, after he'd just won this big zoning battle. She'd hated her husband so much at that point. She was full of bitterness. And there he was congratulating a man who had just snatched a neighborhood away from the people who lived in it.

At first she didn't know why it made her feel so strange to see the Senator with Weyland. This man she thought she liked was having lunch with this man she knew she didn't like. It was as if the Senator might actually be like Weyland. He might be like Phillip Jennings. She wondered if he knew Phillip. If they all three knew each other.

"All of a sudden it occurred to me to wonder why he had known my name in his office all those years before. When I was such a tiny little divorce case."

It had occurred to me to wonder that as soon as she mentioned it.

She thought about that. She thought and thought about it. Her oldest daughter was going out with a law student at the time and she asked him. Could something funny be going on?

He said he didn't know, but that she ought to at least talk to a lawyer. He knew a good honest one. John Auerbach.

Auerbach knew right away that Frank Weyland was the Senator's client. Everybody knew that, he said. He didn't think the whole thing sounded suspicious. He thought it was just a coincidence.

Then she told him about her marriage. That her husband had seen countless other women. One had confessed to her. She caught him with another. Her friends had known of others. That he'd hit her during arguments. The girls had seen him hit her. Auerbach said the agreement she'd signed was to keep her husband from having to pay alimony, that if a man just up and leaves his family, that is grounds for alimony. But there are other grounds as well. Adultery, for one thing. Also physical abuse. Especially in front of the girls. He couldn't believe she hadn't gotten alimony. He couldn't believe the subject hadn't even really come up. He kept asking her if she was sure she'd told her lawyer all this.

"Of course I'd told him," she said. "I sat down in his office and it poured out. I was telling everybody those days." But she didn't remember him making a big thing out of alimony. She hardly remembered him mentioning it.

From that point on she didn't know much. Auerbach made inquiries to Parnell, who eventually admitted he remembered the case. At first he talked about the agreement she'd signed, said he didn't know any other grounds for alimony. But when Auerbach pressed him he said there had been other pressures at the firm; he had been told not to pursue it; there had been all kinds of pressures at that place. He'd been a young man and hadn't been able to resist them. He wasn't going to be blamed in this malpractice case. He was an ethical and competent lawyer. If Anna Jennings sued him he was going to countersue the Senator.

The Senator took the whole thing much differently. He was perfectly at ease, joked with Auerbach, said he didn't remember the case but he remembered Parnell well. There had been other cases like this, where he had overlooked the most glaring details. He'd been a puzzling man. It wasn't that he was lazy or something, more that he was too ambitious. He took on too much, then didn't do anything well. They'd finally had to let him go. The Senator said it sounded as if Anna

Jennings should definitely have gotten alimony, but there wasn't much they could do about it now. He offered a small settlement for the malpractice.

Auerbach was suspicious. The Senator sounded so convincing, Parnell so shaky, but he somehow found himself believing Parnell, for the same reason that he sometimes believed a certain kind of wounded client. Parnell sounded so wronged. So outraged. But at that point it was one lawyer's word against another's. A well-known and well-respected lawyer against a pretty shabby one. For a time he couldn't take it any further. He thought they were going to have to accept the small settlement. Then all of a sudden he found something. His whole outlook on the case changed. He said he could prove the conspiracy. He'd take it to court if he had to.

"Did he tell you what he found?" I said.

"He said I didn't need to know. It would be better if I didn't. But he's been a lot more upbeat about the case ever since. He's been completely different."

Anna had finished her second drink at that point. She had smoked her three cigarettes for that night and started on one for the next night. She didn't seem as glum as she had. But that whole bright friendly side of her was gone.

"I felt terrible when your father got sick," she said. "I have nothing against him. It's my ex-husband who really owes me money. But there's no way I'd ever get that."

"No."

"John Auerbach keeps saying I didn't get what was coming to me. That this little settlement they were offering for malpractice barely scratches the surface. I keep thinking of all those years I worked in crummy places for a pitiful wage. My children had nobody with them."

"Yes."

"Now I have bills to pay. My girls took out huge loans to get through college. Their father wouldn't help them out with that. And I've been almost no help. I'm still feeling the burden of all this. But if that money should have been mine. If I never should have had it so hard in the first place." Her eyes were sad, but determined. "I think I have every right to try to get it."

TWELVE

W hen I first saw Andrea the next morning—standing on the porch of Helen's house as I opened the door—the trace of fear that I sometimes saw in part of her gaze had taken over her face. She looked pale and drawn, as if she hadn't slept. She was wrapped in a raincoat against the chill misty morning, and she held it tight around her. She cowered inside it.

"Charles," she said. "Where were you last night?"

I had found two messages on my answering machine when I got back the night before ("Charles. This is Andrea. I want to talk to you," and "Charles. Andrea again"), but it had seemed too late to call at that hour, and I hadn't thought to call yet in the morning. I had been up since 6:45, working on my column. Helen had only left the house ten minutes before. It hadn't occurred to me that the world was up and about.

"I was out," I said.

"I know you were out."

"I was talking to somebody. This woman."

The problem was that I hadn't told Andrea anything about the lawsuit pending against the Senator. The whole thing had a slight—probably more than slight—air of scandal, and I was afraid she would latch on to that. It was about a woman being taken advantage of, and I knew she would jump all over that. What with her difficult past, I wasn't sure she would understand my feelings for my father. I didn't think she would see that, no matter what he had done, I wasn't going to turn on him.

It was a failure of trust that had kept me from telling her. I didn't know what she might do with it.

"Would you like to come in?" I said.

"Would you like me to?"

"If you want."

"Is your sister here?"

"No. She's gone."

Andrea had never shown up unannounced before. She had always been respectful of my writing time. And she had never looked quite so bedraggled. She liked to make an impression.

We walked into the living room and sat on the couch. She sat on the edge of it, ready to bolt. She had quit holding the raincoat around herself, though she didn't take it off. She wore a plain white jersey and faded jeans.

"So," she said. "Was this woman attractive?"

A question Andrea never failed to ask.

"She wasn't bad. A little on the plump side."

"Did you want to fuck her?"

"I wouldn't have minded."

"Did you do it?"

Andrea had never failed to ask those first two questions. She had never asked the third. We could be talking about a seventy-year-old friend of my mother's and Andrea would ask if I might not, under the right circumstances, want to slip it in her. (Actually, some of those society matrons looked great.) But she had never asked the questions in quite that tone before. They suddenly didn't seem incidental to the conversation. They seemed to be the conversation.

"What do you mean?" I said.

"Did you do it? Did you put it in her?"

The truth of the matter was that I had found Anna Jennings attractive. Not so much the way she looked as her cheerful disposition, and the way—despite the difficult subject—that we had talked, a way Andrea and I never seemed to talk. I had been perfectly relaxed. She had been absolutely straightforward.

"I don't know what you're talking about," I said.

"I'm talking about a man who comes to my house and doesn't want to fuck me. He doesn't apparently find me attractive anymore. Even though I was right there for him. I did everything he liked. Then when I tried to get in touch with him that evening he wasn't there. He tells me he was with another woman. He found her attractive. He wouldn't mind fucking her."

"Andrea. I thought we were talking theoretically. Like when you see somebody on the street. This meeting was not about fucking. It was about business. Something to do with my father. I had to see this woman late because she's a waitress and she works late. It was the only time I could talk to her. Then I didn't return your calls because it seemed too late."

"I was out anyway."

"You called twice."

"I called six times. In the space of about a half hour. I only left two messages. Then I went out."

I had noticed the other calls. I hadn't known they were from her.

"Well," I said. "I thought it was too late to call. I would have called back this morning."

I was sure she wanted me to ask where she'd been. The same way she was asking me. I didn't think it was my place to ask that question. I didn't think it was any of my business.

"I went out and fucked Mitchell Dantry," she said.

I stared at her. Her face was dead white. Her gaze was full of fear and pain. She looked as if she expected me to hit her.

"I was sure you were out fucking some other woman," she said. "I could feel it. I have a sense for such things. You had decided you didn't want me that afternoon. So you went out and found somebody you did want."

"It wasn't that I didn't want you."

"Finally I couldn't stand it anymore. Sitting there trying to get you on the phone when I knew it was hopeless. I had to get out."

"So you went off and fucked somebody."

"Yes."

I liked Andrea's craziness. Probably because I was so fundamentally sane (if you ignored all my sexual perversions), I was attracted to a certain near-insanity in a woman. But this was crazy beyond anything I had ever encountered. I hardly knew what to say.

"Did you tell him why you were doing it?" I said.

"He didn't ask."

"Just out of the blue, you go and fuck this guy, and he doesn't wonder what's going on?"

"It wasn't out of the blue."

"It wasn't?"

"It wasn't the first time."

I was so out of it at that point, so utterly stunned by what she was saying (I wasn't one step behind her, more like five or six) that I didn't understand what she meant. She was halfway into her next speech before I caught on.

"I didn't understand what was going on here," she said. "What you meant by all this. Between us. I knew you loved me and I loved you, that it was the real thing, but I thought the circumstances weren't right. You'd be staying only until your father got better. It might have occurred to me to wish for more, but I didn't think to bring it up. I never thought it was a possibility."

"It took *me* a while to think of it."

"Maybe I should have let myself dream."

"But isn't it always possible that one thing will turn into another? You start off being casual and wind up wanting more?"

"I guess it is. I just didn't know it was happening."

"So you started to see someone else."

I didn't quite see how that followed.

"It's not the same thing," she said. "It shouldn't even be mentioned in the same breath. I've known Mitchell for years. We've done political work together. He's always been around, with this perpetual hard-on, fucking every woman in the movement. Letting me know he was ready when I was. Always in the past I was married. Halfway resenting that fact, since I was so unhappy. Then after Arthur left I was a basket case. I wasn't thinking about anybody. But in the two months since you came along, like a gift from heaven, I've felt like a new woman. I realized I wasn't married anymore. That I'd finally gotten rid of that prick who was making my life miserable. I'm a free woman. I can do what I want. My life isn't ending. It's just beginning."

Jesus. I'm so happy for you.

"So you don't want to be involved with one person," I said.

"I want to be involved with *you*. This thing with Mitchell isn't a love affair. It barely even qualifies as fucking. My involvement with you is completely different. You're the man I love."

I was still having a little trouble following this.

"You took me by surprise yesterday," she said. "You knocked me off my feet. It was a whole new world you were opening up. I couldn't absorb it in the space of a few minutes."

She was so bewildered that she staggered off and fucked somebody.

"So you don't want to be involved with him," I said. Let's come to some conclusions here.

"I've never wanted to be involved with him. It's never even crossed my mind."

"You'll stop seeing him."

"That's what I was talking about yesterday. We both have to decide. If we want to allow each other that kind of casual sex."

I couldn't seem to nail this sucker down.

"You seem to have made up your mind," I said.

"I'm open to discussing both sides."

It is obvious from the perspective of time—looking back on this scene as if it happened to somebody else, which I can almost do at this point—how screwed up it all was. Andrea hadn't thought our affair had a future so she ran off and fucked somebody else. Without telling me. I brought up the possibility of a future and her first reaction was to run off and fuck the guy again, after convincing herself—I have no doubt she was sincere in this conviction—that I was fucking another woman. (I am reminded of the words a therapist once addressed to me: Are you familiar with the phenomenon of projection?)

At the time, however, I had no perspective. I heard what I wanted to hear (after feeling my heart dive into my stomach at the possibility—which I briefly felt—that she was telling me things were over between us). I heard her say that she wanted to be involved with me. That she did want our love affair to have a future. That it might be a good idea to allow ourselves a little casual fucking on the side. Mostly I heard her say she still wanted to see me.

"You must hate me," she said.

"I don't hate you."

"You must want to kill me."

"No."

"I wouldn't blame you if you did. If you were really furious at me. You wanted to take it out on me."

She looked at me from those eyes that were filled with pain.

"I'd understand," she said.

I was actually feeling much more anger than I was admitting. My first reaction is always to deny that I'm feeling anger toward a woman. It boiled around in my belly and tried to burst up through my chest. I didn't know whether I wanted to pick Andrea up and throw her through Helen's picture window or throw her on the floor and fuck her brains out. I reached to touch my hand to the back of her head. She gazed at me, smiled weakly. Without realizing this had been my intention, I grabbed a clump of her hair in my fist. She closed her eyes. I snapped her head back, leaned over and thrust my tongue into her mouth. I brought my teeth onto her mouth and pressed hard. Harder. She moaned.

I pulled back and looked at her.

"It isn't like you to go limp," I said.

"I'd do anything to keep you, Charles," she said. "Anything."

"I don't want you this way. It isn't you."

"All right."

"I want you to resist."

She smiled, slightly puzzled. She had apparently thought I'd want to throw her around like a rag doll.

I slapped her. My hand had been resting on her shoulder, so it didn't have far to go, but it was a hard slap. A ringing slap. I could see the print of my hand on her face.

I had never slapped a woman in my life.

"You really want me to resist," she said.

"Yes."

If she had shown any pain when I slapped her, if she had

cried out or started to weep, I would have collapsed at her feet. I would have called the police and turned myself in for assault. But her face changed in the other direction. It was as if I had slapped the fear right out of her eyes. She took on a calm look. She almost smiled. She knew where she was.

She slapped me back. Her hand had been resting on the couch beside her, and it was a full swing she took at me. It snapped my head to one side. I shouted in surprise.

She tried to jump up but I grabbed her by the hair again—both hands—and threw her to the couch. She screamed. I fell on her as I threw her and she held up her arms to defend herself but I got mine around her and crushed her. Her slap had brought out all my rage. I was holding her with about ten times the force I'd ever used before. Her arms were useless against me. I reached up and grabbed her hair again, pulled her head back. She gasped. She didn't exactly look afraid now—I think her real fear had been that I would throw her out—but she did look, at the very least, cautious.

The strength running through me could have snapped her in two.

"Don't you ever hit me again," I said.

"I won't. I'm sorry."

"Unless I tell you to. Unless I want you to."

"All right."

"Do you feel how much stronger I am?"

"I do."

"Do you feel how useless it would be to resist?"

"Charles." She looked down. "I thought you wanted me to resist."

"I did. So you'd see how useless it is."

She smiled.

I didn't know what I was going to say from one moment to the next.

"Do you feel how weak you are? What a weak little woman?"

"Yes."

"What a weak little girl?"

"You prick."

I crushed her. I squeezed as tight as I could.

"Yes! I feel it!"

"That you're weak."

"Yes."

"Like a little girl. You're under my control."

"Yes."

"We're going upstairs now. And you're going to do exactly what I want."

"All right."

"Exactly what I want when I want it. If you hesitate for even a split second you're going to be sorry."

"I know."

"Your ball-busting days are over."

I had her take off her raincoat before we went up. On a whim I had her take off her jersey too, just so I could see her tits. I walked up those stairs with a mix of feelings. For one thing, I was stunned. Not at what she had said—though that was stunning enough—but at what I had done. I was startled at the person I had suddenly become. A band that was binding my chest—a thick band, which had been around me for years—had just snapped. I felt like a giant. All the same feelings of anger were boiling inside me, but I was big enough to contain them. They weren't going to erupt. I felt as if I could have leaned back and let out a roar that would have blown off the roof.

I had an incredible hard-on. It was standing up in my cotton pants like a flagpole. Andrea—as we had stood from the couch—stared at it in amazement. I let her touch it. I allowed her to take it out of my pants and hold it. I even let her suck it a little. Hell, I didn't hold a grudge.

For the first time in two days she looked happy.

The first thing I told her when we got up to the room was that I was going to spank her. Just to loosen her up a little. It wasn't going to be like the little love pats I might have given her in the past. This time I was really going to do it. I told her these things as I pulled the chair out from my desk and placed it in the center of the room. She was wearing a black solemn expression on her face, like a little girl who knows she's in trouble. I pulled her jeans down (I swear to God I don't know how she got into those pants, with a crowbar or something), got them bunched around her ankles, so they shackled her. I pulled her over my knee and took down her underpants, little white cotton ones with blue flowers on them. Her ass was white and plump. I really walloped her, full swings from my arm, loud smacks on her ass. At first she stifled the sounds, but I made her shout, made her scream. I made her beg me to stop. I didn't do it, though. I kept smacking until her ass was a bright red.

After that I made her take everything off and go stand in front of the window. I told her I was going to leave her there until a crowd gathered in the alley. I was going to go down and sell peanuts and popcorn in the crowd. I made her fondle her tits and play with her pussy. I made her finger fuck herself. I stood up and took off my clothes and made her come kneel on the floor and blow me. I gave her instructions. "Lick the whole thing. Lick it like a big lollipop. Now lick my balls. Use your whole tongue. Make them wet. Take one in your mouth." I made her see how much of my cock she could take down. I told her I expected it to disappear. I took her hand and licked her big thick middle finger, then made her slide it up my ass. I told her to get it in up to the knuckle. I had her pose for me, sat in the chair and made her go through all kinds of lewd contortions. I made her lie on the bed and play with herself, hold it open for me to look. I got a dildo we had bought a few weeks before as a joke—about a nine incher, as big around as a fist—and worked it all the way into her. I made her swear my cock was bigger. I made her masturbate with the dildo inside her. It was hard for her to do with something inside her, especially something that big, but I told her she had to; I told her she had to come. It took her a long time; she moaned and squirmed, screamed when it finally happened. I took the dildo out and made her reach down and taste the juice from her pussy. I made her go way up and get the good stuff. I made her feed some to me. I told her it made me hungry for a tunafish sandwich. I made her roll over and get on her knees, play with herself that way. I got a finger wet in her pussy and slid it up her ass.

"Did he use a rubber?" I said. "This new boyfriend of yours."

"Yes," she said. "But he's not my boyfriend."

"Do you swear he used a rubber?" I said. "Every time?"

"I swear it."

"Did you take his come in your mouth?"

"No."

"Are you sure? You get a little absentminded sometimes."

"I didn't do it."

"All right. Well." I put my hands on her ass. "I'm not wearing a rubber."

The room was silent again. Those words hung between us.

"I've always wanted to fuck you without a rubber. Now I'm going to do it. You can leave if you want. You can leave any time you want to. But if you stay you're going to get the real thing. You're going to take it without a rubber. I'm going to leave my come in you. I'm going to make you my woman."

She smiled. "Yes."

"And I want you to tell him. The next time you see him. Tell that little fag you've got my come in you. Tell him it's running down your leg."

"I will."

She didn't even have to change positions. I just made her move a little closer to the edge, spread her legs a little more.

The woman, as I've said, had a huge cunt, one of the biggest I'd ever encountered, and it was sopping wet at that point, absolutely dripping juice. But it felt fabulous to go inside her without a rubber, slick and wet and hot. She groaned as I entered her, grunted with every stroke. She moved her ass, too, so I barely had to; it was an effortless fuck. We were making little slick squishy noises where we came together. I could hear myself growling down in my throat. My cock felt as if it would stay hard forever. I took my time and just let it happen. When I finally did come, it was far different from feeling it catch in a rubber. It was like dropping my load into an abyss. I felt a part of myself go into her. I left something behind. My knees buckled, and my whole body jackknifed. I fell on her as I finished and held her, lying on the bed. We were both soaked with sweat.

After a few minutes—we hadn't spoken—I felt chilly and got us under the covers. I turned Andrea around and brushed the hair out of her eyes. Her face had regained its color. She didn't look tired anymore.

She was smiling at me.

"Charles," she said. "I swear to God. I didn't know you had it in you."

"I didn't either."

"That's more like what I expect from a man."

I had become the man she wanted.

THE AUTOBIOGRAPHY OF MY BODY

Only a few times in my life had I felt that kind of sexual excitement. From the moment I'd thrown Andrea onto the couch, something had burst free in me. The kind of hard-on I'd had was incontrovertible evidence that I was doing what I wanted. You lay that on the table and rest your case. On the other hand, I was startled at what I'd seen in myself. The capacity for violence and brutality. I'd enjoyed spanking her, quite apart from the sexual excitement. I'd enjoyed throwing her around.

"I'm glad you did what you did," she said. "I loved it." She gave me a little kiss. "I'm just glad you still want me."

I turned her over on her belly and looked at her ass. It was still a bright red. I rubbed it gently with my fingertips.

"Are you going to be a good girl now?" I said.

"Probably not."

We laughed.

"Although I will for a while," she said. "Christ, I won't be able to sit down for a week."

I rolled her over gently and put a pillow under her ass, knelt by the bed and went down on her. I did it slowly, just licked her softly again and again. I could taste my semen seeping out of her. It took a long time, since she had already come once. Finally she did it, with a quiet little gasp and shudder, soft motions from her hips.

"You're a sweetheart," she said, when I got back up on the bed.

Not all the time I wasn't.

We lay together, all entwined. Her head was on my shoulder. "Do you know what turned me on the most?" she said.

"What?"

"Standing at the window. Showing myself. There was a guy down there. Working in somebody's yard. After a while he noticed me. He kept looking up here. I was looking back. We were staring right at each other, but we didn't really acknowledge it. He's probably inside beating off right now."

Either that or breaking into Helen's back door.

After a while Andrea said, "I don't mean to bring up a touchy subject. But who was this woman you were with last night?"

I told her the whole story, the conversations I'd had with Helen, my talk with Mr. Harrold, my trip the evening before

237

to see Anna Jennings. I could feel her grow more attentive as I got to that part. I could feel her come alive.

"They really fucked her over," she said.

"Who did?"

"Those men. The way they always fuck women over. They've been doing it for centuries. This is not a new story, Charles."

"Which men are you talking about?"

"All of them. I'm talking about a group of wealthy powerful men. Who wear expensive suits and meet in boardrooms. They don't need names."

She didn't care to differentiate.

"I'm not saying it was your father," she said.

"People are going to assume, when this comes out in the paper, that he did it. That he has money, and Weyland has money, and they saw a chance to make more money, so they did this thing."

"I'm not assuming that."

"It could have been that young lawyer who screwed up. Or Mr. Harrold could have done it."

"I'm sure what you're saying is true. I am absolutely not making any assumptions about your father. But men with power, men with money, fuck women over. That's as plain a fact as there is in this world. And they do it in all kinds of ways. The system is so stacked in their favor that it's not even hard anymore. This woman's husband was the real shit. He was the one who screwed her. But the system's set up in such a way that he barely has to do anything. All these other men are right there in place to help him."

"I'm worried about my father."

"I know you are."

"I don't want you to be thinking you know what he did in all this. Just because he's a man."

"I don't."

There. We'd established it for the fifth time, or whatever it was. She wasn't making any assumptions.

I still didn't believe her.

"Why is it that you want to find out about this?" she said.

"I don't know." That was a question I'd given plenty of thought to in the past few days. "All my life, or at least a lot of it, I've kept my father at arm's length. I've kept him on a pedestal. It wasn't exactly that I admired him. Most of the time I was fighting with him. I was furious at him. I'd put him on a pedestal that I had nothing but contempt for. Way up there in this prestigious law firm. I don't want to do that anymore. I want to let him get closer to me. Be more of a person to me. Even if he doesn't seem as admirable when I do that. I want him to be on my level, so I can know him."

There was more conflict in all that than I was letting on. A part of me—a younger part, I suppose, maybe from back in my college days—wanted him to be at fault, wanted to bring him down a peg. Another part—probably a still younger part, a child—was scared to death that he was guilty, as if that would shatter our whole life together. The calmly rational adult who wanted to know the truth, wanted to know who my father was, only appeared from time to time. Most often I felt those other parts, first one then the other.

"I understand," Andrea said. "I really admire that. It's more than I could do."

Eventually it got to be lunchtime, or close enough, and we walked down to the Balcony, a second-story glassed-in restaurant that overlooked Walnut Street. We got a table by the window, had sandwiches and a couple of beers apiece. I actually got slightly drunk. I was worn out, and the day wasn't even half over.

"I hope you don't feel bad," Andrea said as we sat over coffee.

"I do, actually." I felt a little depressed. I hated myself in the morning. Except that it was the afternoon.

"Don't. I wanted what we did. I liked it. I like it the more I think of it."

It was thinking of it that made me not like it.

"I've never really liked being spanked," she said. "I probably never will. But I loved doing it for you. Something you really wanted. Something all for you."

I think that was what really bothered me. The fact that it hadn't seemed mutual.

Also the fact that I had been hitting a woman.

"I feel closer to you than I ever have," she said.

In the confusion of what we'd done, that whole issue of monogamy had disappeared.

THIRTEEN

I t had sounded like an informal invitation over the phone—"How about coming over for a drink this afternoon? Four-thirty okay?"—but as soon as I stepped into the apartment I knew something was up. For one thing, the Duchess wasn't around, and on normal days the cocktail hour was almost a ritual for them. The Senator would have his glass of white wine, the Duchess a couple of wicked vodka martinis, and, from what I gathered (though they didn't indulge in this particular vice when I was around) they would listen to National Public Radio and rail at the liberal commentators, a pastime made possible only by the numbing effects of alcohol. (Sometimes Helen would pick up the phone at the cocktail hour to hear the Senator's booming voice: "Did you hear what that horse's ass just said on the radio?") But on this particular day—a Tuesday, following that fateful Thursday—the Duchess was out with some friends, which she never would have been without prior arrangement. And the Senator was different than he'd been with me lately. He had on his lawyer manner.

The Senator was not the same man I had seen when I

stepped into that apartment in January. He had put some of the weight back on that he had lost during his illness, which he hardly needed, but it did somehow make him look healthier, more himself. His face had regained its color, and a certain animation that it had lost for a while. (For a while his face had seemed diminished by fear.) He no longer moved with the exaggerated slowness he had once employed. But the real change was in his manner. He was acting more the way he had in the old days, gruff, hearty, slightly distant, probably less open than he had been at one point. But that had been the openness of a frightened and defeated man who was reaching out to people because he desperately needed them. I was glad he wasn't that way anymore.

I also had the feeling that we had grown close enough that his manner wasn't all that important.

He mixed me a drink, poured himself a glass of wine. The Senator always mixed the drinks in his house. We sat in his study—he in his favorite chair, a saggy old leather one in the corner, I at that end of the couch—and talked. He asked about my work, asked about Andrea. She had remained a shadowy figure in our conversations. He never came out and asked what was going on with her. But he liked her. The Duchess did too, the one time we had all been together. Andrea had a way of making a good impression. She could size people up and deliver what they wanted.

Rather abruptly, after a pause, the Senator said, "I want to talk to you about the problem I've been having at work."

"All right," I said. I was slightly startled. Why all of a sudden?

"It's been going on for weeks now. Months, actually. I thought it was going to blow over. But it doesn't look like it's going to."

The Senator's lawyer manner was rational, calm, and soothing. It corresponded roughly to a doctor's bedside manner. It had nothing to do with the context of what he was saying. He could tell you a nuclear bomb was about to blow us all to kingdom come and make it sound like a minor controllable thing (if we could just get a good jury). There was a look of concern on his face, concern but calm. He would smile gently, hold out a hand to gesture. He was like Socrates discoursing on the nature of truth.

This was the opposite of those grumpy moods he had sometimes shown me after work. He would never have been able to tell me about a problem in one of those moods. He wore his lawyer manner like a shield.

He came at the story from an entirely different angle than anyone else had. It all began, for him, years before, when the firm had hired a young man named Robert Parnell. In many ways, he was a carbon copy of the people they always hired there. Top of his class, law review, graduation with honors. The difference, in his case, was that he'd only gone to Pitt Law School, and before that Bucknell. Up until then they had been almost exclusively an Ivy League firm. That was just the tone of the place. But Parnell's professors had raved about him. And he had really stood out in his class. Head and shoulders above everyone else.

"All the partners interviewed him, as they always do," the Senator said. "I was the one who wanted to take a chance. You only find out so much in those interviews anyway. Everybody's just trying to impress you. You know that some of them will work out and some won't. You try to get a feel for that through the years. It's really just an instinct."

The only problem with Parnell that they could see when they hired him was that he seemed slightly nervous. Almost too eager to please. They wanted their young associates to work long hours, but Parnell never seemed to leave. And he could seem, when he was deep in the middle of a working jag, dangerously high strung. You had a feeling that if you walked over and slapped him on the back he'd shatter into a thousand pieces. "I took all that to be some feeling of inferiority about his background," the Senator said. "Not just the small college but the small town. The ordinary family." (Especially around the aristocratic lineages that peppered the Senator's firm.) But Parnell did know his stuff. It was better for him to be high strung than cocky. And in the courtroom, that crazy relentless energy could be an advantage. It scared the other side a little. "You never knew," the Senator said, "when he was going to uncork a fastball and knock somebody in the head."

Unfortunately, he also made his clients nervous. Sometimes when they were just sitting around the office chatting. You could feel the intensity coming off him. He also didn't react well to pressure. If things went badly he got rattled. "But worst of all," the Senator said, "and this was something I never would have expected, he didn't handle detail well. He had enormous energy, moved at a terrific clip, but sometimes he went so fast that he neglected important things. It was as if he felt so much anxiety that he had to get the whole thing over with."

I knew that kind of person. There were writers, for instance, who couldn't stand to rewrite. The thought that they hadn't been perfect the first time, that they might be able to improve a piece, that they might be able to go on improving it indefinitely, terrified them. They had to cut off such thoughts before they started. In the meantime, of course, that attitude had its own peculiar pressures. You had to get everything right the first time.

"Finally we had to let him go," the Senator said. "That kind of thing is always messy. But we'd heard complaints from several of his clients. And we weren't happy with the results of a couple of his cases. You can't let a thing like that go on too long."

"Were you the one to tell him?" I said.

"No. Mr. Harrold." The Iceman. "He's better at that kind of thing."

The more I heard about this man, the more I thought he'd missed his calling as a mortician.

"How did Parnell take it?" I said.

"He was shattered. He begged for another chance. Even came to me. But when you've made a decision like that, you've finally made it, you have to stand by it."

The Senator heaved a big sigh. "I thought that was the end of it. Just a mistake I made in hiring. One of many, I'm sure. But here we are fifteen years later, and a case he handled comes back to haunt us."

It was interesting the way the Senator related the case. He admitted that Anna Jennings had been wronged and deserved alimony. He had no idea how Parnell could have overlooked the plain facts of the case. He made the whole connection with the zoning battle sound improbable and coincidental, a flight of someone's fancy. He didn't say, for instance, that he had met Phillip Jennings and lobbied him personally. He didn't say how big and important the zoning battle had been. He didn't even mention the name Frank Weyland.

It was just an old habit, I suppose. He instinctively made the best case for himself.

"I don't know what the newspapers will do with all this," he said. "If you told it from the other end it could sound a lot different." He was right. I had heard it from the other end. "You could make the whole thing sound true. I have a feeling that's what they'll do. It's better copy."

"Yes."

"I wanted you to hear it from me. Instead of reading it somewhere. I think the lawsuits will be filed this week."

"I'm glad you told me." At last.

"I wonder if you'd do me a favor."

"Sure."

"I wonder if you'd tell the women."

This was such an odd request—or such an odd way of putting it—that at first I didn't get what he meant.

"The women?"

"Your mother. Your sister."

"You want me to tell Mother?"

"It would make things a lot easier for me."

The Senator had retained his lawyer manner throughout the discussion, but now it was starting to crumble. He blushed slightly, and glanced away. He was turning back into a human being.

I couldn't believe he was asking me this.

"I don't know, Dad. I'd like to help."

I didn't want to deliver bad news to the Duchess any more than he did.

"I keep trying to tell her," he said. "I can't tell you how many times I've sat down with her just like this, thinking I would. But it's much easier to say something else."

"What is it you think she's going to do?"

"Your mother doesn't like the boat to be rocked." The boat being her extremely comfortable life. A luxury yacht. "She likes to just drift down the river."

"But this isn't so bad. You picked the wrong guy for the firm. Years ago." He told it so well.

"That isn't the way the papers will handle it. They'll blow it all out of proportion."

THE AUTOBIOGRAPHY OF MY BODY

"Who cares what they do? We'll know the truth."

"Your mother cares. It's how things sound that she really worries about."

I'm afraid the old boy had her pegged exactly.

"I think Mother can handle this," I said. "She's good at keeping up a front."

She was the undefeated champion of the world.

"I'm sure she can handle it," he said. "I just don't want to tell her."

The Senator and I had the same problem with this. We had both felt the Duchess freeze over as we told her something she didn't want to hear.

He picked up his wineglass and drained it. It should have been a shot of rye.

"When I was a young man," he said. "In that situation I already told you about. That big house, that never felt like mine. The isolation I felt at work. I sometimes used to bring my problems home. I was looking for someone to talk to. I really just needed a sounding board. Your mother tried to listen. She sat there dutifully, with this deeply disturbed look on her face. She would complain that she couldn't do this, she didn't know what I was talking about. I told her she didn't have to know. I would explain if she wanted, but I really just wanted someone to listen. But in time I came to realize there was really another problem. She had grown up in that beautiful house, with a big strong father. He had shielded her from things, as fathers tend to do. Her life had gone a certain way. She wanted it to continue that way. She wanted that same kind of life. That's what she thought her husband's job was, to protect her from the vicissitudes of life. It wasn't that she was unsympathetic. But she thought what I was doing was unseemly. She just wanted to act in the play. She didn't want to know what was happening backstage."

I couldn't have given a better capsule summary of the Duchess myself.

"Did that bother you?" I said.

"At first. Until I understood. This strange kind of horrified look would come over her face, and I'd think it was something about me. Or about my problem. But it wasn't that. It was that I was *telling* her."

He was supposed to be the Daddy.

"I finally gave up," he said. "You get the message after a while. And I lost the ability to tell her things. Anything that wasn't just wonderful. Now I've got something she needs to know. I sure as hell don't want her just reading it in the paper. And I can't bring myself to tell her."

The way the Senator and I arranged things—this was all his idea; I think he'd mapped it out before he talked to me—was that they would have me to dinner the next evening, just the three of us. He had wanted Helen to come too, but I said I'd tell her alone. After dinner he'd hang around and talk for a while, then go in for a nap, as he usually did. Normally I would have taken that as a cue to leave. But on this particular evening I'd stay and talk to the Duchess.

I had to wait until she got through in the kitchen. In the old days, with our large family, she hadn't done much cooking, and hadn't seemed to miss it. Now, when it was just the two of them—and especially because they were in an apartment, where it wasn't too comfortable to have help—she liked to cook and had gotten quite fussy about her kitchen. She didn't even want help cleaning up. (She did have, I hasten to add, the fanciest dishwasher known to man.) It all seemed to relax her, and gave her a way to take care of the Senator. It also, on occasions like this one, got her away from the men for a while.

On this particular evening, when she came back from the kitchen, I was sitting in the living room reading magazines.

"Can I get you something, Charles?" she said.

"No, Mother, thanks. I'm not staying long. I just wanted to talk to you about something."

"All right." Immediately she was on her guard. "Will it take long?"

"I don't think so."

"I'll get my needlepoint."

The Duchess did needlepoint throughout the evening when she was sitting around. It gave her something to do with her hands.

Once she was seated with that—so she could watch it when she wanted to, and not me—I said, "It's this problem Father's been having at work."

When I'd talked to the Senator about my strategy, he said

I ought to present it as my concern, not as something I was doing for him. He didn't want it to sound as if I were doing his dirty work. Even though I was.

She was frowning as she stared down at her needlepoint.

"I really had hoped we weren't going to talk about this," she said.

"I didn't ask him about it. He brought it up. He wanted me to know."

"All right."

"It's going to be in the papers. Not like a big scandal or anything." Another element of the Senator's strategy. "But he didn't want me to just read it."

I told the story differently than the Senator had, more the way I saw it, also in a way I thought the Duchess would understand. A woman in a terrible marriage had come to a lawyer in the Senator's firm about a divorce. He hadn't gotten her the settlement he should have. At the same moment, Frank Weyland was engaged in a major zoning battle. (The Duchess thought Weyland was wonderful, creating all those stylish malls—in place of a lot of old rotten buildings—and making all those millions. She was proud that the Senator was associated with him.) The husband being divorced was also the zoning commissioner. He had awarded Weyland the zoning change. Now, years later, the woman was charging that the whole thing had been a conspiracy.

My personal feeling—and I had been thinking this more and more, ever since my talk with Anna Jennings—was that, if there was a conspiracy, it was Weyland who had applied the screws. Everything I'd heard about him, including some stories Andrea told me, indicated he was a ruthless businessman who would have done anything to get what he wanted. He wouldn't have worried about fucking over Anna Jennings any more than about screwing those people out of their neighborhood. He would have gotten along famously with a real-estate wizard like Phillip Jennings. And a guy like Parnell would have caved in to him in a minute.

The Duchess—who had been staring down at her needlepoint the whole time I told the story, and who still didn't look up when she spoke—saw the problem elsewhere.

"That woman just wants more money," she said.

Her first thought was to blame the woman.

"Apparently she deserves more money. According to what Father says." And everybody else in the world.

"She's a greedy little waitress who wants more money and will do whatever is necessary to get it. Raise a scandal in the press. Tarnish the reputation of a good man."

"But Mother. Everyone agrees. The lawyer should have gotten her more money."

"Why can't she make her own money?"

"It's what the law allows. It's what she should have gotten."

"Why did she marry that man in the first place? If he was going to treat her that way."

Well, it was true. The whole problem wouldn't exist if she hadn't married the guy.

"I don't know," I said. "Maybe she loved him."

"When he treated her like that?"

"Maybe he didn't always treat her that way. Maybe he was nice at first."

"A woman knows what she's got, if she's got her eyes open at all. We have an instinct for that."

Perhaps. But we all—women and men—close our eyes to things we don't want to see.

"Maybe he was good-looking and charming," I said.

"Lots of men are. That doesn't mean you marry them."

Maybe he gave great head, Mother. Perhaps he had an eight-inch dick.

"I don't know," I said. "Why does anybody marry anybody? I wonder sometimes. The whole thing's a mystery."

The Duchess still hadn't looked up from her needlepoint. That craft served a useful purpose. I might have to take it up.

"That does seem to be the way people think these days," she said. "They just throw up their hands. Don't look at what they're getting. They give about as much thought to getting married as they do to crossing the street. In my day it was different. Marriage was sacred. We got married to stay, not because of some brief attraction. And no self-respecting woman in the world would have married a man who treated her like that."

Great. Anna Jennings made one mistake so we should let her rot in hell forever.

I found the Duchess's attitude so exasperating that I said something I never would have otherwise.

"Is that what you think I did?"

"What?"

"Got married like that. Without giving it a thought."

The Duchess looked startled. She actually blushed.

"No, Charles. Of course not. I wasn't thinking about you."

"I wondered."

"I know you tried in your marriage. You wanted it to last. Things don't always work out. Even with the best of intentions."

"I haven't told you much about it. Why it ended."

"You didn't have to. It was none of my business, if you didn't want to tell." The Duchess was nothing if not discreet. "I wondered, of course."

"What?"

"Just what happened. What went wrong."

"It was complicated."

"Of course it was. I never expected to know everything." She paused a moment, staring down at her needlepoint. "I wondered if there was someone else."

The question she'd been waiting to ask for months.

"For me or for her?"

There was a question that startled the Duchess.

"I don't know," she said. "Either one, I suppose. I meant for you."

There were dozens, Mother, legs spread wide, bodies soaked with sweat, faces etched in passion.

"No," I said.

"I didn't think so. I was sure you would have told us."

I wouldn't have told them in a million years.

"I don't know why I even asked that," she said. "I'm sorry."

"It's all right. I brought it up."

"It was none of my business. I wasn't talking about you in the first place. I was talking about this waitress." She was still focused down on her work. She had been focused on it the whole time. She was doing it a little faster now, just as she was hurrying the conversation along—avoiding the depths—now that she had gotten the information she wanted. "I do think some people don't work hard enough at marriage these days. They don't give it enough consideration."

"This woman may have tried."

"She may have. Possibly I'm making a snap judgment. But now that it didn't work out. Now that it's over. She's going to raise a fuss and make as much money as she can."

There was no convincing this woman. All I could say was what I had said before.

"I'll tell you how you confront a scandal, Charles," she said.

"How?"

"You pretend it doesn't exist."

The Duchess used this solution for most problems.

"You go out in the world and face people. You know pretty much what they're thinking. Who's thinking badly of you. You know your friends. Although there are always a few surprises. But you act as if it doesn't exist."

I wondered what scandals she had faced in her life. Perhaps the scandal of having a son like me. A daughter like Helen.

"If they speak of it, and very few people will, to your face, you refer to it only as what you believe it to be. A woman out to get more money." Perhaps that was why she had been so adamant. She was deciding how she would face people. "People who use a scandal are relying on hurting you. If you don't show the hurt they haven't done a thing."

"What if you feel the hurt?"

"You can't help feeling it. You just don't show it."

I was hearing the secret of her flawless exterior. I was hearing her philosophy of life.

I wondered what must be going on beneath that exterior. The tremendous energy that it took to maintain it.

"It's a difficult world your father lives in," she said. "It's also exciting. A world of high finance and greed. It would probably stand my hair on end to know what really goes on. I'm not sure I could take that. But I can stand by him in it."

"Yes."

"That's what he really needs from me."

Anyway, it was what he got.

"It hasn't always been easy. But I've always done it. I've been proud to do it. I'm very proud of your father."

"I know you are."

"I do appreciate your telling me all this. I didn't want to hear it at first. But it would have been harder finding out some other way. I think you should tell him you told me. Just so he'll know."

"I will." Any other messages?

"He's such a private man."

"He is."

"I don't think he ever would have told me himself."

"No. I don't think he would have."

The lawsuits were filed the next week, and the articles appeared in the paper, and I must say that, after all the buildup, they didn't seem too bad. The story was only in the local section, though it was on the front page there, and prominently featured. It told the facts in a dry way and didn't favor either side. The quotations from various parties and factions seemed predictable. Everyone may have been talking about the scandal in the law firms, but I didn't think the average citizen was concerned. Except maybe the ones with a grudge against Weyland.

It was late that week that I was sitting with Andrea in her house, sipping a beer, and the case came up. She had called me that afternoon, said she would whip up an omelet for dinner if I'd pick up a loaf of good French bread. She had put cheese and sautéed mushrooms in the omelet, cut up some fresh fruit for dessert. She'd even picked up some Pilsner Urquell to go with it.

The lawsuit against my father had become a touchy subject after that one discussion we'd had, and we had hardly mentioned it again. I still had the feeling she thought the Senator was guilty, that she thought all white wealthy capitalist men in general were guilty and might as well be hung for one crime as for another. But as we sat there in the living room, Andrea mentioned that she'd seen the articles in the paper. She spoke tentatively, as aware as I of how tender the subject was. I said I was surprised the articles hadn't been worse. She said they hadn't seemed too bad to her either.

"I don't see how this lawyer, this John Auerbach, is ready to take the case to court," I said.

"How's that?"

"As far as I can tell, the whole conspiracy theory rests on some things my father supposedly said to this young associate in his firm. Robert Parnell. But even if you assume anyone on earth could remember things that were said so many years ago. Even if what he was told wasn't in the least ambiguous, so you know he took it the right way. Even if you ignore the fact that Parnell has ample reason to lie at this point, because otherwise he'll be shown up as incompetent. My father is obviously a much more impressive person, in a more impressive position. I can't believe anybody's going to listen to Parnell over him."

"Good. Great, in fact."

"But Anna Jennings says Auerbach is confident. He's ready to take the case to court. He's sure he can win."

"Maybe he's just wrong."

"How can he be that wrong?"

It was a big thing to take a man like the Senator to court. You wouldn't do it lightly.

"There's got to be something else," I said. "Anna Jennings said there was, something Auerbach had found only recently. She didn't know what it was."

Andrea didn't say anything for a while, slumped beside me on the couch. She was also drinking a beer. She had on a large shapeless shift she liked to wear around the house, had her knees drawn up under it. "I wasn't going to say anything about all this," she said. "I didn't think you'd want me butting in. But I could probably find out for you."

"How's that?"

"I know John Auerbach."

I turned and looked at her.

"I didn't know he was the lawyer until I read it in the paper. But I wasn't surprised. He's the obvious person to be suing your father."

"Really?"

"He's kind of the lawyer of the Left around here. Works in some of the same political organizations I do. He's very anti-development. I'm sure he detests Frank Weyland. But he's also a maverick in the legal world. Works alone, doesn't hang out with other lawyers. He'll take on weak cases. Lost causes. He's really quite a piece of work. He hangs around this bar his brother owns and talks about his cases. Gossips about city hall. He's got quite a following. He's a barroom entertainer. He's also got an eye for the ladies. It wouldn't be hard to get him to talk. I'm not sure I can work him around to the things you want to know. But I might."

"You really think so?"

"I'm not a bad little operator myself."

Andrea seemed intrigued by the idea. She liked the thought of working on somebody.

"I'd really appreciate it." I didn't see any other way of finding out what Auerbach was up to. "As long as you wouldn't have to blow him or something."

I don't know why I said that. Probably because I'd wanted to say something—perhaps something a little more tactful—for a long time. The subject of monogamy was another one we hadn't exactly worn out in recent days. Andrea had let me know, in various unsubtle ways, that she was still seeing Mitchell Dantry. She'd spoken of him lightly and deprecatingly, of his incredibly sloppy housekeeping, of the way he mistreated his son. She said she could never see a man like that on a steady basis. But she hadn't said she'd stopped seeing him. (It sounded pretty steady to me.) I had half-convinced myself that I liked her easy attitude, that I'd been looking all my life for a woman like her, that a woman couldn't have her kind of wild abandon about sex without acting as she did.

But I was kidding myself. What I really wanted was for Andrea to be faithful to me. I wanted her to choose between me and that other way of life. I didn't bring the subject up because I was afraid of what she might say.

Instead I blurted out a stupid remark like that.

She was staring at me. "I think he'd come across for a hand job. Although you never know. I'd do what I had to."

At least she hadn't lost her sense of humor.

"Why don't you say it bothers you, if it bothers you?" she said.

She knew it was that larger subject I was bringing up.

"I'm not sure it does."

"It certainly seems to."

"Sometimes it does and sometimes it doesn't."

"What bothers you about it?"

"Well. It doesn't bother me that you want to fool around. I understand that. And it doesn't interfere with us. You never say you want to see him instead of me."

Mitchell Dantry had quietly slipped into the conversation.

"And I never will," she said.

"I guess I'm just afraid you'll fall in love."

"With Mitchell Dantry?"

"With somebody. I'm afraid that if you're out there fooling around, fucking people, you'll find somebody you like better."

The bottom line in all jealousy.

"That isn't what I'm looking for," she said.

"That doesn't mean it won't happen."

"It could happen even if I weren't fucking other guys."

"It's a lot more likely if you are."

"I don't fall in love that easily. I don't see it as a real threat."

"Maybe you'll find somebody who fucks better."

She laughed. "That's even less likely. I've sampled the field. And I'll never find a better pussy-eater. Unless it's a lesbian somewhere."

I was insulted.

She put her arm around me. "I do love you, Charles. I love you more than anyone I've ever known. I'm not looking for somebody else to love. I just want to fuck around a little."

"I know."

I knew about wanting to fuck around.

"I wish I could prove it to you. I wish I could prove how much I love you." She snuggled up to me.

"Actually, I believe you." I felt content with the present. It was the future I was worried about.

"I want to do something. I want to show you."

Well. You could stop seeing Mitchell Dantry.

"Maybe if I get this information from John Auerbach, that'll be a little help."

According to Andrea, we would be able to find John Auerbach any evening at that Oakland bar he frequented. It was like a second home to him. Most evenings he was sitting at the bar with a group of cronies. Other evenings he was at a table with an attractive woman. (The cronies knew to stay away.) She said that as long as we got there before he did she was sure she could get Auerbach to sit with her. There was no question in her mind. The only problem was if he was with a woman.

All this made me wonder, once again, how well Andrea

knew Auerbach, but I didn't raise the question. She suggested I come to the bar with her and sit elsewhere in the room, maybe have dinner. She said the food was excellent. When I picked her up she was wearing a new cotton dress, a bright green number with little black stick figures all over it. Her hair was bright and shiny. The dress was clingy. I wasn't sure I wanted to take her anywhere.

The bar was atypical for Pittsburgh, a bright shiny place with light pouring in the windows, a pale stain on the wide smooth woodwork of the bar, young tan business types sitting around looking as if they'd just gotten back from the health club. The music, in fact—some synthetic kind of rock—sounded like the stuff people do aerobics to. Perrier water and white wine were being consumed in enormous quantities. (Andrea had told me, however, that a number of drug deals were done at that bar. People would make the contact and head back to the bathroom. I didn't see anyone who looked remotely like a drug dealer to me.) I sat at a table and had a shot of Jack Daniel's and a beer. I wanted to distance myself as much as possible from the lightweights who inhabited that place.

Andrea stepped up to the bar and was immediately surrounded by three men. It was like tossing a fresh young tuna into the shark tank. She somehow managed to keep them around her—one immediately bought her a drink—while letting them know it wouldn't be for long. She really was an operator. We probably could have gotten all kinds of information at the bar that night.

By the time Auerbach came in I had ordered dinner. (Grilled red snapper with a side order of pasta in oil and garlic. A tiny portion of zucchini. The food was superb.) Auerbach was a scruffy little guy dressed in a sportshirt and jeans. I assumed he had looked more like a lawyer earlier in the day. He had a tanned, pock-marked face and short brown hair. Andrea hooked up with him instantly; she gave the other three guys a nod and they scattered like a flock of geese. Her greeting to Auerbach was a not-especially-definitive kiss on the mouth. (I'm sorry. I just can't make the call.) They did sit very close at the bar and talk as if no one else were around. Andrea drank two beers. Auerbach was buying. Andrea seemed to be hearing the most fascinating gossip in the world. Auerbach looked as if he were explaining some intricate matter, leaning forward on his bar stool, gesturing with his hands. He also often touched her, the stupid turd. I was feeling the pressure so much that I had a piece of cheesecake with my coffee. It was marvelous. All in all Andrea spent well over an hour with Auerbach. Their kiss as they parted was rather more lingering, but they'd had quite a bit to drink. Her departure was my signal to leave, though it took me a while to get the check. We'd agreed to meet in a nearby drugstore.

When I walked in, Andrea's expression was far different than it had been in the bar. Her face had lost all its animation. She seemed almost solemn. The first thing she said was, "That man really hates your father."

Anna Jennings had said the same thing.

"He seems to see him as a symbol of everything he despises in the legal profession," she said. "You have the feeling he's been waiting for this case for years. Once he got hold of it he's not letting go."

Andrea looked genuinely shaken. I wasn't at all sure I wanted to hear the news.

"Do you think he can prove his case?" I said.

"It certainly sounds that way, if what he's saying is true. But I think I should wait to tell you this until I get to the house."

"What? It's so involved?"

"It might be kind of a shock. I'm not sure."

I couldn't wait until we got back to the house, as it turned out. Andrea told me on the way. It wasn't a shock in the way she was afraid it would be. It was certainly a surprise, but it also—once it had settled in—fit in with everything else I knew. There was more to it all than she understood, plenty to discuss when we got back to the house, but we didn't discuss it when we got there that evening, and as it turned out we never did. There was a note waiting for me at the house from Helen. My father had had another heart attack, and had been taken to the coronary-care unit of a local hospital. She thought I should get there as soon as I could.

FOURTEEN

The dull green carpet in the intensive-care waiting room was faded and worn. The furniture was cheap and sturdy, top-of-the-line at Sears. There were magazines around, *Reader's Digest, Good Housekeeping,* also a number of magazines on health which, if you had read them and followed their advice, would probably have kept you out of the hospital in the first place. In the corner was a huge color television that was left on all the time. The sound was turned down, it was turned almost off, but those images—the strange world of television, which bears so little relation to reality—just kept on coming.

The Duchess, as I stepped into the waiting room and saw her sitting on the couch, looked strong: that was the first word that came to mind. Her face was hard, and fixed in a stoic mask, but it exuded strength and control. Seated on either side of her, dressed in dark suits, were my brothers. Ken is tall and lean, sandy-haired, with a thick mustache that he keeps neatly trimmed, a bland handsome face. He is apparently an intelligent person and a successful attorney, but he is also one of the dullest human beings I have ever met. Barry is slightly shorter, thinner still, with black hair and an olive complexion. He is livelier than Ken, slightly less predictable. He certainly has more physical affect. Ken has all the ease of bearing of a ninety-year-old man. But they were sitting now on either side of my mother, as if to brace her by their example. The three of them formed a kind of phalanx against calamity. They were like the stone busts that you see in front of museums.

Sitting beside them, in jeans and a sweater, and gone all to pieces, was Helen.

She stepped to greet me and collapsed into my arms. It must have been hell to sit there with no one who was sympathetic to who she was. Andrea embraced her with me. She had also started to cry. She must have wondered what was wrong with the stony-faced trio on the couch.

But I didn't. They were like me. Our grief was sunk in us like so many other emotions, like an iceberg. It was frozen all the way down.

I didn't know how to read this situation, whether to take my cue from Helen's grief or my mother's strength.

I put the story together from bits and pieces of what everyone began to tell me. The Senator had gone to work that morning despite the fact that he'd looked exhausted. The Duchess had urged him to stay home, something she never would have done in the past, but he said he was tired because of things that were nagging at him; the only way to feel better was to go to work. He had come home looking worse than when he'd left. His face was a sickly pale that she didn't think she'd ever seen on him, and there were beads of sweat on his forehead. She asked if he felt bad and he said he just felt tired, and slightly nauseous. He seemed terribly anxious, sat down with a glass of wine earlier than he normally would have. Almost reluctantly, he began to describe a pain he was having, actually a feeling you could hardly describe as pain, just a slight feeling of pressure, on his sternum. There was also an ache, really just a kind of heaviness, in one arm and up into his shoulder. It wasn't really a pain. He hardly knew he was feeling it. His arm just felt heavy when he lifted it.

The Duchess listened to these words with a creeping feeling of horror. He was describing the classic symptoms of a heart attack, just as if he had never heard them, though she had listened to a nurse go over them with him only a few months before. The nurses made sure no heart patient left the hospital without knowing them. The Duchess didn't want to alarm him, asked him how long he'd been feeling that way. He said maybe an hour, maybe a little longer. She said she was going to call his doctor, then went into the next room and dialed 911. She came back and said the doctor was going to "send somebody." As soon as the ambulance crew got there (one of them told her later), they knew he was having a heart attack, from his sickly pallor alone. They got him onto a stretcher and started him on oxygen. She rode with him to the hospital, then called Helen. Since then they had told her only that they were running some tests. No one would comment on the Senator's condition. There was nothing to do but wait.

The scene in the waiting room was definitely an awkward one. Ken and Barry had never met Andrea. They didn't even seem to have heard of her. They didn't know whether she was the love of my life or somebody I'd picked up in a bar a few hours before. Ken tried to make conversation with her, like the polite dutiful brother. He asked what she did, and listened as she told him with what seemed to be total incomprehension. All the women he knew were married to lawyers and spent their time chauffeuring children around in station wagons. She also, for some reason, told him about her political work, which must have really stuck like a barb in his ass. This man was one of the bright lights of the local Republican party (you could tell by the vacant expression). The boys asked me about my writing. I asked how things were going down at the office. It was like the most awkward cocktail party you've ever been to in your life, people who might as well be from different planets. But it was a gathering of my family.

After a while a young doctor came in and spoke to us. He said the Senator's condition seemed stable at that point. He was ninety-nine percent sure he'd had a heart attack, though to know that officially they would have to wait for the results of their tests. He said he certainly couldn't tell us there was no cause for alarm, but that the Senator had apparently survived the attack, and that was a positive sign. He was in a safe environment and resting comfortably, but he shouldn't see anyone that night. There was no need for us to stay.

259

There was an immediate consensus that we didn't want to leave him alone in the hospital. We didn't all have to stay, but we wanted someone there. The Duchess didn't want to leave, but we all thought it would be better if she did. We got her to agree to leave if we promised one of us would be there all the time and would call her at the slightest provocation. We decided that Barry would stay until one, Ken until four, and I, God help me, would take the last shift. Helen would go home to be with the Duchess.

It wasn't until we got out of the hospital that I realized Andrea hadn't eaten yet. I had been thinking how difficult all this must be for her, how strange it must seem, but she said it was all right, I shouldn't be giving her a thought. She asked if I needed her, and I said I didn't; she said she was going home to get some food, but that I should call her anytime I needed anything. I should call her the next day in any case. I went back to the house and didn't know what to do with myself. I tried to read and couldn't concentrate. I turned on the television and that was worse: that feeble crap doesn't hold my attention under the best of circumstances. I wanted to go out and take a walk but was afraid I'd miss a phone call. I did a lot of pacing around the house. Around midnight I went upstairs to try to sleep, but it was hopeless. My legs were tied in knots, and my mind wouldn't shut down. I tried to read in bed; I went down and made some tea; I forced myself to stare at a late movie. Somehow I made it through the hours until my shift.

At the hospital, I was the only person in the waiting room. I let the nurse at the desk know I was there. I found out that, oddly enough, you couldn't turn that television off. You could turn it all the way down, but not off. (I asked a nurse about it later, and she said it caused too many arguments, having the choice. I could think of a far better way to eliminate the choice.) Sitting in one of the slightly uncomfortable armchairs, staring at those silent images in the dark, I actually fell asleep sitting up, something I almost never do. I woke up a little after six when a short guy smoking a corncob pipe came in and started to vacuum. He shook his head in sympathy as I snorted and blinked at him. (He didn't offer to come back later.) There was a different nurse at the desk, but she assured me the Senator had passed a quiet night. I went to the coffee shop and had three donuts and a danish for breakfast. The coffee tasted burnt. Helen and the Duchess arrived in the waiting room around eight. They hadn't apparently slept much, but at least they'd had a chance to freshen up and change clothes. The Duchess was allowed to go in and see the Senator at nine. He was weak, she said, but well rested and glad to see her. He seemed pale, but even at that looked better than he had the afternoon before.

I would have said scared rather than weak. Visiting hours were limited in the cardiac-care unit; you could only stay for half an hour, and only two people were allowed in at a time; the Duchess was always one and I was only sometimes the other, but when I saw the Senator he seemed stunned to be there, and frightened. He lay back against the bed and didn't move much. He complained of the various gadgets attached to him, an intravenous and a tube taped to his chest. His heart rate showed on a screen beside the bed. I would try to make small talk when I was there, but he was impatient and distracted, barely seemed to listen. He said he felt like a laboratory animal, lying there with all those things in him, doctors and nurses coming in and out all the time. He said the food was terrible, called it the milk-toast-and-tapioca diet. But I think all his complaints were a reflection of his fear, his extreme discomfort at being there at all. On the third day, much to his relief, he was moved to a private room.

By that time I'd had a chance to talk to the Senator's doctor, Eric Strowd, a man close to the Senator's age who also knew him as a friend. He was a funny-looking old bird, short and extremely bald, with only a few strands of hair running down the center of his skull. He had a fat flaccid face and a huge dent of a dimple in his chin. He was easy to talk to and absolutely frank, told me some things I hadn't known before. He said the Senator's first heart attack had been so mild— the kind that gives virtually no pain, and is discovered only later—that he didn't think the Senator had ever really believed he'd had it. That kind of denial was common among hard-driving competitive types. The Senator had actually told some friends downtown that he'd been hospitalized for exhaustion. He had refused to have a test done that would have checked the blockage of his arteries (there was some risk involved, a tiny mortality rate on the test alone, and he didn't think it was worth it), but he had promised to take his condition seriously and mend his ways. For a while he had followed his diet, and he continued to follow it around the Duchess, but he had confessed to Strowd that he'd been cheating in recent weeks. He hadn't been following his diet down at the Duquesne Club, for instance (he'd had a small steak and a piece of cheesecake the day of his attack!), and had even smoked some. Worst of all, he'd been doing difficult and stressful work. Strowd had told him that was the one thing above all that he should avoid. It was no surprise that he'd wound up back in the hospital.

Strowd thought this heart attack had finally gotten his attention. The Senator was a man whose way of life was deeply ingrained in him, but if he was ever going to change, now was the time. He thought I ought to talk to him. Not to nag him, but to level with him.

At the same time, Strowd was mildly encouraging. He said the recovery rate for people who had had such mild heart attacks was reasonably good. The Senator's condition had stabilized quickly and remained stable since. He needed to get some rest and change his habits. In a few days they would be doing some more tests to see what they might be able to do to improve the situation. But his future was really in his own hands.

Things loosened up considerably once the Senator had moved into his private room. Visiting hours were virtually limitless. The Duchess liked to spend the morning with him, also to come in before he went to sleep. There were plenty of visitors in the evening. But there was a slack time in the early afternoon, after he'd had his early lunch (eleven-thirty) and a short nap. I was through writing and he was ready for some company. He was always glad to have me.

We didn't talk about weighty things; we didn't even always talk. That first week, the Pirates were in Chicago, so we watched a couple of ball games on television. He asked about work, and I spoke of what little I was doing (whenever I wasn't at the hospital, I felt as if I were waiting to go there). We talked about things at his office, studiously avoiding anything serious. Mostly, though, we talked about old times. He had an endless supply of anecdotes about his boyhood and youth, which we had tapped into slightly in the past, but now, with long stretches of time on our hands, one story led to another, and his reminded me of stories from my own past. I don't remember how we got started on all that, but as the days progressed we were falling into it sooner and sooner. After about a week we were talking about nothing else.

There was something sad about those stories. They looked back, for one thing, on times when we had both been young and healthy, when something like a heart attack or a long stay in the hospital was the farthest thing from our minds. There was an unspoken feeling that there were no such good times left. The Senator seemed to have the suspicion, which he expressed only obliquely, that things were much worse than the doctors were saying, that people were talking about his recovery as a formality, a feeble attempt to keep his hopes up. He listened to such talk—at least when it came from me— with impatience and distraction. He wanted to get back to stories of the past. I only sensed this attitude in him, and nothing I said could change it. If he had spoken more openly, I could have addressed what he really felt.

After the Senator had been in the hospital about a week, the doctors did an angiogram, the only-very-slightly danger-ous procedure that the Senator had refused before. It involved entering his body through an artery in the groin (maybe that was why he had refused), then traveling up the arterial sys-tem to inject a dye into the coronary arteries and see where the problem was. They discovered that the Senator's blockage was too diffuse to do an angioplasty (that new procedure with which they clear an artery by inflating a balloon) and that he needed bypass surgery instead. That was a viable, gener-ally successful procedure, and the doctors were still optimis-tic. They would need to wait six to eight weeks from the time of the heart attack to do it.

On the ninth day of his stay—he was scheduled to leave the next morning, to recuperate at home for a while—I said, "Do you think you can do without me for a couple of days?"

"I suppose," he said. "I can always take up the soaps."

We occasionally turned them on for a laugh.

"I've got to do an interview. Down in Florida." I had made sure Ken and Barry would be available to help him move back into the apartment.

"What does Strowd say? Does he think I'll die in the mean-time?"

"He gave me the green light. Said to stay away for months if I wanted."

That was typical of the way the Senator spoke about his health. He wouldn't ask a direct question. He'd talk around it.

"Dad," I said. "You don't think I'd go if there were any danger."

"No."

"All right. Well, I'm going. It's not even an especially important trip. And Strowd did say it was okay. He said I shouldn't give it a second thought."

I did at that point have to invent out of whole cloth the person I was going to interview. I told the Senator it was a preliminary meeting, just to see if I wanted to do the piece, with an aging writer in Florida who had started a comeback. Back in the fifties he had written some interesting and exciting fiction—three books in five years—that had sold only modestly. Broke and discouraged, he'd become a screenwriter in Hollywood, where he'd been a competent craftsman and had turned out a number of successful projects. He hadn't been one of the all-stars, but he'd been a well-paid and dependable utility man. He had also been an alcoholic for years, even while he was a young fiction writer, and he'd gone through five wives in Hollywood. He loved those starlets. When things finally went bust in Hollywood—not because of his drinking, but because he couldn't write about space aliens or upper-middle-class teenagers—he moved back to Florida and returned to fiction as if he'd never quit. He still had some money left from Hollywood and lived on very little, fishing every morning and keeping a garden. He had published two new books and was starting to establish a reputation again. At the age of sixty-four, he was being spoken of in the same breath as writers in their twenties. And his early novels were about to be reissued.

I had made this person up out of two or three writers I'd read about. He sounded like a fascinating subject for a profile. I'd even given him a name. Otis Harvey.

"Is he still on the sauce?" the Senator said.

"That's what they say. As bad as ever."

"Good luck on interviewing him then."

I decided that was what I'd say when I got back. The guy was too drunk all the time for me to work with him.

I still sometimes thought I'd missed my calling as a novelist.

"In the meantime," I said, "I want you to take care of yourself. Get back to that apartment and take it easy. Rent some movies. Read some books. And stick to your diet. Stay off that cheesecake."

"Yeah."

"I want you to get better this time. I want you to do it right."

"It wasn't cheesecake that gave me this problem."

"Not one piece. It was all the cheesecake through the years."

He shook his head. "Not all the cheesecake in the world."

The Senator seemed grumpy that day, restless and preoccupied. It may have been the fact that I was leaving for a couple of days, but I didn't think so. I almost thought it was because he was moving back to the apartment. It wasn't like he was in love with the hospital.

"It was this lawsuit that broke me," he said.

That was the first time he'd mentioned the lawsuit since he'd been in the hospital. We'd been pretending it didn't exist.

I let out a long sigh. "I know."

"This heart attack and the first one. There's no question in my mind."

There was no question in my mind either. But it was easier to talk about some innocuous cause. Cheesecake.

"I just feel trapped by it," he said. "I sit in the office and think about it. All the work I do is working on it. I go back home and it's never off my mind. It sits there and stares at me. The only way I get away from it is to have a heart attack."

"Can't you drop it?"

"How can I drop it? *They're* suing *me.*"

"You've got lots of competent lawyers down there. Let one of them handle it."

I proceeded to launch into an impressive disquisition on how I saw the lawsuit. I was careful to speak only of things the Senator had told me about, but I said what I thought and spoke from the heart. I told him I thought Parnell was trying to throw up a smokescreen and avoid responsibility. He'd been in over his head fifteen years ago, bound to screw up on something, but he hadn't wanted to admit it then and didn't want to now. He was covering his ass. It was his word against the Senator's, but the Senator was a far more impressive person. It wouldn't even be a contest.

I was aware as I spoke that there was one more piece to this puzzle, but I didn't mention that. That was what I was going to Florida to find out about.

The Senator didn't interrupt as I made my little speech. He sat patiently listening to me, his head down, his eyes nearly closed. He said something as I finished that let me know he wasn't going to disagree: he was going to tell me something that made everything I'd said irrelevant.

He said, "The year all this happened. The year of those hearings."

"Yes?"

"That was the year Quentin Robinson retired."

There was a different tone to his words now, different than any he'd used about the lawsuit. He wasn't talking as a lawyer. He was talking as a man.

"Was it?" I said.

He nodded. He was still looking down.

Quentin Robinson was a revered name in my family, the senior partner in the law firm for years. He had been of my grandfather's generation, but had continued to work after the others his age had retired. Even in the old days, when he and his contemporaries had been younger, he'd been the most distinguished member of the firm. By the time he retired he was practically a legend.

"He stood for everything the firm represented," the Senator said. "A cold hard canny intelligence. An old kind of probity. Nobody put anything over on Quentin Robinson. He was a crack attorney. Right up into his eighties. He and my father had started the firm together, but I don't think they were ever really friends. Nobody was friends with Quentin Robinson. He didn't need friends. He had his law books and his bank account. His brilliant mind. My father was a fine attorney, but he was also a human being. He could let down now and then. Quentin Robinson never did."

I'd never heard my father speak of the man this way. He'd only spoken of him in hushed reverential tones, like a minor deity.

"He called me young Bradsher. Even when I was fifty years old and about to take over the firm. He was still calling me that. God knows what he would have called you."

Young Bradsher the Younger.

"Frank Weyland, the builder in this case, was another kind of man altogether. Kind of a sleazy character. He didn't quite do anything illegal, but he also wasn't out for the public good. A man with that kind of money doesn't have to get illegal. Money itself subverts the law. It was a brilliant move on his part to pick Robinson for his lawyer. Like picking Daniel Webster or somebody. It lent an air of uprightness to his enterprise. Nobody questioned Robinson's ethics. But in his own way he was just as ruthless as Weyland. He wasn't money hungry. He was power hungry. He'd do anything to win. He thought it wasn't right for him to lose. He was the prophet of God."

I'd much rather tangle with somebody who was out for cash.

"His retirement marked the end of an era in the firm. Father's death, and his retirement. People thought we were going into decline. All the great old men were gone. A guy like Weyland didn't have any loyalty to a law firm. He'd stick around as long as we could do something for him. He'd be keeping close track. And if you lost a man like Weyland, you lost more than the money he brought in. You lost prestige in the community. You might lose clients.

"Weyland and I went together to lobby this man Jennings. The zoning commissioner. He was exactly the kind of businessman I can't stand. Fast-talking. Good-looking in a slick way. A nasty glint in his eye. Extremely well-dressed. He was full of schemes for making money. Had any number of suggestions for Weyland. He sounded as if he'd like to go in on some of them too. But at the same time, he wouldn't commit himself on this zoning question. He said there were a lot of things to consider. The local businesses that would be affected. All the people in the neighborhood. Jennings was supposed to be the most prodevelopment person on the commission. If he wasn't with us we were in big trouble. Weyland and I kept looking at each other. We hardly knew what to say. Then as we were going out, Jennings pulled me back for a minute. 'Could I have a word with you, counselor?' I hate it when a little dip like that calls me counselor. He was standing there with that slimy grin on his face. He looked embarrassed. For a moment he didn't say anything. Then he said, 'You know, I'd feel a whole lot better about this zoning change if I weren't so worried about paying alimony.' "

Subtlety was not this man's strong point.

"Did you know the connection?"

"I knew about the divorce. It wouldn't have occurred to me to think of the two things together. So it didn't quite register with me what he was saying. I thought he was changing the subject or something. Asking for legal advice. He was standing there with this dumb grin on his face. Then it dawned on me."

"He meant you could be of some help."

"Right."

"How did you react?"

"I don't even remember. I said some stupid thing. I could understand how he felt or something. I hoped it worked out for him. But as I was walking out of the place with Weyland, it occurred to me what had just happened. I'd been asked to do something unethical. Possibly illegal. And I hadn't said no."

"You hadn't said anything."

"I hadn't said no. At first I thought of calling him and saying just that. I would have no part of such a suggestion. I was insulted that he'd even brought it up. Then I decided that would be a needless provocation. I just wouldn't do what he wanted. I didn't have to tell him. But it occurred to me to wonder, what if the wife didn't get alimony for some other reason? He'd think I'd done it. I didn't know how the case stood. I thought I'd talk to Parnell."

Perhaps not the best course of action under the circumstances.

The Senator was staring at the wall in front of him as he spoke. He hadn't looked at me. He was fingering a rabbit's foot someone had given him for luck.

"I was feeling terribly anxious at that moment in my life. I'd never thought it would be like that. I thought I'd move with ease into the top spot. It would feel right. But the weight of the whole firm seemed to rest on my shoulders. I had no one to advise me. I felt I had to win that zoning battle. I had to hang on to Weyland. I was fifty years old, senior partner in the city's best law firm, and I felt like a kid starting out.

"I went to Parnell and asked about the case. I didn't say anything about why I was asking. He started to tell me some things. He mentioned an agreement the wife had signed."

I almost blew my cover at that point. I almost told him—in my impatience—that I knew about the agreement. But I stopped myself. I listened to his whole painstaking legal explanation. It wasn't any different from what Anna Jennings had told me. The agreement was informal, but it was valid.

"Suddenly, when I heard about that agreement, something gave way in me. I must have been under more strain than I thought. I felt as if a whole new world were opening up before me. I wasn't hearing the facts of a divorce action. I was hearing a way out from this enormous weight. A way that Jennings could have what he wanted and I could have what I wanted. The answer to all my problems. It wasn't quite legitimate. . . ."

It wasn't legitimate by a long shot.

". . . but it was at least plausible. It was a possible explanation of why somebody wouldn't get alimony. I started to see all kinds of reasons for not pursuing it. They were blooming around me like flowers. Parnell argued with me. He was an intelligent attorney defending his case. He thought I was crazy at first. Then all of a sudden the light seemed to dawn. You could see it in his eyes. I was talking on a different level. I didn't have to spell it out for him. Parnell wasn't just smart as a lawyer. He was also smart in other ways."

He could see that the Senator was asking him to do something for the firm rather than for his client.

"It didn't seem too bad to me," the Senator said. "The woman would be keeping her house. She'd be getting ample child support. She would probably have had to go out and work in any case. This wasn't going to leave her a pauper or something."

He was wrong about that. I didn't say anything, but I knew. It would have made all the difference in the world for Anna

Jennings to get alimony. Even a small amount of money would have been a huge help.

The Senator didn't understand the way a person like that lived. He didn't know what a tight budget was.

"But what I did was wrong," he said. "Listening to Jennings in the first place. Going to Parnell. I did it because I was afraid. That I wouldn't be able to do what I had to. I wouldn't measure up to Quentin Robinson. I did it because of this empty feeling in my stomach. A hollow feeling down in my balls. The anxiety was unbearable. I grabbed for that agreement as if it would save me."

Instead it dragged him down.

"I know that fear," I said.

It was a man's fear. You won't be able to *do* it.

"It doesn't excuse a thing," he said.

"It helps explain it."

"It doesn't make it any better."

"You were under a lot of pressure. You did the best you could at the time."

"I never thought it would get me this way."

He put his head down and wept. Tears poured from his eyes.

"Dad." I stood from the chair where I'd been sitting and took his hand.

"This was a mistake I made fifteen years ago!" He almost shouted the words, through his sobs, while I held his hand, and he shook with the crying. "For a few minutes, standing there in Parnell's office, I was afraid. Or I didn't face my fear. I didn't see it for what it was. Now I can't escape what I did. It's the one thing people are going to remember about me. It seemed like such a small thing when I did it. A brief moment. But now it fills up everything. It fills up the whole world."

His body was wracked with sobs. I was afraid for him, in his condition, but I also thought it was better for him to cry. It was the holding it in that was killing him.

"It's the only thing they'll remember," he said. "It's the only thing they'll ever see."

"It's not the only thing I'll remember," I said.

I had plenty of time, on my plane trip to Florida, to mull over what that conversation had meant to me. If all I had been interested in was the lawsuit, it might have taken away my reason for going, but by that time I was interested in much more than that. My father had told me some pretty damning things about himself. He had told me he was a part of a conspiracy to defraud, that he—along with a couple of fairly sleazy characters—had cheated a woman out of money she was entitled to. I had met the woman, and knew how much it meant to her. He had told me he'd done it because he was afraid, because he didn't think he could live up to the reputation of an earlier generation of lawyers. I knew the fear he was talking about. I'd had no idea he'd ever felt it. I'd somehow thought you abandoned those feelings when you became a successful lawyer, that you put them off when you put on the three-piece suit.

Hearing those things didn't make me feel further from my father. They didn't make me want to condemn him. I felt closer to him than I ever had. I didn't care what he'd done. I was glad he'd told me, instead of leaving me to find out another way.

I would probably have found out on my trip to Florida.

The story that John Auerbach had told Andrea in the bar on the night of my father's heart attack had been quite dramatic. He seemed to have perfected it at that point. God knows how many of his bar buddies he had told it to. He had been convinced from the start—perhaps just because of his prejudices, his antagonism toward the Senator—that Parnell was telling the truth. He had somehow found Parnell's desperation convincing, but he knew he needed something more than that in a courtroom. He had—in the long interim after the Senator's first heart attack—talked to a number of people without getting any leads. He didn't fraternize with lawyers, but he did know one old duffer—referred to in his story as the Aging Attorney—who invited him to the Duquesne Club for lunch now and then. It was while they were there one day, after the New England clam chowder and the roast Long Island duckling, that the Aging Attorney had said, "You ought to look up Kay Fulton. She was Bradford's secretary for years. I'm not sure where she is at this point. I think she retired somewhere. But she was his closest confidante. She might know something."

The old boy took a sip of his coffee, drew on his cigar. With a perfectly straight face, a matter-of-fact tone, he said, "She was well known to be his mistress."

Auerbach perked up at those words. The idea that the Senator had had a mistress smelled of a scandal to him. It smelled like roses.

It was also of no small interest to me.

But the Aging Attorney hadn't thought it was a big deal. "It wasn't considered immoral for a man like him. Nobody thought a thing of it. It wasn't like he was frequenting whores, or betting on the horses. He was keeping two women. He kept them rather well. More power to him."

Auerbach hadn't had much to go on. He didn't think he'd better call the Senator's firm and ask where Kay Fulton was. But he had an all-star secretary himself, one of those forty-five-year-old ballbusters who will do anything for the boss. She knew a number of other secretaries, and it wasn't long before she found out that Kay Fulton had retired to Naples, Florida, but that she periodically visited her mother in a rest home outside Philadelphia. Auerbach found out when her next visit would be—in February—showed up at the rest home, and asked her if they could meet at her motel later that afternoon. Kay agreed before she'd really had a chance to think about it. She wasn't able to get in touch with the Senator before the meeting.

Auerbach painted a lurid picture of what had happened to his client, a working woman just like her, a middle-aged mother of children in college who was still struggling to make ends meet and who years ago had been cheated out of a substantial sum of money. At first Kay said it had all happened too long ago, she didn't even think about work anymore, but as Auerbach continued to talk about Anna Jennings she finally admitted she remembered the case. She said she had been worried about a conflict of interest at the time, which was more than the Senator had admitted. She hadn't come out and said the Senator had leaned on Parnell, but Auerbach thought there was a certain hesitancy in her manner, a tentativeness. He thought he could probe it on the stand.

Furthermore, it would be a huge embarrassment for the Senator if it came out that Kay was his mistress, a fact that was relevant to the trial because it demonstrated a bias. The Senator would be extremely reluctant to have her testify.

He'd be much more likely to come to a settlement with that threat hanging over him.

I certainly remembered Kay Fulton from when I was younger. She had been so important a secretary to the Senator as to have become almost a member of the family. She had been the first person we saw whenever we went to see him at the office. She was the one who saw to it that we got through to see him. She ate Thanksgiving and Christmas dinners with us. She remembered all our birthdays. We sometimes had a birthday party for her. The idea that she was the Senator's mistress was startling at first, almost breathtaking, but after a few minutes it made perfect sense. You wondered why you hadn't realized it years ago. It was one of those discoveries that opened up a whole new level in your memories. Helen, when I told her, claimed she had known it years before. She had always thought Kay was Father's lover. When I asked her why she hadn't mentioned this little item to me, she said she hadn't been sure. She hadn't thought it mattered (!). She hadn't known how I might react. She wasn't sure I could take it.

I suppose that Kay was an attractive woman in a kind of fifties' way, tall and thin, modest, unassuming. She had moderately long brown hair that she wore up in a bun, and she always wore glasses when she worked. Without them—at our house for a party, for instance—her face looked curiously blank. You wouldn't have described that face as pretty. (She was certainly no match for the Duchess.) It was long and thin, and her mouth was too large. There was a noticeable gap between her front teeth. She did dress tastefully and well. At our family gatherings she stayed in the background, but at the office—in a quiet way—she seemed to run the show. The Senator often said he couldn't have worked a single day without her. She just smiled when he said that. She didn't contradict him.

No one had ever mentioned a man in connection with her (now I knew why). She was one of those women who, when you were young, you thought of as not needing a man, like your old Irish housekeeper, but as you got older you began to wonder. I had never thought of my father as being sexual with her—at a certain age, you don't think of your father as being sexual with anyone—but I had often had sexual

DAVID GUY

thoughts about her myself. She seemed the kind of sweet plain woman whom I could have gone to in those days and plead my case, that I was overweight and shy, I couldn't get anywhere with the girls I knew. All I wanted was a little sexual experience, someone older to teach me a few things. (If I didn't get it I was going to go nuts!) I had actually tried to work myself up into making this suggestion a time or two. I was certainly glad now that I hadn't.

"Do you think Mother knew?" I said to Helen.

"I think at some level she did. Some level she didn't look at too closely or too often. She knew Kay was an extremely important person to Father. She knew she performed some of the functions another kind of wife would have. I think Mother was glad to have her do those things. She just didn't ask herself about some of the others."

This was too weird for words. The Duchess sitting beside the woman at Christmas dinner knowing all that.

When I called Kay to ask if I could come down to see her, there was a long pause after I said who I was. It was as if it were taking time for the name to register, or for the idea to register that I might call.

"Charles," she said. "Is it bad news?"

"No," I said. "Father had a second heart attack, but he's okay."

"I'd heard about the heart attack."

"He's doing fine. He'll be going home in a few days. But I'm coming down to Naples on assignment, and I remembered you lived there, and I thought I might drop in for a visit. I could take you to dinner."

She said that would be wonderful. She was delighted. She did take the opportunity of the phone call to ask me a number of questions about the Senator's condition. She said she looked forward to seeing me.

I didn't know much about that part of Florida. I'd been to Naples once when I was a kid, but I hardly remembered anything. I had the impression it must be a dinky place, because you flew into Fort Myers and had a long drive after that, but it turned out that Naples—at least the part Kay lived in—was a posh substantial community, like an extended country club. I had been picturing her in one of those grubby little Florida houses, the tough scrubby grass on the lawn, a single lonely palm tree out front, but it turned out she lived in a condominium, not a high rise, but a two-story place that looked like a luxury motel. It was much more solid than that, though, and the apartments had multiple rooms, and it was furnished with her own stuff, very much her own place.

Kay didn't really look much different. She might have been a woman in her mid-forties, though she was nearly sixty. Her skin only looked old around her eyes. She was still thin, except for that little swell of a belly women develop. There was a generous sprinkling of gray in her hair, which she wore shorter now. But she still had that curiously blank stare without her glasses, the low throaty voice, the pleasant smile, the grace and calm. She wore plaid Bermuda shorts and a stylish white blouse, served iced tea ("Unless you want something stronger," she said, but it was only 3:45) and cookies. We were sitting in a living room that looked out through a large glass door onto the Gulf.

I couldn't help wondering if it was the Senator's money that had paid for all that.

"How was your father when you left?" she said.

I told her pretty much what I'd already said on the phone, that his condition seemed stable, he was going home that day, that if he'd just start to take care of himself there was no reason he shouldn't make a full recovery.

I wasn't trying to make things sound better than they were. That was how I really thought they stood. Kay seemed to want to hear more than that. She wanted all the details. She wanted a sworn statement from the doctor.

"The things I'm really worried about is this lawsuit he's involved in," I said. "That's what the doctor doesn't know about. I think it's the real problem. More to the point than his blood pressure or something."

Kay had visibly tensed when I mentioned the lawsuit. She reddened, and grew solemn.

"Did you know that attorney talked to me? John Auerbach."

I paused. I hadn't thought she'd be so quick to bring it up.

"I did," I said.

"Did your father tell you?"

"No. I have a friend who knows Auerbach."

"But that's why you came down here. To see me about that."

"Yes. Partly."

It really was only part of the reason. It would have been hard to put the other part into words.

"You're not on assignment."

"That just seemed the easiest thing to say on the phone."

I was slightly embarrassed at being caught in all these lies. She was clearing out the bullshit.

"Did your father send you?"

"He doesn't know I'm here. He thinks I'm in another part of Florida."

"He didn't send you with instructions about how I'm supposed to testify."

"He's not even aware that I know about all this."

"Did he tell you about . . . him and me?"

"No."

"But you know."

"Yes. My friend knew about that too."

I do think it was better to get all this out of the way. Otherwise we'd have been tiptoeing around it.

"I wish he'd been the one to tell you."

That was a puzzling statement when she made it, but I thought I understood it by the end of the afternoon.

"We haven't been that close through the years," I said. "We've only gotten close since he's been sick. He might tell me yet."

There was no telling what might come up.

Kay took a deep breath, let out a long sigh. "It's an awful thing to say, but I've been worried, ever since I heard about it, that I caused your father's heart attack. This second one. I certainly didn't intend that. I didn't know his health was so bad."

"I don't think it is."

"He's a seventy-year-old man who's had two heart attacks."

It didn't sound too good when you put it that way.

Kay told me her version of how she'd gotten involved in the case. It was pretty much what I'd already heard. Auerbach had—the way she told it—somewhat overdramatized Anna Jennings's situation.

She had known all about the Senator's meeting with Robert Parnell. He'd agonized about it for days afterward, and talked about it at length to Kay. He talked over everything with her.

Kay, on the day Auerbach came to see her, held out for a long time before she even admitted remembering the case. She wished now that she never had. Auerbach asked a million questions. Most of them seemed innocent, but she knew she still might be giving things away, or contradicting whatever the Senator had said. In the middle of the questioning, Auerbach let it slip that he knew Kay had been the Senator's mistress. He dropped that into the conversation as if it were nothing, but it made her even more nervous, and probably changed some of her answers. She was more forthcoming about the case to keep him away from that other matter. When he finally left, he said she'd been most helpful. He knew she'd be an important witness at the trial. That made her feel terrible. The whole thing was ironic, because the Senator's wife—who knew absolutely nothing—was protected from testifying, but the woman in whom he'd been confiding for years had to take the stand. And although Kay could be served with a subpoena only when in the state of Pennsylvania, Auerbach knew she came up every three months to visit her mother. She wouldn't miss those visits.

"I wrote your father a letter telling him what had happened," she said. "By that time I was back down here."

"You two keep in touch?"

"We did. Usually once a week. By phone. But in this letter I told him what I've told you. That I hadn't meant to give anything away but I was afraid I might have. I wasn't sure just what I'd said. That Auerbach was aware of our relationship. He was going to call me as a witness."

There was a long pause after that letter, three weeks, during which she had almost called him any number of times. She was dying to know what he was thinking. He finally wrote back to say he was sorry Auerbach had found her but it couldn't be helped. Maybe he should have warned her ahead of time. He hadn't thought Auerbach would be so resourceful. He didn't know what she had told him, but he felt sure—if she hadn't actually talked about his meeting with Parnell— that it couldn't be too bad. He was, of course, concerned about what might happen on a witness stand. Anything could happen in a courtroom. And he was deeply troubled that their relationship would be revealed. It was one thing for people to think they knew in private, quite another for it to be bandied about in public. It would be hard on him, and deeply humiliating for his wife.

She and the Senator hadn't communicated after that for another two weeks. She'd thought of calling, but didn't know what to say. Finally she wrote a brief letter to try to reassure him, saying she felt sure she'd do all right on the witness stand. That sounded lame even to her. The fact was that she had no idea how she'd feel trying to lie under oath. She wasn't sure she could do it. She wasn't sure she wanted to. She'd been dreading that court date ever since Auerbach had talked to her, even though it was still a couple of months in the future.

She heard about the second heart attack from one of her secretary friends. She wanted to call, wanted to come up, but was afraid that would only upset my father more. She felt like the cause of all his troubles. She called her secretary friend every day for news of his condition.

Then she had gotten my call.

"At first I was afraid he'd died. Then I thought you might be coming on his behalf. To coach me or something. I didn't like that feeling at all. I'm glad it wasn't that."

I understood how she felt. She had to be the one who decided how she testified. It was a matter of conscience.

"Do you think I messed things up?" she said.

"I don't see how. You did the best you could."

"I could have played dumb. Pretended I didn't remember any of it."

"Auerbach had already subpoenaed you. He still would have called you. If only to embarrass my father. And you'd have been facing the same dilemma. The same questions on the stand."

She was holding her empty iced-tea glass in her lap, staring down into it. I gazed out at the water, glittering in the afternoon sun.

"I love your father," she said.

I looked over at her. She was looking right back. It was a hell of an experience, to hear those words from your father's illicit lover.

"How long have you known about us?" she said.

"Just a couple weeks."

"You never suspected."

"No. I feel pretty dumb about it now. Helen says she did."

"I knew Helen knew. She's a smart woman."

I could get a little tired of these women and their famous intuition.

"It wasn't what you may think. Some sordid thing. It didn't start one day when I was taking dictation."

Kay said she had always thought of herself as one of the first liberated women. She had liberated herself before the women's movement came along. She supposed the fact that she wasn't a pretty woman (I protested; she brushed me off) had something to do with it, but when she graduated from high school and became a secretary, it wasn't with the idea of finding a husband. She became a legal secretary because she wanted to do something interesting and make good money. She wanted to have a career. She had done exactly that. She made herself into an excellent secretary; she was hired by the best law firm in the city because of how good she was, and when she'd proved herself there she'd been made the Senator's personal secretary. Not for some extracurricular reason, but because she could do the job.

"There were lots of better-looking girls if he just wanted to fool around. Anyway, that didn't come up for years. Four or five years."

I didn't hasten to agree, but she was right. There had always been better-looking secretaries in the firm.

By that time we were having drinks. She had gotten me a beer, and she was having a bourbon. It wasn't some weak little woman's drink. It looked like a double, over ice.

"It had honestly never crossed my mind, as a real possibility," she said. "I might have fantasized or something. But when you work so closely with someone. You work on projects that mean a great deal to both of you. You talk about them at great length. He confides in you. You go through success and failure together. A bond develops that is just like love. The whole thing is like a marriage. It's almost an afterthought when you go to bed at that point. You're already lovers."

I knew what she was talking about. Affairs were common at publications where I'd worked. And they were notorious at writers' conferences. A certain sympathy exists because you're doing the same work. You talk about it, and your spirits mingle. You drift into bed.

"There was never any feeling I was taking your mother's place. He still loved her, and he adored you children. I knew better than to put myself in competition with all that. But I had a big place in his life too. I know I did."

"Did you resent it? That you weren't the wife."

"Of course. There's lots of room for that. Special times when I couldn't be with him. Holidays when I had to go back to my apartment alone, and when I couldn't show my affection in the first place. Vacations. But I thought I had the best of your father in a lot of ways. His most passionate part. The part that connected with his work."

She certainly got the best hours of his day.

"By the time we talked about marriage, I didn't want to do it anymore."

She had dropped that bombshell quietly. It went off nevertheless.

"You talked about marriage?"

"It came up when it often comes up. You children were all finally out of the house. He was alone with your mother. It all started to look empty to him. That's the kind of emptiness a person like me had learned to live with years before. I was also probably a little set in my ways by that time. I enjoyed your father when I saw him, but I didn't want to live with him. I didn't want five angry and resentful stepchildren. I didn't want to be seen as the secretary who stole the boss. I especially didn't want to try to fill that emptiness for him. I think he thought I could do that. But nobody can."

She was right. The Senator had to learn to live with that.

"Then you retired."

"Something went out of our relationship when I didn't want to make that change. We still cared for each other, but I think that hurt him. It drove him closer to your mother. Things at work weren't as exciting as they had been. Your father wasn't doing as much. And I was sick of those Pittsburgh winters. Parking downtown and walking through the dirty snow to work. The bitter wind that came off those rivers. I've always loved hot weather. Always loved Florida. I used to come here for four weeks every winter. I'd make your father take the time off."

He couldn't work a day without her.

I looked around. "You've done all right."

She smiled. "You're wondering, aren't you?"

I blushed. "What?"

"Your father bought this place for me. Years ago. It wasn't all that extravagant then. Naples wasn't the posh community it's become. I used to rent it out except for the weeks I was here. But now I have it. I can live off my retirement benefits, and the money I put away. And this is a wonderful place to live. A dream."

It was some people's idea of a dream. Not quite mine.

"Do you resent me, Charles? All I have?"

"You deserve what you have. It's obvious Father loved you. And you loved him. I'm just glad to know he was happy."

"So we're still going to dinner."

"If you know a good place."

"This is Naples. I know ten places."

When I was back with the Senator in the next couple of weeks, while he was sitting around the apartment, getting strong for his surgery, there were several occasions when the Duchess was gone and I could have told him about my meeting with Kay, but I never did. I made up stories about my encounter with the up-and-coming—though aging—writer Otis Harvey, and never said a word about where I'd really been. He had told me a lot about himself on that last day at the hospital, but he hadn't told me about Kay, and I decided he must not want to. A father shouldn't have to tell his son everything. But I felt much closer to the Senator on those days, both for the things he'd told me and the things I had found out on my own. I wasn't disappointed in him. I'd only been disappointed when I hadn't really known him.

I especially felt closer because of something Kay had told me that night at dinner, after we'd eaten the baked grouper and the tiny potatoes in parsley and butter, after we'd finished a bottle of wine and she had forced a piece of key lime pie on me. We were sitting over coffee.

"There's something I've always wanted to know," I said. "But I'm not sure I should ask. I don't want to be obnoxious."

DAVID GUY

"You haven't been so far."

"Maybe I'll just ask, and you can decide whether or not to answer."

She was smiling. We were both slightly drunk. If I was ever going to get an answer to this question, now was the time.

"Was my father a passionate man?" I said.

Kay paused when I asked that, still smiling, looking down in her coffee cup, trying to decide, I suppose, how much to tell me.

"He was a very physical man."

"I know."

"He was a man of hearty male appetites."

"I know that too."

She raised an eyebrow, as if to say I might not know quite as much as I thought I did.

She gazed at me, trying to decide how to answer my question without saying more than she wanted to.

"Sometimes," she said, "after we made love, he would lie in my arms for hours. Just talking, and caressing me. He always had his hands on me, always had his body against me. He didn't want to let go. I think that was the thing I liked best about him, that he would give so much time to that, not actually making love, not really talking, but just being together, with our bodies. He'd cancel his appointments and give the whole afternoon to that. Let the world go to hell."

He sounded like me.

"That's what I think of as a passionate man," she said. "A man who loves women. Who loves to spend his time with women. Who will give up other things to do it."

She had told me exactly what I wanted to know.

FIFTEEN

T hree weeks after my trip to Florida, on a Saturday afternoon, I was sitting in Helen's little dining room eating lunch while she was out in the kitchen making a shopping list. She was wearing a tennis outfit, planning to stop at the store on the way home from the game. The phone rang, and she came out to the dining room to answer it. "Yes," she said, "of course," as the caller identified himself. Then she turned to look at me, and her mouth fell open. She covered it with her hand. I had never seen a look like that on her face in my life. I knew what it meant before she told me.

The phrase that Eric Strowd used to describe what had killed my father was a ventricular arrhythmia. It is one of the distinctly possible causes of death in the first weeks after a heart attack (which Strowd, somewhat to my annoyance, kept calling an infarction. I think that doctors use these terms to distance themselves). What happens, he said, is that the heart's pacemaker goes haywire. It virtually stops functioning. This is not the same thing as a heart attack. It happens instantly, and there is no pain involved. "There would have been a moment there when he knew he was going out,"

Strowd said. We were standing in the middle of a large crowd at the funeral home, and that was the first sentence he had spoken that wasn't full of medical jargon. It startled me. "But he wouldn't have felt any real pain."

My parents had been sitting together after lunch. They had eaten from trays that Mother brought into the study. Father was about to watch a ball game, and had turned on the television, but he was slightly early, and a teenage dance program was on. Nowadays they pan around among the dancers (who all look like budding rock stars) with one of those hand-held cameras while the kids sneer into the lens and violently jerk their bodies around. My parents laughed. "Isn't that awful," Mother said, standing in the doorway with the trays before she carried them into the kitchen. She spent only a short time out there, rinsing off the dishes and putting them in the dishwasher. When she returned to the study, Father was lying back against the chair with his head to one side. For the briefest of moments, she thought he had dozed off. Then she knew he was dead. It wasn't like before, when she thought she had to rush around and do something. Her husband was dead, and there was nothing to be done. She went to the bedroom and sat by herself for a while before she called an ambulance.

I think that the odd confusion that follows a death—the sudden busyness, in which everyone's lives stop as they devote themselves to this single event—is functional. It is better for the bereaved not to be alone at a time like that, and as far as I can tell they never are. Helen and I rushed immediately to the apartment, but we weren't the first people there. Already two of Mother's neighbors—two couples—had arrived, making coffee for her and for the others who would be coming. It was one of those neighbors, a Mr. Holyfield, who had called Helen. Mother was certainly not herself, more than a little stunned, but she seemed past the initial shock, well beyond where Helen and I might have expected. She was sitting between her two friends, sipping coffee, looking a little absent but holding herself together. Her face was cold when I kissed her. Mrs. Holyfield made room on the couch for Helen and me. Soon my brothers were there with their wives, and the minister from church (he greeted me as a total stranger, which I certainly was, though I'd had any number of chances to meet him in the past few months). A man came from the funeral home, and the reporter who was going to write the obituary. All through the day neighbors from the building stopped in, and toward evening my third brother, Todd, arrived with his wife from Cleveland. I spent the whole day greeting people and talking to people and looking after various details. I didn't have a moment to think.

The next three days have all run together in my mind. I have always been struck by how the days surrounding a funeral turn into the most wonderful party you could imagine. Everyone comes together whom you'd like to see (also, of course, a few people you'd rather not), and they hang around for hours; they don't dash off somewhere. They really want to talk to you, to know how you are and what you're doing. They are all, whether fully conscious of it or not, celebrating life, because they have just taken a cold hard look at death. I couldn't help thinking, again and again—and this was a sad thought, of course—how much Father would have liked to be there.

I heard countless stories about him that I'd never heard before. Without ever quite putting it into words, I had always felt like an outcast in my family, in that whole class of people, because of the way I'd lived, but I had no feeling of that in the days surrounding the funeral. I wondered to what extent I'd imagined the whole thing. People seemed glad to see me; they spoke glowingly of articles I'd written, asked what I was working on now. They told me how proud Father had been of my writing, how much he had talked to them about it, insisting they read certain of my pieces. I'd never had any idea he had done that. He was proud of all his children, people said, but especially tended to talk about Helen and me, because what we did was so offbeat. He fiercely defended Helen outside the family, spoke of her right to live any way she wanted.

It was only around us, apparently, that he vented his frustration.

Helen herself was staying pretty close to Mother those days. Mother seemed fine, welcoming people to the apartment, talking to them at length, but Helen had the feeling that, beneath all that, she was teetering on the verge of collapse. It was good that she had so much to do, Helen thought, and so many people around, but she wasn't sure how she'd be when all that was over.

In any case, from the moment we went over there on Saturday until the funeral Tuesday afternoon, we were constantly busy. There were visiting hours at the funeral home in the afternoon and evening, and people at the apartment almost around-the-clock. Many had brought food, and our old cook Emily had come to be with us for as long as we needed her, and every meal was a banquet, with a crazy mix of people and all kinds of delicacies. The day would start at nine or ten o'clock, often with a trip to the airport to pick someone up, and would end twelve or thirteen hours later, with people around and talking to us the whole time. It was exhausting. All that continued until the funeral service Tuesday afternoon, the graveside service after that, then an enormous family meal. It wasn't until I got back to the house alone that night (Helen was going to stay with Mother for a while) that I began to feel the emptiness.

I haven't said much about my feelings in all this. They were overwhelming at the time, and I am still trying to sort them out even now, months later. It is amazing, in a way, to think of what happened between Father and me. We had the kind of reconciliation, though not perfect or complete (whatever is?) that most men only dream of. We had a prolonged period of adult time together that fathers and sons rarely have. It was also true, of course, that we'd had a lot of catching up to do. Our life together had barely begun. For a few brief months I felt connected to my source as I had never been. It is impossible to say all I gained, then suddenly lost, in that time I had with my father. I am also aware that, if he hadn't died, his immediate future would have been difficult. It would have been terribly hard for him to go through that lawsuit, however it came out. It would have been a time of great pain. I can't feel sorry that he missed that.

In any case, during the week after his death, none of that had even begun to register with me. I was going from moment to moment, doing the next thing that needed to be done. I was numb, and not especially conscious. Things didn't begin to slow down until after the funeral.

I also haven't said a word about Andrea, not since that night when she talked to John Auerbach and we wound up at the hospital. She had nevertheless been as much a part of my life as ever. I had seen her two or three times a week—even with all my visits to the hospital, we only missed one Thursday afternoon—and if she wasn't quite as much the focus of my attention as before, that was understandable under the circumstances. As soon as I called her on the day my father died, she came to the apartment, and she was around almost constantly during the next few days, helping with the food preparation and the cleanup, looking after me, explaining to countless people her connection to the family (many of them didn't know my marriage had ended), comforting Helen and Mother. Andrea was good in a crisis. She always had been.

But I didn't emerge from that long dark tunnel I'd been in, that tunnel full of endlessly chattering people, until the Thursday after the funeral. Andrea and I had missed our Thursday afternoon that week (I wasn't ready for sex, I suppose, but I longed just to be held, a long naked embrace with no words) because she'd had to make up for time she had taken off around the funeral. But on Thursday evening we went to a Chinese restaurant—a second-story place in Squirrel Hill, overlooking Forbes—then drove back to her house. It was a late dinner. I had picked her up at work an hour after the store closed because she'd had some things to do. She had a terrible—almost blinding—headache when I got there, but she had taken a heavy dose of a pain reliever and thought it was starting to work. Andrea often had headaches. That was the way tension got to her.

We hadn't talked much at dinner. She asked after Helen and my mother, caught me up on her political organizations and how things were going at the store. She talked some about her son. If I could have talked about anything, I would have told her what I'd been thinking over the past few days, that—despite my father's death—I still wanted to move back to Pittsburgh. It felt like home again. My family felt like my family. My life seemed centered there in a way that it never had when I was in North Carolina, and a major part of that was my relationship with her. One way or another—however we worked it out—I wanted to be there with her. But I didn't bring all that up, primarily because of the way she looked. I didn't think her headache was getting better. She still seemed exhausted, and closed up, and in pain.

I hadn't often been at her house in the evening; we had mostly met there in the afternoon. There were only a couple of lights on, for some reason, two lamps, which lit up large circles of light but left the rest of the house in shadows. We were moving back toward the bedroom, or at least I thought we were, when she stopped, and said, "I need to talk to you about something." I turned back, and she was standing near one of the lamps, so that her face did seem, oddly, half in light and half in shadow. It was the way her face had seemed in general that evening, only partly there.

She said, "I don't want to be your lover anymore."

At first the words didn't register with me. They made no sense. I must have gone pale or something, I must have looked as if I were about to keel over, because she reached out and gripped my shoulder, as if to steady me. She had stepped out of the light to do that, so we were both in shadow, we could barely see each other. Why doesn't somebody turn on some lights in here? I was thinking. What the hell are we doing in the dark?

I hadn't been shocked by my father's death. I don't mean that it wasn't a terrible moment, one of the worst I will ever go through. I mean I had known deep down inside me that it was coming, that that long talk we'd had before I went to Florida—though it was far from the last time we spoke—was his deathbed conversation with me. But Andrea's words that night were an utter shock, the worst shock, I think, of my life. You will say—people did say—that there must have been signs, I should have seen it coming, and I'm sure there were, but they had come during an intense and difficult time, when I hadn't much been noticing things. They also seemed—what things I could look back on and see—a natural part of any relationship, when the rush and passion of romance begin to give way to something deeper and more lasting. In any case, I was terribly shocked; I took a step back, and almost fell. She gripped my shoulder, and looked into my eyes, and her own eyes softened just slightly.

"I don't understand," I said.

She got me into a chair. She should have done that in the first place. I might have fallen over and hit my head or some-thing. Then she'd have had all that blood to clean up. She sat me in a chair off in the shadows, while she sat in the light of the lamp and started to talk. It was a strange sensation. On one level, I didn't hear a word she was saying. I just sat there and watched everything I'd wanted, everything I thought I'd had a week before, disappear before my eyes. The ground had fallen from beneath my feet and I was falling, falling, into the vast spaces of the empty abyss, no up, no down, just blackness all around, and silence, and my body slowly tumbling head over heels. On another level, I heard every word she said; her words are etched on my brain forever; I could repeat them verbatim this very minute. I can see her sitting across from me, her face relaxed for the first time all evening, now that she was saying what had been on her mind. She looked much relieved. She was in an unassailable position. She didn't want the man who wanted her.

It had all happened quite suddenly, she said. She could see now that she had been vaguely troubled for some time, but it was only that morning that she'd woken up and realized she didn't want to be involved with me anymore. She had learned to trust such insights. They had guided her all her life. Next week marked the one-year anniversary since she and her husband had split up. Everyone had told her that would be an important landmark, and she could see now that it was. She had been through a year of mourning. It had had its crazy highs and its dreadful lows, but it had all been mourning. She hadn't been herself.

Her love affair with me had been an enormously important part of that. I'd come along at a crucial time, like a gift from God. She could never have gotten as far as she had without me. But she realized now that she was starting to feel hemmed-in and restricted. Her life wasn't her own. She didn't want to commit her Thursday afternoons for the rest of her life, or her Saturday nights. She needed more space. She didn't like the emotional demands that were being placed on her. I had gotten too clingy. I was dragging her down. She realized she didn't want that kind of all-consuming primary relationship. She had tried that and it didn't work for her. That was why her marriage had been so fucked up.

My friendship, of course, was terribly important to her. She wanted always to be my friend. She might be ending the sexual part of our relationship, but she wanted the rest of it to continue. Not, perhaps, with quite the same intensity. She didn't want to see me quite as much. But she wanted to remain close, intimate friends.

In other words, she said the same old shit everybody says when they're dumping you.

I didn't know quite how to react during that long monologue, during which—apparently overcome by her own words—Andrea cried twice. Most of what she said concerned her own feelings, so I couldn't contradict her, except to say that I'd never meant to hem her in. She could have called off the Thursday afternoons anytime. I hadn't expected them to go on for the rest of our lives. I probably had been clingy lately, but I thought there was good reason for that. I didn't expect that to go on forever either.

There had been a time when she was a little clingy herself.

All I could think about while she was talking—all I could speak about as I began to speak—were the plans we'd made, the places we'd said we'd go together. Cape Cod and Cape May, the beaches and mountains of North Carolina. San Francisco. Seattle. Spain. Italy. The Caribbean. She said those things had never been practical. They were just pleasant stories we were telling ourselves. I talked about the life we'd planned, the way we'd said we'd live on the same block but not in the same house (unless we could find a fabulous duplex); we'd sleep together by invitation only, so it would never become habitual and boring; we'd share shopping and various chores and child care. She said she'd realized she needed more space than that. (I was starting to hate that fucking expression.) I said I didn't understand why she'd said all those things when she didn't mean them, and she said that bothered her too, it sounded as if she had deceived me, but she had meant every bit of it at the time. She had never spoken an insincere word to me. She reminded me that she had never promised this would be a monogamous relationship, or that it would last forever. That was true. She hadn't gone before a notary public or anything. But when a woman tells you five times a day that she loves you; when she spends hours talking about all you're going to do together, in the near and far future; when she tells you she's never had a relationship like this, she'd never known a man and woman could be like this, she's never loved anyone so much in her life, it doesn't occur to you to get it in writing. You don't expect her to end the whole thing because of a mood she wakes up in one morning.

"I don't want you to think this has anything to do with Mitchell," she said.

Of course not. The thought never crossed my mind.

"I'm feeling the same way about him," she said.

"You're breaking up with him too?"

"I'm not breaking up with him. That was never as intense as this. But I'm going to keep it at arm's length. I'm going to keep it under control."

She'd been saying that all along.

"I don't love him," she said. "I've never loved him. I do love you. I'll always love you."

There was that word again.

"That's the whole problem," she said. "That's why I can't be involved with you."

I stared at her. I didn't know how to answer something as ridiculous as that. I was starting not to want to. But in a single moment of clarity, I did say the one thing I was feeling most strongly.

"What a time to do this," I said.

"I know." For the first time since we'd been talking, she blushed. She smiled slightly, in embarrassment. "The timing is bad."

That was how she referred to one of the most difficult moments in my life.

"But what was I supposed to do?" she said. "Wait a few days, when I felt this way? Wait a few weeks? The feelings would have gotten worse. They would have come out in the relationship. What do you want me to do, fuck you when I don't want to?"

She had me there. I certainly didn't want that.

I wanted her to want to fuck me. The way she had a week ago.

There may have been more that we said. More words, but nothing new. We hadn't said anything new since the first two sentences. She didn't want to be my lover anymore. I didn't understand. At some point in all that I stood. I walked toward the door. She may have stood and embraced me. Knowing her, I feel sure she did. I honestly don't remember. I only remember closing the door behind me, walking down the steps to my car.

It is hard to describe what happened to me at that point. I

don't mean at that particular moment (though it started then; it started as I walked down the street to my car), but over the next few days, the next, say, fifty-six hours. One word that comes to mind is dissociation. You somehow remove yourself from whatever is going on. What I think actually happens is that your mind separates from your body. It is like one of those modern works of art, where a guy is walking down the street holding his head in his hands. He's got it tucked under his arm or something. Or he has a long neck, his head is off in the clouds at the end of a huge giraffe neck, while the body is down here on the ground, trying to make its way.

The problem is that the pain is too great. Your feelings are in your body, your thoughts in your mind, and if—in some imaginary saintlike person—we picture an exact correspondence between the two (the sages describe this as having a mind empty of thought), most of us are lucky if our thoughts and feelings even notice each other now and then. We walk around all day worrying about paying our bills and wonder why we have such a backache when we get into bed. But when something happens that is extraordinarily painful, when your feelings are really wrenched, you shut them off altogether. You "feel numb." And your mind, also in order to avoid pain, tries to get as far from your body as possible. Your thoughts come to bear almost no relation to your feelings. Your experience "makes no sense." You don't "believe" it. You can't "accept" it. It is "unreal."

All of these reactions are natural. It is natural to try to avoid pain. That is why ancient cultures had rituals to help you face your pain. The town elders would come around and force you to get down into your body, where you needed to be. You could moan, for instance. You could scream and wail. You could roll around on the ground. You could pour dirt on your head and weep. You could pound the walls, stomp the earth, throw your limbs about crazily. You could break into a wild dance. I'm not saying these things would make the experience easier. They might make it harder. But at least you would feel what was going on. You would express it with your body. You could do that for days, weeks, months, whatever it took. You could really experience what was happening to you. Your body and mind would be as one.

You can't do that alone, of course. You might take things too far: bash your head against a wall, or throw yourself off a cliff. The town elders have to help you. I, unfortunately, didn't have any town elders. The three people I had been close to in Pittsburgh—my father, Helen, and Andrea—were all gone.

I have wondered how things might have turned out if I'd had Helen to go to. I've wondered specifically if I might have avoided the thing that I did at the end of those fifty-six hours. I feel that somehow, despite her own pain, she'd have gotten me what I needed, even if she'd had to find someone else to give it to me. But she was with our mother the whole time. She was quite worried about her, and didn't want to leave. She didn't want to come home. I didn't feel I could intrude.

That first night, I knew that sleep was out of the question. I didn't even go upstairs, stayed on the first floor and left the lights on. I spent much of the night, hours I suppose, brooding on what had just happened. I went over and over what Andrea had said, trying to find a way it didn't mean what it seemed to. I put it beside the events of the past few weeks, the past few months, tried to see some way it all made sense. I tried to see what I should have done differently. I felt horribly horribly sad, about half an inch off the ground (I knew I had to keep from falling that last half inch. I had to summon all my strength). I still felt in shock. My body ached. It was hard to get my breath.

At some point far into the night I decided I couldn't keep brooding on all that. It was getting me nowhere. I turned on the radio to an all-night jazz station. A slow muted blues came on and made me cry so hard I thought I wouldn't be able to stop. I switched to talk radio. The intensity there was just as great in its own way. I couldn't believe the energy people were giving to the utterly trivial. At some point in there my mind blew a fuse. It kept going around and around—I'd gotten that motion started and it wouldn't stop—but it couldn't continue to dwell on that subject that was going nowhere, so it dredged up a whole load of other things. Popular songs, lines of poetry, television advertisements, radio jingles, remembered conversations, bizarre sexual fantasies, dialogue from movies, dreams of athletic prowess. They flew around in my head like clothes in a dryer, anything and ev-

erything to keep me from facing the silence. Talk radio began
to make a certain amount of sense in that context. I almost
called up myself during a dispute about sixties' rock and roll.
Those stupid assholes didn't know what they were talking
about! I was there, by Christ!

Around four I turned on a late movie. It was some kind of
gangster comedy. Edward G. Robinson was in it, and William
Bendix, and a very young and rather trim Jackie Gleason in
a cameo role. I thought I must be hallucinating. I watched
the farm report, and an exercise program, and all two hours
of the *Today* show. That meant it was the next day, of
course, but such distinctions no longer seemed especially important. I spent the rest of that day downtown. I somehow
felt that if I was out among people—not talking to them or
anything; I couldn't stand the thought of talking—but just in
their presence, I would be all right. I walked the streets for
hours. I walked through department stores, bookstores, record stores, five-and-tens, anywhere I figured I would be left
alone. I sat at lunch counters over cups of coffee. I walked
down to the Point—where the rivers converge—and sat on a
bench for a while. I stood for a long time at the end of the
block staring at Andrea's store. I crossed a bridge to the North
Side and walked around there. At some point late in the afternoon I walked into Father's office building without quite
realizing I had done it. I was standing in front of the elevator
that used to take me up to his office. I started to cry and had
to walk back out. I rode the little Pittsburgh subway for a
while. It doesn't cover much ground, just goes around under
a few streets. I rode it again and again.

That night I made the mistake of trying to sleep. As long as
I was out in the daylight, I could stare at the old ladies with
their shopping bags, watch the bums down by the river scratch-
ing themselves, whatever, but once the lights were off I had
nowhere to look but inside myself, and I was afraid that—from
beneath that load of garbage that was flying through my mind—
some demon would rise up and devour me. I also thought I
needed sleep, I had to have it, that if my subconscious didn't
have a chance to sort things out I might go crazy. That strange
restlessness of mine was surging through me. It was ridiculous
to get into bed when I felt that way. I couldn't sink into the
mattress. I kept flopping down, but I never did. I would toss

around for what seemed like an hour, look at the clock and find that it had been ten minutes. I turned on a light and tried to read, but the words wouldn't come into focus. I went downstairs and turned on a movie, but it was a sentimental romance. I couldn't stand at that point to listen to a bunch of lies about love. I also couldn't go back up to bed. Finally I just turned on a light and waited for the dawn.

I was out on the streets by 6:30 that morning, which made for a long day. I walked around Shadyside, the quiet residential streets and the back alleys. Families were starting to awaken, voices coming from the kitchens, from elsewhere the muffled sounds of television. It seemed eerily quiet until I remembered it was Saturday. My father had been dead for a week. I sat for a long time in a breakfast place on Walnut Street. I walked from there—actually walked up Negley Hill—to Squirrel Hill, where by midmorning the old Jewish men were already starting to appear on streetcorners, wearing business suits and smoking cigars, taking the morning air. I walked down the long hill where the kosher butcher and other Jewish stores were. I felt as if I were walking through my past, as if people were not actually seeing me. I was a ghost. I think it was my father's death I was mourning—that was the dark hole I was staring into—but it was Andrea I kept thinking of, partly because that was easier to face in some ways, partly because it was more immediately shocking, it made less sense. I had known people died, I was aware of death as a fact of life, but I had never thought anyone would treat me the way she had.

That afternoon I walked down Forbes into Oakland, spent some time at the museum, looking at the dinosaurs. I sat around the newspaper room at the library. I eventually decided that what I needed was a swim, if I could just wear my body out I would be able to sleep that night, so I went back for my car and drove to the Y, but when I got there I just couldn't do it. My body was so tight that I couldn't swim at all, a couple of laps wore me out, but I couldn't swim long enough to reach that other kind of exhaustion, where my muscles stretched out and were ready to rest. I only spent about ten minutes in the pool. I had a hamburger in a bar and decided to spend the evening at the movies. I didn't care what I saw as long as I passed the time. I found one theater with a 7:15 show, another with a 9:30. The crowds were decent, since it was Saturday night. I had people around me. One downtown theater had a late show. It was mostly young people who came to that, having been one place and probably on their way somewhere else, but also around the theater I saw men—and one woman—like me, sitting alone, staring vacantly at the screen, staying in their seats through the credits, looking around quickly—an odd mixture of fear and sadness in their eyes—when the lights came on.

It was as I left that third movie that I found myself, a little after 2:00 A.M. on a Sunday morning, on the street where—as the expression goes—my story began, the one street in the city that is always open. I am aware even as I say that how much of a lie it is. I have made it sound as if I came downtown to go to the Y, I stayed because of the movie theaters, I walked from the movie theater to Liberty Avenue because I was trying to escape the night, the solitude of my house, the chaos inside my head. But it was also true that I knew the evening was headed for that street; it was always going to wind up there. It would be just as true to say that I did all those other things in order to get there. I turned onto that street with a hollow feeling in the pit of my stomach, a weight like dread in my chest, because I knew my story ended there. It always ends there. It never really goes away.

A little drizzle was falling, the pavement soaked from an earlier, harder rain. Lights flashed garishly above the streetfronts and shone in the puddles. The street itself wasn't busy. One pale woman in a storefront beside an adult bookstore, her lipstick as bright as the lights, stared at me as I passed. Every time I looked back she was still staring. The two or three men I saw didn't meet my eyes. They walked slightly faster as we passed. The doorway I was looking for was halfway down the block, the same worn sagging steps, the narrow corridor of badly plastered walls, the smells of urine and old garbage.

Things hadn't changed upstairs either. The guy who buzzed me in from the desk was big and blocky, short-haired. His nose had a dent in it. His knuckles were mangled. He must have decided at some point that sitting at that desk all night was easier than bouncing people from a bar. The lighting was dim, the decor garish—scarlet and black—the carpet thick. An odd embarrassed hush fell over the room as I entered.

Four women in bathing suits and net stockings stood to greet me. They looked sleepy and bored. I picked the best-looking one, an extremely dark black woman, slightly taller than I. She wore red lipgloss and a sparkly turquoise eyeshadow, but her body, squeezed into a bathing suit a size too small for her, was spectacular. She had a little smile to her eyes that I liked. Her hair was fluffed out and natural, grew down to her shoulders. She took me back to the room and told me to get comfortable; she would be back.

The room was plush, with an enormous bed and shag carpet; one wall was mirrored, and along the other were a sink and a huge bathtub sunk into the floor. When Alicia came back—she had told me her name on the way to the room—she took off her platform shoes, bringing her closer to my size. There was that initial awkwardness of being there, which always exists, and which had taken the smile out of her eyes. I hoped it wasn't gone for good. She took me to the sink to wash me off—my cock was tiny, still scared—and ran through a list of what they did, French, Greek, English, Swedish. She also mentioned restrictions that had never come up before. I had to wear a rubber. I couldn't come in her mouth.

A man was like a rattlesnake in that place. You had to avoid his venom.

"How much to do all that?" I said.

"What do you mean?"

"I don't want to decide right now. I want to do whatever comes up. I want to pay and get it over with."

She stared at me, wondering what crazy thing I wanted, how much she could ask.

"Two hundred," she said.

I took it from my wallet and gave it to her. I had stopped at a bank machine a couple of blocks away.

"This is anything within reason," she said.

"I just don't want to talk about money anymore."

She really did have a fabulous body when she took off her bathing suit, almost a caricature, huge shapely tits that were nevertheless firm, a flat belly, one of those big round jutting-out asses that only black women seem to have. For a long time after she got onto the bed with me I just lay in her arms. I buried my face in her jungle of hair. She really hugged me, as we lay there. When I squeezed her, she squeezed me back. It made me want to cry. After a while, I pulled back and looked at her. The light was back in her eyes, but she also looked puzzled, the way women do with me. They expect me to want more. They don't know what it is I'm doing. They expect me to grab for their crotch.

I touched my lips to that large garish mouth of hers.

"I don't kiss," she said. "Really kiss. I'd be glad to use my mouth somewhere else."

"Maybe later," I said.

I moved down her body, licked her nipples. They were brown and tough, quickly got hard. "Easy," she said, when I started to suck them. There was so much tit behind them it was hard to get hold of them. I moved down farther, between her legs, got her to spread them wide. "Be careful," she said. I assured her I would. I gently pushed her knees up to her chest, lay there and stared at her pussy. It was a dark brown, but lighter than the rest of her, moist and well shaped. It gave off a strong scent, one I hadn't really smelled before. She didn't have that little fishy odor white women have.

The way things are these days, of course, I was probably about three inches from death. I was playing Russian roulette with three bullets in the barrel. I didn't especially care. I was also, in terms of my life, at the heart of the mystery. Maybe if I lay there for a few minutes and spoke to that dark opening, it would speak back, finally answer the questions I'd been asking it for years. I wished I knew why I loved it so much, why it had occupied such a huge space in my life, taking me over and taking me away, until it sometimes seemed to blot out the whole world. It was the world. It seemed to me that other men had—pardon the expression—handled it better. What was it about a pussy that had always driven me crazy, led me into sordid places and compromising situations and was now just about killing me with grief? I had loved it and longed for it before I ever saw it; I loved it even more after I saw it; I'd spent most of the years of my life sniffing after it like a bloodhound, and I knew right now, about three inches away from one—even after all I'd been through—that I would always love it, I would never be done with it; I loved the way it looked and the way it smelled, the way it felt inside to my fingers, the way it tasted and its texture against my tongue; most of all I loved the way it felt when my cock went inside it, like no other hole in the world; there was nothing to compare with it. That funny-looking little hairy spot on a woman's body, so pretty and wet and defenseless, had ruled my life. I could see now that it *was* going to kill me, one way or another.

"You had enough of that, sugar?" she said.

An interesting question, in light of all that had been going through my mind.

I moved up beside her. "Listen," I said. "I paid you that money so I could do what I wanted. Now, whatever I do, you're trying to stop me."

"I don't know, sugar. I've come in here with lots of guys, lots of them rougher-looking than you. I've done lots of different things. I'm not usually scared. But you scare me, honey. Something's wrong."

"My girlfriend left me."

"I knew it was something."

"My father died."

"Jesus, honey. You don't need to be here. You don't need to be here at all."

"I've got nowhere to go."

"You must have some place."

"I just want to hang around for a while. I'm not going to hurt you. I just want to be here."

"All right. Do what you want. I won't say a thing."

I went back to where I had been. She pulled her knees up. I got her to touch herself. She did it very delicately, with one finger, one bright red fingernail, that just kept sliding down and going up. She held herself open with her other hand. Her pussy got wetter and wetter.

"Are you careful in here?" I said.

"You know I am," she said. "None of that stuff gets into me."

"How about out of here?"

"I don't do nothing out of here." She laughed. "I'm too tired."

I won't pretend that what she said reassured me. I don't know why I even asked. What was she going to say, she'd fucked a million guys (as she probably had)? She'd fucked every guy who had ever asked her? The truth of the matter was, I didn't care. I didn't care about anything that night. I was going to do it. I took her fingers away and started to lick her, softly at first, then harder. She had a strong briny taste.

It was almost too much for me. She was squirming around on the bed, holding herself open with her hands. I started to suck. "God," she said. I worked a finger into her, two fingers. She was smooth and hot and wet inside.

"Let me get a rubber," she said.

Unfortunately, my cock was still about half an inch long. I hadn't felt a thing from it the whole time I was there. It still seemed small and scared.

Maybe my cock was smarter than the rest of me.

"You sad, honey," she said. "You just too sad."

That was probably true too. But if I didn't get this energy out of me somehow I didn't know what would happen. I'd go crazy.

"Will you beat me?" I said.

"What?"

"I want you to whip me. With my belt."

"Oh, honey, I don't know."

"I'll kneel right here on the bed. You hardly have to move."

"If that's what you really want."

It was like that time with Becky, years before. I knelt on the bed with my head lowered, my ass in the air, and she stood above me. She did it halfheartedly at first, but after a minute I yelled at her and got her cranked up. I just wanted to feel something. I wanted to whack my body out of this numbness. Alicia was much stronger than Becky. She was taking huge swings with the belt, hitting me a solid smack every time. She grunted as she did it. I shouted with the pain. It all started to go together after a while, my shouts and her grunts and the loud smack of the belt and the terrific pain, I was finally feeling something, but in the middle of it all she stopped and fell down on the bed beside me.

"Please, mister," she said. "I can't do this anymore. Don't make me do it. Don't do it to yourself. I can get it up, I can suck any dick in the world up, I swear to God I can. But please don't make me do this. I can't stand it."

I let her try. She was good, no question about it. She was great. She used her fingers beautifully, her tongue and her lips. It was soft and warm and wet, what she did. Her hair tickled my belly. But it was no use. She must have worked on me for fifteen minutes. My cock was dead to the world.

"You got to go home," she said. "You got to get some rest."

She was right, of course. But rest was something I couldn't seem to get.

I don't know when it was that I decided what I was going to do at that point. It was as if I never did decide. Something inside me just knew. I got my clothes on and walked out of that place as if I knew where I was going. I knew I wasn't going back to the house. I couldn't stand the thought of that. I had certainly decided by the time I got to the parkway, because I had to wait for a different exit. I felt that old sense of dread in my chest, the same dread I had felt when I stepped onto Liberty Avenue. I also felt a need to hurry, as if the thing I was going to do might disappear, as if I had to do it before I thought about it.

The lights were off, of course. All the lights on the street were off, and it was dead quiet. I walked up the driveway and around to the back. I didn't have my key anymore—I'd taken it off my keychain and thrown it into the river that day I was down at the Point—but she kept a spare under a rock in the garden. I picked it up and let myself in the back door, moving slowly and silently. I seemed—in my sudden resolve to do this—to have inhabited my body again. I felt cool and deliberate. I shut the door and took off my shoes. I stood in the kitchen until my eyes got used to the dark. The rain had stopped, the night had cleared, and moonlight shone through the windows. I walked through the kitchen in my stocking feet. Chris was asleep in the first room I came to. His body was all twisted up in the sheet, and he lay on his back, snoring softly with his mouth open. I quietly shut his door. I walked into Andrea's room, closed and locked the door behind me. She was sleeping alone, and naked, one nipple just showing above the sheet. I don't know what I would have done if she hadn't been alone. I stood there for a long time, looking at her. I stepped over to the bed and sat down beside her. My weight on the bed awakened her. She opened her eyes and started, tried to jump away, but I grabbed her arm and yanked her back. She gasped as I did that, lay awkwardly crumpled on the bed. I felt as if another hard snap at her arm would have yanked it out of the socket. I half wanted to do it. I relaxed my grip and she straightened herself out on the bed. She looked up at me. I turned on the bedside lamp, and she blinked against the light.

"Charles," she said. "I didn't know it was you."

"It's me," I said.

The fact didn't seem to relieve her. Her eyes, once they got used to the light, were full of fear.

"You should have called," she said. "You should have knocked."

"I didn't feel like it."

She was just talking. She knew this wasn't a social call.

"What are you doing here?" she said.

"I don't know."

I really didn't. All I knew was that I had no place else to go, and I had to do something to ease my pain. It was going to drive me crazy if I didn't do something.

She tried to jump away again. She actually almost made it, but I caught her by the hair this time—that beautiful head of burnished red hair—and pulled her back harder, really slammed her head against the bed. She let out a loud gasp, almost a yelp. I put my hands on her shoulders and held her down. I moved to straddle and sit on top of her. I felt as if I had the strength of twenty men, as if I could have picked her up and thrown her around the room like a doll. As I straddled her I felt my cock—which hadn't felt anything for a week—stir in my pants.

"Don't try to get away again," I said.

"I won't."

I hated the feeling that she wanted to get away from me. After all those times she had wanted to be there.

"Please don't hurt my little boy," she said. "Please don't hurt Chris."

"I'm not going to hurt Chris."

"I'm afraid he'll hear this. I'm afraid he'll come in and see it."

"I closed his door. I locked yours. He's not going to come in."

She lay very still while I got off her and took off my clothes. Tears were pouring from her eyes, and she kept sniffing. I took off everything. My cock had come to life. An hour before I couldn't get a thing out of it, and now it was as hard and heavy as I'd ever seen it. It stood there like a big dumb animal. When I lay on Andrea, she put her arms around me, but she didn't really hold me. Her hands were like ice. Her mouth as I kissed her was soft, and wet, and tasted of tears, but she didn't kiss me back. She opened her mouth and let me use it.

"Kiss me," I said.

"I can't," she said. "I'm too scared."

I tried to kiss her again but she still wouldn't. I moved down her body. I had always loved that place at the top of her chest where the skin was smooth and led down to her tits. I put my head there for a moment and, strange to say, started to cry myself. It was because of the way she smelled. I had smelled that smell that I loved so much—strong because of her fear—and it just got to me, the way I had always loved that, and how happy I'd been when I smelled it, and the thought that I would never smell it again. It was some kind of visceral physical grief I was feeling. We were both sobbing. Her hands were on my back as if to comfort me, but they were cold and clammy. I cried for a long time. There was a box of Kleenex beside the bed, and I brought it over and we both kept blowing our noses, then sobbing some more. Finally I felt all cried out. My body felt heavy, relaxed as it hadn't been for days. My cock felt huge.

I pushed her arms up above her head and buried my face under one of them, that luscious thick clump of hair, the wonderful smell, like ripe pussy. I licked it and made the smell stronger, licked until all her hair was combed down. I did the same under the other arm. I moved down to her tits and sucked on them for a while. I sucked hard. I bit them. Andrea was groaning and squirming around. "Oh Christ please, Charles," she said. "That hurts." I went down between her legs and shoved her knees up, put my tongue inside her, way up inside. I lapped away at her like a bowl of milk. I got a good mouthful of the soft squishy fishy hairy flesh of her cunt and sank my teeth into it—"Jesus!" she said--sank them harder and harder until I felt her thrash around. I started to use my fingers on her. I got two inside her as if it were nothing; three were no real problem; I got pretty far with four. I probably could have worked my whole arm up there if I'd wanted to take the time.

I turned her over. I went down and licked her asshole, worked my tongue up her ass. I used the juice from her cunt and got a couple of fingers up her ass. I worked them in and out while she lay there and groaned. "Give me the stuff," I said. She reached up the bedside table and handed a tube of lubricant back to me. We had used it on each other before, penetrating that way. I got her good and slippery. My two fingers went in easily now. I positioned myself behind her and shoved her legs wide open. I rested my hands on the small of her back and leaned on her.

"You're not going to stop me this time," I said.

The one time we had tried fucking that way, it had hurt her too much.

"I know," she said.

"No matter how much it hurts. How much you want me to stop."

"I know."

"I should have done this before. I should have gone ahead and done it."

She didn't say anything. She was sobbing into the mattress.

"I want it to hurt. I'm going to make it hurt. I'm going to fuck you blind."

She tried to turn and look at me. She was still sobbing. She couldn't get her head all the way around.

"Are you going to kill me, Charles?" she said. "Are you going to kill me after you do this?"

The question stopped me. I hadn't thought about it.

"I'm afraid you're going to kill me, and you're going to leave me here, and Chris is going to find me." A sob caught at her throat, and she had to stop. "Please don't do that." She sobbed again.

I leaned back from where I had been pressing with my hands. I didn't say anything.

"Please don't leave me here for my little boy to find," she said.

Feeling had returned to my body. It had surged through me the moment I'd thrown her to the bed. My mind had cleared long before that, before I'd gotten to the house. What I was doing at that moment occupied my whole consciousness. My body and mind were one. My cock was enormous. I could have fucked an army of women with it. And I wanted to. More than anything else at that moment I wanted to be inside her, hearing her groan and feeling her squirm, sinking my teeth into the soft flesh of her shoulder, smelling her sweat and her fear and the odor of her hair, holding that body I had loved so much and giving pain to the woman who had hurt me. My feelings were a jumble, but they all went together.

But her question stopped me. It was like a problem of logic, a philosophical conundrum I couldn't answer. It took me out of the realm I'd been occupying, where we would have been just bodies, and into that human realm which, most of the time, I was looking for in sex. It made me picture the scene she was talking about, Chris coming into the room and finding her. It also made me ask myself the question she was asking. Is that why I had come there, to kill her? Was that what this was all about?

I really did want to fuck her. That was the problem with the question: It took me beyond the moment, when all I knew was the moment and what I wanted, to go inside her and lose myself forever. But I also saw, as I knelt in front of that act in which I had so often lost myself, that if I did it now I would also in some other way be losing myself. Not because it was rape or murder or whatever it was, but because I had done it. I would have given myself over to her. And somehow, in that moment when everything had come together, I didn't want to do that. I didn't want to lose my *self*. My self felt precious, more important suddenly than getting laid. It was stunning to feel that way. I had never felt that way before in my life. I loved my self. I didn't want to give it to her.

I got off her. I rose from the bed and just stood there a moment, staring at her, then started to put on my clothes. Andrea was lying very still. I hadn't said a word to her. It wasn't easy getting my pants buttoned and zipped, my cock still standing there like a flagpole. I unlocked and opened the door and looked back at her. She still hadn't moved. I walked down the hallway and opened the door to Chris's room. He was still sleeping, lying on his side now, his mouth still hanging open. I walked through the kitchen to the back door, where I had left my shoes. While I was putting them on, Andrea came and stood at her door. She leaned against the doorjamb. Her face looked weary and washed out. I stared back at her, that pale soft body I had loved so much, the thick bush of hair that always drew my eyes. I didn't have the slightest wish to go back. I turned away from her, and opened the door, and walked out.

SIXTEEN

Helen and my mother came to North Carolina to visit me in August, four months after my father died. I wasn't surprised at Helen—she had been threatening to visit me for years—but my mother was a real shock. In all the years I had lived elsewhere than Pittsburgh, she had never visited me anywhere.

"What's going on?" I said to Helen on the phone before they came down. "Why now, all of a sudden?"

"I think she just wants to get away."

"What's wrong with Cape Cod? It was good enough all those other years."

"Too many memories. She's also just been getting around more. She went to Cleveland to visit Todd. Now she wants to come see you."

She was reversing the tendencies of a lifetime.

"It's not especially comfortable," I said. "The place I'm living in isn't air-conditioned. It's hot as hell."

"Mother loves the heat."

"I'm sweating buckets even as we speak."

"Charles. Please. Your mother doesn't sweat. It's been bred out of her."

I cleaned the house more assiduously than I normally do, went to some pains to find a motel that my mother would consider passable. (There was no suggestion that she would *stay* with me.) I tried to get in the appropriate kind of food and drink. Finally I just gave up. My mother traveling to North Carolina was in itself an astonishing concept. There was only so much I could do.

I had left Pittsburgh on the Wednesday following that Saturday night with Andrea, after I'd finally been able to get a few decent nights' sleep and pull myself together. I had checked with Helen and my mother, and they seemed to be doing as well as could be expected. I knew that, in the shape I was in, there wasn't much I could do for them anyway. It didn't take long to get my things together. The drive to North Carolina takes a day. I had rented out my house down there, so I had to find another place to rent for myself, but that isn't hard in a college town in the summer. I notified my editors that I was back. They seemed to find all my moving around quite amusing.

Not long after my return to North Carolina, I wrote Mr. Harrold to tell him what I knew about the lawsuit against my father. I told him what my father had told me, that he had, in a moment of weakness, spoken to Parnell about lightening up in the divorce case. There had in effect been a conspiracy. I told him that John Auerbach was planning to call Kay Fulton as a witness, that she knew what my father had done and—now that he was dead—would almost certainly tell it in court. I told him I thought the fact that she had been Father's mistress would come out at the trial, causing considerable embarrassment to my mother and to the law firm. I told him my personal feeling that Anna Jennings had been cheated out of money that was rightfully hers and that the firm had a moral obligation to compensate her. I knew it was ridiculous to speak to Mr. Harrold of a moral obligation, but I wanted to do it anyway. I wanted to do it just because it was ridiculous. The letter I got back from him was extremely dry. He thanked me for my letter. He said that even before they had heard from me the firm was reconsidering its position on the lawsuit in light of my father's death. He felt sure now that it would be settled out of court. He thanked me for my concern, and for the information I had given him.

The old boy wasn't giving away a thing. I'd always thought he knew more than he was saying. I heard later from Helen that Anna Jennings had received an enormous settlement. At least it sounded enormous to me.

The Duchess had a different look when she came to see me. She still seemed sad, and slightly stunned, and she looked a little older, all of which was to be expected. But the real difference I saw in her was subtle, and hard to put into words. She just seemed more present, less aloof. In the past I'd always had the feeling that talking to me—or to most other people—was an onerous chore for her, which she tried to keep at arm's length and confine to as little time as possible. Now she seemed willing to have the conversation. She seemed to want to have it.

She stepped into my cluttered little two-bedroom house with real interest—"You do have the books, Charles"—and sat on my secondhand sofa as if she belonged there. (It was true. Even in a silk blouse and a long skirt, she didn't sweat.) She drank three vodka martinis—I had gone to a bartender friend for precise instructions on how to mix them—with no apparent effect. She insisted on taking Helen and me to dinner ("I didn't come down here to be a lot of trouble"). And it was while we were sitting at dinner, at the one really gourmet restaurant in town, that she made her most startling statement. "I'd like a chance just to be with Charles sometime." She turned to Helen. "If it's all right with you."

"Of course." Helen didn't miss a beat. "I can find some way to amuse myself."

This whole thing had gone too smoothly between them. It was looking like a conspiracy.

"We can go somewhere to lunch," the Duchess said. "You can treat me."

I was still reeling from those two suggestions when she said something that almost knocked me off my chair.

"Why don't we try one of those barbecue joints?"

We actually did that. I can't say that the Duchess ate one whole hell of a lot, but we did sit down to a table of barbecue, fried chicken, and Brunswick stew. She said it was all delicious. I didn't tell her of the rumors I'd heard that there was possum and squirrel in that stew. She ate hush puppies. She had a piece of chess pie. Her only real problem came when she tasted her beverage.

"What did they *do* to this iced tea?"

"They like things a little sweet down here," I said.

"I think you'd better get me some water. Unless they fill that with sugar too."

I had plenty of time, as we sat over coffee, to ponder the change in my mother. It seemed too easy to say that it was a new awareness of mortality, a wish to take notice of things that she hadn't before, but I do think that was part of it. It seemed also to have something to do with the fact that my father wasn't around. She had become more her own person in his absence. The funny—and slightly sad—thing was that I think he would have liked her that way. He would have enjoyed doing those new things. He would have torn into that barbecue.

"Helen and I were talking on the way down," she said, "about how much we enjoyed having you in Pittsburgh."

"I enjoyed being there."

"Your father especially liked it. It meant a lot to him that you had that time together. I'm so glad it worked out that way."

I had come perilously close—just a few months—to not knowing him at all.

"I'd actually thought you might stay," she said.

"I was thinking of it."

"Helen and I would love to have you."

I started to speak, then didn't. I was still at the point where the idea of seeing Andrea—even just setting eyes on her—was too much for me. I didn't think I could handle it.

"You left rather suddenly."

"I know. I'm sorry."

"It was all right. I had Helen to look after me." She was smiling gently. I looked down at the table. "Something happened with Andrea," she said, "didn't it?"

I don't know why I felt so ashamed, facing that fact. It was hard facing it with anyone—the few people I had told—but hardest of all with my mother.

"Yes," I said.

DAVID GUY

"She didn't want to see you anymore."

I nodded. I was perilously close, if the truth be known, to crying.

"That must have been terribly hard."

I nodded again.

"On top of everything else. I'm so sorry." She shook her head. "I've been worried about you."

If anything was going to make me cry, that was it. That my just-widowed mother, with all she had to face, was worried about me. But I didn't do it. I swallowed it back.

"I'm all right," I said.

There I was, still telling my mother I was all right. She seemed to be ready to hear something else.

"I know you're all right," she said. "But it must have been hard."

"It was."

"I didn't know why you hurried back here."

I wasn't entirely sure myself. I had to go somewhere.

"I thought you might be coming back to Sara," she said.

"Good Christ." For some reason, the very suggestion infuriated me. The ignorance it showed about my life. "No."

The Duchess looked startled. "I'm sorry. I didn't mean to say the wrong thing. I wasn't sure how things stood."

She was bringing up my other major failure with a woman. Two in one day.

"You never really told me what happened," she said.

"I drove her away." I had started to speak out of pain and anger. I hardly knew what I was saying. "I did it on purpose. She was my first girlfriend, I'd never really had a girlfriend, I didn't believe I could have one. I didn't believe I could be loved. At some level I didn't think I should be. So I set out to prove it. I made myself unlovable. I worked at it."

That was my most—shall we say—savage interpretation of my marriage. I had grown up with a woman who was cold to me (she happened to be sitting across the table at that very moment) and I had, once I married, set out to make my wife cold to me, by withdrawing from her, and being angry all the time, and making impossible demands. I had picked out a woman with a tendency toward coldness, toward distance, and I had made her more that way. I had driven her away.

310

"I don't believe that," the Duchess said. "You're very lovable. You couldn't make yourself unlovable."

"I tried."

"You're too hard on yourself."

That was my favorite pastime that summer. Being hard on myself.

The Duchess said something then that surprised me. I hadn't even thought she'd been noticing such things. What she said was at least as true as what I'd just said to her. It wasn't the whole answer. It was another piece of the puzzle.

"Sara was so young," she said.

She was gazing off at the wall as she spoke, thinking back.

"She had so little confidence when you two got married. She didn't know who she was. You were both a little young to be taking that step, but she was younger than you. She didn't know herself well enough to be with someone else."

It was true.

"She's seemed a different person in recent years. So much more confident. More herself. That's why I thought you might be coming back."

"She has someone else."

The Duchess nodded.

"I don't think we'd get together now anyway. We're so different."

There hadn't been enough of us to know that, in the old days.

"Now Andrea," the Duchess said. "She's another matter."

I had looked down, but I looked back up. The Duchess was staring straight at me.

"You were hoping things would work out with her."

"Yes."

"Well. It's an awful thing to say. Especially now. But I never thought they would."

"Mother." I couldn't believe my ears. "You hardly knew the woman."

"I know. I saw her, what, three or four times. I hardly spoke to her. And I know men get tired of hearing about these things that women *just know*. But this didn't take any great powers of intuition. Andrea was a far different creature from Sara. Terribly confident. Sure of herself in any social situation. What's behind all that I don't know. But she's the kind of woman, and you'll have to trust me that I've met a few of them, who never gets serious with anyone. Even when she gets married. She just does that to complicate her entanglements. She's looking for brief romances. High drama. Grand opera."

The Duchess had seen a lot in those few meetings.

"She's the kind of woman you don't trust around your husband."

"Mother." I had to smile. "What a thing to say."

"It's true."

"Why didn't you tell me this six months ago?"

"I had no idea you were so attached. I thought you were just having a fling."

"I was in love."

"Oh, Charles." She covered my hand with one of hers. "What a mistake."

"I know."

"I *should* have warned you."

"I wouldn't have listened."

"Any woman could have told you. There's a look in Andrea's eyes." She shook her head. "That woman is trouble."

I had seen the look in her eyes. I had seen it as pain.

"Ask your sister," she said.

I intended to.

The Duchess, as it turned out, took a nap after lunch—you could hardly blame her—so I had some time alone with Helen that afternoon. I had told her bits and pieces of what had happened to me in Pittsburgh, but that was the first time I really went into detail. I told her everything, from the day I walked into Andrea's store until that last Saturday night when I left her house. It took us much of the afternoon—sitting out on my little screened-in porch—and a whole pitcher of lemonade. I sat in a cushioned lounge chair (I do better on my back, so my stomach doesn't get riled up) and she in a rocker. Helen didn't say much as I was talking. She is a superb listener. She does it for a living.

I also told her what the Duchess had said. She thought it was quite perceptive. Helen was more specific with her reasons—she didn't think I should have gotten involved with a woman who was so close to the end of her marriage, and who seemed so emotionally unstable, and who obviously had a problem with men—but she basically agreed. She thought Andrea was bad news.

"Why didn't you tell me?" I said.

"I was like Mother. I thought you were just fucking."

Not that our mother had quite put it that way.

"The next time you start going out." Helen paused. "Have you started going out yet?"

"No."

"Good." It might have been too late. "The next time you start going out, pick a happy woman. One who likes her life. And who doesn't run through all the crimes of the male gender in the first fifteen minutes. There are such women in the world."

"I know."

"You don't make people happy, Charles. People make themselves happy."

That was a hard thing for me to learn.

"I just don't see how she could do what she did at a time like that," I said. "When things were so hard for me."

"She didn't do it in spite of the time. She did it because of the time. Everything was fine when she thought you were just in Pittsburgh for a few months. She could lavish you with affection. Send you flowers, whatever. But things started to get antsy when you talked about moving to the city. That sounded a little too close for comfort. And when this major thing happened in your life. When you really needed her. When the relationship got real. She couldn't handle it."

By that time Helen had stepped over to sit beside me on the chaise longue. She had taken my hand in the two of hers. I must not have looked too good.

"It was so cruel," I said.

"I know."

"It was like a cruel joke. A big cosmic joke. Like the whole world was laughing at me."

"It was bound to happen sooner or later. It was too bad it had to be at such a traumatic time. I'm sure it would have happened if you'd moved to Pittsburgh."

I was certainly glad I hadn't done that.

"There's one more thing I have to tell you, Charles." Helen said. She touched a hand to my cheek, gazed into my eyes. "Can you take it? Or should I wait?"

"I can take it."

"May I lapse into the vernacular?"

"Be my guest."

"The problem with you is, you're cunt struck. One of the worst cases I've ever encountered in my life."

That wasn't the expression you expected a professional therapist to use. Wasn't there some Latin term?

I smiled. "Does this problem show up among your clients?"

"Hell yes. It's terribly hard for women to get together as lovers in our culture. A certain kind of sweet timid woman gets a little pussy and she thinks it's the moon and the stars. She's ready to move in the next day. But I swear to God you're just as bad. I know your emotions were involved. I don't question that for a minute. But what you really liked about this woman was the way she fucked you. The way she came on so blatantly. The way she sucked your cock. It means so much to you. It's incredible how much it means. And when you lose it, it's like the world's coming to an end. You think nobody is ever going to blow you again. Believe me, Charles. There are thousands of women out there who are looking for a nice man like you. They might not chase you back to the hotel room the first night. It's probably a bad sign if they do. But if everything else is right, and things are going well, they'll do the things you want. They'll be happy to suck your cock."

This was music to my ears. "Will they tickle my balls while they do it?"

"They'll tickle your balls all you want. They'll tickle your balls with feathers."

Jesus. Helen was into some refinements even I didn't know.

"Will they beat me?" I said.

"Absolutely. Hell, *I'm* going to beat you, if you don't shape up."

I laughed. Helen would be a formidable partner.

"Well," I said. "I hope I find that woman someday."

"You will. She's right around the corner."

"I don't know. I've been around the corner. I didn't see her."

I wouldn't have said so up in Pittsburgh—I thought I had really settled in—but as I look back on it now my time there

seems to have a strange interim quality. It doesn't quite belong to the rest of my life. It started at a decisive moment—
the moment, I think when I was finally through with my
marriage—but it wasn't a new beginning. It was more like a
brief pause, a crazy interlude, when I was more at loose ends
than I cared to admit.

What I felt most when I got back to North Carolina was a
need to find a new direction for my work. Just writing—any
writing—has always brought me a deep kind of satisfaction,
but my successive small projects were starting to feel dilet-
tantish. I wanted to do something more substantial. So I have
started to work on a biography, of an obscure but fascinating
writer whose name I don't care to mention, in case some graduate student starts nipping at my heels. He was an avant-
garde artist, a brilliant social philosopher, a ragged and
idiosyncratic poet. He led a difficult life as a sexual renegade
that I don't think anyone has adequately explored. He was a
multifaceted and oddly eccentric man, whose life seems well
worth my attention.

I have stuck to my old schedule—I treasure my afternoon
time at the gym—but part of my afternoons and much of my
evenings have been given over to researching my book. My
workday has expanded to take over my life. I wanted it to. I
still give long mornings to writing. For some time—obviously—
I have been exploring my own life, especially the months up in
Pittsburgh, trying to understand the way in which they reflect
all the rest. I feel ready now to turn outward again. I want to
write about someone else.

It was some time before I started to go out with women.
For months, I didn't have the slightest inclination. I think I
was afraid, if the truth be known. Afraid—strange to say—of
women's bodies, which had fascinated and obsessed me and
been the object of my intense admiration all my life. I was
afraid of what would happen if I took one in my arms, afraid
both that nothing would happen—as it had with Alicia, who
had about as beautiful a body as I had ever seen—and that
something would happen that I couldn't handle. I was afraid
both of being humiliated and of losing control. That whole
area just held too much pain for me.

A comparison is sometimes made between sexual obsession
and other kinds of destructive behavior, and though in some

ways the comparison is apt—the wounds are probably similar, and the need—in other ways it makes no sense at all. It is as if an alcoholic could actually take a drink, and if he did it in a certain way—in a certain spirit—everything would be fine. It would actually be good for him. But if he did it in another way it would be deadly. It would lead back into his illness. And those two ways of taking a drink are almost indistinguishable.

It is one thing to want comfort now, to seek an embrace as a consolation for all the difficulties life has to offer. It is quite another to be rooting around in the past, trying to get some physical affection that you didn't get then and can't get now, because it had to be then. I'd thought I was through with all that, I had given up that impossible task, but I found that it all comes back. In a difficult moment you feel that need as desperately as the six-year-old boy did, when his mother didn't hug him and he wanted to roll around on the floor and scream. Your mind has a new understanding about all this, but the old feeling is still in your body, and your body is an elephant that never forgets. Your whole past exists in your body, waiting to be awakened.

It is like what my old friend Becky said, that time I called her up at work to say good-bye. You'll be back. They all come back.

I don't think the only time I was buying back into that old need was the night I went to see Alicia. I think I'd been buying into it with Andrea, not all the time, but sometimes. I'd been plugging her into that old wound, trying to heal it. But you can't heal that wound by trying to get what you missed in the past. You can only heal it by accepting that you didn't get it, that you never will. You have to open the wound and let it bleed. You have to feel the pain.

The other thing that is strange in my life at the moment—and I think this has only partly to do with what I've gone through, much more to do with the stage of life I've entered—is that the things that used to excite me no longer do. Stunning bodies, soft milky skin, lewd conduct, dirty talk, a perverse imagination: all those things still delight my mind, like memories of an old dream of paradise. But they do nothing for my body. They leave it cold. My body is looking for something else, but I'm not sure what. I miss the old days, to be perfectly honest about it. I know I was a little weird. But at least I knew where I was.

I did finally start to go out, after all those months. There is—as Helen mentioned—no shortage of nice women my age. There are even a number of younger women who seem to enjoy my company. I can see that their faces are lovely, their skin young and soft, their bodies firm from all the exercise they do. But they don't attract me. I'm looking for a certain wisdom in the eyes, a face weathered by experience. That kind of face has become beautiful to me. I want a woman who knows what I know, so we'll be starting out roughly together.

They're all over the place. I see them everywhere.

There is still considerable anxiety around sex for me. The funny thing is that, now that I'm cautious, the women are the other way. A couple of times, when I'd settled into some kissing—I've always had that thing for kissing, and these forty-year-old women *know* how to *kiss*—the woman would be the one, before I was ready, to make a suggestion. "Should I go turn down the bed?" one woman said, when we had finished a couple hundred kisses and I was ready for several thousand more. (What's the hurry here?) Another woman, after the *third* kiss, when we were sitting on the floor of the living room—and when we'd known each other for a grand total of about two hours—said, "Do you want to make love out here or go into the bedroom?" I had to explain, without, of course, really explaining (I hardly knew the woman!) that I had to go more slowly than that. I was still getting over something. I had some bruises that needed to heal.

There is a certain historical irony to all this. These women tried to be understanding, but it hurts to be turned down. I don't think they understood any better than I did, when we were in college and I was in their place. That second woman, after I'd done my best to explain and she had really tried to get it—her brow knit in concentration, a puzzled look in her eyes—said, in all sincerity, "Couldn't I just blow you a little?"

The sex has been okay. It's really been just fine. I'm not quite there yet. I'm like an aging ballplayer who's gone back to spring training for what is probably the last time. You can see he was great in his day. He's got all the moves. He's just a step or two slower.

There is also the matter of this uncharted territory I'm in. The feeling that my body is through with the old ways. I'm not sure what the new ways are. But I'm starting to get some hints.

I was with my new woman friend the other night, she of the knit brow and puzzled expression. She is bright and cheerful and energetic; she has—even in middle age—the body of an acrobat and a contortionist; she has as intricate a knowledge of sex as Havelock Ellis and Mae West put together; she has a great capacity for fun. The other night she used all her wiles, her amazing body and her remarkable mind, her mouth and hands and the whole texture of her skin; she did everything she could to make the sex spectacular. And it was fine, as I've said. It was just fine. I'm really almost there. It's been a rough spring, but everybody looks for me to be ready for opening day.

The next day—a Sunday—we were sitting out in the living room, reading the paper and drinking coffee. We were drowsy and slightly grumpy, and probably—if the truth be known—a little hung over. (It's shameful.) We were talking about what we were reading, war in various parts of the world, homeless children, radioactive waste, the greenhouse effect, about as unerotic a conversation as you could possibly imagine. She seemed somehow to be enjoying that, just sitting there feeling the way we were (women never cease to amaze me). You would almost have said—if the mood of the whole conversation hadn't been so glum—that she was happy. The difference for me, I think, the way in which this was different from the past, was that I wasn't trying to make it otherwise. I wasn't trying to divert the conversation so we could maybe get a little romantic and get laid before she left. I was letting it be. I didn't really feel like having sex. (That had never stopped me in the past.)

In that vague mood of discontent and sorrow, wearing my ratty old bathrobe and a tattered nightshirt of her own, she came over and sat in my lap. She collapsed into my arms. She needed to be comforted. And that—in a way that all the things she had done the night before hadn't—excited me. That single thing, the feeling of her small sad body collapsing against me. My excitement excited her. We went into the bedroom and made love, for an extremely long time, and there wasn't the slightest bit of anxiety in it for me. I knew I was all right. I wasn't even thinking about it. Afterward, while she was touching herself—she likes to do that, while I embrace her from behind and egg her on—I got excited again, though it was only minutes before that I'd come. It was partly the way she got all tight and quivery, her muscles popping out all over her body, also the way she gave a little cry and went suddenly limp. It made me see her as a girl. It touched me. We made love again. But this time, because we were so exhausted, and because we didn't want to take up the whole day with this, I came quickly. That was no problem either. I could have gone the other way if I'd wanted.

This wasn't like the old ballplayer at spring training. This was like the aging Zen master who is playing for his delight a game that the young people don't even know about. Most of them will never discover it. And though the fucking is better than any they ever do, the fucking isn't the point. The Zen master can't say what the point is. If you have to ask you'll never understand.

This is where my confusion lies. The old things no longer excite me. What excites me now is a sad woman in an old bathrobe on a Sunday morning, her kisses tasting of coffee.

Some people will say I've discovered love. I've finally realized its spiritual dimension. But I believe that I've loved many times—just because I didn't do it well doesn't mean I didn't do it—and that the new dimension I've discovered, this uncharted territory I keep talking about, is in my body. It bypasses the higher spheres altogether. That's why it's so hard to talk about. That's why it seems so strange. The real wisdom is in what has been here all along, while we were looking elsewhere.

I do have one other woman in my life. I found her name on a bulletin board at the university and made an appointment with her on a whim. It was one of those fortuitous accidents in my life. She is a dark woman, dark-complexioned, her long black hair streaked with gray. She is extremely strong, especially with her hands. Sometimes it feels as if she could snap me in half. But she is also gentle, with a soft healing touch. It is her softness you notice first, her quiet compassionate soothing presence. I start to feel calm the moment she walks through the door, lugging her massage table in a huge canvas carrying case slung over her shoulder.

Interestingly enough, she is a witch. She practices the Goddess religion and celebrates the cycles of nature, something I learned about when I was writing that article up in Pittsburgh. She isn't obnoxious or defensive about that; she mentions it casually, as if telling you where she went to school or something. She believes, as she touches me, that her energy comes from the ground, that it flows into her feet and through her body and her hands into me, but she doesn't care whether I believe that or not. I definitely feel the energy. It makes sense to me, since I was wounded by a woman, that it might be a woman who can help me to heal. There is no question in my mind that she is a healer. She has magic in her hands. I don't think she has any idea how much magic she has. But she has picked the right way to make a living.

It is a fascinating experience for a person like me—whose body is a minefield of past events—to have a massage. The one part of my body that I have spent my life trying to get women to touch is not touched. That is a premise of the whole experience. But every other part of me is lovingly and soothingly touched, anointed with oil and—as it were—blessed. The touching never stops. She always has a hand on me somewhere. The undeniable message of this experience is: You are worthy of being touched. You deserve to be touched. It is a revolution in consciousness for me to feel that way. It turns the world upside down.

She goes over my body systematically, feet and legs and back and shoulders and neck and chest and belly and arms, but also all of my toes, one by one, every finger, the lobes of my ears, my scalp (with her fingernails), my face. I am utterly passive while she is touching me. I feel like a baby. Once, in fact, she was touching a place on my neck—a long slow steady pressure, to release the tension—and I fell asleep for a moment, as I sometimes do. When I woke up, I was in the midst of a memory, one earlier than any other I'd ever had, certainly earlier than that moment at my mother's dressing table. I wasn't having the memory up in my head; I was living it, in my body. A nursery rhyme was going through my mind, one I hadn't thought of for years, and that I hadn't been aware had ever been said to me. (Pease porridge hot, pease porridge cold . . .) I was about to be rolled over on my back and picked up by my old Irish maid. The feeling that I had at that moment was utterly blissful, as if I were in the womb again, as if I were in paradise. I couldn't remember ever feeling anything even remotely like that. I wanted it never to end.

One other interesting reaction I had came the first time she gave me a massage, when she touched my stomach. I wouldn't have been more surprised if she had grabbed my cock. I had known in theory that she was going to touch my whole body, but I hadn't thought she was going to touch me *there*. It seemed almost obscene to me. I hadn't realized until that moment how much I hated my belly, how much I thought other people hated it. I couldn't believe she wanted to touch it. But she was touching it with that same gentleness, that same feeling of imparting a blessing, as she touched me everywhere else. I felt a rush of gratitude for what she was doing, an overwhelming feeling of love for her. She, of course, didn't know any of this was going on. She was just giving the usual massage.

I told her how I felt, and she said we should concentrate on my stomach. I obviously had a wound there; we should probe it gently and see where it led. Every time she touched my stomach, I felt that rush of gratitude and love. Often I felt a yearning to be held, and she was glad to hold me; she would hold me as long as I wanted. I nearly always got a hard-on when she touched my stomach, and she said that was natural too; sexual feelings were obviously a part of this experience, however far back it went. I wasn't having such feelings specifically for her. My eyes were closed, and she was just this wonderful pair of hands. She was Woman. It was also true that, as she approached my belly, having done the rest of my body, much of my tension had been released, and energy was flowing through me. There was no telling where it might go. She touched my belly and it flowed into my cock. It was as natural to get a hard-on as to take a breath.

Once I had an appointment with her when I was just getting over the flu. I almost told her to skip my stomach that day, it was so tender, then I decided not to say anything. I would see how it felt. She somehow knew to be gentle. Her hands just seemed to feel what was going on. In any case, on that day, because I was tired and my belly was so tender, a barrier was missing that was usually there, and she got to a place she didn't normally touch. She seemed to go deeper. And there was a particular spot, far down on my belly, that seemed—like that place on my neck—to have a memory associated with it. She touched it and I was immediately, overwhelmingly, sad.

I told her how I felt and she said we should touch it some more. She probed it gently. Suddenly, as she pressed slightly deeper, my body seemed to go into convulsions. I buckled at the stomach, my head and shoulders bouncing off the table, then flopping back down again. That reflex had happened to me before when she touched my stomach, but never more than a few times; now it kept happening again and again. She continued to probe the spot. I had a tremendous erection, which had no reference to anyone outside myself, but was a reflex, like the erections you get when you're asleep; nevertheless, the physical motions were so violent that I felt as if I might spontaneously ejaculate, the way you do during a dream. My body was trembling and shuddering, totally out of control; I felt scared but also exhilarated, as if years of tension were flying out of me. Before long I started to cry. I was bawling like a baby. I was very much like a baby, in fact, lying on my back and convulsed with the sobbing. The most interesting thing about the whole experience—which went on for twenty minutes, until I was utterly exhausted—was that it had no specific memory associated with it. I was having this extraordinarily violent reaction, but I had no idea what it was about. It was as if that sadness had been living in my body, and something about the way she touched me released it.

What I realized that day—it came to me as she was probing that place, just before the fit began—was that normally I keep a layer of anger in my belly, like a belt I can cinch tight, but on that day, because I was sick and weak, the anger wasn't there. I keep that anger wrapped around my belly to protect me from the sadness, but also to guard a tender place associated with it, and where I once was hurt. I have often felt anger well up from my belly like a cyclone—I've known for years that I hold it there—but I had never felt that tenderness before. I hadn't known it existed. But I recognize it now as mine—from my distant past as a sweet little boy who wanted to be held—and I want to feel it as a part of me again. I understand why I have protected it, but I don't want to do that anymore. I don't mean that I want to feel nothing but tenderness—love is much more than that—but that I want tenderness to be a part of what I feel. I believe it will make a great difference. It will be as stunning a revelation as that belief that I deserve to be touched. It is an exciting thought for me. I am convinced that a whole new world is waiting. There is another way to love in me, lying in my body waiting for me to find it.